Praise for

Our Italian Summer

"The novel is carried by the rich interactions between the women, as well as the lush Italian landscape, city descriptions, and culinary pleasures. Probst consistently charms."

—*Publishers Weekly*

"*Under the Tuscan Sun* meets *Divine Secrets of the Ya-Ya Sisterhood* as Probst (*Searching for Someday*, 2013) explores the dynamics of womanhood between three generations against a picturesque Italian backdrop. . . . Filled with family drama amidst a lush setting, plus a touch of romance, *Our Italian Summer* will provide a delicious escape for readers."

—*Booklist*

"In *Our Italian Summer*, Jennifer Probst captures the essence of Italy and celebrates the bond between mothers and daughters. With food worthy of an Italian grandmother's kitchen and descriptions to make the Travel Channel jealous, you'll want to join the Ferrari women on their unforgettable journey."

—Amy E. Reichert, author of *The Kindred Spirits Supper Club*

"*Our Italian Summer* beautifully navigates the complicated relationships between families in a heartfelt manner in this multigenerational novel set against the splendid backdrop of Italy in all of her glory. Jennifer Probst whisks readers away on an unforgettable journey. The perfect novel to satisfy your wanderlust!"

—*New York Times* bestselling author Chanel Cleeton

PRAISE FOR THE NOVELS OF *Jennifer Probst*

"Achingly romantic, touching, realistic, and just plain beautiful."

—*New York Times* bestselling author Katy Evans

"Tender and heartwarming."

—#1 National bestselling author Marina Adair

"Beautiful . . . and so well written! Highly recommend!"

—*New York Times* bestselling author Emma Chase

"Jennifer Probst pens a charming, romantic tale destined to steal your heart."

—*New York Times* bestselling author Lori Wilde

"Probst tugs at the heartstrings."

—*Publishers Weekly*

"I never wanted this story to end! Jennifer Probst has a knack for writing characters I truly care about—I want these people as *my* friends!"

—*New York Times* bestselling author Alice Clayton

"For a . . . fun-filled, warmhearted read, look no further than Jennifer Probst!"

—*New York Times* bestselling author Jill Shalvis

"Jennifer Probst never fails to delight."

—*New York Times* bestselling author Lauren Layne

The Secret Love Letters of Olivia Moretti

JENNIFER PROBST

BERKLEY

New York

BERKLEY
An imprint of Penguin Random House LLC
penguinrandomhouse.com

Library of Congress Cataloging-in-Publication Data

Names: Probst, Jennifer, author.
Title: The secret love letters of Olivia Moretti / Jennifer Probst.
Description: First edition. | New York : Berkley, 2022.
Identifiers: LCCN 2021039445 (print) | LCCN 2021039446 (ebook) |
ISBN 9780593332894 (trade paperback) | ISBN 9780593332900 (ebook)
Subjects: LCGFT: Novels.
Classification: LCC PS3616.R624 S45 2022 (print) |
LCC PS3616.R624 (ebook) | DDC 813/.6—dc23
LC record available at https://lccn.loc.gov/2021039445
LC ebook record available at https://lccn.loc.gov/2021039446

First Edition: March 2022

Printed in the United States of America
1st Printing

Book design by Katy Riegel

This book is dedicated to all of the emergency workers and first responders who sacrificed to help others at the expense of themselves. Whether it was to stock grocery shelves, administer medical care, or hold a patient's hand, I appreciate and respect every single one of you.

A special shout-out to my brother, Steve, and sister-in-law, Dana, who were in the trenches every single day while I wrote this book.

Thank you.

Your task is not to seek for love, but merely to seek and find all the barriers within yourself that you have built against it.

—Rumi

Lovers don't finally meet somewhere. They're in each other all along.

—Rumi

The Secret Love Letters of Olivia Moretti

PROLOGUE

Dear R,

I dreamed of you again last night.

It's always the same one. And not the usual memory of the night we first kissed, or the time we got caught in the rain and I lost my shoe and you carried me up all those stairs and I realized I loved you. No, it was when we met. Aunt Silvia introduced me to your father and you were standing behind him, your head kind of ducked down like you were shy. You had these dark, beautiful curls and I got this crazy urge to run my fingers through them, but I was shy too, so I pretended it didn't matter you wouldn't talk, but your father said your name and you looked up.

Did you know like I did in that moment? Or was it only me that sensed I'd never be the same? Your dark eyes, soulful and calm. I felt like I could look at you forever and find all the answers I was always searching for. And then you smiled, showing off your crooked front tooth, and when I smiled back my heart was bursting with something big, something I didn't know yet. I'm glad we were friends first. I needed time to process all those feelings I didn't understand. I think I dream about that moment so much because it was the beginning of endless possibilities. You were the only one who truly knew me. My husband knows I must sleep on the left side of the bed, and I never remember to put the toothpaste cap back on, and I'm allergic to strawberries. But you have known my true heart and soul from the very first moment I met your gaze.

I know I said I'd never write. I meant my vow, I take my marriage seriously, but it's like each piece of me has been slipping away a little bit more with every passing day, like sand in an hourglass, and I'm afraid. Afraid there won't be anything left if I keep going on. So, I'm writing to you to save myself. It's selfish, but I always told you, R, that I wasn't as good as you. I wanted bigger and better and I got them.

I didn't realize the extent of the sacrifices I'd make. For both of us.

I don't expect you to write back. Maybe I won't even mail this letter, but tonight, as I write this in the quiet of the night and my bed, I needed you. And I needed you to know that I remember.

I will always remember.

Buona sera,

Livia

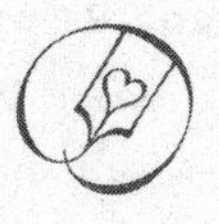

CHAPTER ONE

Priscilla

Priscilla Hampton wondered if every daughter who buried her mother suddenly became swamped with regrets.

She'd never been one to question her decisions or linger on actions she'd taken that couldn't be changed. But staring up at her childhood home, facing the task of cleaning out her mom's personal belongings, she was pretty much sick with what-ifs.

The overly large Tudor house still seemed as if it was judging her as she walked up the curvy pathway leading to the sweeping arched doorway. Pris had never liked the way the two giant windows gave off an eerie yellow glow from the sage-green stucco, like eyes stuck in a deep-set face. The balcony dead center reminded her of a flat nose and had been the bane of her mother's existence—a perfect escape route for teen girls to sneak out at night. The lower brick should have lent an elegant, timeless tone, but it all ended up looking like a mishmash of old and new. Still, it was the only family home she'd ever lived in. After the divorce, Dad had given the house up without a fight, moving on and moving in with his newest love interest. She'd blamed him, of course, until she realized her mother hadn't seemed to care, which somehow made Pris angrier with her than with Dad.

It would've been easier if Mom wanted revenge, or insisted her daughters hate him. Instead, she'd snatched Pris's right to bitterness and swept all the messy emotions away with her usual sunny smile, encouraging them to have a healthy relationship with Dad and not worry.

Did her mother ever get exhausted by the endless pursuit of perfection? Always having to be nice, and forgive, and put everyone else first without resentment?

Pris trembled as she thought of her beloved mother alone in her hospital bed. Once again, refusing to ask for help, hating to bother anyone with her issues, even sickness.

And dying alone.

A wave of emotion battered her body, so Pris held her breath, sensing she was on the verge of either a breakdown or a breakthrough worthy of an *O Magazine* feature article.

Her sister bumped her from behind and Priscilla stumbled forward. "Dude, you're blocking the pathway. Why do you have that dumb look on your face?"

Pris shot her an annoyed look. Her fleeting come-to-Jesus moment departed faster than a conservative trapped in a room with liberals. "I was thinking."

Bailey rolled her eyes and kept walking. "No time to think. I've gotta be at open mic tonight."

The sound of her middle sister's voice floated in the air with a tinge of annoyance. "Really, Bae? We cleared this day to pack up Mom's stuff and be together. You can't even hang with us for one lousy evening?"

"I gave you my day. Don't pretend if you had one of your important meetings that you wouldn't ditch us without a thought."

"Maybe for a job I get paid for," Devon said. "Not to read some crappy excerpt of another poem you'll never publish."

Pris tried not to wince, but once her sisters got going, not even a naked Jason Momoa could stop them.

They stepped through the carved mahogany doors together, their shoulders deliberately bumping, while Pris trailed behind.

"Real nice," Bailey said. Her sleek golden ponytail bobbed in protest. "Go ahead and judge my life, but at least I'm not pretending to be someone I'm not."

"And I'm not wasting mine doing nothing worthwhile while I pretend to search for meaning," Devon retorted.

They'd just arrived and it was starting already. Her temples throbbed with the beginning of one of her migraines. Not today. She refused to let them hijack this day for their familiar arguments. When they'd been younger, Pris had been jealous of her younger sisters' close relationship. Being five years older than Devon forced her to be the leader, even though Devon had always been bossier. But like everything else, Pris had taken on the role believing that was what was needed. It also erected an invisible barrier between her siblings she'd never been able to overcome. "Guys, can we just focus? The estate handlers come tomorrow, so all we need to do is Mom's bedroom. They'll take care of the rest."

"Feels weird to think nothing will be here," Dev said with a sigh.

"Did you ever wonder why Mom never sold this place?" Pris asked. "She always complained it was too big for one person."

Bailey waved her ink-stained fingers in the air. "Us, of course. She told me once there were too many memories to ever give it up. Maybe I'll move some stuff in and live here."

Devon snorted. "Don't think so. You'd turn it into some hostel for your broke friends. We'll sell it and split the proceeds like Mom wanted."

Bailey huffed with her usual drama. "Mom always said I could have the house if I wanted. I bet she'd rather have it stay in the family."

"Did you get that intention in writing?" Dev asked, her gaze sweeping over the spacious foyer to the crystal-dripping chandelier. Pris could practically hear her brain clicking with how much they could get for the place. Her role as tenured professor in the finance department at NYU was impressive, but she had a tendency to see things in stark black and white. Money was serious business, and Devon had made sure they all agreed to sell so everyone would get a fair share.

"Seriously? That's messed up," Bailey said.

"So is this." Devon's gaze cleared, her hazel eyes glinting with a new hardness Pris had never seen before. Like there'd been additional layers that crusted over during the years they'd grown apart. "Let's not pretend this is what any of us want right now."

"Mom's death?" Pris asked, her insides clenching at the rising tension in the air. They formed a semicircle together. A memory flashed of the three of them ready to play hide-and-go-seek—squeezing into a tight knot while they picked who'd be it, back when they not only loved but liked one another.

"No. Being together. I'm not playing the role assigned to me, okay? So, let's just agree to tackle the house piece by piece without getting all sentimental for things that no longer exist."

Even Bailey sucked in her breath, a shadow of pain flickering over her delicate features. "Why are you so cold?" she whispered.

The air shimmered; softened; quieted. Pris waited for the answer too, wondering when the real turning point had been, when they'd decided being apart was better than trying to make the fragments of each of them fit into one clear puzzle. Two years ago? Five? Or had their relationship deteriorated so slowly no one had cared enough to count?

For a second, Dev opened her mouth and the words hung unuttered in the air, like an overfull balloon ready to pop.

Then she turned and the moment floated away.

"We better get started," Devon said.

They watched her climb the grand staircase and disappear.

Bailey muttered something under her breath. "I need to use the bathroom," she said, marching down the hallway. Left alone, Pris looked around, wondering if her mother's presence would show itself. A brush of cold air. A sound. A wave of charged energy that announced Mom's arrival to help smooth all these jagged edges between her children.

But nothing happened. Just a terrible empty sensation in the pit of her stomach and a familiar tension behind her eyes.

Pris dragged in a deep breath, set her shoulders, and headed up the stairs.

CHAPTER TWO

Devon

Dev muttered a curse under her breath and opened the first empty box. Why did she have to act like such a bitch? At least when Bailey lost her temper, people accepted it as her artistic streak. She'd grown up with her parents shaking their heads at Bailey's tantrums as if they were amused. But when Devon lost it? She was called ugly and out of control.

And right now?

They were right.

She yanked the top drawer of her mother's nightstand and began to sift through an array of junk, making neat piles. One for garbage. One to sell in the estate sale. And one for treasures she or her sisters wanted to keep.

She heard Bailey's stomping footsteps echo up the stairs and tried to push the sliver of guilt aside. Bailey was too old to be treated like a child. Why did everyone cater to her? If Devon hadn't taken control, this house would still be sitting on the market, rotting away like all their potential money. Pris had her rich husband, and Bailey still relied on their father's generous dole outs, but Dev made sure to make her own way.

Living in New York was damn expensive. Sure, being a tenured professor at NYU was a respectable career, with a decent salary. But there was still so much she craved—like scoring that elusive dean position and gaining a spot on the board. Being respected by her bosses, colleagues, and students on a higher level. Dev had a voracious appetite for success and sensed the victory she craved was close.

Dev refocused, finished the top drawer, and started on the next. Most of the stuff was throwaway remnants of cast-off makeup, holiday cards, empty notebooks, broken picture frames, and a mishmash of collectibles that had meant something to Mom once. The calming scent of lavender drifted in the air, soothing some of the jagged edges of a grief she'd not been willing to steep herself in. Not yet. When she got back to her place, she'd take some time to cry and mourn.

Alone.

"Nice going," Pris drawled, sitting down on the edge of the bed. Crossing her long legs with a natural grace that spoke of all those days she used to dance, her oldest sister gave a deep sigh, clasping her hands on her knees. Dev took a moment to study the large, glittering rock on her finger, her French-manicured nails without a chip. Even at forty, she held a youthful beauty, from her swanlike neck and long blond hair to her wide powder-blue eyes that still shaded an onlooker from her secrets. Pris was the peacemaker but also the most secretive. Dev wouldn't have been surprised if she'd learned her sibling danced in the fairy world when everyone went to sleep and had never breathed a word to anyone.

Both her sisters had inherited Mom's looks—light hair, blue

eyes, fair skin. Dev resembled her father with his dark hair and hazel eyes. He was a handsome man, always had been, but somehow the features she'd inherited didn't work on a female as well. Dev always felt a bit too stocky in the hips and bust, a bit awkward in her gait, and a bit dull with her coloring. It was hard growing up with the golden sisters and the constant comments about how Dev looked so different. Sometimes, she'd had to grit her teeth to keep from slugging those nice old ladies who gave her a slightly sympathetic look.

She refocused and shrugged. Time to defend herself for being cruel to Bailey. "Sorry, but we all need to be grown-ups now. It's not good for her to depend on Dad, or have grandiose ideas of keeping this house for fun. Can you work on the closet? I've got some not-for-profits coming to collect her designer labels, but the rest can be donated."

"Don't you want anything?" Pris asked. Her gaze flicked around the room as if cataloguing every personal item. "I'd like some pieces of jewelry she wore. And that red-gold sweater."

Dev lifted a brow. "I think we should all take what means the most to us. I won't fight anyone on it. Why would you want that sweater, though? God, it was awful."

Bailey interrupted their conversation, her ponytail bouncing as she walked into the room. "For once, I agree with Dev. I begged Mom to throw it out every time I saw her, but she'd only wrap it closer. It's old as dirt and ugly as sin. So bright I couldn't even look at her when she wore it."

Pris laughed, walking to the closet to search. "I know, but there was something she loved about it. I think she treasured it more than the few diamonds she owned."

"Can I have her wedding ring?" Bailey burst out. At Dev's sharp look, her pixie face turned stubborn. "Not for the value—because it reminds me of when we were all together. And happy."

The slice of pain surprised her, along with her sister's words. When was the last time they'd felt happy together? Holidays were now strained affairs, with all of them desperate to leave as soon as the turkey was eaten or presents opened. Dad had his own family and always looked uncomfortable when his old and new families collided. As the youngest, Bailey was stubbornly optimistic, seeing the tension through rainbow-colored glasses, which was part of her nature. If only Devon could blot out the bad stuff as easily. But it lay in wait every night, whispering in her ear. Taunting.

"Sure," Dev said. Her sister relaxed, the tension between them slowing from a burn to a slight simmer.

"Thanks."

"Found it!" Pris pulled the sweater from the closet with a triumphant grin. The fabric was worn—once a wide, loopy-type knit that reminded Dev of a handmade afghan. It was oversize, and the pattern was a swirling mix of bright sunset colors that was overdone, making an onlooker a bit dizzy. Pris slipped it on. The sleeves stretched out over her delicate hands, and the large rust-colored buttons only added to the clownish image.

Dev and Bailey burst out laughing. "It's just as horrible as I remember," Dev said with a grin.

"I don't care, I'm going to take it," Pris said.

"Enjoy," Bailey said with a wave of her hand. "I'm sure Mom would be happy someone actually wanted it. We'd better get working—I need to shower and change before my reading to-night."

Dev swallowed her retort and reminded herself to relax. It was a short weekend and then she'd be back to her busy life. For Mom's sake, she'd hold her temper. "Why don't you work on the bureau?" Dev suggested.

They focused on the work, mostly in silence. Each object

Dev touched was like a sharp memory bursting into her brain, leaving shimmers of grief trickling through her body. She pushed forward with the methodical precision that had served her well. A lone silver-handled hairbrush. Mini albums filled with wallet-size photos collected over the years, mostly stuffed with awkward school pics. A bottle of travel perfume still in its box. Dev removed it and took a deep whiff, the floral scent light, with notes of citrus. Definitely a scent Mom would wear. Perhaps it'd been an extra, thrown carelessly in a drawer for later, because wasn't there always a later? A tomorrow?

Her fingers gripped the smooth glass tighter. If only Mom had told them she was sick. Why couldn't she reach out and ask for help? Why did she have to die alone in a hospital when all of them would have been there if she had told them?

The words escaped her mouth before she could bite them back. "Mom should have told us."

Pris kept her back turned as she gathered clothes off the hangers. "It happened fast, Dev. No one knew it would turn into pneumonia."

"No, before that. She'd been sick for a damn week and hadn't even seen a doctor. God, why couldn't she just have called for broth, or Mucinex, or anything?"

"Because she was afraid no one would come."

Bailey's voice whipped her head around, shock barreling through her. "What are you talking about? I'm under two hours away—I would've driven here right away. And you're under an hour! Why didn't she contact you?"

Bailey's shoulders stiffened, but she refused to meet her stare. "Not sure. Probably afraid we were all busy, which we were. She was stubborn like that."

"She didn't give us a chance." The frustration writhed in her belly like pissed-off cobras. "Not to say goodbye, or that we were sorry, or anything."

Pris cocked her head, a frown furrowing her brow. "Why would you need to be sorry? Did you guys have a fight or something?"

Or something. Like the thousands of patronizing questions she'd ignored, hating always being compared to perfect Pris and adorable Bailey. And God knows she despised her whining mind, which tortured her, but the truth was too terrible to avoid.

Somehow, her mother had made her feel completely unworthy.

And now there was no more time. No hope they'd finally have an honest dialogue about why Dev had been the one to disappoint her. Life wasn't a chick-flick rom-com with a neat ending.

It was more like a shit show.

"No fight," she said, dumping the perfume and shutting the last drawer. "Just a random thought. I'm just mad at the way it happened."

Pris gave her a sympathetic look. "Can't blame you. Getting a call from the hospital that Mom died was like a nightmare. I kept thinking someone would jump out and say, 'Kidding!' and I could hate them for a terrible prank."

"I didn't believe you," Dev said. "When you called me. It was too much."

Bailey's voice trembled. "I ran. I was in my pajamas at the hospital because I didn't stop to even change. I think I figured if I got there fast enough I could prove it was a terrible mistake."

The memory of Bailey in sleep shorts and an old black T-shirt, hair unbrushed, with those blue eyes wild with grief, would haunt Dev forever. Her sister had collapsed on the floor and let out a wail that brought goose bumps. Was it easier for her to pour out her emotion at all times? To empty herself like a vessel until it was filled up again with feelings, and then tip it over and spill them out—like the little teapot song? Dev had always wondered. Because her insides were like a devastated forest—quiet, dehydrated, with perished trees standing in even lines.

Silence settled over the room. Everyone seemed lost in their thoughts, so when Pris called out their names, Devon jumped.

"What is it? Did you find the Gucci suit?" Dev asked, trying for some sarcastic wit to break up the heavy sadness thickening the air.

"No. I found a trunk."

Dev watched her sister drag out a cedar trunk with beautiful gold carvings. It was medium-size, with pedestal feet and an intricate lock. A shiver raced down her spine as they all gathered around the piece, staring at the object as if it held the answers to something instead of some carefully preserved blankets or linens.

Dev was the first one to speak, ignoring her suddenly racing heart. "Open it up."

Pris hesitated, her hand like a fragile bird, hovering midway in the air. A strange foreboding swept through Dev.

Then the lock clicked and she lifted the lid.

The scent of must and cotton and wood drifted to her nostrils.

They stared down at a quilt.

Her shoulders relaxed. The quilt was ivory colored, hand stitched, and quite beautiful, but still a boring reveal after such anticipation. It was obvious from her sisters' relieved sighs they'd done the same thing. Expected something else.

Bailey smoothed her hand over the soft material. "Pretty. I would've saved my dibs for this, Pris. Better than the sweater."

Pris grinned. "You and Dev can fight over it, or we can donate it. I certainly don't need another quilt in my life."

Dev lost interest and turned back to the second bureau. "Not sure why Mom needed a trunk to store bedding. This place has a huge linen closet that's only half full."

"Maybe she liked the beauty of it," Bailey murmured. "I'm always attracted to those pretty hatboxes, but I've never owned a hat in my life. It's kind of romantic."

Dev gave a snort. "Mom was the least romantic person I've ever known."

"Why would you say that?" Bailey asked. "She probably had dreams and fantasies like everyone else."

"I agree with Dev on this one," Pris said, her voice a bit brisk. "Mom was practical. She preferred stability and smart decisions over passion. She wasn't the type to date a bad boy or ditch a logical plan over an impulse."

"Well, I disagree," Bailey said.

"What's new?" Dev muttered. She practically felt Bailey's glare, so she concentrated on her task. A rustling rose in the air, along with her sister's voice.

"Um, guys. I found something."

Dev turned, expecting to see more quilts, but Bailey was holding a fat manila envelope in her hands. "It's probably copies of important financials or old pictures," Dev said, peering over her sister's shoulder.

Bailey opened the clasp and pulled out a stack of letters tied with a purple ribbon. Dev watched as her sister tugged on the ribbon and flipped slowly through the papers. No envelopes. Just one letter after another with dates at the top and the same salutation repeated.

Livia, amore mio.

"What is it?" Pris asked, turning from the closet.

"Letters. A lot of them," Bailey said.

Dev picked up the envelope and slid her hand inside. "Nothing else in here. Are they to us?"

Bailey shook her head. "They're from someone named R. And they look like love letters."

The sudden silence seemed to crackle with electricity. They shared a look. Pris shook her head. "Impossible. She wasn't dating anyone after Dad. And she got married at twenty-three, so there wasn't tons of time to have love affairs."

"Maybe they were from a college boyfriend?" Dev suggested. "Maybe she forgot they were in there."

Bailey's fingers tightened around the papers as she scanned through some of them. "These seem kind of intense."

Pris reached inside the trunk. "I found something else. It looks like a certificate."

Dev waited while her sister examined the document. When she looked up, shock carved out the lines of her face. "It's a deed for a house. That Mom owns. In Italy."

Bailey gasped. "Wait—Mom has a house in Italy? That's crazy! She would've told us."

Head swimming, Dev tried to focus. "Can I see that?" Pris handed it over. "Oh my God, Pris is right. Mom owns a place in Positano, Italy."

"Is that on the Amalfi Coast?" Bailey asked, frowning. "We don't even know anyone from Italy. Has she ever mentioned it to one of you?"

They shook their heads. "There has to be some explanation," Pris said. "I'll get in touch with her lawyer and see if he knew about it."

"And Dad, of course," Bailey added. "Maybe it was Dad's and he gave it to her in the divorce?"

"Doubt it. Don't you think we would've taken a trip there?" Dev asked.

"I don't know what to think," Bailey said in a strangled voice. "It's so weird."

"Maybe she left us a letter?" Pris suggested.

Bailey split up the papers. "Good idea, let's look. I only glanced through them."

They each shuffled through their pile, but Dev found nothing addressed to them.

Pris sighed. "I don't see any letter to us. They're all from this R guy," Pris said. "But we need to go through the rest of her things. Maybe the explanation for the house is somewhere else and we missed it. Did Mom keep a diary? Journal? Special folder of personal items?"

"We found those already, remember? We needed all that stuff for the funeral and death certificate," Dev said.

Bailey waved her hand in the air. Her voice sounded highly pitched. "Guys, you need to hear this."

She began to read.

Livia, amore mio,

Today, I climbed onto the roof and watched the sunset and thought of you. The way you smell like lilacs, and the way your blue eyes light up when you smile and the way you say my name in a whisper after I kiss you. I count the days until summer and wonder if you will think of me the same. If another semester at college will cause you to realize you can have so much more than this simple life I can offer here. Yes, it would tear me apart to lose you, but can I be enough? This woman who sets my heart on fire and brings the world to its feet with just a smile? And even worse—I am too selfish to warn you away, dolcezza. If you will have me, I will wait for you. I will make sure you find the type of happiness you deserve by the way I love you, and I will force open the cities like an oyster to give you the things you need. I'm not surprised you are at the top of your class, especially in art history. There are many museums and art curators who will be lucky to have you. Soon, you will arrive with Aunt Silvia and my life will truly begin again. Until then, the fish and the tourists keep me company during the day. And you keep me company in my dreams.

Il mio cuore sarà tuo per sempre,

R

Bailey finished reading and lifted her head.

Dev had never heard such words from a lover—the way the raw emotions seemed to wrap around her and squeeze. Who was this woman who'd inspired such heartfelt vows? Certainly not the mother she'd grown up with. And why hadn't she ever spoken of him—even as an old boyfriend?

Her thoughts knotted into a tangle. Pris looked like she'd been sucker punched, her face dangerously pale. Bailey had that dreamy expression, like she'd been carried far off somewhere outside reality. Probably romanticizing the whole thing, when there had to be a rational explanation. Dev just needed to find it.

"It's just a silly college crush," Pris said firmly. "We all keep memories of old boyfriends. She probably hid them from Dad and forgot they were even in here."

Dev bit her lower lip. "This guy was from Italy! What about the house? And who's Aunt Silvia?"

"I don't know," Bailey said. "It sounds like she traveled there every summer. Why wouldn't she have mentioned this to us?

Grandma and Pop Pop never said anything about Aunt Silvia either. Was she some type of secret? A black sheep or something?"

"Don't know. But they both died when we were young so we never got a chance to ask," Dev said.

Pris kept shaking her head and murmuring under her breath, like she refused to accept their discovery. "There must be an explanation. Mom is not the type to hide a secret life and an Italian getaway. It's not possible."

"Anything's possible," Bailey pointed out. "This must've happened before Dad, though. Do you think she looked this guy up after the divorce?"

Dev lifted a brow. "Well, Dad was the one who had an affair. Maybe she got back in touch with this guy for revenge? Or from loneliness?"

A strange sense of anger made Pris snap. "I think we're overreacting and there's a rational explanation. Let's read another letter. The latest one. What's the date?"

Bailey flipped to the end of the pile, careful of the ink on the crisp white paper. "No date." She hesitated. Dev held her breath, sensing they were all caught on the precipice of knowing too much. Once they fell off the cliff, there'd be no turning back or pretending it didn't happen. Did they want what they knew about their mom to change forever?

But it was already too late to turn back. They had discovered these letters, and Bailey had already begun to read.

Dearest Livia,

For too long, I was unable to accept your letters. It was best for both of us—to finally let go of a past that was too beautiful, it may have ended up destroying us both. I had done my best to keep those summers locked away. Even that one precious week when I believed you'd come back to me is a memory best not to revisit. I convinced myself our time together was a dream, but when I saw my name on those envelopes, I realized I alone could ruin a life that I'd rebuilt after you left. I couldn't do that, dolcezza. Not even for you.

But now, I find myself at a crossroads. I still think about you. I still wonder what could have been. I still want to gaze upon your face one more time.

So, yes, I will meet you here for your 65th birthday.

R

Bailey dropped the pile of papers. They gazed at one another in stunned silence.

Dev's mind clamored to understand, and she stumbled over the timeline. Her mom had passed in February. Her birthday was in May—which meant she'd died before this meeting could have taken place. After the funeral, her sisters had taken time to settle paperwork and the will, putting off the house to the last task.

Had this man been waiting for her in Positano on Mom's sixty-fifth birthday? Did he know she passed? Or was this a secret kept from everyone?

Dev was the first to break the silence. "I think we need to read all these letters and figure out what's going on."

Bailey slowly nodded. "I think I'll cancel my reading tonight."

Pris gave a long sigh. "I think I'll run out and get us some wine."

CHAPTER THREE

Olivia

On the last day of school the summer I was nineteen, I didn't score a graduation party or new car like many of my friends; instead, Mom took me aside and asked if I wanted to go to Italy for the summer with Aunt Silvia, her sister, whom I rarely saw. At first, I thought she was joking, but the sour purse of her lips as she offered told me the truth. I knew then, it was bad at home. Either my parents were going to try to work it out while I was away for a last-ditch attempt to salvage their marriage, or I'd return home and Dad would be gone. My stomach hurt and I wanted to cry, but I was also pissed off with both of them. So, I barely hesitated to jump at my aunt's offer. The next day, I met her at JFK Airport and we flew to Italy.

Aunt Silvia had a loud, vibrant personality. Her golden-red hair was long and thick, and makeup perfectly accented her high cheekbones, full lips, and elegant nose. She wore high heels, bright colors, and elaborate jackets with sequins, embroidery, or fur. At first, I was intimidated, feeling like a mousy teen with my plain face, dirty-blond hair, and too-thin frame that held no interesting curves. But she kissed and hugged me like we'd spent forever together, and chattered nonstop until I relaxed.

"Tell me about Positano," I asked as I sipped my Coca-Cola in a large glass with ice. First class was an experience in itself. The seats were plush and reclined fully, and we were treated like customers in a fine dining restaurant.

Aunt Silvia sighed with pleasure. "Darling, you're going to adore it. The town is on the Amalfi Coast, with spectacular views, beaches, and amazing restaurants. Tourists flock there for the season, so it will be very crowded, but perfect for a beautiful young girl ready for an adventure."

I tried not to blush.

"Your uncle's house is a pretty little cottage amid the hills. It was handed down to your uncle Richard and has been in the family for generations. I'm sure everyone was devastated when he passed and found I was the one to inherit, since we had no children. But who knows—if you like it maybe you'll be my beneficiary," she said with a twinkle in her golden-brown eyes.

I grinned. "It sounds amazing. Do you speak Italian too?" She impressed me when she rattled off a string of Italian words that I couldn't decipher. "Wow, I'd love to learn. But I kind of suck at languages. I've been taking Spanish for three years now and I still only know the basics."

"You need the immersion method, darling. When everyone is speaking the language around you, it's easier to pick up. But everyone I know speaks English, so don't worry. I will introduce you to all the neighbors and you will make new, wonderful friends."

I pushed my parents' troubles and thoughts of college aside. I intended to enjoy this summer as the experience of a lifetime. Maybe in Positano I'd gain some clarity in what I wanted to do with my life. I loved to draw and write. I loved art and history. I popped from subject to subject, gathered information, then moved on. But Mom and Dad said that was a failure of mine—a lack of focus and goals—and that I needed to pick one thing and stick with it.

I watched Aunt Silvia flip through a glossy magazine and hoped this summer would give me some answers I desperately craved.

I think I fell in love with Positano the first time I laid eyes on the gorgeous outline of brightly colored homes and terra-cotta rooftops sprinkled over the steep hills. We'd arrived by water taxi, and I soaked in the crowds on the dock, the lilt of rapid Italian peppering my ears, the pungent scents of damp earth, water, and a mixture of faint florals scenting the air. The sun burned hot on my skin, and I was overwhelmed by the significance of being away from home for the first time. Here I was in another country, with an aunt I barely knew, ready to spend an entire summer without having an idea of what was to come.

~~~

It was the most exciting and terrifying experience of my life.

A few men helped carry our luggage and we began the steep hike. Halfway there, I was huffing and sweaty, but my aunt kept chattering and pointing things out, her heels not slowing her down as we climbed. She cheerfully informed me we'd climbed 181 steps and said by the end of summer, she was always in the best shape of her life. The idea of living far in the suburbs to drive half an hour to a mall used to scare me. Now I wondered if I'd live without pizza delivery.

"Here we are!" Aunt Silvia announced, her hands sweeping outward in a welcoming gesture. "Our cottage for the summer!"
~~~

I gasped. If this was a cottage, I wanted to live here my entire life.

The bright blue door emphasized the sunny yellow shingles and quirky, sloping roof. Lemon trees burst from the sides and framed a gorgeous garden, overflowing with blooms that seemed to explode from the ground in a happy mess. She ushered me inside and I was struck by the coziness of the place. The floor was a gorgeous hand-painted tile of florals. An overstuffed sectional and love seat with curved lamps created a cozy reading space. A square, carved pine table lay in front of me, with bright blue cushioned chairs. The kitchen was open, with butcher-block wooden counters. White-shuttered arched windows were flung open so the spectacular hillside view could be seen from every angle.

I poked through the rooms, taking in the gorgeous bathroom with an old-fashioned tub, and the full-size bedrooms with private wrought-iron balconies.

I was living in a paradise.

"It's so beautiful." I breathed out. "It almost hurts to look at."

Aunt Silvia smiled with pleasure. "I always have the place cleaned and opened up before I arrive. Now, why don't we rest, have something to eat, and then I'll take you into town to meet a few people."

Nerves tingled in my belly, but I readily agreed. If I was going to be spending my summer here, I wanted to meet as many people as possible. Hopefully, they spoke English like my aunt had said.

Later, I changed into denim shorts, a white lace top, and my pair of comfortable sneakers. We made the long trek back down the hill, stopping here and there for my aunt to call out greetings and introduce me to a few neighbors. My senses were overloaded as I tried to take it all in: the crowded, zigzagging narrow streets, the endless displays of shops and outdoor cafés, the whizz of scooters on the main road. Aunt Silvia maneuvered deftly around and we headed back toward the pier, where the light caught the water and the smooth movement of the boats.

"I'd like you to meet someone special," Aunt Silvia said. Her eyes shone mischievously like she had a secret. "He's a good friend of mine, so we'll be spending time together. You'll adore him, and his son."

I cocked my head and studied her elegant profile. "Is he your boyfriend?"

She let out a booming laugh. "Something like that, but we're not in a serious relationship. For now, we just make each other happy."

I thought of my mother's accusations that Aunt Silvia had loose morals and enjoyed the thrill that skated down my spine. I hoped I'd find my own adventures like her. I hated being socially awkward and shy in front of people and was trying to push myself out of my comfort zone.

"Eduardo!" she called out, waving her hand in the air. "Over here!"

I turned and watched a stocky man walk over to us. His dark hair was short and glossy, and his smiling face seemed kind. I noticed his dark eyes lit up when he stared at my aunt. His nose dominated his face, and his skin was a warm, toasty brown. He broke into a litany of Italian and kissed my aunt full on the lips. When he looked down at me, his eyes crinkled when he smiled like he'd been out in the sun too long, and his teeth were blindingly white. "*Signorina*, welcome to Positano! Your aunt told me all about you and we are so happy you have come to visit. Your aunt desperately needs a chaperone."

I smiled and he took my hand, dwarfing it with his grip, making me feel immediately welcome. "*Grazie.* I'm so happy to meet you."

"How are the tourists today?" Aunt Silvia asked.

"Keeping me busy. We had a fishing trip this morning, and a general sightseeing tour."

"Oh, you have a boat?" I asked.

"*Sì*, hopefully you will join me one day for a tour. I give you good rate," he said with a wink.

"Is Rafe here? I'd love for him to meet Olivia," Aunt Silvia said.

"Of course, he will be happy to show a pretty girl around." Eduardo called out while I tried not to blush, and a young man strode down the dock, pushing his sunglasses to the top of his head as he closed the distance.

"Olivia, this is my son, Rafael. He is my assistant in our boat business and knows everything about this enchanting city. I'm sure he'd love to show you around. Rafe, this is Silvia's niece, Olivia. She is staying for the summer."

I couldn't have known at the time how often this moment would play out in my mind. How I'd pick apart every second of my reaction; the way his chocolate-brown curls hit the light, or the shy smile curving his full lips, or the way he shifted his hips in an almost nervous stance, as if he was just as tongue-tied as me. He ducked his head, and his father repeated his name, as if he needed urging to look up. I'd remember that, when he reached out to shake my hand, his fingers were warm as they enclosed mine, and lingered just a few seconds too long, enough that I'd obsess over whether or not it was deliberate. He was tall, with broad shoulders that stretched out the navy-blue T-shirt he wore. Jeans rode low on his hips. Battered boat shoes clad his feet. And he smelled of the sea, and sunshine, and laundered cotton—all the things I wanted to bury myself in and savor.

But it was his eyes that mesmerized me. Thick eyelashes framed a dark, sooty gaze that seared right to my soul. The rings around his irises were so dark, his eyes seemed almost black, with a bottomless depth that gave me goose bumps.

I blinked; my tongue tangled so much I could spit out only one word. "Hi."

"*Ciao.* Is this your first time in Italy?"

I nodded a bit too vigorously. "Yes. I love it here. I think it's one of the most beautiful places I've ever seen."

He grinned, ducking his head again, and I fisted my sweaty palms. "I'm glad. I'll be happy to show you around when you're free. *Mi dispiace*, I have another appointment to get to. I will see you later, no?"

"Yes! Um, yes, whenever. I'm good."

He nodded, said goodbye to Aunt Silvia and his father, and walked away.

Did my heart already recognize that nothing would ever be the same again?

CHAPTER FOUR

Pris

Pris stared at the perfectly set table spread before her. She'd gone with the fine china, pairing the place settings with Lenox candlesticks and linen napkins. The rib eye was rare and crusted with peppercorns. The earthy smells of rosemary and garlic wafted through the air from the roasted potatoes. Steamed asparagus had reached the perfect shade of green. Her fork bit into a stalk with a firm crispness that should have given her pleasure. She'd spent two hours in the kitchen prepping and hoping to achieve some sense of normalcy between them. Tonight, there was no messy hair or dirty jeans—she'd cleaned herself up, applied makeup, and managed to slip on a skirt. Even her legs were shaved.

The empty chair at the head of the table mocked not only her effort but the denial she'd been trying hard to force down.

She was losing her husband.

Pris forked up a piece of meat, tried to chew, then gave up and reached for her wine. The ruby-red Cabernet was rich and complex on her tongue but had turned more into a goal than a pleasure. Maybe if she got drunk enough, she'd begin to feel something other than the sense her entire life was slipping away.

Even better?

Maybe she'd care.

A humorless laugh spilled out and broke the heavy silence. Even though Thomas had been away at college, knowing he wasn't coming home for the summer threw her into empty-nest syndrome all over again. The sweeping open spaces of the high ceilings and massive rooms only added to the loneliness. She remembered when he was a toddler and one afternoon she'd locked herself in the pantry to cry, overwhelmed by one little boy's mischief and the energy he sustained for endless hours on little sleep. He had flung open the door and giggled with delight, thinking they'd been playing hide-and-go-seek. Pris had stared at her precious child, tears running down her cheeks, and laughed so hard she'd almost peed her pants. Even then, Thomas had the ability to drive her nuts and inspire such love, it was as if the cells of her body would split open and break with the power of it.

Once, his father had teased out the same reactions.

What had happened to them?

The sound of the door interrupted her thoughts. She waited for him at the table, sipping her wine, while his footsteps echoed on the shiny mahogany floors and stopped beside her.

"Oh shit."

The wry admission swung her gaze up, colliding with his. The denim blue of his eyes still pierced right through her, but now there was nothing left to unearth. No surprises left for him to discover and meet with delight. She just had a vast space inside that felt as empty and lonely as her house. "I hope you didn't use that language in court," she said.

He rubbed his head, the salt-and-pepper strands lending an

air of distinguished authority that was still sexy. How many times had they lain together, naked limbs entangled, while she ran her fingers through the thick, mussed strands. Her fingers clenched in muscle memory, but the impulse to reach out died away. She hadn't wanted to be touched in a while. Another issue to deal with. Another fault of hers to chalk up to the disintegration of their marriage.

"I'm sorry, Pris. I forgot you were cooking tonight and stopped at the DA's office. Lost track of time."

She gave a half shrug. "I understand. You can stick it in the microwave if it's too cold."

He shot her a half smile, shed his suit jacket, and slid into the chair. "Nope, I'm starving and that meat looks so good, it'll be better cooled. How are you doing today?"

Pris watched him pile up his plate, still in his dress clothes. Lines of weariness bracketed his eyes. She was wrong to think he wasn't affected or was ignorant. As much as she'd like to blame him for all their problems, it wasn't fair. She'd made her own choices, using him as a guidepost for her happiness instead of herself.

"Okay. Spoke to Thomas today. He loves London a bit too much. I don't want him to become a transplanted Brit."

Garrett laughed and cut into his steak. "It's still new. He'll get tired of the accents and stiff upper lips soon enough."

A smile ghosted her lips. Father and son were so alike, in looks and build and humor. "Hopefully. But he's happy. That should get me through a lonely summer."

"You have me."

The words fell between them, along with an awkward silence. Once, it would have been uttered with a wink and a laugh. They would have talked of a few weekend getaways to put on their calendar, excited to spend time traveling together.

She forced herself to nod, but an honest reaction shot out of her mouth. "Not really. You're never home."

His deep sigh said they were off and running. "Pris, I told you before, I'm slammed at the office. They doubled my caseload since I made partner."

"Funny, for the past few years all I heard was you have to work this hard to make partner. Now, it's the same story, even though we passed that goal months ago. I'm beginning to think it's you, not the company."

One silver brow shot up. "What are you trying to say? That I love working all hours on little sleep and dealing with a testy wife twenty-four seven?"

She flinched but held her ground. God knows, some hard things needed to be said. Might as well be over a cold hundred-dollar steak and fine wine. "Yes, that's exactly what I'm saying. Because you don't want to come home. Why don't you finally admit it?"

For a moment, she thought she'd won. His blue gaze grew flinty, and he opened his mouth, ready to shoot the truth out at her like a missile to blow up her safe, orderly, cold life. Pris poised, ready for it, but then his shoulders slumped and he rubbed his head. His voice grew softer in sheer weariness. "I don't want to fight. I'm sorry I'm not here more often. It's just . . . a difficult time."

"My mother recently died, Garrett. I just found out she has a secret house in Italy and a hidden lover from her past. My sisters are freaking out trying to decide what to do, so I'm having a difficult time myself."

"I know. I'll be happy to do some research for you at the firm and see what we can find."

"No, I'd rather do it myself. Bailey's talking with Dad, and Devon's digging into Mom's financials in case she was sending money somewhere and we didn't catch it."

"Do you think she was having an affair?"

An icy chill skated down her spine. He'd said it so . . . casually. Like it didn't mean anything. "Of course not." Pris tried not to sound shrill. "It was obviously a relationship she had before Dad. He's the only cheater in the family—Mom would have never betrayed him."

Garrett leveled his gaze at her. Once, she'd been able to read all the secrets in his eyes. Now it was like looking into foggy ocean waters, choppy and gray. "How do you know that? People make mistakes all the time. Your mom wasn't perfect."

Her heart sped up, but she calmed herself by taking a slow, deep breath. Why was he trying to bait her? Her sisters also seemed to think Mom might have betrayed Dad, which was ridiculous and wrong. She wasn't about to allow her mother to be torn apart for an act she'd never commit. "She was close to me," Pris clipped out. "She prided her family above all else. We came first at all times. Plus, she never snuck away to Italy, or left us for any period of time. There's no way she had an affair."

Garrett's mouth softened. "You would have made a great lawyer."

"There's only room for one of us to have a thriving career. Don't you remember?"

She didn't mean it. His broad shoulders stiffened, and now there was nothing soft about him as he concentrated on his plate. "I remember it differently. I remember you convincing me I was what you wanted."

Emotion roiled through her in waves. She ached to go to him and be held. To feel safe as she told him every secret of her heart. He'd listen like the old days, and the connection would reignite, giving her something to fight for.

"You were," she said softly. "I just didn't realize I'd be competing with another, more important mistress."

Annoyance flickered over his strong features. "I've never cheated on you, Pris."

"You cheat every night and weekend. Every holiday and canceled vacation."

He muttered a curse and shook his head. "I can't do this tonight. Not again."

He was right. Neither could she. Pris paused, returning to an idea she had considered for the past few days. "I'm thinking I may fly to Italy. To close up the house. Maybe sell it."

He cocked his head. "When?"

"Soon. There's no one who needs me here right now, so it's a good time."

"What about your work with the foundation? And the library fundraiser you've been developing? There's plenty to do here."

The familiar unease wrapped around her belly and squeezed. All the stuff she'd busied herself with in the past decade had once given her focus and purpose. Tommy needed her. The charities she worked with needed her. She'd re-created herself into a strong leader in the community, always willing to volunteer, mentor, and run various auctions, fundraisers, or parties. When she'd given up ballet, she'd focused on creating a new woman—one who had purpose and passion. But lately, Pris realized it was like looking at an empty shell. Nothing seemed important anymore. It was like playing a role while she watched at a distance, untouched and unfeeling while she went through the motions like a puppet.

This is your reward for doing it all right, the voice whispered bitterly. *You get to stare down the barrel of a full midlife crisis for your big prize! Congratulations!*

"They'll do fine without me," she said. "We have committees for a reason."

"How long will you go?"

"Not long. Just enough time to take stock of the house and see if we can figure out who this mysterious R is."

Garrett hesitated, twirling the fork in his large grip. "Does it really matter anymore, Pris? She's gone. Maybe it's best you don't go digging and find something that you won't like."

She blew out a breath. "I owe it to her! Why should her life get picked apart when she did everything right? I refuse to let anyone believe something false that could paint her as a bad wife or mother."

"Sometimes, lying is the only way to keep what you love together."

She jerked at the words and stared at her husband. There was something beneath the statement, a hidden meaning. But she also knew if she poked, the answers she discovered might destroy what was left of them. "What you love?" she asked. "Or who?"

He seemed to realize he'd been led deeper into a dialogue he wasn't ready for. Was that what was happening now? Were they too terrified to drag their troubles into the light because neither of them was ready to face the end?

He dropped his head and concentrated on the food. "I'm just noting we don't know what your mom's real story is. And I know things have been tough around here, with more work responsibility and Tommy being gone. Maybe we can just use this summer together to reset. Try and figure things out. Spend some quality time together."

Suddenly, she was exhausted by the mental games and denial, which were beginning to break her apart. "Is that what you really want, Garrett?" she asked softly. "To be together? Or do we need to talk about something else?"

Her husband jerked his gaze upward, blue eyes wide with

surprise. She'd finally asked it aloud. They'd grown so distant these past two years, she wouldn't know where to begin to find her way back to him. The couple they were when they'd first met, young and passionate and ready to take on the world, had softened into a reality she'd thought she wanted. Now, though, she wasn't sure.

God, she still did love him. His laugh and his kindness and his sharp wit. She loved the way he looked at his job as something bigger than making money, but actually helping people. Loved the way he interacted with their son and how he cooked her perfect French toast on Sunday mornings, and how he could walk into a room and command it without saying a word.

But lately, it wasn't enough. She was haunted by her past choices—there was a rising resentment she couldn't rationalize or wish away. And it wasn't on him.

It was her.

Odd, that the decisions that gutted your life could barely be seen when looking back. She thought it was often the daily, minute decisions and choices along the way that eroded the foundation to broken crumbles.

"What do you mean?" he asked carefully.

Pris placed her wineglass down. Dragging in a deep breath, she gazed at him and tried to face him honestly. "Things haven't been good with us in a long time, Garrett."

His jaw locked. "We're going through a rough patch. All marriages do."

"So, we just keep ignoring the issues and it will all go away one morning?"

"I don't know, Pris. It seems I don't know much anymore except my wife is unhappy, distant, and recoils when I try and touch her. I'd be happy to hear if you have any other answers."

The jab hit hard, stealing her breath, but she was tired of

pretending. "We don't even talk," she said, curling her fingers into a loose fist. "And when we do, it's like you look through me. I feel like you're already anticipating my answers and are just biding time until you can escape, either to work or to one of your many golf games, or even those video games you're addicted to."

His body stiffened, turning his gaze to stone. "I leave because it's obvious you don't want me around. When was the last time we had sex?"

She blew out a breath. "Why does it always have to revolve around our physical relationship? Do you think I'm a robot, ready to get hot and heavy just because you ask? How can I give you my body when we can't even have a conversation?"

His laugh was full of derision and scraped her nerves raw. "Great, here we go. It's always my damn fault, so, fine. I'll own it. Tell me what you want and I'll do it. Do you want to have date night? Do you want me to whisk you away for a romantic long weekend? Buy you something so you feel valued? Give me the steps, so I don't feel like a goddamned stranger with my own wife!"

The silence exploded like shrapnel, scattering fragments of pain throughout the room. If only she could do just that—tell him exactly what she needed to make things the way they used to be. If she could go back to the woman she'd been, before time and regrets and what-ifs eroded her happiness.

But she couldn't. Pris didn't even recognize who she was or what she'd become while her husband forged ahead on his path, never questioning if he was enough. They were both coming apart at the seams, but if they were sewn back together, would he want the new version?

Her head bowed in surrender. "Garrett, this isn't about a date night or me needing attention. I wish it was. I wish I knew a quick cure, but all I can say is we've lost our connection. I remember I used to look into your eyes and find my answers. Now there's a barrier between us I don't know how to scale. We've both checked out of this relationship."

He nodded slowly, meal forgotten. Even now, looking at him from across the formal dining room table, she could only measure the yawning gap and mutual weariness at trying to figure the other one out. It was no longer an exciting puzzle, with the reward of falling into each other more fully. Instead, she looked forward to an empty room, a relieved quiet where she didn't have to force herself to play along.

She was lonelier with Garrett than by herself.

"What do you want to do? Counseling?"

"I don't know," she said honestly. "I just don't want to pretend any longer. I think taking a trip to Italy is a good idea. Maybe we both need some space to think."

"Maybe you're right. Take some time away to be with your sisters. Hopefully, we'll gain a fresh perspective on what our next step is." He paused, as if trying to decide if he should say the next words. "I still love you, Pris. But I don't want to feel like the one making you unhappy all the time." He pushed his chair back and stood. "I'm going to shower. Thanks for dinner."

She watched him go. For a few seconds, she wondered if she should run after him. When they used to fight, she'd always be the one to run after him, until sex became the go-to plan for both of them to forgive and forget. Once, that passion had ruled her, and she'd embraced it with a tight-knit focus because it made sense. Physical intimacy eased the bumps and hidden potholes of a marriage.

Until its lack became one of the biggest road blocks. A weapon; a curse; a living thing to be negotiated instead of a welcome relief from the hard stuff. The glue had come undone and left a sticky mess that neither of them had been able to figure out.

Garrett had first caught sight of her when she was dancing, caught up in the passion and focus of an art she'd been studying for many years. Her decision to walk away from a career that might have torn them apart had been a sacrifice, but one she'd been willing to make.

But now? It was time to acknowledge the empty ache inside her that had been slowly growing like weeds choking healthy grass. Pris had no idea how to fill it, or stop it, so she'd ignored the feeling and hoped it would eventually pass.

Until her mother's death. The grief had only added to the brutal cocktail mix and pushed her over the edge. She didn't know who she was anymore. And God, she was tired of pretending she was okay. She needed some direction. Some quiet and space in her soul.

Maybe if she could figure out how to make peace with herself, she could bloom under her husband's touch again.

Maybe Italy was the only answer left.

The thoughts roiled in her head while she sat in the empty room, sipped her wine, and began planning her trip.

CHAPTER FIVE

Olivia

I learned early that my aunt gave me free rein, of both the house and my social life. She encouraged me to go out and meet people, citing that it was the best way to immerse yourself in a new culture. I watched her spend time in the early evening getting ready to go out, most of the time with Eduardo or visiting friends. The bathroom filled with the scents of rich sandalwood and exotic musk, along with various spiked heels and flowing dresses baring her shoulders or running into a deep V to show off cleavage. There was an air of excitement and adventure when I was around her, and I ached to absorb her beauty through my skin, to become even a tad like her.

Many times, I stayed behind, sketching nonstop in the garden or reading, content to watch the shadow of the sun fall on the hills in its slow descent. I'd journal my up-and-down emotions, from my increasing attention toward Rafael to the agony of believing I'd never experience love in the forms my aunt had. I didn't want my life to be limited like my parents', full of daily tasks and an increasing boredom. I scribbled madly, trying to figure things out by catching the words on paper as if it would finally free the secret.

When I joined the get-togethers or parties in town, Rafael was always there. He'd quietly slip in and out of various groups, cradling a beer, laughing easily at whoever was trying to secure his attention. Girls hung on him, but he didn't seem to have one in particular he dated. Once in a while, he'd meet my eyes and something inside me melted and flamed at the same time, this itchy need to get closer to him. But I tried to give off a cool, detached vibe like I was comfortable in this new world where most of the language slipped past me and my peers seemed so much more exotic and alive than the ones back in high school. Too soon, his gaze would slide away and he'd turn, as if to let me know he was here if I wanted to seek him out. But I refused. I wanted him to come to me, even if it was torture. Plus, I was too shy and confused to strike up a conversation. I'd only make a fool of myself.

I tried to relax and make friends in Italy. When I spoke with Natalie and Julia, two girls my age currently enrolled in university, they seemed not to worry about grades or school or the future with the tense anticipation that usually stole my sleep. When I asked if they wanted to make a mark in the world, they laughed, tossing their long dark hair over their shoulders, raising a pint glass of beer in a sloppy salute, and telling me to chill, at least for the summer.

I was ashamed at my constant need to make sense of things, so I turned to drawing. My fingers cramped and my feet hurt as I walked and explored and recorded the things I saw and how they made me feel. For the first time in a while, I began to forget about what could happen and what I should be doing and enjoyed the climbing wisteria that framed the cottage, or the scent of lemon in the air, or the slow, lazy cut of boats drifting in the water. I indulged in the eye candy of buff men, with dark gazes and lilting voices that seemed to hypnotize me. I baked in the sun and lazily dreamed hours away and learned how to stop feeling guilty.

One night, Julia invited me to meet for dinner with her friends. I dressed in dark-wash capri jeans and a black halter top that showed off my burgeoning tan and left a patch of my stomach naked. I stuck with flat sandals because I knew heels would make me trip on the uneven streets and steps, but added a gold ankle bracelet. My hair was a riotous mess with the humidity, so I pinned it up. Gold hoops and red lipstick gave me extra confidence.

I faced the steps with a deep breath and paced myself as I made my way down. The night was balmy, and I was a bit sweaty by the time I reached the restaurant. The place was packed, and I had to weave in and out before I found Julia. She waved me over to a large table outside by the marina.

"*Ciao!*" she said, smacking my cheeks in an enthusiastic kiss. "You look amazing!"

"*Grazie.* So do you."

Julia had braided her long hair, and it looped over one shoulder. Her white shorts and creamy top showed off her perfect body and lean legs. I tried not to fiddle with my halter top and forced a wide smile at the group she introduced me to.

Marcus, one of Julia's friends, immediately sat next to me, chatting me up with a casual confidence I liked. But his gaze kept sliding over my exposed stomach, touching on my breasts, and I almost wished I'd brought a jacket. Usually, I loved when a guy looked at me in admiration, but there was something about him that made me a bit uncomfortable. I tried to shake it off. He ordered me another drink, touching my arm while he spoke in decent English.

"Have you seen the secret caves yet?"

I shook my head. "No. My aunt has been busy, but I'm hoping to do some exploring. I'd love to see the Blue Grotto in Capri."

"Overrated," he snorted. He had an abundance of muscles in a compact frame, but his face seemed a tad too big, with a prominent forehead and a slanted, jutted jaw. Light brown eyes held a glint of sharp interest. "I can take you out if you want. Show you more stuff."

"Thanks, I'll let you know."

"This Saturday. I've got my dad's boat." His fingers wrapped around my wrist.

I laughed and pulled away, reaching for my drink. "I'll have to see. My aunt is careful who I go out with."

"Doubt it. She's known to have a good time herself. What do you say?"

I opened my mouth to tell him no way, not after he'd insulted my aunt, but another voice interrupted.

"Back off, *cugino*. When you insult Silvia, you insult my father."

Rafael stood beside me. Immediately, my skin began to tingle and that hot, melty feeling slid through my veins. He was dressed in a plain white T-shirt, denim shorts, and boat shoes. His chocolate curls spilled over his forehead. He didn't even glance at me. His gaze was glued to Marcus, his jaw clenched, and a thrill coursed down my spine.

"Ah, come on, Sartori, you know I'm joking." Marcus jerked his head, a slight smirk on his lips. "Have you two met yet?"

"Yes," I said, sliding away from Marcus. I nodded at Rafe. "It's good to see you again."

Did his face soften when he looked at me, or was it my imagination? There was such gentleness in his eyes, but also a male intensity that made my throat close up with longing. "You too."

Marcus laughed and the waitress came back with our drinks. He lifted his in a mock salute. "Guess the three of us can become best buddies this summer. I was just inviting Olivia on my boat this weekend."

Rafe broke into a litany of Italian, and I watched in fascination as Marcus's face morphed into anger. He shot some remarks back to Rafe, and I tried to catch a word here and there, but it was too fast for my ears. Finally, Marcus lifted his hands high in the air and shook his head.

"Not worth a fight. Not for this." He shot me a look, scooped up his drink, and headed over to the far side of the table.

My cheeks burned as I watched, uncomfortable that I'd done something to make a scene, but then Rafe was touching my hand, his voice soft. "I'm sorry. I hope I didn't mess up your night. I just know Marcus, and he's a bit . . ." He trailed off, seemingly just as embarrassed as I was. "He comes on very strong sometimes."

I smiled with pleasure. He'd actually worried about me. "I'm glad you did. You were right, I wasn't feeling very comfortable. Is he your cousin? I can't understand much Italian but it sounded like you called him that."

He let out a breath. "No, it's just an expression. I call many of my friends my cousins. Marcus is known around here for his love of new women, but he has a girlfriend he always goes back to. I didn't want you to get hurt."

Giddiness gripped me. This was the first time we were having a real conversation. At all those previous parties he'd kept his distance until I figured he'd never be interested. But now I read the situation differently. "Well, I appreciate it. The last thing I need is a pissed-off Italian girl beating me up for trying to steal her man."

He grinned. "I thought Americans were tough. Don't you take classes like kickboxing or karate?"

I laughed. "I did tap dance when I was young. I could jump all over her feet."

Rafe shook his head. "That's terrible. It is a good thing I saved you."

"Yes. It is a good thing."

We stood together in the shadows while laughter and chatter and clinking glasses swarmed around us. Julia came over and interrupted the moment, waving him to take a seat with everyone. "Rafe! About time you decided to talk to Livia!"

Was that a patch of red on Rafe's cheeks or my imagination?

He laughed and shook his head. "*Sì.* Usually you are doing all the talking, *chiacchierona*."

With a mischievous wink, she spoke to Rafe in rapid Italian, glancing back and forth between us, then floated away.

"Uh-oh. What did she say?" I asked, fiddling with my straw. I hated the fact that Julia or her friends were mocking me and my crush on Rafe. Was it that obvious?

"She said it was a good thing I took care of you. We get many Americans here for the summer. Many are a bit—how do you say—snooty? Acting as if we are less because we don't have money, or a fancy education. But you are different."

A rush of relief poured through me. It was nice to know Julia honestly liked me. In just a short time, I was beginning to trust her more than some of the mean girls at my high school. "I'm glad because I think she's super nice. And beautiful."

The words popped out before I could stop them, and I tried to fight another blush.

"*Sì.* But so are you."

"Sorry. I didn't say that to fish for a compliment." I took a long swallow of my drink. "I'm just glad everyone doesn't think I'm a bitch."

White teeth flashed in his sunbaked face. "Silvia would have never brought you for the summer if she didn't like you—whether or not you are family. I don't think you could be a bitch if you tried." He leaned in and our gazes locked. "And I know you weren't fishing. I just tell the truth."

My breath got trapped in my lungs. My nose tingled from the delicious scent of him, a combination of sea and sun and wind I wanted to steep myself in. Something hummed between us, an energy I'd never experienced before. I heard my name called from a distance, and then I shook my head to refocus.

"Liv! Come over here. I want you to meet someone!"

Julia motioned me over, and though I hated to leave, I knew she was being really sweet, trying to make me feel more comfortable with the group. Rafe seemed to catch my hesitation, because he smiled and jerked his head toward them. "Better get over there. I'll catch you later?"

"Yes."

I felt his gaze on me as I grabbed my drink and joined Julia and her friends. She introduced me to Ava, another American who spent the summers with her parents in a house close to mine. Her curvy figure, pin-straight black hair, and gray eyes gave her a unique look that seemed a bit intimidating, until she opened her mouth. Then she launched into a warm greeting, peppered with a lot of curse words and crass humor that made me immediately crack up. It didn't take me long to relax and enjoy the chatter of fashion, crushes, and stuff we wanted to do this summer.

We wrapped up at the bar and headed to a house to continue the party. The stars sparkled in a velvet sky, and the girls linked arms as we maneuvered through the crooked streets and away from the bustling crowds gathered by the string of shops and cafés. The boys were loud behind us, singing off-key an Italian song as we moved deeper into the shadows and stopped at a mint-green home with an outdoor terrace and an array of white lights strung around the trees.

The group quickly set out some chairs, rickety tables, and the cooler of wine and beer. Someone set out a radio and fast-paced music blared out into the night. I spent the first hour getting to know Ava better, and the other girls in the group, occasionally chatting with some guys who approached.

Marcus stayed away.

The entire time, I was tracking Rafael from my peripheral vision and hoping he didn't seem too interested in a particular girl. I had just refilled my wineglass when I felt the back of my neck prickle.

"Hi."

I tamped down on a silly grin and tried to be cool. "Hi."

"Want to go for a walk?"

I barely hesitated, elated at some alone time. "Yeah, sounds good."

I followed him down the path at a slow pace. Our arms swung casually back and forth, our shoulders close to touching. We both held our drinks and I stopped myself from gulping the alcohol to calm my nerves. Vomiting on him tonight would not be a good look.

"Tell me about yourself, Olivia Moretti," he finally said, his voice touched with teasing.

"What do you want to know?" I asked, wishing I could have uttered something witty or sexy.

"Anything. What are your summers usually like when you're not with your aunt?"

I thought of my parents back home, deciding whether or not to get a divorce. I thought of the lonely days, and how I always felt like an outsider in my own life, and that I was more comfortable around my sketch pad and books rather than people. "Pretty boring."

He laughed, a deep rumble in his chest that made my heart launch in my chest. I wondered if I could ever get tired of hearing that sound. "You're talkative, huh?"

"Sorry. I guess I'm used to being alone a lot. Kind of lame, I know."

"Nope, sounds like me. My favorite place to be is on the water. Something about it makes me feel really free and at home at the same time."

"You do tour charters, right?" I asked, relieved he didn't seem to think I was a weirdo.

"Yes, me and my dad. At first, Dad was just a fisherman, but as Positano became more and more active, he invested in a good boat and began doing tours. Smart move. As you've seen, we seem to be a playground for the rich and famous."

I took a sip of wine, tilting my head upward to catch the faint breeze. "I guess when I think of Italy it's more of statues, museums, and the pope. I've never seen so many yachts in my life, or designer clothes."

He laughed again. His arm swung and brushed mine. "Unfortunately, most of the locals aren't as well-off. We get invaded for the summer, so shopkeepers and restaurants make most of their money in season. I prefer when I can get a seat to drink my espresso and not fight for space on the sidewalks. Where are you from?"

"New York, but not the city. About two hours north. There's a lot of farms in the neighborhood, so I'm not used to crazy crowds either."

"Sounds nice."

"Have you ever been to the States?"

He shook his head. "I haven't been anywhere. One day, I may be able to travel, but the business takes up all of my time now."

"I think it's cool you work with your dad," I said. "Do you like the work, or did you feel like you had to do it?"

He looked surprised by my question and I wondered if I'd probed too deep. "Hmm, I never thought about it. I've been on the water since I was little, and after my mom died, it was like Dad and I were a team. It was the only way to get through it."

My heart squeezed. I stopped walking and touched his arm. "I'm sorry, Rafe. I can't imagine how hard that must've been for you guys."

"It wasn't easy," he admitted, not trying to brush me off or pretend he was okay. "I miss her all the time, but I guess my answer is I like where I am. I'm my own boss—other than my dad—and I get to experience different people every day and be outside. I never had the itch to go to college."

I liked how honest he was, and I felt the connection between us tighten. We began walking again, the lights from the boats flickering in the distance. "I'm going to college to figure stuff out. I hate how everyone is constantly asking me what I want to be. I feel like I should know. I love writing and art, but I don't think I can make a living doing creative stuff, so I also want to study business. I'm heading to New Paltz to stay in the dorms." I gave a mocking laugh. "Even I know it's a pretend independence. But it's not like I can backpack across Europe to find myself or apprentice at a studio to learn a craft. My dad works for an insurance company, and Mom is an office worker. Neither one of them seems very happy. "

"Sounds like this summer is a gift. A chance to learn more about yourself before you head to college."

I glanced over and smiled. "Yeah. I'm pretty lucky. Now I just have to make sure I take advantage and push out of my comfort zone. I've been staying close to home with my sketch pad."

"Maybe I can help. I can show you some places most tourists don't find."

"Secret adventures?" I teased, instantly pumped at the idea of spending more time with him.

"Unless you want to double-date with my dad and your aunt."

I laughed at the image. "Sounds hot."

He laughed with me. "My days are pretty full, but I can call you about this week's schedule. Maybe we can grab a few hours on a late afternoon?"

My heart sped up. "That'll work. I have nothing going on, so I'm flexible. Do you need my number?"

"I'll get it from my dad."

"Cool." I swayed a bit on my feet, giddy with the warm night air and the stars streaked overhead and the warmth of his male body so close to mine. I studied the shape of his hooked nose and chiseled jaw, his dark brown eyes and heavy brow. Faint stubble clung to his chin. The white T-shirt stretched across his broad shoulders, and my fingers curled with the need to reach out and touch him.

Voices echoed in the air, and Rafe shook his head. "Better get back before they try to track us down."

I nodded and followed his lead.

But I knew that simple walk with Rafael Sartori had changed everything.

I just didn't realize how much.

CHAPTER SIX

Devon

"I'm sorry, Dev. You didn't get the dean position."

The words were like a harsh slap across the face. She blinked, trying desperately to compose her face into a smooth mask. "I see. Who got it?"

Jordan Turner, current chair of the Accounting and Finance Department, regarded her from across the desk with a level gaze. "Elliot Feimer."

The name made her gnash her teeth together. Typical. Besides being male, Elliot was front and center on some of the most important committees. He was a decent teacher, but his arrogance was legendary. He gave mansplaining a whole new definition. Dev couldn't help the bit of sting in her words. "I shouldn't be surprised. Did I even have a fair shot?"

She never would've challenged someone from the interview board, but Jordan had always been a champion of her work. Once he decided not to run for the position himself, he'd encouraged her to go for it, even though her administrative background was light. She had the most publications and committee experience and consistently scored at the top tier of student surveys.

Jordan gave a sharp nod. "You were our second pick. Great interview, but Elliot has been here longer and served on a few more boards."

She let out a breath. "I understand." After all, she knew how things worked. There was a hierarchy, and cliques were huge in the academic world. Still, it burned her that no matter how hard she worked, Dev was scolded for pushing too hard, too soon by the big boys. It was frustrating as hell.

"What's the next step?" she asked briskly. Better at this point to focus on the future and play nice for the team.

"Glad you asked." Jordan shifted his weight in the squeaky chair. He was an overlarge man; his muscled body always seemed to stretch out his suits, which added to his riveting presence when he stood in front of a group. Ruthlessly intelligent, he'd helped spearhead the department in new directions. His cultured voice held a hint of accent from his native country, Trinidad. He reached across his littered desk and grabbed a folder. "There's an opportunity this summer to teach an advanced course in corporate accounting in the global economy specifically for work professionals in the industry. I've got demand for a diverse group of high-profile CEO types, Wall Street brokers, and admins who need a hands-on workshop but with big-level reach. I thought you'd be perfect for it."

She took the file he handed over and began to flip through it. "Nothing like this has been done before from our department."

"Exactly. It's a rare opportunity to connect with some powerful contacts outside our normal efforts. Very high-profile—there's already been some buzz, so you'll be closely watched. You up for it?"

A bloom of pride cut through her. Dev realized this was not

just about teaching another course. Jordan had been working hard on leveling up the Finance Department at Stern School of Business to compete with the stellar reputation the college had for fashion and creative arts programs.

She mentally sifted through her schedule but already knew she'd do anything for the opportunity. "Of course. Looking forward to it."

"Good. The course starts in August, but there will be a ton of prep."

"No problem. I'll be ready."

"Excellent. Hope it won't be ruining your summer plans."

She shook her head. "Why would anyone want to leave this crowded, hot, overpopulated haven in the height of summer?" He laughed as she got up, the file firmly closed in her hand. Then she suddenly remembered. "Oh, I will be going away next week. Did you need me to cancel?"

"Don't be silly, even you need to take a break sometimes, Professor. Where are you off to?"

"Italy."

He raised a dark brow. "Nice. What part?"

"Positano. I recently found out my mother owned a house there, so my sisters and I are going to check it out. Probably sell it."

His voice softened. "I'm really sorry about your mom, Dev. You doing okay?"

She shifted her weight, uncomfortable whenever she talked about personal feelings. "Fine. I'll only be gone about a week."

Jordan dismissed her with a wave of a hand. "Take two—you'll probably need it. I have a feeling this course will help you in a lot of ways. And hopefully soon, I'll be out of here and you can take over as chair."

"Oh, I'm not looking for that at all! I'm—"

"Kidding, Professor. Have a good time, but don't come home

with any of those hot Italians. I hear they're good at breaking hearts."

Dev rolled her eyes and headed to the door. "I'd prefer a hot bath, a healthy profit margin, and a good night's sleep."

His laughter followed her out the door. She nodded to his secretary and headed to her office, mind buzzing.

Finally, she'd have an opportunity that could be a big help with her career. She had no issue with leaving NYU eventually if the right positions didn't open up. There was so much more she wanted to do; she refused to be limited for too long. Dev had never been afraid to push her way up the ladder of success instead of waiting her turn.

The memory of her last conversation with her mother rose like a cloud of dirt kicked in her face.

"I can't understand why you have no respect for my academic career." Her voice shook with frustration and resentment. "Pris never graduated because she was dancing. Bailey got a degree from an arts school and barely scraped by. Yet, I sacrificed to get my PhD, work at a top college, and published numerous articles. But I don't have a boyfriend, right? So that negates everything else."

"No! That's not what I'm saying at all, sweetheart. You know how proud your father and I are of you. I'm just worried you shut yourself off from any other part of life—friends, travel, love, experiences. When was the last time you went out on a date? Or to one of those fun clubs to dance?"

Dev groaned, barely restraining herself from bashing her head on her kitchen table. "I'm working so I can get ahead and secure a future for myself. So I don't have to depend on anyone else for my own happiness. I'm sorry it's not enough for you, Mom."

"I want it to be enough for you. I don't want you to have regrets when you look back at your life."

"Like Pris?"

Her mother's soft sigh echoed over the line. "All of you girls are unique. I don't want you to be like anyone else but you, Dev. I just . . . worry."

The rest of the conversation faded away. Dev paused in the empty hallway, trying to get her bearings. She hated their last exchange—hated the idea that that was the last time she spoke with her mother before she'd died. More than how she'd sniped at Mom was the fact that underneath it all, Dev only wanted her mother to be proud of her accomplishments. But it always felt as if her boring, staid, logical life was a huge disappointment compared to the excitement of her siblings.

Dev straightened her shoulders and marched toward her office.

She wouldn't think about that conversation or her wishes, or even regrets. She had a job to do in Italy—take stock of the house and get it sold. Their mother's financial records showed no strange deposits or withdrawals, and she'd kept to a reasonable monthly budget. She'd definitely not been renting out the house for extra income, so maybe it had been willed to her and she'd forgotten. Or hadn't gotten around to telling any of her daughters about it. A bit financially lazy, but Dev would take care of it. She'd already researched prices and they'd all make a tidy bundle.

Cracking the identity of the mysterious R was a bonus. Deep inside, she didn't believe Mom could have an illicit romantic affair and hide it from them. There was a reasonable explanation, and when they figured it out, they'd all return home and things would get back to normal. Bailey probably romanticized the entire thing as a dramatic end to a play or romance novel.

But Dev sensed the true secret had nothing to do with an epic affair or love letters.

It was about loneliness. Mom had been cheated on, her trust shattered by their father. So, she'd made friends with what-ifs. Dreams of who she once was, and who she could have been before she married, had kids, and gave up herself for everyone else.

Dev would never do that.

Dragging in a breath, she calmed down, cleared her mind, and got back to work.

CHAPTER SEVEN

Bailey

She stood outside on the front lawn, naked, staring up at the stars.

Toes curling in the soft grass, Bailey took a breath, slightly drunk on the sweet night air while the symphony of crickets hummed all around her. The slight danger of someone walking by and catching sight of her added an edge of excitement she seemed to constantly crave. Not that she'd be embarrassed. She'd made peace with her body and treated it like a lesson in kindergarten.

You get what you get and you don't get upset.

She liked her gentle curves and long blond hair. She disliked her small breasts, big feet, and the mole on her left cheek she always had to check with her dermatologist. She had been gifted with vision to see things others didn't that fueled her creative passion. Whether it was a scene to enact in a play, a drawing to etch, or a scene to capture on canvas, she was always driven forward.

Bailey lifted her arms in the air, wide, a smile playing on her lips. She'd always felt so different from her family—her mother, who'd stayed in that big empty house because she was afraid to go anywhere else and explore; Dev, who seemed married to work, as if it was the only true thing to cling to in the world; and Pris, who walked away from her dancing career to be a wife and mother and now looked like she was only half alive.

Now, though, she wondered about Mom. Her thoughts drifted to this past afternoon.

When Bailey arrived at her father's house, she was hopeful the mystery would finally be solved. Dad seemed puzzled, rubbing his head back and forth in his habitual gesture of deep thinking. They'd sat at the overlarge dining room table that was decorated with fancy china as if the queen was dropping by for a visit. His new wife, Tabitha, was young and hot and loved expensive things. Bailey always wondered if Dad would have married her if she hadn't gotten pregnant, but that had sealed the deal. Bailey's half sibling was now a spoiled teen who wanted nothing to do with her half sisters.

Dad was definitely beginning to look more tired than usual.

He spoke slowly, as if trying to think hard. "Your mother never mentioned a house in Italy. I think I met her aunt Silvia at our wedding, but I don't remember when she passed. I know we didn't go to her funeral. Are you sure she inherited a house in Italy?"

"Here's the deed." Bailey handed it over. "Dad, it seems really weird she would have kept this a secret from you. I mean, isn't that also communal property for the divorce settlement?"

He shook his head. "I wouldn't have fought her on that anyway," he murmured. "I know I was at fault."

"Okay, but what if you'd wanted to take a vacation? She had a whole house in Positano available! Was she taking secret trips there or something? Renting it out and pocketing the money? Dev is looking into her financials."

"No! Geez, your mother practically never left the house without you kids, and I can guarantee you never went to Europe. As for money, we had plenty. It makes no sense." He stared at the papers in front of him for a while. Suddenly, he lifted his gaze and looked at her with a hint of shame. "To be honest, Bae, there *was* one time she left by herself."

"To Italy?"

Dad nodded. "Yeah, but I never thought she had a house to stay at. We were having some . . . issues. She decided to take some time to think things through and said she wanted to see some art. She ended up going to Italy for two weeks. You know, to do museum tours and stuff like that in Rome."

Misfit pieces still lay abandoned in the full puzzle. Bailey thought of the letters they'd read and tried to focus on the big picture. "Do you know if she actually went to Rome? Or you're not sure?"

His lips tightened. "Not sure. I assumed, I think. We didn't speak when she was away. I tried to give her space."

Bailey bit the inside of her cheek. She didn't want to ask but had to. "Why, Dad? Why did you guys need that time apart?"

He hesitated, and she didn't think he'd answer. He seemed to struggle with telling the truth but then finally blurted out the words. "I cheated on her."

Bailey groaned and dropped her head. "Oh God, Dad. Again!"

"It was just once! We were having some issues—things I'm not about to discuss with you—and I slipped up. Of course she was devastated and said she needed some time alone."

"Did this happen when I was little and I don't remember anything?"

"No, you weren't born yet. Pris was about four at the time and went to Boston to stay with your grandmother."

"What happened?"

Dad sighed. "She came back and we both decided our marriage was worth saving. I knew I had to earn her forgiveness and I did. Shortly after, we found out she was pregnant with Dev."

His amber eyes held shadows from the past. "We were happy after that for a long time."

"Until you cheated again."

He winced. "I know. Don't think I don't regret it every damn day. But we weren't happy, Bae. I wish I could explain, but until you're in that same position, it's hard to see my side of the story."

She stared at her father. Obviously weary, he was still a handsome man with his thick hair, beautiful brown-gold eyes, and robust personality. When she was growing up, he had laser-like focus that made Bailey believe she was the most important person in the room. He played hard and never acted like one of those fussy dads who refused to get dirty. He never made her feel like he missed out by not having a son—he took her skiing and skating and taught her how to pitch a wicked softball.

When he was home.

Even though she hated what he'd done, Bailey knew her father was a decent man. He'd been a solid father, supportive and loving, even if he was also a workaholic. Bailey also knew her sisters would freak if they heard this story. They barely had a decent relationship with him, not able to get over his cheating.

But at least they'd believed it only happened once. Knowing he'd betrayed Mom previously would make things even worse. Bailey swore to never tell them.

Some secrets weren't meant to be told.

But the more Bailey dug, the more questions she had. Had her mother seen her secret lover during that missing week? Had she cheated on Dad to gain revenge?

A familiar ache grew and spread in her gut. The moment she'd unveiled the deed to the house, Bailey realized it could be the key to truly understanding her mother. Not as a type of role she played to her daughters, but who she was at her core. Bailey wasn't afraid to find out. Not like Pris and Devon, who'd put

Mom on a pedestal and tried to make her proud by following in her footsteps. Yet, now, maybe they questioned their choices because Mom had surprised them all.

A secret lover. A hidden house in Amalfi. A mystery to solve.

Yes. It was time to go.

"What are you doing out here?"

The male voice hit her ears at the same time strong hands wrapped around her naked waist and pulled her against him. She leaned her head against his shoulder and let her body relax into his. "Stargazing. Getting some air."

His husky laugh rumbled in the night air. "Buck naked? Ever heard of cell phones? There could be a video rolling as we speak."

"It's too dark, I'd see the flash. Besides, I'm tired of all the puritanical judgment of the female body. If they want to make something sexual out of my time with nature, they don't deserve my attention."

Will tightened his grip. "Maybe I just don't want anyone enjoying the view of my woman," he said.

Bailey knew he shot for a teasing remark, but the slight ruffle of possession filtered through. He was getting attached. She'd been wary when they first dove into their affair. After all, he was the theater director in a small town, so most of their time was spent together in rehearsals. It was common for relationships to form between the cast and production crew. She enjoyed Will, with his full beard and intelligent dark eyes, and his perspective on the world fascinated her. He was a people watcher, a perfectionist, and these past few weeks she'd soaked up his knowledge and presence and sexual prowess with enthusiasm.

But now it was getting too intense. Expectation simmered in his gaze, and though a shred of her—ego?—savored the excitement of being wanted, Bailey wasn't about to commit herself to one man or one relationship.

Maybe she never would.

A deep discussion wasn't her style, so she turned in his arms, reaching up to kiss him at the same time she gently berated him. "Chauvinist. I belong to myself. Now, why don't you ditch the clothes and dance with me under the moonlight?"

He lifted her up and walked back toward the house. "I prefer a warm, dry bed rather than getting grass stains on my ass."

She laughed against his lips even though he'd failed the test. Bailey craved a man to match her inner soul—a man who'd never cage or try to leash but rather would run beside her. Will was a good man. It'd be better if she disappeared for a while and let him find someone else. The play closed in a week. He said he'd been working on a script just for her, but she was afraid that would bring further attachment between them. Better to dive into something else and give acting a break for a while. Maybe painting again, where she could lose herself in wild colors and shapes and visions. Things that needed to be captured in something bigger than a simple photograph.

There was nothing to hold her back. Pris wanted to figure out who R was, and Devon wanted to sell the house. Maybe they'd go together, put things in order, and she'd take a break. Reset and decide what to do next. Besides, she liked the idea of gaining a glimpse into her mother's past.

Italy was calling and she was ready to answer.

"Where'd you go?" he growled against her neck, placing her down on the soft comforter.

A pang of emotion she couldn't name, and didn't want to, coursed through her. His gaze promised her more if she only asked. But Bailey never did.

Instead, she smiled and lifted her arms. "I'm right here."

And for tonight, she was.

CHAPTER EIGHT

Olivia

I kept myself busy with my sketch pad, books, and hanging with my aunt. She'd take me to long lunches and let me sip Prosecco at Caffè Positano while we feasted on mussels, pasta, and fresh prawns, gazing out at the magnificent view of water and sky from the wrought-iron balcony. She dragged me shopping and bought me my first pair of real Italian sandals, buttery soft with a block heel and crisscross straps. Aunt Silvia seemed to know everyone—the shop owners, café workers, and pedestrians filling the walkways—stopping quickly to introduce me, then flitting on with a dramatic wave of her hand.

I grew closer to Julia and Ava. We hung out at the beach—which was unlike any I'd ever visited, full of pebbles rather than sand. I learned quickly that water shoes were crucial after the first time I cut my foot, and the sandy strip was narrow and overcrowded. But I got used to it, my fingers hurriedly trying to capture the scenes before me—rich women in tiny designer bikinis and floppy hats; the brown-skinned Italian men, stocky and muscled, walking on the shoreline in briefs that revealed more than concealed; striped teal and lemon beach chairs and umbrellas lined up in perfect rows; the crush of summer people like me, giggling and gossiping in small groups as we lazed away hot afternoons, just waiting to get to the thrill of nighttime parties.

I wondered if the locals despised the tourist invasion each season. Wondered if they mocked this bright peacock-like strutting in their streets, contradicting all the simplicity Italy was supposed to stand for, or if they relished the fresh flow of money and interest in their home.

Either way, it didn't matter, because the tourists were here to stay.

At night, Rafe and I would get together with the group. We'd start off kind of shy with each other, almost as if we believed the connection between us would simply disappear like smoke and one of us would be left feeling awkward. But eventually we'd maneuver ourselves close together in the crowd, start talking, and pick up where we left off.

For two weeks, the tension between us was hot and sweet. We never kissed or even held hands. Just broke off from wherever our friends were to go for a walk, shoulders brushing together, me breathing in deep gulps of his scent, obsessed with his every movement and the erratic beat of my heart in his presence.

Rafe finally managed to wrangle a late afternoon off and we made plans for him to take me out on the boat. I never asked if he'd invited anyone else, but when I arrived that muggy afternoon, we were alone.

"Do I ask for permission to board?" I called out, watching him confidently stand on the boat deck, fiddling with some thick ropes.

He stood and squinted in the sun, smiling. "I don't understand."

"Never mind, I think it's an American thing I've seen in too many movies."

He offered his hand to me. "Jump on."

My fingers closed around his. Besides the tiny shock of awareness, I felt completely safe when he touched me, as if nothing would happen as long as he held my hand. He didn't let go right away when I stood beside him, and we stared at each other for a few moments, recognizing the wild energy that was eventually going to push us together.

Slowly, he released my hand, then cleared his throat. "Ready to take off?"

"Yes. Just us?"

He nodded. "That okay?"

I smiled. "Very okay."

Pleasure shone from his dark gaze, and a touch of red appeared on his cheekbones. I loved the easy way he moved from confident man to a tad shy; it made him so much more authentic than any guy I'd known before. I watched him ready the boat to pull away from the dock, his strides purposeful, every movement deft and focused. I took a seat and relaxed, taking in the beauty of Positano from the distance.

"Was your dad okay with you taking some time off?" I asked.

He nodded. Dark curls tossed in the wind and fell over his forehead. "We had a cancellation and decided not to book a new appointment. My dad is with your aunt right now. Enjoying some alone time."

The knowing quirk of his lips confirmed they were definitely doing it. As much as I loved my aunt, the idea of her being intimate with Rafe's dad freaked me out. It must've showed on my face, because Rafe began laughing.

"Don't worry," he said. "We'll take our time. Maybe grab some dinner if you're up for it?"

"Sounds good."

We fell into easy chatter as he showed me how to drive the

boat. Something flickered on his face, a pride and peace I wished for myself one day, as if he was happy with what he did and who he was. Why did everything inside me always feel jumbled up and empty at the same time, as if I was looking for a missing piece?

I pushed away the questions and concentrated on enjoying our time on the water. Rafe pointed out the various sights, giving me a hint of his tour-guide savvy.

He cut the engine. "We can lie out here and relax a bit. Enjoy the view."

My breath caught at the stunning visual of giant carved rocks thrusting from water to sky. The shoreline was littered with jagged boulders, giving a glimpse into gaping holes that led to numerous caves, making me shiver in the hot sun. Lone individuals sunbathed on towels spread out on rocks.

I stripped down to my bikini and we laid out our towels on the bow of the boat. I felt his gaze sweep over me, taking in my bare skin, and hoped he liked what he saw. I was never confident in my body—who was?—but the energy from my surroundings gave me bravery and a need to show him I wasn't afraid to let him see me. When his eyes finally met mine, there was a heat and admiration that made a thrill jump through my veins.

Yes. He liked what he saw.

I dreamed of him kissing me. I dreamed of sliding my hands around his neck and sinking into a kiss that would finally satisfy me, instead of experimentation or a dare by friends. Mostly, boys didn't excite me like I wished.

But Rafe did.

I pulled myself out of the daydream. "How did this thing with my aunt and your dad get started? They seem so different, but when they're together, I feel like they fit."

"Ah, my father was eating alone at a café when he overheard

an argument. Your aunt's friend was pretty drunk and got really loud and rude. She was trying to get him to calm down. Dad thought things were getting out of hand, so he asked if she needed help, and she said yes. He tried to escort the guy out, and he took a swing at my dad."

"Oh my God! I didn't hear this story!"

Rafe grinned. "The fight was brief and my father laid him out quickly. He arranged to get him home and walked your aunt safely back to her house. She kissed him at the door, he asked her out, and she agreed. That was last summer."

"That's amazing and kind of romantic. Well, without the drunk, violent guy." I treasured his laugh. "I'm surprised it lasted the entire year without seeing each other."

"She's flown here now and then, but mostly they write letters."

I raised a brow. "Like old-fashioned paper with a pen? No phone?"

"Guess so. My father has a drawer filled with her letters. Maybe we're missing out on something. Didn't you mention you write?"

"Oh, just journaling and poems. I guess you're right. You can get more intimate in writing than speaking. I just never pegged my aunt for the love-letter type."

"They are both happy. I'm not sure if it's exclusive—my father probably knows that would be hard to ask—but when they are together it's real."

"I like that," I said slowly. "You're right. My aunt is happy and that's what matters."

I ached to know everything about this man and the way his mind worked. He was so different from anyone I'd ever met. "What was it like growing up here?" I asked curiously.

He cocked his head. "Lovely. Simple. Sometimes hard. Losing my mother made me spin out for a while. I was angry and fought a lot with my father. I remember I came home drunk one night and blamed him for ruining my life. Told him I didn't want to end up like him, stuck catering to rich people all day while we had nothing."

He winced at my expression. "Yeah, I know. But I was so mad and there was no one else to take it. Dad listened to me yell and told me he understood. That I was free to go make a life for myself. That he'd pay for college or help support me if I wanted to travel. He said he only wanted what my mother did—that I was living a life that satisfied me."

"Your father sounds amazing," I murmured.

"He is. Eventually, I worked my way through the mess. And along the way, I realized I didn't necessarily crave what all those rich people have. I'd watch them with their fancy clothes and jewels and how they seemed to worship everything outside themselves. And it made me sad. For me, a boat gliding on the water, or the pull of a fish on my line, or drinking a *caffè* in the sun gives me more happiness. Sure, they buy the experiences, but I always wonder how much pleasure they gain. Half of the time they're taking pictures or have this bored expression like they're afraid to show excitement." His crooked smile and his reflective words kept me transfixed. "Do you think I'm silly?"

I shook my head, charmed at the adjective he chose. "No! I think you're right. I can't tell you how many people I know, my parents included, who are so unhappy all the time. Like they look at their lives and wonder how they got there. I don't want that."

"Are you close to your parents?"

I gave a snort. "No. Oh, don't get me wrong, they don't do anything bad. But . . . the reason I'm with Aunt Silvia this summer is to get me out of the house while my parents figure out if they want to get a divorce." Raw pain punched through my chest. "They may be better apart, but I don't want to see it. I don't want to deal with separate households and new boyfriends or girlfriends. I don't want to be replaced one day. I hate it. And I blame them because they never seem to listen to each other—just accuse and yell, and then there's days of silence."

Tears burned my eyelids. I realized I hadn't expressed my true thoughts to anyone, keeping them locked up tight. To my aunt, I pretended I understood. To my parents, I tried to be the peacemaker, believing if I tried hard enough maybe I could force them to realize they loved each other again. To my friends, I said it was cool, because so many of them had divorced parents already.

Rafe touched my knee, his fingers a gentle brush of heat and comfort. "I'm sorry, Livia."

He said nothing further. I settled into the understanding silence and felt something loosen inside me. He didn't try to tell me it would all be okay, or offer any superficial condolences. As if he realized words couldn't take away my hurt, but he'd sit with me in it, and be my friend.

I wasn't alone.

We spent the day talking, swimming, and sun worshipping. Finally, he restarted the engine and turned the wheel, easing around a crowd of boats docked and packed with a group who waved and shouted to us. I waved back, catching their joy at being out on such a beautiful day.

As it got later, Rafe guided the boat to Praiano, a small fishing village that wasn't as crowded, situated a few miles away from Positano. He secured the boat, once again helping me down with his hand in mine.

When we began walking ashore, he didn't let go.

He took me through the village and to Kasai, a restaurant in front of a B and B that offered stunning views. Scoring a table next to the balcony, we sipped Pellegrino and caught our breath from the heat and walk.

He spoke in rapid Italian to the waiter, asking a few questions about the menu, then translated. I ordered my traditional favorite—spaghetti and meatballs—and a Coke. Rafe ordered the pasta in truffle oil and insisted I had to taste it. "You speak English so well," I said after the waiter left. "I've been trying to get better at Italian, but I think I suck at languages."

He laughed. "I learned English young, so it was more natural. I'm just no good at certain words—called, um, slang?"

"Yeah, we love making up cool words for the older generation to figure out."

His dark eyes sparkled. "I hope you don't consider me ancient at twenty-three."

I gasped. "Are you that old? I'm jailbait."

He lifted a brow. "Jail what?"

I laughed for so long, he laughed too. "I'm sorry, I'm kidding. I just turned nineteen in May. I don't think we have anything to worry about."

"Especially since we are friends."

I stiffened. Suddenly, my mood crashed. Were we just friends? But he'd held my hand on the walk over. Was it just a casual thing? Was he not interested in more? Had I been an idiot thinking an older guy who lived in Italy would look at me romantically rather than as a buddy to hang with? I forced a smile to hide my misery. "Yes. Friends."

We lingered over dinner, and I tried to enjoy it, but my mind kept going over his words. I shouldn't be so disappointed, and I hated myself for believing we were doing more than casually flirting. Why did I have to be so awkward with guys? Another girl would up her game and make sure he knew I was interested in more than friendship. Instead, I felt tongue-tied and craved being safe at home, where I could figure things out. I was quiet on the way back, and this time he didn't take my hand.

We got back on the boat and lay out on our backs to stare up at the stars. It was like a massive pattern of crackled lights smashed against a velvet background. I breathed in the warm air, being rocked gently back and forth by the water, and tried to savor the moment. If this was all I could have from Rafe, I'd take it. I had no choice.

"Livia?"

"Yeah?"

His voice sounded hesitant. "What if I feel more than friendship?"

My heart ratcheted to a rapid pace. This time, I refused to hesitate. This time, I'd jump right in and take the chance. "I'd like it."

He let out a soft puff of air. "I don't want to mess up. I like this. It's been a long time since I felt this way about someone."

"Me too. But I don't want to pretend either."

"We only have the summer. I don't want anyone to get hurt."

I knew I wanted to see what happened and not care about consequences. But he was right. I only had a month left and then I wouldn't see him again. If we defined this differently, it could be heartbreak for both of us. "Neither do I," I said softly.

"What if we see what happens but don't rush? Be friends for now. I don't want to lose that by trying for more too soon."

My insides lit up and I smiled in the darkness. "I like that."

"Good. Friends?"

"Friends."

Our pinkies brushed. Slowly, he tangled his fingers in mine and we lay looking at the stars, holding hands, and thinking of possibilities.

CHAPTER NINE

Pris

The moment her gaze took in the magical house wedged into the hillside, Pris experienced a sharp sense of déjà vu, as if she'd been here ages ago and was now rediscovering a place she'd once been.

The sunny yellow paint with bright blue shutters, sloping roof, and spill of wild surrounding gardens coaxed an instant smile to her lips. The July afternoon was hot and sunny. Sweat pooled under her armpits from the steep climb, as she lugged her lone suitcase while listening to Devon bitch nonstop regarding the lack of help, the sting of the sun, and the long flight.

But as she stood here, her gaze sweeping past the fall of fuchsia bougainvillea that clung to the structure, the lemon trees giving off the delicious waft of citrus, and the magnificent view of Positano from their perch, all her discomfort drifted away.

"Thank God, we're finally here!" Devon announced, dropping her bag to the ground. "Wow, what a view. And it looks nicely kept, so the lawyer hired someone decent for maintenance."

They'd tracked down the lawyer from the envelope that held the deed. Dev learned there was a small amount of money set aside for monthly expenses to a keeper who made sure the cottage was well-kept and maintained. Pris couldn't believe it had been vacant for all those years, held by her mother but never shared. Why? Hadn't Mom felt the pull to come back or bring her daughters to Italy?

The lawyer couldn't give them much more information. Pris figured it was up to them to gain the details.

Dev marched to the left flowerpot, dug around, and fished out the key. "We're definitely not in New York anymore," she said, opening up the door. "I doubt anyone would want to rob any of the houses up here. Not worth the effort of the climb."

Bailey was circling around, her arms flung out. "This is so beautiful," she whispered. "It's like a dream."

Pris agreed but kept quiet. The trip had been stressful, full of last-minute doubts and worries about leaving her husband, and about the things she'd discover here. The continued snark between Dev and Bailey only ratcheted up the tension. She didn't know how they'd spend a week cramped all together. It was as if they'd once been a unit, and now each of them had no idea how to work with the other.

"There's only two bedrooms," Dev called out. "Who's taking the couch?"

"I will," Bailey said, following them both in. "Maybe one night I'll sleep outside in the garden under the stars."

Dev shuddered. "And wake up with giant bug bites all over your body? Whatever floats your boat."

Bailey shot her an exasperated look and began poking around. "I love the décor. All that hand-painted tile, watercolor paintings, and tapestry. The bedrooms have their own private balcony. Did you see the views?"

"You can have the master, Pris," Dev said. "It has its own bathroom. Bailey and I can share this one."

Pris studied the queen-size bed covered by a white lace-stitched quilt and matching pillows. The walls were painted buttercream; a floral throw rug cushioned the hard floor. Light spilled in and the room smelled of sunshine and citrus.

She walked to the balcony and took in the tumble of blue sea, fluffy clouds, and giant yachts in the distance. A tingle fell over her, imagining Mom standing right here, happy in this magical place that seemed so far removed from the daily stresses of normal life.

An image of Garrett rose in her mind, and her heart twisted. What would happen between them? Maybe a break and time apart was best for now. She didn't want to give up on their marriage, and counseling might be the answer. Yet, something inside her whispered there was a bigger answer.

And it lay with her.

"Pris, come out and have a drink with us," Bailey called out. "I found a bottle of wine."

She glanced at the bed longingly. She craved a nap, real food, and quiet. But it'd be good to start the trip with some family bonding. "Okay, I'm in. But then I need to rest."

Dev deftly uncorked the bottle of red, fished out wineglasses, and poured. "Agreed. I think we should go out for dinner tonight, do light exploring, then seek out our generous neighbor who's been paid to keep up the house."

"As long as you're not scheduling every minute of this week," Bailey said. "I don't do well with time charts, remember? Italy is for discovery and adventure."

Dev stiffened. "Only trying to keep us on track. We have limited time before we need to get back to our responsibilities." She directed a pointed look at Bailey. "Some of us, that is. Isn't your play over?"

"That's right. I'm gainfully unemployed for now," Bailey said cheerfully. "Let's sit in the garden. There's some chairs out there."

Pris rolled her eyes, already weary of their bickering. But she followed them out, took a seat, and gave a sigh of relief. Her legs still smarted from the climb. She stretched them out and sipped the wine. The fruity taste of blackberry and spice slid over her tongue. "What's the name of the maintenance guy?" she asked.

"The lawyer sent me his contact info," Dev said, fishing out her phone. "He's a long-term resident and knew Aunt Silvia well. I just can't believe we had this cool aunt in our family and Mom never even mentioned her."

"Maybe because she passed so young," Bailey said.

"Here it is. Roberto Ferrante."

Pris stared at her sister in shock. "Roberto? R?"

Dev shook her head. "Okay, I feel *stupida*. I didn't even put that together. Could it be that easy? It'd make perfect sense he'd want to take care of the place for Mom!"

"Why don't we go see him in person rather than a call?" Bailey suggested. "It'll give us an opportunity to ask more questions."

Dev recited the address. "Good idea. Better to spring all of us on him rather than give the man time to build a defense."

Bailey laughed. "A defense against an affair with Mom? I doubt he'd worry at this point."

Annoyance flickered. Pris tried hard to ignore it. "An affair points to cheating, and Mom didn't cheat. The letters point to being with him during college—before she was married to Dad. There's no other proof."

"Except the letter that confirmed they'd meet on her sixty-fifth birthday," Bailey said.

"Mom was already divorced. That's not cheating. Plus, maybe she just wanted to reconnect and visit a place she loved again."

Bailey sighed. "More questions than answers, that's for sure."

Dev lifted her phone. "I gathered a list of clues from the love letters so we can narrow down certain items we're searching for."

"Of course you did," Bailey said.

Dev ignored her and ticked off the list. "Mom was in college, so that gives us a solid timeline of nineteen seventy-six through nineteen eighty when they met. I'm not sure of his age, though, so that could throw us off a bit. Also, R mentions fishing and tours, so he must have been employed by a boat charter. Maybe the ferry? His dad, name unknown, got sick and R had to step in. Which means they could have owned their own business, or he got promoted at a company." She fell silent and looked up.

"That's it?" Pris asked, a bit disappointed. "Not a lot of info to go on."

"He mostly wrote about feelings and philosophy and memories they shared. Not a lot of hard clues within the letters. Bae, what else did Dad say?" Dev asked. "He had to give you some other information."

"Not much. He didn't remember Aunt Silvia and knew nothing about an actual house in Positano. He assumed Mom went to Rome when she—" Bailey broke off. A look of horror crossed her face before a mask slammed down. "I mean, Mom mentioned visiting Italy now and then, but he thought she meant Rome. Mom was big on art, remember?"

Pris narrowed her gaze. Her sister was holding back. "You said he assumed she went to Rome. Come on, Bae, don't lie. Not about this."

Bailey chewed on her lower lip, looking uneasy. Then spit out a curse. "I wasn't going to tell you because you'd freak. Dad said there was a time when they had a brief separation and Mom went to Italy for a few weeks."

Dread overcame her. "When?"

"When you were really young, Pris. Before kindergarten.

Dad said they never discussed it because they were out of touch at the time, but he assumed she was in Rome and Florence. He didn't know about Positano."

"And he didn't know about this guy either?" Dev asked.

Bailey shook her head. "Guess not."

"Why were they separated?" Pris asked. "What happened?"

It was Bailey's guilty silence that did it. Dev let out a humorless laugh and swished her wine. "Because Dad cheated. Of course."

Pris wondered why disappointment cut through her. It wasn't a stretch to think Dad would have cheated once before. "Did he say that, Bae?"

The uncomfortable look on her sister's face pegged the truth. "He confessed they'd hit a difficult point in the marriage and he made a mistake."

Dev huffed out. "Another one. Typical. Poor Mom never had a shot."

"Poor Mom seemed to be just fine with her own secret lover," Bailey cut in.

Pris raised a brow. "I can't believe you're trying to blame Mom for this."

"I'm not! But you both have her in this box where she's this perfect, fragile figure, and I think there was more to her than that! I mean, look at where we are now. Would you have ever believed she could have hidden such secrets from us? If we're going to track down R and learn more about Mom, you both need to be more open to the possibility she made her own mistakes."

Dev shook her head. "Why are you always defending Dad?"

"Why are you always so quick to blame him for it all? He may have cheated, but he was a good father. He never abandoned you or made you feel unloved, did he?" Bailey challenged. "Isn't it time he's forgiven for not being perfect?"

Pris sighed. "Maybe she's right. I certainly don't remember Mom crying about feeling betrayed after their divorce. It was almost like she'd accepted it a while ago. They grew apart. Mom never bashed him to me, not like so many of my other friends' moms who divorced."

"I don't believe this. Dad was selfish. He destroyed their marriage and made us all feel like crap." Dev blew out a breath. "Don't you remember how we cried when we found out about the divorce? How we thought our lives were over? You can sit there and spout about how he should be forgiven, but I would've had more respect if he'd just left Mom because he wasn't happy. Why cheat? Why hurt someone you love?"

Pris studied her sister, who seemed even angrier than her. Steam practically snorted from her nostrils. Dev had always seemed to take Dad's betrayal the hardest, but Pris wondered if it was something deeper. Dev kept her secrets close and rarely shared, putting all her energy into her career. There had always been a wall around her sister, as if she was desperate to protect herself, yet she gave off such a tough, cool demeanor. You had to look hard to find the emotions swirling under the surface.

Once, Pris had both seen and respected her sister's feelings.

Now? She had no idea who Dev really was anymore. She'd been too wrapped up with her own life and struggles. Guilt hit. Once, they'd all been so close.

She opened her mouth to console Dev, but Bailey interrupted.

"I didn't forget. I just decided to forgive. But what if you found Mom also had an affair while she was married? Would you blame her as much as Dad?"

Dev jerked her gaze away and sipped her wine. "Yes. Cheating is a lie. Is it too much to demand truth from this family? Lies make you question what's real and what isn't. I'm not about to live that type of life. If Mom did, I'd be just as upset."

A short silence fell. Pris thought about her sister's words. In a way, she was right. It was easy to look to parents to learn relationships and morals. To decide what one wanted to be and what was right and wrong. Mom had always been their beacon, the one steady figure that all of them counted on. If she'd been lying about who she was, did that invalidate everything else?

Pris thought of all Mom had done for her family with little complaint. No, it was impossible she'd be anything less than an extraordinary woman, mom, and wife. Pris had to prove the truth so Mom's legacy wouldn't be tainted.

Pris owed her that.

It must have been a young romance where they kept in touch. The letters they'd torn through and read like guilty gossip magazines had only shown how much R had loved Mom over a few idyllic summers. Maybe Mom wanted to meet him for her birthday for completely pure purposes. Like wanting to see an old childhood friend who'd known you best.

Dev stood up. "I'm going to lie down and then get changed for dinner."

Her sister marched away, shoulders stiffly set. Bailey sighed and leaned back in her chair. "Well, that went well. Hopefully we won't end up killing one another by the end of the week."

"Bae, what really happened with you two? Is it still about that boy years ago? And if so, don't you think it's time you both got over it?"

Bailey stared out at the tangle of bright blooms and curved trees that made up a natural privacy wall from the neighbor next door. Her finger absently tapped against the rim of her glass.

"Dev can't seem to forgive me. I think it's ridiculous—I told her over and over I had no idea she was that serious about him—but she blames me for the breakup. Like I'd ever want to steal her boyfriend."

The details were cloudy. Being five years older than Dev, Pris was removed from their daily fights and interactions. She only knew the bare bones of the situation. "Tell me your side of the story so I can be in the loop. Maybe we can have an intervention and get Dev to let it go."

Bailey groaned. "I hate conflict."

"Who doesn't? It's part of life. Now, tell me."

"Not much to tell. Dev was dating the guy—Liam—and when he came over, he always invited me to hang with them. Join them for ice cream or an occasional movie. Silly stuff. I thought he was just being nice."

"I'm assuming Dev didn't like it?"

"Yep. Told me to get my own life and my own boyfriend. So, I began leaving the house when he was around. And a few weeks later, Dev said they broke up."

Pris cocked her head. "Was she upset?"

"No, that was the whole point. She was her usual stoic self. Told me it was good because she had no real feelings for him anyway."

"What happened?"

"I was at a club one night with my friends. Liam was there. We'd been drinking and we ended up hooking up." Bailey gave a long sigh. "I wasn't thinking it was a big deal. They weren't together, and it was just sex. It wasn't like I wanted him to be my boyfriend."

Pris thought about how her sister would have viewed the scenario. "Yeah, but maybe there were bigger feelings there that she didn't tell you about."

"I know. I figured I wouldn't see him again, but he came to the house and Dev caught us. I was telling him to leave and that I didn't want anything more, but she still went apeshit."

"For someone so cool and composed, that girl has a temper."

"You're telling me. I figured the whole thing would blow over once I explained. I had no idea she meant what she said."

"What'd she say?"

Bailey paused. Her voice hitched a bit as she said the words. "Told me I wasn't her sister anymore. That she'd disowned me."

A shiver raced down her spine. Normally, it was a vow that'd make Pris laugh, a silly sibling threat that disappeared the next morning. But something told her Dev had spoken the truth that day, and now Bailey was paying the price.

"Ridiculous, right?" Bailey asked. "I mean, she's crazy."

Pris rubbed the back of her neck. "I'm already stressed and we just got here. Maybe we should just focus on finding out about Mom. The other stuff may work itself out."

Bailey agreed and they went back inside to get ready.

But Pris wondered how easily the past could ever really be changed. Or forgiven.

CHAPTER TEN

Olivia

The summer raced by so fast I was afraid it was going to be a fleeting memory. But I knew, even then, as sweet as the experience of living in Positano, diving into a new culture, and spending time with my eccentric aunt was, it was Rafael who made the difference in changing me.

My feelings grew for him daily, but we still hadn't even kissed. We held hands and sat close. We spent hours conversing on the most ridiculous of subjects, then switched to sharing things I'd never opened up to anyone else about. I sensed he was holding back, afraid to cross the line, especially when I'd be gone soon. The thought of leaving made me slightly nauseous. I was supposed to be excited about going to college and being back home, but these past two months had only strengthened the bond between my summer home and the boy I was falling hard for.

So, we remained in this strange twilight of a zone, not together but not casual buddies.

On my last Saturday, Julia and Ava arranged to take me out to the special caves of Grotte di Suppraiano. Rafe usually worked, but when I met them all at the boat, he was already there, laughing at something one of the girls, Lauren, had said. She wasn't a core member of the group, so I didn't know her well, except she was pretty and had a flirty energy that immediately attracted guys. Rafe's dark eyes seemed intent as he leaned in, their faces a few inches apart.

The jealousy bit hard, but I tried to seem casual as I waved hello at them both and headed straight to my friends.

Why was he here? Wouldn't he have told me if he'd gotten the day off and wanted to join us? Not that he owed me anything—they were his friends. I was just the summer interloper. I hugged the girls and tried to pretend I was excited, but I was too focused on the couple behind me. Did Rafe like Lauren? Was I really only a friend after all, just a silly teen to flirt with this summer?

God, I hated my doubts and the way I always questioned myself. Rafe deserved a confident woman who wasn't afraid to speak her mind. And though I had definitely grown this summer, able to decipher some conversations in Italian, and making friends who seemed to genuinely like me, I would always be an outsider. Maybe even to myself.

I kept tight to Ava and Julia while we took off, sipping Coca-Cola from a bottle and concentrating on the light chatter. I refused to turn my gaze and look at Rafe, especially since I could hear Lauren's giggling. I pictured her hand on his arm, her long, sleek hair blowing glamorously in the wind while mine seemed to curl like crazy in the humidity.

The boat veered a hard right, and everyone screamed as the water splashed over the side. Ava laughed while Julia called out reassurances.

Suddenly, his rich, deep voice came close to my ear. "*Chiacchierone*, are you trying to kill us? Do you want me to take over?"

I stiffened and pressed myself against the side, trying to put some space between us.

Julia launched into a colorful stream of Italian. Many of the curse words didn't need translating. "Go take care of your *ragazza*, Rafael," she said, a sly look on her face. I saw the red dig into Rafe's cheekbones and helplessly stared at him. Why was he blushing? What did she say?

Rafe said something back, making her laugh, and suddenly he was in front of me, his dark gaze pinning mine. My breath exploded from my lungs, and it was as if Lauren had never happened. When I was around him, it was like magic. Was this what love was supposed to feel like? If so, it was too much to feel all these things. It was too . . . dangerous.

"What does *ragazza* mean?" I asked curiously.

He cleared his throat, looking embarrassed. But then his jaw clenched, and he was staring at me again like he could swallow me whole. "It means girlfriend."

"Oh." I wanted to die but refused to show him. "Well, Lauren is really pretty. And nice." My throat closed up. "You should get back to her."

He blinked, looking confused. "Lauren isn't my girlfriend."

"Who was Julia talking about?"

His lower lip quirked. "You."

My belly dropped to my toes. Palms suddenly clammy, I stared back stupidly, having no answer, but thank God, Ava announced we'd arrived.

"Who's swimming and who wants to be in the boat?" Julia called out.

Rafe and I were pushed to the side as the group pressed forward in a mad rush, calling out their preferences and stripping down to their bathing suits. My head still spinning from Rafe's response, I followed them and looked over the edge of the rail.

My breath caught. A wall of jagged rock thrust from the deep blue sea toward the side, creating craters of space where both swimmers and boats glided in and out of the opening. The stunning view of earthy colors created a giant wall of stone, moss, and occasional gleaming white buildings of hotels or cafés. I turned to Rafe. "This is where we were before, right?"

"Yes, Praiano. But I didn't take you to the grotto. Do you prefer to swim or take the boat?"

Julia's voice called out. "Livia, everyone wants to swim. Are you good to come with us?"

I hesitated. Damn, I wasn't the best swimmer, but I felt completely lame being the only one who wanted the boat. I didn't want to ruin their good time, but I was worried I couldn't make it. And that'd be even more embarrassing—needing a rescue. My cheeks burned. Maybe I could stay on board? But I knew Julia and Ava would never let me. Maybe—

"We're going on the boat," Rafe suddenly yelled. "You guys go ahead."

"You sure?" Julia asked.

He waved her off. "*Sì*, now go jump, *chiacchierona*."

She made a face, grabbed Ava's hand, and jumped off the side. "What's that word mean?" I asked.

"Someone who talks a lot."

I grinned, liking the way they teased each other. "Chatterbox."

"Exactly."

I watched the group leisurely swimming toward the cave. I didn't want Rafe to get stuck because I was a lousy swimmer. "I'm sorry. I know you wanted to swim. Why don't you go with them and I'll hang here? It's a gorgeous view—I don't need to see the inside of the grotto."

He reached out and touched my cheek. My body stilled, savoring the feel of his skin against mine, the gleam of male interest in his dark eyes. "I'd rather stay with you. Alone."

With a smile, he let his hand drop and took his position by

the wheel. He guided the boat toward the gaping mouth of the cave, and we waved and hooted as we passed by the swimming crew. The sun burned hot and bright, gleaming on the surface of the water so it dazzled like diamonds. Kayaks cut back and forth to our side, and we waited a while for our turn.

As we entered the cave, the dank, earthy scent rose around me, and I gasped at the vast space. A quiet, almost reverent energy pulsed around us. We didn't speak as we sailed around the circumference, and I leaned over to study the strange gleaming turquoise of the water. It was like the liquid was alive, glowing with an eerie presence that sent shivers down my spine. Shadows played across the rock from the weak strains of light that managed to penetrate the opening. It was as if we'd sunk into a whole new world untouched by people.

I loved the stillness, and I itched for a sketch pad to try to capture the essence of the cave. Too soon, Rafe exited to make room for others, and he cut the engine a long stretch away from the tourists and our friends. "We'll circle back and pick them up when they're done," Rafe said, walking to stand beside me. "What did you think?"

"Oh, it was beautiful. I've never seen water actually glow before."

"There are a lot of natural caves around here. The Blue Grotto is the most famous, but I've always loved this one because it's not as touristy."

"I went to Howe Caverns once. It was upstate and we climbed down a ton of stairs to see these cool caves that all linked together. It was pretty cold because you're below the ground."

I realized I was babbling, but he only smiled. "That does sound cool. Want to sit on the bow for a bit?"

"Sure."

I settled in with his familiar presence, reveling in the scent of him, the slight brush of our heated bodies as we adjusted on the gently bobbing boat. He wore sunglasses with gold frames that made him look even sexier. His chocolate curls blew over his forehead from the wind.

I realized I was happier than I ever had been. Right now. With Rafe.

His words kept repeating in my mind like a mantra.

Girlfriend.

My fingers curled into fists. I wished he'd take my hand or finally kiss me. I was leaving in two days and my emotions were a tangled mess.

"Is your dad sad about Aunt Silvia leaving?" I asked, desperately trying to sound normal.

"Definitely. They're good for each other. Dad gets lonely. Hasn't met someone who he can really settle down with. Silvia makes him laugh."

"Think they'll try to do something more permanent?"

He smiled. "You're a romantic, huh? Honestly, I don't know. Things work between them well for now. Neither of them may be ready to risk blowing it up."

I'd be leaving in two days. Did I really want to waste more time because I was afraid Rafe might reject me? I had nothing to lose. I might not ever make it back here—lose my opportunity forever. God knows, I didn't want to be one of those old people regretting not kissing a boy one summer in Italy. I sucked in a breath, ignored my racing heart, and went for it. "Is it the same with us? Are we afraid to take that next step in case we blow it up?"

He stiffened. His head cranked around so we were super close. I studied the full curve of his lip and hoped I hadn't made a fool out of myself. "I didn't know what was best. Have you wanted me to make a move?"

My heart pounded so loudly I knew he heard it. "Yes."

I met his stare and tumbled deep, finally seeing the raw want there, the firm set of his jaw that told me he'd been holding back. Relief rushed through me. "Livia," he breathed, my name dancing on his lips like the most beautiful sound in the world. "I'm crazy about you, *dolcezza*. I've been dying to kiss you, but I didn't want to push when I knew this was all we had. I wanted you to remember this summer like I did."

"How will you remember it?" I whispered.

He leaned in close and cupped my cheeks with his warm hands. His forehead pressed against mine with pure intimacy. "The season I met the girl of my dreams and my best friend," he said. The declaration shook me to the core, and then he was kissing me, his lips warm and soft and patient. I looped my arms around his neck, my fingers in the dark silk of his hair, and kissed him back. Slowly, over and over, learning each other's taste and texture, his lips slid over mine, then sipped me like I was fine wine. I shuddered and my insides fell apart, opening up for more space to allow him in, and I knew in that moment I loved him.

We broke apart slowly. The heat of his body was like fire, drawing me in, so he tucked me against his body and held tight, the boat rocking us in a gentle embrace.

"What's *dolcezza* mean?" I asked.

"Sweetness."

A smile curved my lips. "I like that. Will you write to me?"

A half laugh rumbled his chest. "With a real pen and paper?" he teased.

"Yes. Exactly like that." I tipped my chin up to study his face. "I'd like us to write letters to each other. I think there are things I can say I may not be able to over the phone."

He grinned, kissing me again, and desire rolled through me, gripping and sweet and terrifying in a way I'd never experienced. It was as if his touch had seeped not only into my skin but into my blood and caused this need. I wondered if I'd ever be the same or if he'd ruined me for everyone afterward. "Yes, I'll write you. But, Livia, I need you to promise you won't feel guilty if there's a guy you like. I don't want to hold you back."

"I won't want anyone else."

"But if you do. That was another reason I didn't want to start something between us. We live in two different countries and this is the time for you to be free, not saving yourself for a summer romance when we may never see each other again."

The words hurt and tore, but at the same time, I was filled with gratitude. Rafe was right. We couldn't give promises to each other right now. It had just begun, and I'd be gone before we could see what came next. I owed that to both of us, even though my heart screamed there would be no other like Rafe.

"I promise. Same for you. We'll see what happens, just like we did this summer."

He nodded. "Promise."

The night was magical. We spent it with our friends, celebrating the end of summer, but Rafe and I had crossed the threshold. When I kissed him for the last time, I knew he was different from any casual crush. He'd stolen my heart this summer.

I returned home. My parents informed me they'd decided to formally file for divorce. I packed up boxes along with my father, who was moving to an apartment. Mom dropped me off, helped me set up my room, introduced herself to my roommate, and waved goodbye.

All I could think about was Positano and the man I'd left behind.

CHAPTER ELEVEN

Bailey

Positano reminded her of a perfectly wrapped Christmas present, complete with bows, crisp, colorful paper, and sparkle. With each turn of a narrow street corner, or glimpse of a stunning view, the box revealed layer after layer of delightful surprises, increasing its initial value.

At first sight, the packed crowds wearing designer clothes, glossy yachts docked at sea, and shops filled with extravagant goods gave Bailey a sense of indulged tourism. She'd seen the same type of photographs from Monaco and Paris—rich cities where the entitled could laze and play before departing to their real lives. But as she looked deeper, she discovered so much more to unearth—secrets woven into a gorgeous landscape of a simpler culture.

The lone Italian sipping at a café in silence, seemingly beyond the dim chatter of the crowd below. The old shopkeeper with the thick accent and gnarled fingers, nodding enthusiastically as Bailey lifted a distressed leather bag, the sharp, oily scent curling around her nostrils. The pair of lovers with hands entwined, caught up in their own world, walking down the steep stone steps as each plateau of Positano revealed itself in glory. The crush of narrow side streets leading to endless stairs and revealing private treasures such as quirky, colorfully painted doors and the wild bloom of flowers and lemon trees. The handsome boy on the scooter, zipping through the crowds with an expert ease, brown skin gleaming in the sun.

It was a place of scents and sounds, of tastes and textures that flooded her senses and overwhelmed. She itched to sketch and draw what buzzed around her, to capture the fleeting feeling of beauty that was a daily fixture to the locals.

She talked her sisters into eating at a tiny café tucked down a zigzag alley, farther away from the stunning balcony views. It was crowded and loud, but Bailey snagged the last empty table on the street and ordered a glass of red wine.

Dev wrinkled her nose and opened her menu. "Really, Bae? We have an opportunity to eat at a fancy place overlooking the water and you drag us to a pizza place?"

"We can do your choice tomorrow," Bailey said firmly. "This spoke to me. Sometimes, the pricey, touristy ones are a trap."

Pris laughed. "Says someone who's never been to Italy, but what the hell? I'll have the pizza. It does smell good."

Dev obviously didn't like it but gave up grudgingly. "Fine. I'm starving."

They ordered and sat together for a while in silence. Bailey relaxed, taking in the leisurely street crowd and the lilting sounds of conversations in Italian drifting in the air. "I wonder if they have a theater in Positano," she wondered aloud.

Dev snorted. "Are you thinking of trying to get a job here? You'll need to learn Italian first. And don't think you can stay at the house. I have a real estate agent coming tomorrow to give an appraisal."

Bailey tamped down on her irritation. She refused to be drawn into an argument while eating dinner on her first night in Italy, but damned if Dev didn't hit her hot buttons. "This isn't just your choice," she reminded her. "Pris and I also have shares—it's not like Mom left it just to you. Maybe we don't want to sell."

"Trust me, you could use the money," Dev said. "Give Dad a break from paying your bills."

"I don't know what you think you know, but Dad doesn't support me. I made decent pay from my past few plays, and I have low rent that's split with a roommate."

"For now. You don't stay in one place for long."

Bailey stared at her sister intently. "So what? Why do you care so much, Dev? I don't need a fancy title and a cool Manhattan loft to be happy. I also don't need everyone else's approval."

Dev narrowed her gaze. "What's that supposed to mean?"

"I think you know."

"I only meant eventually you need to settle down. Pick a lane. You're an actress, you sketch constantly, and you write. Don't you worry about your future at all? What if your car breaks down or you get sick or the play gets canceled? If you want to be a serious actress, go to Manhattan, get an agent, and focus. You live with no backup plan," Dev said.

"The universe will catch me," Bailey said simply.

Dev widened her eyes. "Are you fucking kidding me?"

Pris cleared her throat. "Okay, let's change the subject! Where does Roberto live? What questions will we ask him?"

Bailey wanted to finish their conversation but sensed it wasn't the time. Things between her and Dev were coming to a head, and it was time they tore apart the seams of their relationship to see if it could be mended. She'd avoided the confrontation this long because she was terrified Dev had meant exactly what she'd said all those years ago.

That Bailey was now nothing to her.

The pizza arrived and they dug in. The sweet scent of basil, the richness of mozzarella, and the fresh tomatoes tasted incredible. They groaned between bites, blissfully silent and bonded together in a way they hadn't been for a long time.

"Why are carbs so good?" Pris asked amid shoving cheese into her mouth. Bailey almost laughed at her elegant sister's sudden primitive hunger.

"There's nothing wrong with carbs," Dev said, nibbling on a chunk of crust. "They took something women love and spun it so it was evil. The world is always afraid we'll rise to complete power if we figure out our bodies are perfect just how they are."

Bailey nodded. "You're right, I completely agree. Patriarchal society keeps us locked into fear mode, afraid of our own success."

Dev looked surprised. "Yes, agreed."

Bailey wondered if a sudden hailstorm would cut the moment short. When was the last time they had agreed on anything, let alone had a civil conversation? She decided to push her advantage. "Speaking of success, tell me about your job, Dev."

Her sister squinted with suspicion. "Why?"

"Because I'm interested. Do you still like teaching at NYU?"

Dev spoke reluctantly, as if she suspected ulterior motives from her simple question. "Yes, I do. Unfortunately, I got passed over for the dean position."

"I'm sorry. I'm sure you'll get it next time."

"Doubt it. Elliot the Mansplainer will keep that job till he retires or dies."

Bailey laughed. She'd always enjoyed Dev's sharp wit and wry humor. Very different from her and Pris. "What does that mean, then? Go for another job or title?"

"I'm teaching a new type of hands-on course in August for

some bigwigs in the financial community. I think it could be a starter ground for me to feel other jobs out. I like academia, and NYU has been good to me, but I'm just looking for . . ." She trailed off, letting the words float away in air like mist.

"More?" Bailey asked.

Dev nodded. "Yep. A bigger leadership role. I love teaching, but I sense a private company might be what I need next. I could always teach part-time."

Bailey watched her face turn thoughtful, as if it was the first time she was vocalizing her wants. Dev had always been the most ambitious of the three of them, driven from an inner need to excel and compete. Even Pris in the cutthroat world of dance had never taken well to that type of lifestyle. For the first time, Bailey wondered if it was hard on her sister being so different from anyone else in the family. She'd cut Dad out, and he was maybe the only member to understand loving work above all else. But their personalities had always clashed—Dev's edges a bit too sharp for her father's vibrant energy and people-pleasing abilities.

"I think it's wonderful. We have too few women out there looking after the financial world amid stuffy old men. You've accomplished so much in your career—more than Pris and I ever have. No wonder Mom favored you the most."

Bailey lifted her wineglass, then stopped mid-sip. Her sisters stared at her as if she'd just sprouted horns and wings. "What did you say?" Dev asked.

Bailey blinked. "Mom favored you. You know that."

Pris cleared her throat and pushed away her empty plate. "We should get the bill and head out."

"Are you trying to piss me off or are you really that clueless?" Dev demanded.

And just like that, the brief closeness exploded. "I'm trying to be nice! God, can't I say anything to you without getting my head bitten off?"

"Okay, maybe you are clueless. Mom has disapproved of every choice I've made right up until her death. *You* were her favorite, along with Dad. Pris was always second choice."

"Gee, thanks," Pris muttered.

"You never saw it," Bailey said in surprise. "Mom always talked about you nonstop. Your degree, your teaching, your publications."

"Riiight. She spoke to me about how I'm wasting my life because I'm too afraid to go after love. Asked me to back off a bit and find real happiness, like everything I've done so far has been because of this empty, gaping place inside only a man can fill." Her laugh was bitter. "Pris made the big romantic sacrifice and you're the artist Mom always wanted to be."

Pris blew out a breath. "Mom was proud of all of us in different ways. And I'd appreciate if you didn't draw me into your arguments. I have my own crap going on."

"Oh, please. Did your color-coordinated china get messed up for one of your charity functions?" Dev mocked. "Just own it, Pris. Your life is perfect, and you have everything you always wanted. Mom frickin' revered you."

Bailey sensed a sudden undercurrent at the table, as if an earthquake was beginning to form. Instead of taking the warning, Dev only aggravated the burgeoning break. Pris's face had turned white, her bloodless lips curling as if she was talking, but no sound emitted. But her eyes burned with a mad gleam Bailey had never glimpsed before—as if Pandora's box had broken open.

"Listen up, little sister. You know nothing about me, my life, or even how Mom felt. Maybe if you'd stop looking at what everyone else seems to have, you'd see a clearer picture. Until then, keep your opinions to yourself."

Dev stared back at her with a slightly open mouth. Pris slammed her credit card on the table. "One last thing. Neither of you bother to ask me any questions about my life. Next time, take a few precious moments from your busy schedule and try it. You may find the answers surprising."

She stood up, her face back to a tight mask. "I'm going to the restroom. Try to keep from killing each other with your juvenile comparisons."

Pris marched off without a backward glance.

Bailey and Dev stared at each other, then looked away. A tiny curl of admiration bloomed in Bailey's belly.

She had rarely seen Pris lose her temper. Her sister funneled all her emotions into ballet, then taking care of her family. It had been easy for both Bailey and Dev to distance themselves, caught up in their own little worlds.

But damned if a pissed-off Pris wasn't a sight to see.

This trip was already filled with surprises.

CHAPTER TWELVE

Dev

Dev concentrated on the steep climb as they made their way to Roberto's home. Was this how people stayed thin while eating pasta and drinking wine? Because she'd never exercised so much in her life just by trying to get from place to place.

But she refused to complain. She was done. No matter what happened, she was tired of earning the reputation as the bitcher. After Pris's startling outburst, she was beginning to feel a trickle of an emotion she despised.

Guilt.

Yes, Pris wasn't one to pick up the phone either, but her sister had a point. No one ever checked in on her. Bailey and she always assumed Pris was fine, and thriving in her perfect life. Was Dev wrong? Were there cracks behind closed doors Pris kept hidden? And if so, wasn't it her sister's responsibility to share or offer bits to her family?

She was always so . . . serene. Smiling, putting on the graceful hostess facade, and playing peacemaker between Dev and Bailey. Dev got pissed off because she never seemed to lose her temper, or fight with her husband, or complain about her son. She took things as they came with a poised acceptance, which was technically wonderful but only made Dev feel like a subpar human.

So, the guilt wriggled and made her uncomfortable as she climbed toward the man her mother may have had an affair with. Part of her wished he was the secret lover. They could get on with their lives, sell the house, and she'd return home to normal. At least work didn't give her all these horrible feelings about herself and make her question her existence.

Only her mother and sisters did that.

Now there were only her sisters.

Dad was more of a distant figure, a forced responsibility around holidays or birthdays. She didn't have the close relationship with him like Bailey, and even though it had been Dev's choice, lately she'd been thinking of him. Of what it would be like to just hang with her father like the old days and laugh. To enjoy his vibrant personality and funny stories and see the warm affection in his gaze. To slough off the bitter anger and appreciate the good again.

For the past few years, Dev only allowed phone calls and short visits to his new home and family. Each time her father tentatively reached out, Dev slammed it down until Dad stopped asking.

Wasn't it better that way, though? Rather than pretending he hadn't replaced them all and moved on?

They finally reached the small, crooked umber-colored house, and she was saved from answering her own question.

Bailey and Pris looked over and waited. Dev stepped ahead to knock on the door.

The man who answered was about her mother's age. With close-cropped white hair, he squinted at them with dark eyes, as if trying to place who they were. His stature was short but solid, with muscled arms and no hint of a belly. Definitely in shape. Definitely handsome. Definitely a possibility.

Dev smiled. "Signore Umberto? *Mi chiamo* Devon. *Parli inglese?*"

He nodded. "*Sì.*"

"You've been taking care of my mother's house—Olivia Moretti?"

His face cleared. "Ah, *sì*! Silvia's house. Is all okay? The house is good, no?"

"It's perfect, thank you so much for all your help. My sisters and I wondered if we could talk to you for a bit about the house and our mom. If you don't mind?"

He threw up his hands in delight. "*Va bene*, come in, come in!" He bellowed a litany of Italian and a stout woman suddenly appeared.

Dev shot a look at her sisters. Uh-oh. They hadn't thought of the awkwardness of having a spouse around. Would Roberto even want to mention her mother in front of his wife? They'd have to be careful of the way they phrased things. The pile of letters suddenly seemed heavy in her leather bag. She clutched it a bit tighter to her hip and smiled at his wife.

Wiping her hands on her apron, she motioned them in, her eyes sparkling behind her glasses. Her hair was short and curly, and her curves were generous. The house was tiny, with a family room featuring a worn gray couch and chairs and a red area rug, and knickknacks littered every surface. The short hall led to a cramped kitchen. But it seemed sparkly clean, and the scents of lemon, basil, and garlic wafted in the air.

"This is my wife, Adriana," Roberto said.

His wife's hand was weathered with age but held a strong

grip as Dev shook it. "Nice to meet you, I'm Devon. This is Priscilla and Bailey."

They got through introductions and their hosts motioned for them to sit. "You must eat with us," Roberto boomed.

Dev's overfull stomach gave a groan of protest. "Oh, thank you, but we just came from dinner. We're really full."

"We didn't want to interrupt," Pris cut in. "We can come back later when you're free to talk."

"Nonsense, you will join us. It's only a little pasta, sit, sit."

Adriana began loading the tiny table with extra plates and dragged over additional chairs. Roberto grabbed glasses, filling them generously with red wine. Dev shared a look with her sisters, but they all seemed helpless to try to get out of the situation. It would be rude to walk out. Maybe Dev could manage a few bites and keep them distracted by conversation.

They all sat.

A plate of sliced bread with a thick crust was passed around, along with a dish of golden olive oil, pepper, and olives. Adriana served them heaping portions of pasta with fragrant tomato sauce and grated Parmesan. The smell was heavenly, so Dev picked up her fork. What the hell. While in Italy . . .

"Tell us all about yourselves," Roberto invited, sipping his wine and beaming at them like they were royalty. "But first, let me say how sorry I am for the passing of your mama."

"Thank you," Dev said. "It was a bit of a shock to lose her so quickly."

"What was a bigger shock was to find she left us the house," Bailey added, dipping her bread in the oil and nibbling. "We had no idea Mom even owned this place. We were hoping to get more information about her and Aunt Silvia. Anything at all."

Adriana shook her head with sympathy. "You poor girls. It's

so hard to lose a mother, and even worse when there are questions you don't have answers to. Here, have some sole—it's freshly caught. It will make you feel better."

Dev began to put her hands up to politely decline, but Adriana slid the fish onto her plate. Fresh parsley, lemon, and garlic created a masterpiece that would have gone for fifty bucks at a New York restaurant. "Thanks," she said weakly. Her sisters seemed to have the same issue—there was no declining food here.

Roberto frowned as he regarded his pasta. "I am afraid I won't be able to tell you much. Houses in Positano are mostly very old, handed down from generation to generation. There is much history in the family lines. I know your mama's house belonged to Richard Agosti, who married your great-aunt Silvia. After he died, Silvia inherited and would stay here for the summers. I remember her as a beautiful, vibrant woman with a big laugh."

Bailey leaned in eagerly. "How did you meet Silvia?"

A grin curved his lips. "She dated my uncle for a while. I met her at a party and my uncle introduced us."

"Were they in love?" Pris asked.

Roberto laughed. "No, they had a good time together, but it was never love."

Adriana cut in. "Silvia was a bit of a celebrity in Positano. Everyone wanted her at their parties because she was so much fun. Oh, how the men adored her! But she loved your uncle Richard very much. Something inside of her died with him."

Dev wondered about this great-aunt she'd never heard of who'd made a place for herself here. A place she'd shared with Mom. Did Mom get wrapped up in a summer romance because of her aunt? It definitely made sense. What didn't was the number of letters collected in the hidden trunk. She was still thinking of this boy so many years later. That had to be much more than a summer crush, then, right?

Dev studied Roberto under her eyelids. Time to poke. "And what about Silvia's niece?" she asked. "Our mother. Did you ever meet her? We're trying to find out when she came to stay in Positano."

Roberto shook his head slowly. "No. I never met your mama."

Dev searched for any flickering emotion that would indicate an intimate memory. But his gaze was direct and he seemed to be telling the truth. Disappointment crashed through her. She should have known it would be too easy if Roberto was the one.

Adriana dumped some roasted potatoes next to her sole and made a clucking noise. "Silvia spent many years here before she died, but after that, no one ever came. The house remained empty."

"Did you know her, Adriana?" Pris asked, forking up a bite of the flaky fish.

"No, I'm sorry, I did not."

"May I ask how you got the job as caretaker?" Dev asked. "If you didn't know Mom, I was just wondering how she chose you for the job."

"Roberto has taken care of many houses here," his wife said. "There are many summer people who leave from October to April, and he has made a living making sure each house is well-kept." His wife shot him a loving look, one that spoke of simple emotion and respect. It made Dev's heart twinge a bit in her chest, the idea that after so much time, one could still feel those things for a partner. "He takes his job very seriously. Silvia's lawyer said she requested he be the one to look after her home."

"He's done a wonderful job," Pris said gratefully. "The place looked not only lived in but happy."

Adriana beamed. "*Sì*—this is what is important. A home has

energy and it must be cared for, even in absence. The stories still live on and should be cherished. This goes beyond checking pipes and brushing off some dust. It is . . . holding the space. That is what my Roberto does."

Her heart squeezed again. She'd never thought of a home like that. It had always been an asset or a liability, something to sell or invest in. Sure, she loved her family home, but many times she wondered if she also wanted to move on from those memories, the memories of a past that defined her. The way Adriana explained things, though, felt different. More . . . accepting.

Bailey sighed. "That's beautiful."

Roberto winked and refilled his glass. "My wife is a poet. To me, I just make sure the house doesn't fall apart."

They all laughed.

"Since you've been taking care of the house, you never saw my mother use it?" Dev asked curiously.

"No, not once. It has been empty since Silvia passed. I am glad it will now be filled again with family."

"Me too," Bailey said. "It's too special to remain vacant."

Alarm bells went off in Dev's head. She tried to speak carefully. "It's true, but the problem is we all don't have the time to truly use the property. We don't have summers off to visit, with all of our responsibilities. It may be better to sell it to a family who can enjoy it."

Roberto jerked. "You want to sell your mama's house?"

Dev nibbled at her lower lip. "Yes."

"No," Bailey cut in. "We don't."

"We're discussing it," Pris said firmly. "There's been no decision made."

Adriana gazed at them with distress. "But why would you

want to sell your family heritage? Are there no children you'd leave it to?"

"Only my son," Pris said. "He's in London now at college."

"But there could be more children later on," Bailey said. "Children who deserve a chance to grow up in Italy or spend summers here like Mom."

Dev tried not to gnash her teeth. Bailey would be thrilled to keep a house for no real purpose while the trust paid the bills. She never wanted to think practically or for the future. Why was it always Dev's role to be the unfun one?

"We're discussing it," Dev repeated.

Adriana quickly lifted the plate of bread. "Would you like more to eat? I have plenty!"

Dev stared at her half-filled plate and wondered how she'd managed to stuff in more food. She felt pleasantly bloated and a bit buzzy from the wine. Thank goodness no one had to drive.

"No, thank you. It was delicious," she said.

Her sisters agreed. She noticed they'd also eaten at least another half portion. They'd definitely be returning home next week with more curves. Especially if they rented those scooters and began to skip the stairs.

"Roberto, would you do us a favor?" Pris asked. "If you have any friends or co-workers or family that may have known my mother, would you ask around? We're looking to see when she came here, who her friends were, things like that."

"Of course! I know many people and will ask."

Adriana began quickly clearing, shooing them back down when they tried to help. "I will do the same. Someone here must know—there may be many tourists, but we are a tight-knit family here. Do you have any idea about the time frame?"

Dev quickly calculated Mom's age and when she'd been in

college. "Nineteen seventy-six to nineteen eighty is a good estimate. We're not sure after that."

Roberto nodded. "Is there a number where I can reach you while you're here? How long will you be staying?"

"Only for the week."

Pris handed him a scribbled note with their number. "You can text or call anytime. We can't thank you enough for taking such good care of the house and inviting us to dinner."

"Don't be silly," Adriana sang, "we adore company. And you can't leave yet. I couldn't send you out the door without dessert! I have fresh pastries and gelato!"

Dev swallowed. "Um, I'm so full, I don't know if I could."

Adriana's face fell. Disappointment beamed from her gaze, which was a complete match of Roberto's expression. Oh no. Maybe saying no to food in Italy was an insult?

"Gelato helps you digest," Roberto said hopefully, cutting a concerned glance at his wife.

Dev forced a sickly smile. "*Grazie.* It sounds . . . wonderful."

The couple immediately relaxed and fell into excited chatter while Adriana served.

Maybe she'd be able to roll down the steep stairs when she left.

CHAPTER THIRTEEN

Olivia

I finished my first year of college with a solid 3.7 GPA, which satisfied my parents, and a burning desire to leave academic life behind for the summer. Rafe and I had been writing letters regularly to each other throughout the year, and after a conversation with Aunt Silvia, she'd agreed to help convince my parents to let me go back to Italy with her.

I tried to tamp down on the frantic panic at the thought of not being able to see Rafe, and I planned a meeting with Mom and Dad over dinner where I launched my plan. Even though they'd expected me to hold down a summer job, I'd been working regularly in the work-study program and had saved up enough money to pay for my expenses. Aunt Silvia had already bought my ticket as a late birthday present. I got the most pushback from Mom, who didn't like the idea of missing out on my company, but she'd been forced to find another job due to a layoff and I think she finally realized she'd have more time to settle into her new position without worrying about me.

I'd been smart to set up a PO box so Rafe's letters got sent either to school or there, and Mom had no reason to think a boy was the reason I wanted to go back so badly. Eventually, both my parents agreed, and I found myself at JFK the very next week, headed back to Positano.

Rafe and I spoke on the phone and planned to meet later that evening. His voice sounded excited, but my stomach felt like a flock of birds taking flight. Would we feel the same about each other once we were together again? Had I built something up in my head from a perfect summer meant never to be repeated? I knew I took a risk going back when everything might change. My mind churned as I tried to keep up with my aunt's chatter and excitement. I'd asked if she was still with Rafe's dad, and she said he was a treasured friend she always looked forward to seeing.

Guess she wasn't sure either.

I wondered if Rafe and I could have that type of relationship. Free to date and build relationships for those ten months, while coming back together for the summer. I think I'd seen a movie like that once—*Same Time, Next Year*—where the couple met for a weekend each year to be together, even though they were married to others. As romantic as the idea sounded, I didn't like the image of Rafe kissing another girl while I wasn't there. Maybe monogamy was too important, after all.

I fiddled with my outfit that night, settling on a casual white sundress and flat sandals. I rarely wore dresses, but tonight felt special. I left my hair loose and borrowed Aunt Silvia's perfume, spritzing a cloud of it in the air and walking through like I'd seen my mom do.

I headed down the familiar trek of steps from the house toward the village and waited outside Santa Maria Assunta. The old church was a landmark, the gorgeous ceramic roof and dome towering above as a marker for me while I learned the ins and outs of the Positano streets. Last summer, we'd spent a quiet hour there. While Rafe prayed, I soaked in the spiritual silence and gorgeous white and gold décor. When we reemerged, I'd felt closer to him than ever before, as if within our silence we shared a deeper bond.

Would it be the same? Would I still experience that jolt when he touched me, the leap in my chest when his eyes met mine? Or was ten months apart too much for anyone to overcome?

And then I spotted him.

His legs ate up the sidewalk as he walked over, dressed in khaki pants, a black button-down shirt, and his good boat shoes. Chocolate curls spilled lower on his brow and over his ears—he'd let it grow longer. I gazed hungrily at his body, still lean and broad, taking long, graceful strides until he stopped a few inches before me. His dark eyes were intense, a bit shuttered, as if afraid to let me back in. My nostrils tingled at his familiar earthy scent. We stared at each other, both half smiling, obviously nervous, and I held my breath. My fingers curled into tight fists. Oh God, was he happy to see me? I couldn't tell—his face seemed distant, as if he was about to tell me his feelings had changed. Maybe this was a mistake. I should have stayed home and not been so stupid to think—

He closed the distance and whispered, "I've missed you, *dolcezza*."

He lowered his head and kissed me.

And just like that, I fell apart and fell for him all over again.

• • • •

RAFE AND I adjusted back into a routine, and the past year seemed to melt away, as if we'd just left each other for a long weekend. We hung out when he wasn't working, and I spent more time with Julia and Ava, who was back for the summer.

One lazy late afternoon, we lounged on chairs in the garden, surrounded by the scent of lemon trees and the vivid blooms of wisteria and bougainvillea. I'd asked if I could sketch him and he agreed. "Can you tilt your head to the right?" I instructed.

"Do I look dumb?" he muttered. "I feel dumb. Don't get my profile."

A giggle threatened to escape. "Why? The moment I met you I thought you were hot."

He brightened. "Really?"

"Really. Plus, you have a great profile. Very Romanesque."

"I have a big nose."

"It's perfect." I loved the tinge of vulnerability he shared. I guess I never figured men were hard on their bodies like women. "No man wants a petite, feminine nose, right?"

"I guess. I made plans for us tonight."

"Oh, a surprise date. Where are we going?"

He looked pleased with himself. My fingers raced over the pad, trying to capture the elusive expression of male pride. "We're going dancing tonight."

My eyes widened. "Like club dancing?"

He laughed. "Of course. Do you think Italians only waltz to Sinatra?"

I laughed too. "You're right, that was silly. Are we going with the crew?"

"Yes, they're meeting us at Music on the Rocks. It's usually jammed from the tourists, but I know one of the guys working there, so he'll get us a table."

"Ah, big-time. Like the Mafia, you have connections."

His brows drew down in a frown. "There's no such thing as Mafia. It's just a fictional story to explain away how hardworking Italians became successful."

I paused. "Hm, interesting. I didn't mean to insult you."

His shoulders and face relaxed. A hint of red stained his cheekbones. "No problem. I just have this thing with people calling every Italian who makes money part of the mob."

I bit my lip. No need to challenge him when he was sensitive. Maybe the articles I'd read about mob wars and all those popular movies weren't true.

I focused on the sketch, which had taken on a life of its own. He leaned back in the chair, one leg bent, hand resting on his knee as he stared back at me. I'd used extra shadow to give him a bit of a moody look, emphasizing those fierce brows and intense eyes, his overlong hair and slightly stubbled jaw. But softening the angles of his face gave him an overall aura of a man who loved; a man whose heart I wanted to capture because he'd already captured mine.

Sweat beaded on my upper lip. It was so obvious how I felt about him by looking at the sketch. For a moment, I decided to crumple it up and tell him we'd try again another time. I knew he wouldn't fight me. Rafe respected my privacy, especially around my art.

"Is it done?" he asked.

I nodded, still hesitant. "I don't know if you should see it."

Another guy would push or tease. But Rafe nodded. "Sketching is personal. I'd love to see, but I understand if you're not ready, Livia."

His gentle smile changed my mind. On shaky legs, I rose and brought over the pad, turning it over to him.

He studied it for a long time, his gaze almost caressing as he took in every pencil stroke of his very essence staring back at him, an essence I saw because I was in love with him.

Then he tipped his head up and slowly smiled. "Damn, I'm hot."

I laughed, and he grabbed me by the loop of my jeans and

pulled me onto his lap, kissing me. It was hard to be around each other and not touch, as if our flesh craved contact at all times. I kissed him back. Instead of feeling vulnerable, I felt like he'd given me a gift. The gift of having another person see me for who I really was.

That night, we danced at Music on the Rocks for hours. The place was an open structure, with no windows, situated at the top of the cliff overlooking the sea. Couches and chairs surrounded the space. Rafe's friend had saved us a long sofa where we all crowded in and ordered expensive drinks, then squeezed onto the dance floor to move to techno and pop hits that reminded me of the clubs in New York. Afterward, sweaty, a bit giggly, a tiny bit tipsy, we stumbled out and down to the beach, where we could still hear the music drifting in the breeze. Breaking off from everyone else, we sat on the rocks, our bare feet in the surf, my head against his chest, arms wrapped around each other in perfect harmony.

My blood ran hot and fizzy like champagne. And I knew in that moment what I truly wanted in my life. "Rafe?"

"Hmm?"

"I don't want to go back at the end of summer. I want to stay."

I held my breath as I waited for his reaction. Of course, it was crazy. My parents would say I was a silly teen girl with a crush. My aunt would wave her hand and smile and say love was wonderful but fickle; to grab the moment and not to worry about the future. But the thought of leaving him to spend another year alone, when I knew I belonged with him, was torturous.

His dark eyes were serious and gleamed with emotion. "I don't want you to leave either."

"What if there's a way I could stay? Transfer to a school here? Or, I don't know, find a work program or something. Maybe Aunt Silvia can help."

He pressed his forehead against mine, his breath ragged over my lips. "Livia, your parents would never allow it. And right now, you need their financial support. You are not ready to be on your own yet."

My stomach dropped. "Okay. I'm sorry—I thought—never mind."

Humiliated, I tried to move away, but he held on to my shoulders, forcing me to look at him. "No, *dolcezza*, you don't understand. I want you here with me more than anything! The idea of you returning home and knowing I won't see you for almost a year breaks me apart. But there's too much for you to lose right now. You need to finish college and get your degree. Your parents would never forgive me, or your aunt, if you just quit school and ran off to live with me. We have to look at the future."

I knew he was right, but my heart didn't want to be rational. I craved to steep myself in these feelings with him, to explore a different life than I ever imagined. I shut my eyes against the image of leaving him behind. "I know you're right," I whispered, "but is it so wrong to know what you want, even if I'm young?"

"No, but I am older than you. Even my father would disapprove. If we can stay strong until you graduate, then we can be together. It will be on our terms."

"And if you don't want to wait for me anymore? If you get tired and fall for someone else?"

Oh, I hated how my voice broke, making me sound like a whiny child. I hated the doubt that burned in my chest and the jealousy at the idea that Rafe could find a woman to replace me. I expected him to tell me to believe in us more, or shake his head with exasperation, but instead, he tipped my chin up and looked deep into my eyes. Within those sooty depths, I found a twinge of sadness that startled me.

"No, Livia. It's you who may change your mind. I know who I am already, and the life I want here in Positano. I've made my choices. But you have more options. You may decide you don't want such a simple life here with me, when you can have so much more. Be so much more." He dropped his gaze and paused. "It's happened before."

I frowned. "What's happened?"

His shoulders lifted in a half shrug. "I was dating someone seriously two years ago. I met her on a tour-boat trip with her friends. She was attending university in Napoli."

Jealousy clawed at my insides. Knowing Rafe had once loved someone before me hurt, but I also realized I couldn't voice the feelings. Then I'd look like some crazy American trying to erase his past to make myself feel better. He deserved someone more mature than that.

So, I fought the poison back and remained calm. "What happened between you?"

"We managed to make it work for a while. I juggled my work schedule with her college classes. Naples isn't too far. But she wanted to transfer to Milano—her dreams were to work with fashion. It became harder to see each other, and eventually, she got frustrated with me."

"Because you couldn't see her enough?"

He gave a slow shake of his head. "No, because she was leaving me behind. She liked the vibrant, crowded cities and didn't want to settle here. Didn't want me to run a tour boat with my father. She asked me to enroll in college with her to start a brand-new career. I did not want that. Yes, many of my friends have gone on to have exciting jobs and travel. But I have never dreamed of that type of life. Perhaps something is lacking inside me. An ambition or need for more."

"There's nothing wrong with you." Outrage flowed through

me. "She wanted you to change, Rafe, but refused to compromise. Why should wanting to stay in this beautiful place, with your family, not be enough? Everyone has different dreams. We shouldn't judge."

A faint smile curved his lips. "She did. Maybe she was right."

My heart broke for him. I reached out and stroked his rough cheek. "I'm so sorry, but maybe she didn't love you enough. She wanted things for herself. She was selfish."

He raised his chin and looked at me. Beneath the sadness was a fear I didn't understand, a knowledge that challenged my statement and made a shiver course down my spine. "No, she just couldn't imagine herself with me in the future. Most women don't want such a simple life, *dolcezza*."

"What do you dream of, then?" I whispered.

His voice deepened with passion. "A great love who becomes my wife. Children. A simple, fulfilling life on the water, in the home where my great-great-grandparents lived. Not what most Americans would want. Who can blame them?"

I shook with the need to convince him he was wrong. I wanted everything he dreamed of. To be away from the trappings that eventually withered a marriage like my parents'. To be free to sketch and write and love on my own terms.

"You're wrong, Rafael. Because I want those things more than I can explain. Nothing is ever going to change. We belong together and I will always choose you."

Heat blasted from his gaze. His jaw clenched as if he was desperate to hide his emotions. "Livia."

The tortured rip in his voice moved me to pull him down close and kiss him, trying to allow my body to convince him this wasn't a passing fling or a summer crush. An image of us together, sailing on his boat, making a life together in this perfect Italian town, caused my insides to light up with joy. He kissed me back, and we were caught up in the moment. Caught in the possibilities of true love and happy endings and a place where the ugliness of the world could never touch us.

It was only much later that I learned how wrong we both were.

CHAPTER FOURTEEN

Bailey

"That was fun. *Not*," Dev muttered as they reached the top of the hill by their cottage. "God, my body feels like if the Goodyear blimp and Violet from *Charlie and the Chocolate Factory* had a baby. Why is it an insult to Italians to be full?"

Bailey couldn't help laughing. "You're not purple," she pointed out. "And I think they were excited to have company to fuss over. They were really sweet."

"Yes, but Roberto was not our mysterious R," Pris said. "It may be harder than I thought to track him down. He could have moved, or died."

"Or used a fake name," Dev added. She leaned forward and put her palms on her knees. "When I get home, I'm joining a gym. It's embarrassing. That old guy passed me on the steps and gave me a pitiful look that screamed *tourist*."

"If we used the house, we wouldn't be tourists," Bailey said. "We can have Positano as part of Mom's heritage. I think we really need to talk about this. I don't want to sell."

Her sister straightened up and shot her a glare. "Of course

you don't. In your mind, this is a romantic getaway and Mom's hideout. But we need to be practical here. This could sell for a crapload of money and we can have it in our accounts for the future. Let's be smart and not emotional."

Bailey softened her voice. "Maybe it's not wrong to be emotional sometimes. It doesn't always have to be weakness, Dev. I think Mom wanted us to have this place. It was special to her."

Dev jerked her head. "Pris, what about you?"

Once again, her oldest sister seemed torn between picking sides. She was the steady peacemaker, the final vote, and the only one able to navigate the strained relationship between them. Bailey was tired of it. She'd already lost Mom, and she had to find a way to repair this relationship with Dev on her own.

"I think we should wait the week out and make a decision then," Pris said. "Both of you have good points. Let's see how we feel then."

Dev seemed satisfied with the answer, and they headed toward the cottage. Darkness had fallen and the evening was alive with heady floral scents, the soft chirps of insects, and the shower of stars high in the sky. The moon was a thin sliver of orange-gold, a tiny peek of light hovering over the cottage like a guidepost. As they drew closer, Bailey squinted and caught a towering figure a few steps from the porch. Head tipped back, hands propped on his hips, he seemed to be staring at the roof. Soft mutters echoed in the air.

Bailey looked at her sisters, who just stared back at the stranger as if they had no idea what to do.

"Hey, can we help you?" Bailey called out.

He didn't jerk or move. Just cranked his head around to stare back at them. "My cat's up on your roof."

They reached him all at once, flanking the man on both sides as they all peered up. Bailey caught a darker shadow creeping along the slanted lines. "I thought cats were good climbers."

"They get stuck in trees, though," Pris said. "Has she ever done this before?"

"He. And yeah, once before when we had a fight. But he came down quick. This time, he's been stuck up there for almost half an hour. He's making a point."

Dev tilted her head and regarded him with interest. "You had a fight with your cat?"

"Yep. He's a pain in the ass, but he's mine. I think I have to go up there."

Bailey was caught between concern for the cat and fascination for this stranger. "We don't have a ladder. Can you climb up?"

He blinked. "I'll have to. Can't leave him."

"Should we call the fire department?" Pris asked.

Dev sighed with impatience. "For goodness' sakes, Pris, I'm sure it doesn't work like it does back in New York. Before Tarzan goes up on his vine, just hang on a sec. I'll be right back."

She marched inside the house with her usual purposeful strides. A soft meow cut through the air. The cat's tail swished back and forth as he hovered on the edge. Bailey watched with worry and hoped he didn't get stressed and try to jump. But wasn't that whole cliché true about a cat landing on his feet? Or was that the nine lives thing?

"Sorry about this," the stranger said. "Didn't mean to interrupt your evening."

"No problem. My name is Bailey. This is Priscilla."

Pris nodded.

"I'm Hawke," he said. His voice had a sexy rough gravel tone. "I'm your neighbor. Live right past that garden wall." He pointed to the right, where a thick cluster of trees made a natural privacy barrier. "Surprised to see someone here. This place has been vacant for a while."

"It was our mom's," Pris said. "She died and left us the house."

He nodded. "Sorry for your loss."

Dev came out with a small plate filled with food. "Roberto had put a few things in the refrigerator for us before we came. I think fish may do it—there's no tuna." Without waiting for Hawke to take over, she began making "Pshhhh" noises and put the bowl on the ground in front of him.

The cat meowed louder.

Dev shook her head and addressed the animal. "He got the point, cat. Now, come down and eat and we can all get on with our lives."

Bailey pressed her lips together. Her sister was so damn bossy. There was no way the cat was just going to listen to a stranger who put out a bit of . . .

The cat jumped to a tree and then down to the ground in two smooth, graceful leaps. Stalking over to the bowl, he ignored Dev and his keeper and began to eat.

"Well, I'll be damned," Hawke muttered. "Good idea."

Dev turned on her heel with a pleased smile. "You gotta talk their language. Now, who are you?"

"Hawke," Bailey cut in. "He's our next-door neighbor."

"I appreciate you helping me and Lucifer out. Can I invite you over for a nightcap or coffee?"

Bailey paused, tempted to find out more about their new neighbor. He didn't look Italian and was about her age, give or take a few years. Dressed in jeans, a white button-down shirt, and sneakers, he still exuded an air of power, like he was used to getting things he wanted. His aura interested her. She opened her mouth, but Dev interrupted.

"Sure. It's still early, why not? You guys good with that?"

They nodded. Hawke walked over to Lucifer and scooped him up with a commanding grip, murmuring something in his ear. The cat twitched, then settled in. "Follow me."

They did, trotting behind him to keep up with his long strides. "Why'd you name him Lucifer?" Bailey asked.

"Because he's the devil incarnate. Was a stray around here who pissed me off. Messed up my garbage, woke me up too early whining, and broke in twice to raid my kitchen. Finally, I gave up and kept him."

"That's so sweet," Pris said.

Hawke grunted. "It wasn't voluntary. I think he was eventually planning to smother me in my sleep."

Dev barked out a laugh. "Those are the best types of pets. Keep you on your toes."

"Maybe you're right."

He led them up the short pathway and to the porch. The glowing lamp illuminated the white and powder blue exterior, with a stone wall shielding the high curved front windows. As they climbed the steps, she noted the generous number of potted plants and herbs; the cozy corner where a table and chair had been set up with a laptop humming; and the half-empty glass of wine on the ledge.

"It's a beautiful night, not too hot. Do you want to stay on the porch?" he asked.

"Sure." Bailey figured he didn't want three strange women traipsing through his place and it'd be more polite to wait out here. "Do you have any limoncello? I've been dying to try some."

He gave a sharp nod. All his motions seemed extremely efficient, requiring the least amount of effort. "For you ladies?"

"Red wine is great," Pris said.

"I'll take a limoncello. Need any help?" Dev asked.

He shook his head. "Be right out."

They stood on the porch with the one chair a bit awkwardly and looked at one another. "Think he's hiding a mess in there?" Bailey asked her sisters. "I didn't see a ring, so he's probably single."

"He doesn't seem like the bachelor-pad type," Dev said.

"We need to ask him questions," Pris whispered. "Maybe he knows Silvia and Mom."

"He's a New Yorker," Dev said.

Bailey cocked her head. "How do you know?"

"Obvious in his tone when he said *C-A-W-F-F-E-E*. We can't hide it for long, especially with our kind."

Bailey grinned. "You should have been a detective, Dev. You're just suspicious enough to be successful."

Bailey enjoyed her sister's short laugh and relaxed in the comfortable ambience of the warm night. Bailey was good at ignoring the pieces of herself that hurt, able to refocus on the moment and happier things, but being with Dev reminded her of an old wound that ached when probed.

Hawke exited without the cat and leaned three chairs against the door. "Here you go, be back with the drinks."

They unfolded the chairs and positioned them in a semicircle around the table. He walked out with a bottle of red wine, another of limoncello, and three wineglasses. "Want any snacks? I have some bread, cheese, and prosciutto."

Dev gave a groan. "God, no. We just realized being invited to eat dinner here means you leave strung out on carbs."

Hawke's lip quirked. "Italians highly regard experiences of pleasure. Carbs, sweets, and wine are all important parts of daily life."

"And cheese," Bailey added.

"Of course." He settled back in his chair and poured everyone's drinks. He refilled his own glass with red wine, picked it up, and swirled it around like an expert. "How do you like Positano?"

"It's stunning," Pris said. "We only got here today, though, so we have a lot more exploring to do."

Hawke stretched his legs out and regarded them thoughtfully. Bailey had the impression he was comfortable in group settings. A natural confidence shimmered around him. "Will you be staying long?"

"A week," Dev said. "We should be able to cram all the sights in by then and decide what we're doing with the house."

His gaze narrowed and pinned on Dev. "This place isn't about sightseeing. You should spend your time being bored. That's when you experience the best moments."

Bailey caught her breath. "I agree. Life shouldn't happen on a schedule. Why is it so hard to convince others we shouldn't focus on checking experiences off like a task?"

Annoyance hummed in Dev's voice. "Because without tasks or schedules, the world would fall apart. I'm surprised to hear that view from a fellow native New Yorker. You must have been here a long time."

In the outside light, Bailey appreciated Hawke's strong features, from the bold slash of a nose to the carved cheekbones and hooded gray eyes that seemed the color of a misty fog. His dark blond hair was thick and slicked neatly back. He was more than handsome. He was interesting, and Bailey prized that higher than other traits. Her mind flashed to Will, and a strange trickle of longing kicked in, surprising her.

Will had been texting her. At first, she'd been trying to avoid a male temper tantrum after he realized she'd run without explanation, but he surprised her. His last message was long, a litany of intellectual emotion that fascinated her—a modern love letter stating he'd wait for her, that the play he'd written for her to specifically star in would be shelved because she was the only one who could bring the role justice. It was rare that a man surprised her. She seldom missed the ones she left behind, but Will had gotten under her skin. Images of him snuck into her brain, even as she reminded him not to wait for her. Still, she knew it'd been the right choice to leave him behind. She had no idea where her new path lay and she didn't want to hurt anyone. It was better for both of them this way.

Bailey shook off her thoughts and refocused. Hawke arched a brow. "How'd I give it away?"

"You said coffee," Dev said.

"Ah, that does it every time. Or *D-A-W-G*." He adjusted his weight, sipped at his wine, and seemed to ponder his answer. "Been here about two years now. Have nothing against schedules, as long as you remain in control and not them."

Bailey puffed up with satisfaction. "That's what I'm always trying to tell Dev."

Dev rolled her eyes. "Oh, please, that's only because you don't have anything scheduled."

"How do you like the limoncello?" Pris asked.

"It's good," Bailey said. "A little sweet, but I like it." She crossed her legs and didn't bother to tug down her skirt, which rode up high on her thighs. She felt Hawke's gaze slide over the expanse of bare skin, but he didn't linger.

Dev caught the gesture and shot her a look filled with judgment. Bailey looked away, hating her sister's automatic assessment that she used and discarded men. Pris seemed to catch the whole vibe and cleared her throat. "Um, Hawke, we're actually trying to find out more information about our mom. She stayed here a few summers back in college—our great-aunt Silvia owned the house before. We wanted to try and track down some of the people who may have known Mom. Maybe she knew the previous owners here?"

"This is my father's house. It's been in our family for years, but like you, I rarely visited after he passed." His eyes flickered. "I was too busy."

His words inspired more questions within Bailey. She wondered about his past, and if it was too outrageous to ask him.

Dev didn't have such issues. "Yeah, making a living can get in the way of Italian dream homes. I get it."

He jerked in surprise. Bailey let out a sigh.

"Dev!"

Dev put up her hands. "Sorry."

"It's okay. What do you do?" he asked.

"I'm a professor at NYU. Finance."

He nodded. "Good job. What about you, Pris?"

Pris stiffened as she always did when the topic came to careers. "I do work for various charities."

Bailey cut in. "She used to be a ballerina with the New York City Ballet. She was a beautiful dancer."

Pris waved her hand. "Too many years ago to count. But I make a difference in my own way."

"I'm sure you do. Bailey?"

She caught her breath a bit at his intense stare. Her heart tripped a bit, then slowed. Hmm, interesting. Attraction was so important to her, the push/pull of a man and woman engaging in the delicious dance. The first flush always enthralled her. It was only later that she ran, when things began to get real. "This and that. The play I was acting in just finished, so I'm in between projects."

"Go where the wind takes you, huh?" he asked.

"For now." She offered a brilliant smile. "Until the next adventure is discovered."

He smiled back.

Dev cleared her throat. "Would your dad have known our mom? Olivia Moretti. They may have spoken or hung out if they were neighbors. Or Silvia Agosto—she was the one who had the house before that."

A furrow creased his brow. "The names don't sound familiar, but I didn't visit that much. I spent two summers here when I was a kid, but then I fought to stay at home. I didn't want to leave my friends, and then I was in college and making a career for myself." He winced. "I guess I was an ungrateful kid—not wanting to go to Italy seems like a foreign concept today, huh?"

"I could understand," Pris said. "My son is attending college in London and building a life. If I asked him to uproot for a month, he wouldn't be happy."

"Sounds like you have a smart kid."

"Did your mom stay home with you, then?" Dev asked.

"Yes. My parents were divorced, so my father came here and I stayed back with my mother. He died about a decade ago, and I inherited the place."

"So, your dad has been coming here regularly, then, since he was young. Our mom would've been about twenty years old in the mid-seventies. That's the period we're looking at," Pris said.

"Yeah, that's about right. My dad would've been college age then and coming here with my grandparents. Definitely possible they knew one another."

"Do you know if he had any serious relationships when he was young?" Dev asked casually.

Hawke scratched his head. "Specifically? I don't remember him mentioning any names, but he told me he fell in love a few times in Italy when he was younger. That was another way he tried to convince me to come."

Her heart ramped up. It would make perfect sense! They

were the same age, and neighbors, and his dad was divorced. Bailey took the plunge. "What was your dad's name?"

Bailey held her breath as she waited for the answer. Dev and Pris leaned forward.

He regarded their anxious expressions for a few moments before answering. "Gio."

Disappointment mixed with relief. Another dead end.

Hawke let out a short laugh. "I'm going to assume I didn't utter the name you were hoping."

"I'm sorry," she said. "You must think we're a bunch of wackos, asking you a million questions when we've just met."

"You rescued my cat—I owe you." He finished the last sip of his wine. "Besides, I haven't had such an exciting night in a while."

"Oh, I don't believe that," Bailey said with a touch of sass. He looked at her again, and they assessed each other in a frank, bold way. Bailey sensed he wasn't a man to jump into anything without thinking about it.

"We better get back." Dev stood up and shot him a tight smile. "It's late and I'm still jet-lagged."

Bailey stood too, and they all shook hands again. She liked his firm grip and the no-nonsense shake. Too many men tried to press a thumb to her palm or interlink her fingers in a forced connection. "Let me know if you have any questions about the area for your sightseeing. The ferry will take you to some nice day trips like Capri, or there's some beautiful walking paths to explore."

"Thanks," she said.

"I'm home most of the time. Feel free to stop by. It's nice to have company."

His words made her wonder if he was a bit lonely. She wanted to know more about Hawke's story.

They made their way back to the cottage in silence. Bailey was hoping to cuddle up on the couch together in their jammies and indulge in some girl talk. It had been so long since she had both her sisters alone, with no other stresses or tasks pulling them away. But Dev headed straight to the room without looking back. "Going to bed."

The door shut.

Bailey looked at Pris. "What happened?"

Pris sighed. "Who knows? It's been a long day. Let's get some sleep and regroup tomorrow. Night."

Bailey heard the second door shut. She stood alone in the living room, in Positano, with her sisters down the hall, and had never felt so alone.

CHAPTER FIFTEEN

Pris

She sipped her coffee in the garden. The sun was high and bright, and the vivid colors of blooms and sky hurt her vision even behind her sunglasses. The run should have cleared her mind—she'd gone a full five miles this morning—but she kept thinking of last night and how it had been another dead end. Was she crazy to think they'd track down R? After all, they had nothing to go on. He was old, or dead, or living somewhere else and moved on with his life.

Who cared if her mother had come here for a week when Pris was young? It meant nothing.

But the little voice inside kept nagging. *What about his last letter? The one agreeing to meet your mother on her sixty-fifth birthday?* It sounded more serious than a past crush. Had he showed up here on her birthday, wondering why Mom hadn't shown?

A flare of regret coursed through her. Mom had passed in February, just three months before her birthday. She hadn't gotten the opportunity to see him or tie up loose ends. Would she have told her daughters about the trip to Italy? Or had that been another secret she meant to keep?

The questions were a nonstop mix churning in her mind. Underneath was the mounting concern that she'd never truly known her mother at all. Maybe no one had except for R. Until they found him, that part of Mom would remain a mystery.

Pris took a big gulp, burned her tongue, and spit out a curse.

"Morning to you too, sunshine." Bailey flopped into the seat beside her, tucking her knees up. "How'd you sleep?"

"Pretty good—I was exhausted. Dev up?"

"Yep, already in the shower and getting ready to take on the day. What time were you up?"

"Six?"

Bailey shuddered. "What do you do with all that time?"

"I run every morning."

"Hmm, interesting. I never knew you liked running."

Pris thought about it. "I never thought so, but Thomas asked me to do this charity run with him a while ago. I realized I couldn't even make it a mile without collapsing, which pissed me off. So, I started running and began to like it."

"I shouldn't be surprised; you've always been competitive with yourself."

She cocked her head. "You think?"

"I know. I think you need it. It's how you feel worthy." Pris was startled by her sister's observation, but she had no time to process. Bailey was already moving on. "Do we have any specific plans for today?"

Pris snorted. "Dev has the agenda, but I had an idea. We know R worked with boats—touring and fishing. I was thinking we can go on a boat trip. Poke around and see if we find any information."

Bailey looked amused. "Your plan is to go and ask a million boat operators if their name begins with R?"

"No! I mean, maybe. I'm not the expert here. Damn it, I probably should have asked Garrett for help. He wanted to hire a PI and do an investigation. We're amateurs."

"Smart idea but not as much fun. Plus, this is personal."

"That's what I said."

The thought of her husband made her stomach clench. She'd just texted him briefly that she'd arrived and everyone was fine. He'd politely answered. Since their talk that night, nothing had been resolved or uncovered. It was as if they were both hoping this trip to Italy would clear their heads so they could decide what to do next.

"Pris? I was thinking about what you said yesterday at dinner. About us never asking you stuff."

She stiffened, hating that she'd showed that vulnerability. It was better to keep her sisters out of anything serious. "Forget it, I was just cranky and tired."

"No, you're right. I never ask you anything about your life, but it's not because I'm not interested. It's just . . ." She trailed off, ducking her head.

Curiosity peaked. "Just what?"

"You're kind of like Mom. Hard to really know."

Her eyes widened. "Me?"

Bailey nodded. "You have this amazing capability about you—like you can handle anything and you don't need anyone's help. It's like you know yourself to the core and it gives you an inner strength that's sometimes intimidating. Maybe it's from finding ballet was your passion so young? But even when you got married, you just marched forward without seeming to question anything."

The image her sister painted was laughable. Her mouth hung open, half in shock, half in wonder. She actually gave off that impression, when inside she was full of doubts? How could her own sister not sense it was an act—a way to quell the doubts and regrets that haunted her?

"Maybe you weren't looking hard enough."

Bailey stared at her for a while. "I don't think I did. Every time I tried to ask, you always made light of it. Whether it was ballet or your husband or when you got pregnant, you'd smile and say things were good. Always good. How long was I supposed to keep asking, Pris? Why wouldn't you trust me?"

She jerked back. Was it a matter of trust? Or was she so used to her role of protector, she began to minimize her own problems? After their parents divorced, everything seemed to fracture. As the oldest sister, she worried about them all—Mom's hidden sadness, Bailey's wildness, Dev's anger . . . There was nothing left for her. Because she was good.

Good.

Her marker for everything. If things were relatively good, how could she complain or ask for more? Her thoughts spun as she tried to get a handle on a million lightbulbs exploding all at once. "Why do you think I'm like Mom?"

"Mom took care of all of us without complaint. Always with a smile. But when I began to ask questions, or try to dig into her past because I was curious, she shut me down. She never talked about her college days, or her life before Dad. It was like it never existed, and now we found so much more. A house in Positano and a love affair we never would have known about. What don't we know about you, Pris? What are you hiding?"

Thank God she didn't have to answer the awful question. Dev marched into the garden with a planner, pen, and cup of coffee. "Hey. We need to go over the day's schedule."

Bailey turned. "Dev, do you think Pris hides things from us like Mom?"

Dev slid into the last seat. "Sure. We only know the bare bones of your life, but you had a point last night. We haven't asked much. That's on us."

Her sister's admission tore through her. The casualness of the remark surprised Pris the most.

In her head, they didn't care, so she'd spent her time building a shelter where she could live completely self-sustained. But was that what she really wanted?

"Dude, you look really freaked out," Dev said.

"I thought you didn't care what was going on with me," she said slowly. "It became easier to stop talking."

Her sisters shared a pointed look, and for once they seemed in agreement. "That's our fault," Bailey said. "It was easier with Mom around. She kept us all connected. Now that she's gone, I think we need to make a conscious decision about what we want our relationship to be."

Dev remained silent, usually uncomfortable with emotion, but Pris took up the olive branch. "I haven't liked how we've been treating each other. I'd like us to be better. We only have each other now."

"We finally have the time together uninterrupted," Bailey said. "Let's use it to get to know one another again. What do you think?"

A lightness shimmered through her. "Yes, Mom would have wanted that."

Dev's features tightened, as if she was holding back, but then she gave a sharp nod. "I'll try. But let's not expect us to go all sunshine and roses just because we had one chat."

"Yes, Ms. Balloon Popper," Bailey said, but it was obvious she was teasing and Dev rolled her eyes. "What's our day entail?"

Back in her element, Dev flicked open the notebook. "I think we should have an early lunch in town—Caffè Positano looks perfect. Highly rated, budget-friendly, and great views close to the beach. We have time for some exploring and maybe we can make reservations for a boat tour tomorrow."

"Yes, we should ask around by the ferry. R may still be in the business."

"A long shot but definitely worth some research." Dev scribbled a note. "Then the real estate agent is coming at four p.m. for an appraisal. Once we get the figures, I can punch them into the spreadsheet, do a risk calculation, and we can see what each of our shares would be if we sell."

Uneasiness washed over her. It felt wrong to sell Mom's house. She'd only been here one day, but already she was beginning to connect to this place. She opened her mouth to tell Dev, but Bailey interrupted.

"I don't want to sell Mom's house. What if I buy out your share?"

Dev snorted. "You don't have the money. Unless you're going to ask Dad, which is many shades of wrong."

Bailey's face turned stubborn. "You can't make us sell if Pris says no. Can't you see this is more than money? It's our heritage."

"We agreed to get the figures, discuss rationally, and make a decision later in the week." Dev's tone was crisp and cool. "What's not fair is if we refuse to be open-minded about all our possibilities."

Knowing Dev was right, Pris stepped in. "We'll stick to our promise. No decisions or fighting until we have a frank discussion."

Bailey blew out her breath. "Fine. But I'm not changing my mind."

"Thanks for being so helpful minutes after we agreed to try harder with each other."

Bailey glared at Dev. "Because I know you won't be open-minded either! You'd have the FOR SALE sign on the property this morning if we let you!"

"Oh, please. Now that you've got your eyes on our new neighbor, you won't be able to see reason."

"I knew this was about Hawke! I didn't do anything wrong; you are impossible to deal with."

"Oh, like I didn't see the flip of your hair? It's your trademark move—you need some new material."

"You're vile," Bailey whispered. "Completely—"

Pris stood up. "Enough. Get up and get ready—we're all going out."

"It's too early for lunch," Dev said, glancing at her planner. "I was going to catch up on some email and work before we left."

"No work. I think we all need an activity guaranteed to bond us together."

"What's that?" Bailey asked.

"Shopping. I've got an American Express Gold I need rewards on, so it's my treat today. Anything goes."

Bailey paused. A gleam lit her eyes. "Anything?"

Pris smiled. "Anything. Dev?"

Her sister tried not to show her interest, but she was female. "You may regret that statement later."

"Just remember—whatever we buy, we need to haul up and down those stairs," Pris said.

That got Dev to grin. "I knew there'd be a catch. I'm in."

"Let's do this." Satisfied that she'd managed to defuse the rising argument, Pris made her way into the bedroom to finish getting ready. Reaching into the back of the bureau drawer to where she'd stuffed her underwear, her fingers closed around a paper folded up in the back corner.

Frowning, she opened it up and began to read.

Dear R,

I feel like I've spent this summer stealing and trying to stop time.

I'm writing this a few days before I plan to leave, but I'll never send it. I want to be able to revisit my words each time I come back to you, and remember we've always been meant to be together.

I know you're right about me not dropping out of school to move here, but every moment spent away from you feels empty. How can I explain how much this summer meant to me? Aunt Silvia told me she knows about our secret but swore she wouldn't tell my parents as long as I stayed in school. I think she believes distance will eventually break us up, but she doesn't know the truth.

I can't stop thinking about our night together. The way you greeted me at your house and cooked me my favorite dinner of spaghetti vongole. The way the rain beat against the window and locked us into a world of our own. The candles you'd lit everywhere and the soft music that played and the way you undressed me with hands that trembled. The way you whispered my name in my ear. It was like falling in love with you all over again, a slow, easy slide until I became part of you, and the ache inside me was finally filled.

I tried to memorize your face that night, stockpiling images so I could remember every detail when I was away from you. I wondered if I'd ever feel like a whole person again. Is the way I love you the greatest gift or the most awful curse?

You said you loved me but you're still afraid I'll leave you. I knew you were thinking of the girl who'd hurt you before, so I swore I'd always come back, no matter what. I promise you can trust me. I'll prove this to you, my love. Every summer, I'll return, until we're finally together. Because you're my soul mate, my other half, the man I want to spend the rest of my life with.

Until then.

Love,

Livia

Heart frantically pounding in her chest, she reread the letter and called her sisters in. "I found this in the drawer," she said, her hands shaking. They both read it, then stared at one another in shock.

"This wasn't a casual crush," Bailey finally said. "This was so much more than that."

Dev remained silent. Pris's insides churned. This was proof there truly was a part of her mother she'd never known—a life she'd once dreamed of spending with another man, right here in Positano.

Dev shook her head. "Come on, let's go. We'll talk about it at lunch."

They finished getting ready, each lost in her own thoughts.

CHAPTER SIXTEEN

Olivia

The second year of college got better.

I got a new roommate, Sonya, and liked her immediately. She ended up becoming my trusted confidante and the only one who knew about Rafe. She was also the only one to get me to go out and socialize, insisting that being true to one's heart didn't necessarily mean being isolated and alone.

I got to take more electives and found I had a love for art history. Slowly, I began to creep out of my shell and enjoy college, even though my heart ached for Rafe. I figured if I kept my high grades and my work-study job and dropped hints to Mom and Dad that I was getting more involved in group activities, they'd allow me to go back to Italy this summer.

Aunt Silvia had already confided that my dad wanted to have me for a good portion of my vacation so he could spend more quality time with me. It sounded nice, but I also knew my father was a workaholic, and it'd mean getting stuck at his tiny house with no friends and no car and waiting for him to get home so we could have dinner together. Then I'd watch him fall asleep on the couch way too early.

I had to change their minds.

I used Thanksgiving and winter break to plant the seeds with both of them, talking excitedly about my decision to switch my major to art history with a minor in business, and how my summer in Italy had helped jump-start my new passion. They both fought me at first, citing the inability to gain employment with a liberal arts degree, but I remained stubbornly persistent. After I talked to my art advisor about opportunities to study in Italy, he gave me a packet of information where college students can complete extra study credit. They assigned a few mentors to the students to help them transition from college life to reality. Basically, it was a clear path to create contacts in art work environments so when I graduated, I'd have a job waiting for me.

That was a language Mom and Dad understood, and they finally agreed to send me off again with Aunt Silvia.

Rafe and I continued to write letters and spoke on the phone. I'd hold the pen in hand, close my eyes, and picture the busy streets and packed restaurants in Positano slowing to a trickle from the loss of tourists. He'd been taking the boat out more with his father, but the fishing hadn't been as productive this season. I'd read his words, hearing his lilting, husky voice in my ear while he talked about the books he was reading, and the hours spent hunkered down in his house thinking of me. I felt a bit guilty at my suddenly booming social life and packed schedule—sometimes there didn't seem enough time to breathe—but then pushed away the thought. This was temporary. I'd work hard, graduate, and find a job in Italy. I never really thought past finally being together. My mind conjured up glamorous images of me working in an art gallery while Rafe came to visit me. Cooking meals together in our cozy kitchen and sitting outside watching the stars light up the sky. Sailing on his boat while I helped charm the tourist guests. It all seemed like a fabulous, passion-filled, romantic life, so different from the one I'd be trapped in within the States.

Was that the beginning of things changing but I just never noticed? Or had we always been fated to struggle to combine two very different worlds into one?

The third summer I returned to Italy I didn't pause when I caught sight of Rafe. I jumped into his arms, and we fell into a passionate kiss, my hands clinging to his hard, familiar body as I breathed in the sharp male essence of his scent. He whispered Italian in my ear, and I recognized some of the affectionate phrases, but it was the *mio amore* that thrilled me.

Giddiness bubbled in my veins. I was back.

Aunt Silvia was no longer seeing Eduardo on a romantic basis. The conversation that unfolded between us caused a tiny seed of worry.

"But why did you break up?" I'd asked, trailing her around the cottage as she got ready for her evening out. She wrapped her favorite sweater around her—a gorgeous, vibrant mix of reds and golds that was as bold as her. She'd let me borrow it one night and I felt like a movie star. "I thought you were so happy."

"Darling, I was! Eduardo is a lovely man and we'll always remain close friends. Things change with romantic relationships." I must've looked crestfallen, because she gave her booming trademark laugh and pulled me into a tight hug. "How can I explain so you understand? Oh, you're so young and passionate—I remember all those wonderful feelings that ripped me apart and put me back together." She took a step back and studied me. "Olivia, I already had the great love of my life—your uncle. I'm happy now to explore the world and meet new people. Eduardo loves his place here in Positano, but he rarely ventures out. He's happy being in his home, leading a simple lifestyle."

"But why is that wrong? Did you want someone more exciting?"

"It's not wrong—it's just different. Rafe is much like his father, my love. He's set roots deep in this place and doesn't have the lust for travel like some others do. Eduardo is fine with the breakup, I promise."

I sighed, still hating the idea that it didn't work out. Sure, there were obstacles, but didn't love conquer all? "Who's this new man?"

Aunt Silvia shivered with delight. "Maximus Garner. Isn't that such a strong name? He's an actor who will be in Rome for the next few weeks shooting a film. He invited both of us to visit. You'll come with me, won't you, darling?"

I didn't want to sacrifice any precious time with Rafe, but he was working so much, it would be a perfect opportunity to see the sights. "Yes, I'd love to! Can I check with Rafe on his schedule first?"

A flicker of concern flashed in her bright eyes, but it was gone just as fast. "Yes, darling, I would never think to take you away from the man you love."

I smiled and hugged her back.

I ended up visiting Rome many days with my aunt. I loved seeing a live-action set, and then I'd roam the museums, taking pictures and sketching, lost in the gorgeous world of art I was beginning to love so much.

Rafe and I fell back into our summer routine, but I began to notice something had changed. I couldn't articulate what it was, but I felt a restless energy nipping at me. Before, I'd been thrilled to spend hours in the garden, drawing, daydreaming, waiting for Rafe. I'd sip a *caffè* at one of the overcrowded restaurants and people watch, content to be a bystander rather than a participant. But once I hooked up with Julia and Ava again, we began hanging out more with a bigger crowd. My Italian was stronger, so I participated in get-togethers at the beach, jumping on Julia's boat to party at various hot spots, and dancing most evenings at Music on the Rocks and Africana Famous Club. I was accepted into the group now, a regular like Ava, and didn't need Rafe as much to feel comfortable.

I was growing into myself and enjoyed the new self-confidence both school and Rafe gave me. But I also noticed how the man I loved would look at me now, with a haunted worry when I cut my gaze to his. He seemed to crave more alone time with me—especially since his days were filled up with back-to-back tours. His father had been having knee issues and needed more help, so Rafe stepped up. I admired him and understood. I just decided to fill my time a bit differently than I had my past two summers. I pushed for us to be more social, when before I was thrilled to cozy up alone with him.

I never realized it had begun to cause a problem.

One late night, a bit tipsy, the girls struck up a dare and threw off their clothes, diving into the sea naked, screaming and giggling. The boys finally followed, but I kept to the side with Rafe. If this had happened before, I never would have been tempted—way too shy and awkward to want to involve myself in their mad games. But this time, I sent a mischievous grin toward Rafe. "Wanna join them?"

He blinked, obviously stunned. "You want to skinny-dip?"

I laughed. A surge of adrenaline rushed through me. "Yes, let's do it!"

Before I could change my mind, I tore off my clothes, but left my bra and underwear on. Then I raced over the rocks, wincing at the sharpness, and dove into the water. Cries of support rang in my ears, and I laughed with delight as my friends circled around me.

It was a while before Rafe joined me. I noticed he moved slower, kicking off his shoes and peeling off his shirt and pants, the moonlight highlighting his beautiful lean muscles and dark curls. He swam over, cutting into the girl circle and grabbing me by the waist. His strong legs scissored back and forth to keep us both above water, and my friends splashed us and swam off. "Are you okay?" he asked.

I wrapped my arms around him. His body was slippery and hard against mine. "Yes. Did I surprise you?"

"I worried you had too much to drink. I didn't want you to get hurt."

I grinned, delighted I'd managed to take him off guard. It was about time I loosened up and did more fun things. "I'm fine. I just thought it would be nice to be a little wild. Show you a different side of me."

I expected him to laugh and tease me, but his dark eyes were serious as he stared back. He hesitated, as if not knowing how to tell me something. A shiver shook through me that had nothing to do with the cold. I kept catching an unease carved into his features, gleaming from his gaze. Was he bothered that I joined in the skinny-dipping?

"Rafe? Did I do something wrong?"

He shook his head. "No, *dolcezza*, you didn't. I love seeing you happy and free and laughing. It makes my heart just as happy."

"Then why have you been acting strange? Like you're seeing me for the first time?"

A smile touched his lips, but his eyes remained sad. "Because I think I am. You're changing, and I'm being selfish. I want you to stay the same and that's wrong of me. I'm sorry."

I blinked, not understanding the apology. "I am the same," I insisted, cupping his rough cheeks. "I would have never done something like this before. Since I met you, I've been braver. More sure of myself, because you love me."

He kissed me gently, his hand shaking a bit as he pushed back my wet hair. "You're so beautiful. You don't see how special you are, Livia. You're blooming like a flower and it has nothing to do with me. You can do anything with your life, and I hate myself for getting worried and jealous that I'm going to lose you. I picture your life back in New York, and the new friends you made, and wonder if you'd ever be able to give all that up to settle here with me." He blew out a breath and his next words broke my heart. "I'm afraid I won't be enough for you."

"You are," I said fiercely. The moon glowed bright above us, squeezed amid the burst of stars. My friends' voices carried in the air, light and carefree, separate from the sudden intensity of our conversation. "The plan hasn't changed, Rafe. Yes, I'm enjoying school more. But I'm enjoying Positano—my second home—just as much. I love the friends I've made here, and how I'm better at the language, and how I don't get lost anymore or panic when I'm alone. Remember my promise? I meant every word. Don't give up on us."

His face relaxed, and relief poured through me. He believed me. For now, his doubts were clear. I knew there were going to be ups and downs with us as we navigated a long-distance relationship. I had my own insecurities—sick with jealousy when I saw Rafe talking or laughing with another girl, spinning stories of how she was trying to take him away from me. But I was busy enough to distract myself.

Rafe was alone here with his thoughts and ideas of what I was doing at college. Plus, he probably kept thinking of his past and the woman who left him. I burned with anger at her. She'd been the one to tear him apart. That was why he questioned our commitment—he was afraid it would happen again.

But it wouldn't. We were halfway there. In two years, we'd finally be together.

He sighed in my ear and goose bumps prickled my skin. "I'll never give up on us, Livia. Even if one day you end up leaving me. My heart will always belong to you."

His words made my head spin. We kissed, the worry fading away for both of us, and then our friends motioned us out of the water. We held hands and ran to the beach, donning our clothes, high on the moon and the midnight swim and the feeling we had the world captured and laid at our feet.

And for that one beautiful night, we did.

CHAPTER SEVENTEEN

Dev

The shopping trip was epic.

She was careful with her expenses because living in New York City was a budget breaker. The future was as important as the present, in her mind, so every dollar she made needed to stretch to accommodate savings, Roth plan, bills, and fun. Dinners out were critical due to needing a social network for dating and staying abreast of current news at NYU. Usually, frivolous stuff like clothes, shoes, and jewelry were cut.

But not today. Today, they were on her sister's dime.

She didn't even feel guilty indulging in the gorgeous handmade leather sandals at one of the shops. The lady only spoke Italian, but her products spoke a universal language. Fashion. They all grabbed a pair—Pris going with classic camel brown, Bailey snatching up pastel beaded slingbacks, and Dev choosing a beautiful fringe with no heel.

Stalls with vibrant-colored pottery demanded a viewing. They fingered the smooth, glossy textures of hand-painted lemons on ceramic and urged Pris to buy a full set of pasta bowls to be shipped back home.

As they walked down the sloping, narrow streets crowded with tourists, a sense of contentment settled over her. The buzz of Italian in her ears, the leisurely pace that settled her nerves, reminding her that at this moment, no one needed her attention. The slight breeze caressed her cheeks. Scooters zigzagged in and out. The blue of the sea stretched before her in magical glimpses as they explored.

She'd forgotten what this felt like. In New York, she adored the bustling city full of excitement and possibility. It was her home. But right now, there was only the moment unfolding before her, and her responsibility was to just be here to witness. It had been a long time since she experienced this odd sense of freedom.

"Oh. My. God." Bailey gasped and pointed. "Moda Positano! We are so getting our jam on—let's go."

They tested fabrics in cool cottons and elegant linens, spun from the best in the fashion world. The clean smell drifted to her nostrils, reminding her of one of the special candles she loved to light to make her apartment smell like fresh laundry. Dev helped her sisters compile outfits, pulling out light and airy lacy dresses; fancy cover-ups with beads and tassels; long skirts that skimmed the hips and fell in soft folds around the ankles. Each piece was a vision of beauty.

Dev couldn't resist.

Hands full of bags, they stopped and bought perfume—a delicate floral scent tinged with citrus—and matching new wallets in deep burgundy leather.

Finally, they stumbled to Caffè Positano and grabbed a table overlooking the sea. Dev ordered a limoncello spritzer and gazed out at the water softly lapping at the shore; the crush of bodies on the rocky beach; the slow, smooth slide of boats as they made their way out of the harbor. It was pure magic, too much for her to take in, and a nest of emotions stirred deep inside her, desperately looking for a way out.

She frowned and sipped her drink.

"What's the matter?" Bailey asked.

She turned sharply, surprised her sister had noticed anything. She'd forgotten how sensitive Bailey was to the moods of others. Probably a wonderful asset for her acting career. Or job. Bailey never seemed to focus long enough to make anything a career. "Nothing."

"Come on, tell us the truth." Her blue eyes sparkled with happiness. "I'm drunk on shopping and Italy. We promised to try and open up to each other, remember?"

Ah, crap. Feelings again. She hated them. They were so . . . messy. "I'm just happy."

Bailey blinked. "That's what made you look so intense? Isn't that a good thing?"

Usually, she'd jab back at her sister and shut down the entire conversation. Opening herself up never seemed tempting, but with the sun shining down and contentment buzzing in her veins, she decided to answer. "Yeah, but it's also uncomfortable. I'm not like either of you. Big ups and downs aren't my jam. I like routine, order, and steadiness. I know it sounds crazy but . . ." She trailed off, not wanting to share the rest.

Pris leaned in. "No, go on, Dev. Tell us."

"I try to avoid things that make me too happy. Because I figure anything that good will eventually lead to something really bad. It's easier to keep to my lane, where I can control things." Her cheeks heated with embarrassment. "Forget it."

"No, I get it," Pris said. "Makes sense to me. Even growing

up, you always loved order. It satisfied you. Remember your Legos?"

Bailey laughed. "Oh my God! She created these amazing cities and spent hours on those things. I hated when you got new Legos because I didn't see you for days."

Dev gazed at her suspiciously. "Is that why you always tried to destroy them?"

"Yeah, I missed you. I got bored."

"That's so messed up," she said, but it had no sting. In fact, a tiny bit of pleasure snaked through her at the idea of her sister missing her.

"You craved organization. Probably why you chose a math and finance career. Your brain works differently from ours," Pris said.

"But being happy shouldn't be something you're afraid of," Bailey said. Her tone was soft and held no judgment. For the first time, Dev analyzed her reaction and her past. Is that why she always steered away from intimate relationships and made work her world? Even her friendships were controllable—a group she enjoyed seeing but didn't have to invest too much in.

Had she always been like this, or had something changed her? She remembered being devastated by the divorce and feeling betrayed by her father's cheating. It had really seemed he'd cheated on his family and not just Mom. When he remarried and had a child, she'd been sick with jealousy at being replaced. Had that screwed her up regarding relationships? God knows, she hated sitting too long with her thoughts and trying to do self-therapy. But it might be time to dig a bit more, and her sisters would be the safest place to start.

It was something worth thinking about.

"Is anyone else thinking of the letter Mom wrote?" Pris asked quietly. "I can't get it off my mind."

The shopping had distracted her, but Dev had been sifting through her mother's words too. It was as if she was meeting a different person, and she couldn't tell if it was Mom's youth, the excitement of being in Italy alone for the summer, or if R had truly been her soul mate. What did that make Dad? And why had Mom left R?

"She seemed so happy," Bailey murmured. "I've never heard her talk like that before about anything."

"Or anyone," Dev finally said, trying to ignore the ache in her chest. "Maybe we should look for more hidden letters when we get home. Or a journal."

"Good idea," Pris said. "I feel like it brought me more questions than answers."

"Me too," Bailey said. "I keep thinking about that type of romantic love. It seemed so intense yet completely fulfilling." A flash of yearning flickered over her face. "I always thought I'd experienced love until I read that letter. Now I'm wondering if I've just scratched the surface."

"At least you've been in love before," Dev said. She tried not to sound accusing, because she owned her choices and loved her career. "I can't even relate."

Suddenly, Pris pinned her with an intense gaze. "Are you happy, Dev? Really, truly happy?" Pris asked.

She jerked slightly and stared at her sisters. The question unsettled her. "Is anyone *really* happy?"

She held her breath, hoping they'd take her lead. Her sisters shared a glance and began laughing, and Dev relaxed. "Good point," Bailey said, lifting her glass. "A toast. To . . . feeling good enough."

Dev grinned and they clinked glasses. The waiter dropped off their lunch. The buffalo mozzarella was rich and creamy, setting off the tomato and basil salad fragrant with herbs. They dipped crusty bread in pungent olive oil and quickly finished half the loaf. Steamed mussels and clams held the salty tang of the ocean, which danced over her tongue. They ordered a bottle of Prosecco to share and spent the next hour eating and chatting about nonsense subjects while looking over the balcony at the spill of sea and cliff and sky.

Dev had forgotten how nice it was to be with family—the ones who knew every quirk and secret of her past. And even though it had been a long time, she began to fall into the ease of being with her sisters, the push/pull of teasing, affection, and shared memories. In her deepest heart, a flare of longing touched off, and she realized how much she had really missed them.

If only she could find a way to transcend the past for good. But it would mean opening up to the monsters in the closet and cleaning house. It would mean facing old emotions that she hated to revisit.

It would mean having a heart-to-heart with Bailey.

On cue, her sister gave a long sigh. "Do you think Mom sat here at this restaurant years ago? Maybe planning her future with R?"

Her nerve endings prickled, as if a new energy had drifted by, touching her as gently as a whisper. She imagined herself seated in the same exact place as her mother, full of hopes and dreams for an undeveloped story. Did Mom have regrets? Did she ever wonder if she chose the right path—especially if it was a choice between this R and her father? Mom never seemed the type of woman to question herself—she'd told her daughters on a regular basis how much she loved her life. But underneath, were there doubts slithering like snakes, and she'd shut them all away like the letters in the trunk?

Pris spoke up. "Mom fell in love here, but I'm sure it was a summer romance that eventually faded. I don't think she would've married Dad if she was in love with someone else."

"How do you know?" Bailey asked curiously. She propped her elbows on the table and laid her chin in cupped hands. "I guess I saw her so differently. I'd catch her, many times, staring out the window with this sad look on her face, like she'd spotted something she lost."

Pris shook her head. "Because she used to tell me stories about her and Dad and how crazy they were for each other. Plus, she never got really mad at us, remember? All of my other friends used to hear their moms bitch about all the tasks they had to do and how much they hated it. Mom was always happy and involved. That proves she wasn't living with regret for this guy who wrote her a few romantic letters." Her jaw tightened in pure stubbornness. "And I don't like the idea of us ruining her memory. She wouldn't like it."

"Then why do you want to pursue looking for R?" Dev asked.

"To prove everyone wrong."

Dev wondered why her sister seemed the most passionate about defending Mom's choices. Dev wasn't as much on Bailey's side, believing Mom had an affair while married to Dad, but she also didn't believe Mom was a saint like Pris believed. Somehow, smack in the middle seemed more of a natural place. After all, Mom was only human.

"And if we find out differently?" Bailey asked. "Will you be okay?"

A short silence fell. Pris stared out at the cliffs, her eyes filled with a mix of emotions. "I don't know," she said slowly. "I just know we won't."

Bailey cocked her head. "Is there something else going on with you, Pris? Are you and Garrett okay? I know we've been selfish. I think Dev and I always assume you're okay, but we're here now. Ready to listen."

Pris tangled her hands in her lap. Various emotions flickered over her delicate features, and Dev was once again struck by her innate beauty. She still reminded Dev of a doll, graceful and willowy and trapped in her own snow globe. It was as if she looked out at the world through a pane of glass, sometimes wishing she could be out there, but content to dance within the constraints of her entrapment.

Some kind of energy shifted between them. Pris seemed poised for a breakthrough, and suddenly, Dev held her breath, almost wished her sister wouldn't say anything.

Because it would shatter the image Dev had clung to for her entire life.

The practiced smile curved her sister's lips. "Nothing. Really, everything's good." She glanced at her watch. "We better get going. We'll be late for the real estate agent."

No one pushed and Dev was relieved. So much had already happened in the past two days. She needed time to process.

They paid the bill, took their shopping bags, and headed to the house.

With each step they climbed, Dev thought about not only her mother's secrets, but her sisters' as well. And she wondered if any of them would finally be revealed.

CHAPTER EIGHTEEN

Olivia

When I began my junior year, I was slammed with the pressure of achieving high grades, taking on more credits, and still keeping my part-time job in order to go to Italy next summer. Sonya and I managed to remain roommates for another year, and I was consistently battling between my responsibility and my burgeoning need to be with my friends. Work usually won. I tried to save my socializing for weekends, but as my daily hours seemed to shrink, something more alarming began to occur.

I began to think less and less of Rafe.

Of course I still loved him. The plan hadn't changed at all. But as we'd miss each other's phone calls due to the time zone differences, and he'd send me three letters to every one of mine, I realized I was under serious pressure. I could tell his tone was a bit sharper when he asked why I hadn't written to him. I tried to explain, but even to my own ears, my explanations seemed like excuses.

My heart remained loyal and committed. But being away from him, stuck in this world with the goal to graduate, began to feel stressful. I noticed we'd fight more often, with differing opinions setting us off. We always made up, and then I'd stay up late writing to him, my fingers gripping the pen as I spilled out all my emotions on the paper and right into his heart.

He mentioned trying to come see me for the holidays, but I knew my parents would flip and shut my travel down for next summer. The goal was to keep them believing my trips weren't focused on Rafe. The moment they believed I'd be giving up my life for a boy, they'd try to stop us. I didn't have enough money to support myself right now, and neither did Rafe. Aunt Silvia was honest about what she'd do for us. I'd spoken to her at length to confess my feelings and was surprised when she seemed to understand and not try to talk me out of my plan to move. Instead, she informed me she wouldn't tell my mother yet, because it was my responsibility as a grown adult. I was twenty-one, old enough to make my own decisions. Unfortunately, she also let me know she wouldn't be able to help me financially because she knew my mom would never forgive her. Basically, I had Aunt Silvia's emotional support, and full use of the cottage, but I was pretty much on my own.

One dreary winter afternoon, I attended a recruitment seminar for a company called International Business Machines—IBM. It was a cutting-edge computer business that was rapidly expanding, especially with the rise of floppy disks. To satisfy the minor in business, our professor encouraged us to attend to get an idea of what opportunities were out there for graduates. I was desperate for a change of pace outside the classroom and gladly went.

The guy who ran it was young—definitely midtwenties—and dressed in jeans, a button-down blue shirt, and a striped tie. I pegged him for a nerd at first, with his glasses and goatee, but then I spotted the sneakers as he walked up to the stage and addressed the small crowd.

"Hi. I'm Adam Clayton, I've worked for IBM since I graduated from this college, and I'm here to make sure I recruit the best. By the time I'm done, every single one of you will be applying to work and get in on the ground floor of something amazing." His voice was deep and commanding, and suddenly I was listening intensely, fascinated by his powered confidence and broad smile.

The time flew by as he dazzled us with statistics, employment benefits, and the goal for the company. By the end, I think he'd won over the whole audience, and there was a line to talk to him when he finished his presentation.

I fiddled with my bag, ready to go, but something stopped me. Of course, I wouldn't be working here. I was an art student going to Italy. But a gut instinct guided my feet toward the front, and I took my place at the end so I could get my time.

"Hi. I'm Adam. Nice to meet you—"

"Olivia Moretti." Up close, his eyes were a beautiful shade of brown-gold and gleamed with a sharp intelligence that intrigued me. "I enjoyed your presentation."

He rocked back on his sneakered heels and regarded me over the gold wire rims. "Good, because I have a quota to reach. If I don't get enough applications . . ." He trailed off, doing an imitation of slicing his hand over his throat.

My eyes must have widened because he laughed and shook his head. "Just kidding. Tell me about yourself, Olivia Moretti. Majoring in business?"

"No, minor in business."

"Concentration in marketing, management, or finance?"

"Marketing."

"And why a minor not major?" He tilted his head as if he was seriously interested in my answer.

"I'm majoring in art history. I'm hoping to work for a curator, or private art gallery, or museum. Any place that will hire me. As for marketing, I find it more creative than management. I think I'd be a poor manager."

"Hmm, I'll have to ask why again. I sound like a parrot."

I smiled. "I'm not good at telling people what to do. Plus, marketing has some artwork involved, so it's more my speed."

He nodded. "I like your answer. Knowing your own strengths is key. Just make sure when you interview, you act like if they don't hire you, it will be a big mistake. Leave the weaknesses at the door."

"Got it. Thanks."

"Welcome. Want an application?"

I laughed. "No. I just wanted to let you know I enjoyed the presentation. Definitely more interesting than sitting in class."

His eyes glinted with pleasure. "Appreciate it. Hey, are you done for the day? I've got the rest of the afternoon free and I'd love to get a cup of coffee with you. Chat a bit."

I hesitated, confused. Was it a date? Or a casual coffee thing? A flush came over me as he waited patiently for my answer. Was it a betrayal to Rafe to spend time with the man, or was I overreacting? Frustrated with my doubts, I decided to treat it like a mentoring thing. He seemed smart and interesting. Nothing wrong with having a talk over coffee. "Sounds good. There's a café down the street that's much better than the cafeteria."

"Thank God. I like my coffee strong, black, and unapologetic."

I laughed. "Me too."

"We're going to get along just fine, Ms. Moretti. Maybe even at the end, I'll have your application in hand."

I was surprised at how easily our conversation flowed. Two hours passed in a blur as we loaded up on caffeine. I learned he was an up-and-comer in the company and had big ideas on how to recruit not only technical business majors but a bigger variety of creative people to think outside the box. He spoke with a passion about his job and his dreams, thinking big, and I was swept up in his ambition to have it all. I'd always leaned toward a simpler existence, content with my thoughts, my books, and my art. But lately, I was getting pulled into the lure of the world and its other possibilities. As I became more comfortable in social situations and gained more friends, a strange longing for something bigger kept twisting my gut.

It scared me a bit because I didn't want anything to change. But I wasn't sure how to stop it.

Adam fed that longing, and when we finally broke apart, I was reluctant to leave. "Hey, I had a great time with you. Can I take you out to dinner sometime?"

His invite was simple, but his gaze was bold as he stared at me. A shiver raced down my spine. My instinct was to say yes, but it had definitely sounded more like a date. I had to let him know the truth. "Honestly, Adam, I'd like to, but I have a boyfriend."

Surprise flickered across his face. "Oh, I'm sorry, I didn't know. Then again, kind of stupid to think you'd be free." I blushed at his compliment. "Listen, I won't push and we can keep things as friends. Here's my number." He pushed his card into my palm and treated me to one of his sexy smiles. "Call me if you want to hang out as a nondate. I promise I won't cross the line. I just like your company."

Pleasure sprang up. I nodded. "Okay. I'll let you know."

We parted ways at the café. I tucked his card into my purse for safekeeping. There'd be no harm now in calling. He might be a great friend to cultivate since he was in the business world. College taught us anyone can have a contact somewhere. Besides, I'd been honest and he knew I wasn't available. My conscience was clear.

If I'd known that night would have changed the course of my future, would I still have called him?

I'd never know.

CHAPTER NINETEEN

Dev

The real estate agent was quick and efficient. Her eyes widened when she spotted the place, and Dev watched as dollar signs pretty much flashed in her gaze as she took in the remodeling and perfect condition.

"I could get you top dollar for this property," she promised, her short dark bob swinging under her chin. "How fast do you want to sell?"

"Soon," Dev said.

"Never," Bailey shot back, giving a death glare.

Dev ignored her and sent the alarmed agent a smile. "We needed to start with initial figures before we move forward."

"Of course. I think you'll find my sales history is top-notch in the area. This is a rare find with such updates. Is this a straight sale or are you looking to rent?"

"Give us both options," Dev said.

The agent calculated some numbers and left after Dev was satisfied she'd answered every last question.

When she turned to her sisters, Bailey crossed her arms

across her chest, disgust sketched on her features. Pris just seemed confused. She'd have to be careful navigating the conversation. "These are hefty numbers," Dev said, trying to start off on a high note.

"I don't care," Bailey said. "My vote is no sale."

Dev let out an annoyed breath. "You promised to go through every suggestion rationally first, remember?"

Pris glanced over. "You did promise. Why don't we sit down?"

They all convened at the sturdy pine table. Dev opened her phone calculator and her notebook. She'd been calculating various scenarios to find the one that satisfied everyone. "Hear me out before we go any further. If we sell the house for this price, minus fees, we each pocket this amount." She tore off pieces of paper and slid them across the table. Bailey didn't react, but Pris widened her eyes.

"That's a lot of money," Pris said.

"Exactly. Think about the nest egg this can bring us. That's what I believe Mom wanted for us. There was a reason she never came back here. She wanted us to have this inheritance not for the house but for the investment."

Bailey rolled her eyes. "Are you serious? You *would* think like that!"

"Look, I'm sure this house was important at one time in her life, but she literally never told us about it. Never brought us here, never wanted to share it. Don't you think that's saying something?"

Pris let out a breath. "She's right. Why was Mom so intent on not having us find out? I mean, it was locked up in the trunk with those love letters. Maybe the house held bad memories instead of good but she felt guilty about selling it."

Bailey jumped from the chair. "Guys, this is crazy. You have to listen to me. The reason she didn't tell us is so much bigger—can't you see? This house was special because it was just for her. Her memories. Her summers with Aunt Silvia. Her romance. It was something she didn't have to share with her husband or her children or anyone else. This is a legacy of happiness, and I will not sell it off to the highest bidder just so I can fatten my stock portfolio."

"You don't even have a portfolio," Dev muttered.

Bailey jabbed a finger in the air. "That's what I hate! I want my sister back—the one who went to lunch with us and admitted she had issues. Not this snarky, defensive woman who has so many walls I can't get through. Why do you have to pretend to know everything? Please, Dev. Let's keep the house and we can figure out logistics later. If you want help with the maintenance or finances, I'll give it to you. Please don't sell Mom's house."

The raw emotion in her sister's voice hit her full force. Dev froze, staring into those pleading bright blue eyes, and her heart cracked open. It was the first time she realized Bailey needed this for much more than a place to crash or a summer vacation. She believed it was one of the best parts of Mom.

Dev had no problem fighting impulse or bad decisions. She relished trying to help Bailey have a bigger, better future, whether she wanted it or not. But how could she fight her sister's need to connect to Mom?

Pris cleared her throat. "I vote with Bailey," she said firmly. "I don't want to sell either, but I am open to compromising on how we pay for the upkeep and taxes."

Usually, Pris siding with Bailey would ignite her temper, but this was different. Something was changing between them, and Dev didn't want to fight anymore. The shopping trip and lunch had given her a glimpse of the old days—when they cared about one another as a unit more than themselves as individuals. Before their relationships had withered and died while Mom looked on, unable to stop it.

It was all their faults in different ways. But if Dev pushed and fought to sell this house, she might never get another chance with her sisters.

And right now, that was most important.

A tightness squeezed her chest, practically strangling her. Oh God, it was too much. She needed to get out of here.

Dev managed a nod and stood up. "Majority rules. We'll talk more logistics later. I think I'll go for a walk."

"No, Dev, don't go like this. We don't want you to be upset," Pris said.

How could she tell them it was this new closeness that was driving her away, rather than the sale she lost out on? She needed repetitive motion to gather her thoughts.

Dev forced a smile. "I swear, I'm not mad. I really just need some air."

Bailey stared at her for a while, then slowly nodded. "Okay. Want company?"

"No, why don't you both take a nap? I won't be long, and then we can get changed for dinner and head out for the night."

"Sounds good," Pris said.

Dev grabbed her phone and fled.

She sucked in a lungful of air but instead got a choking mass of heat. Damn, probably wasn't the best time for a hike, at the peak of afternoon, but she needed alone time to figure things out. She'd expected the fighting but not the longing to heal their rifts—not like this. It was hard to explain the things she felt, especially with her sisters. Some time alone might help.

"Hey."

The familiar voice made her pause and spin on her heel. Hawke closed the distance between them in a few long-legged strides. Towering over six feet, he had a powerful physique, but he didn't give off the arrogant ego she'd expected. His clothes were relaxed and casual—khaki shorts, a white T-shirt stretched tight over his chest, and sneakers. His skin was a tanned brown. She'd enjoyed their conversation last night. He was direct, which she appreciated, but what was he doing in front of their house? "Hi, Hawke. What's up?"

"Not much. Was going to knock on your door, actually. See if you wanted to take a walk."

She stared at him, confused. "Oh. Well, um, Bailey and Pris are grabbing naps now."

"What about you?"

She blinked. His direct stare was a bit much for her. Those blue-gray eyes reminded her of both a storm cloud and the Listerine blue of the sea. The combination intrigued her, but she got stuck somewhere within his gaze and it was a bit of a jolt. She shook her head to dissolve the weird trance. "I was already going out for a walk."

"Great. Mind if I join you, or did you want to be alone?"

His words confused her. "You want to go for a walk with me?"

His lower lip quirked. "Yeah. That okay?"

"Sure. Come on, let's go. It's hot as Hades and I need some shade." She didn't know why he'd want to walk with her and not Bailey, who he was obviously interested in, but what the hell? As long as he realized she walked fast and hated a leisurely pace. Then again, if he was a New Yorker he'd be able to keep up.

"Would you like me to lead? I know some good paths off the main beat."

She gave him a humorous look. "That sounds great, thanks. I guess you can tell I'm a bit of a control freak."

Their shoes made a steady, soothing rhythm over the path. "Nope. But us numbers people have a certain love for order, which sometimes pushes us to lead. Let me ask you this: would you rather delegate to have more free time or do it yourself even though you'll work nonstop hours?"

"The latter."

"See? That's how I used to be."

Curiosity burned as hot as the sun on her skin. "What's your story? If you don't mind my asking."

He gave a shrug. "Not very interesting. Worked in finance in New York for years. Reached burnout. Had a come-to-Jesus moment and decided to walk away and live here for a while. That's it."

She gulped a breath. "Um, dude, that's a lot. Where did you work?"

He paused and Dev knew something big was coming. "Delmar & Associates."

She tripped. His hand darted out to steady her. His company was one of the ones she'd be teaching in August—a pool of some of their brightest executives. How strange. "They're one of the most successful investment firms in New York."

"Yeah, that's them."

His face was serene as he spoke. She tried to see if there was any tightness in his jaw, or if he seemed disturbed talking about his past, but his energy didn't seem to change. "Did you have a big position?"

"I'm on the board, so yes, I was high up."

Dev shook her head. "Wow."

She let his words settle and they walked in silence down the flight of steps. Finally, he looked over, one blond brow raised. "That all you got?"

"I never said I was an English major. I prefer numbers."

He laughed then, and a wash of pleasure rushed through her. He had a good laugh. Masculine, robust, and without apology. "Do you like living in New York?"

"I love it. I seem to thrive in busy cities."

"I did too. I still miss New York. The crowds and smell. The bagels you can get when the bakeries open at five a.m. All the busyness that makes you feel important."

"I know why you didn't mention missing the pizza."

"Thank God for that."

They passed burnt-orange houses with wrought-iron balconies. An elderly woman was shaking out a big rug, and when she spotted them, she called out. Hawke stopped, his head tilted up, a grin wreathing his face. They spoke back and forth in rapid Italian. Dev enjoyed the almost musical flow of sound from their lips; the obvious affection between them; the feel of connection on a back side road across the world.

The woman pointed at Dev, dark eyes lighting up, her head nodding enthusiastically. Hawke laughed again and waved goodbye, continuing on the stroll.

"Who's that?"

"I don't know."

Dev cocked her head. "You spoke with her like you knew her well."

"I see her on my daily walks. She's part of the community here. It's something I was uncomfortable with for a long time after I moved from New York. Speaking to strangers used to be a waste of my energy—too unproductive unless there was a goal. Now I've learned every person has something to give, even if it's a few moments of realizing we're connected."

The simple way he spoke touched her, stirring a bee's nest of emotions she hadn't even realized was buried within her. How many times had she rushed past a colleague or person without making eye contact—too behind schedule to see them as people? They were always a block or obstacle keeping her from getting to her goal. "I do that a lot. There never seems to be enough . . . time."

"Yes. I liked that before, though. I even thrived because it gave me a reason for my actions. Until I looked around me and found I had no one I could truly trust and be myself with. Hell, I didn't even know who I was separate from my job, so how could I even share myself?"

"What made you want to change?"

He led her down a zigzag path with flowering trees drooping low like umbrellas, casting precious shade. The distant sound of children's laughter floated on the breeze. "A few things. I lost a big account and got my ass kicked. My brilliant reputation got knocked around, and suddenly, I wasn't the hot up-and-coming big shot anymore. I started drinking too much because there was no one left to talk to. My friends were all like me—basically married to the job. I'd already lost my previous relationship due to my schedule, though she did like my money." His quick smile took away the sting. "For the first time in my life, I felt lost. I had all this stuff, but I didn't even enjoy it. I didn't know if I liked the business anymore. So, I yank open this drawer in my desk and I find the deed to this house. And I knew right then and there, that was my answer. I needed to find myself. All those years my father visited and I refused to come hit me like a bullet. I decided to get to know the place he loved and go on my own journey, so I bought a ticket."

Fascinated, she stared at his strong profile, the carved slash of cheekbone, the square jaw, the slight scruff clinging to his chin. "You just left?"

He gave a sharp nod. "Just left. Put in my resignation, packed a bag, and got a flight out. Now I've been here for almost two years."

"What about work? Did you take another job?"

"I do some consulting work when I choose. I was lucky to have made enough to step away for a while."

Dev wiped the sweat off her brow and Hawke handed her the water bottle. She gratefully took a sip. "What do you do all day when you're not working?"

"Walk. Eat. Meet new people and visit old friends. Think. Read. All the things I've never done before. I needed to figure myself out. Figure out who I was."

She stopped, needing to process this revelation. Heart madly beating, her voice was a whisper. "Do you regret it?"

His smile was brilliant, a ray of light that pierced through her very soul. "No."

The possibilities exploded around her. The idea of being able to change her life with one decision. The strength it took to be so brutal with your truth, instead of always rationalizing actions to match the answers.

"You're a very brave man," she said slowly.

His eyes darkened and gleamed with sudden intensity. "I have a feeling you're brave too."

She jerked slightly, not knowing how to respond. Hawke didn't wait for an answer, though. He continued walking, and she followed.

They traced a leisurely path through the neighborhoods, up more stone steps, and away from the busy center village. Vespas roared along the main road. The blur of earthy Tuscan colors spread out before her, but she enjoyed studying each individual house as they passed, families busy with their day's activities, caught up in their own agendas. Dev wondered what it would be like to live here. To begin to appreciate the simple mechanics of living and find pleasure here, instead of rushing endlessly ahead toward a moving goalpost.

She'd never questioned it though, not like Hawke. She loved her life and excelled at achievement. But a voice rose inside her, coming from nowhere, and whispered in her ear.

Because you've never allowed yourself something else.

"I'm very sorry about your mother," he said. "Were you close?"

"I think we could have been closer. We had issues."

"Who doesn't? Family relationships are complicated."

"Do you have any siblings?"

He shook his head. "Always wanted one, though. Mom couldn't have any more children, so I think I was a bit spoiled."

"That's how I think of Bailey," she said automatically.

She sensed his gaze prodding her. "Is she the youngest?"

"Yeah. She's this wonderful free spirit who always lands on her feet, while the rest of the world plods through their boring must-do's. Maybe I'm resentful. She always seemed to be my parents' favorite."

"Was that one of the issues with you and your mom? How you related to her?"

"Probably. I'm the middle child. Jan from *The Brady Bunch*. 'Marcia, Marcia, Marcia.'"

He laughed. "Figured you'd be too young to know that sitcom."

"It's iconic."

"Are you close to your sisters?"

This question was harder to answer, writhing with complications. "We used to be. We're trying."

"That's all you can do."

They walked. Chatted about nonsense things. Hawke brought up some popular activities they could experience before they left. Dev figured that would be a good thing for her sisters to do together. She whipped out her phone and typed in her Notes, inputting all Hawke's suggestions. She'd block tomorrow morning for a hike and make reservations for a boat tour. Hopefully, they'd be able to poke around and maybe find someone with the name R at a company. A definite long shot but worth pursuing.

When they passed a bright painted bench, Dev looked at it longingly. Hawke grinned and dropped down, and she sat gratefully beside him. "Now I know why Italians live so long even with all those carbs and alcohol."

"Everything in balance. You truly can have it all that way."

"Very un-American," Dev teased. "We've mastered the art of more is better."

"Took me a while to like it."

"Will you ever go back?" Their shoulders brushed as he shifted his weight. A funny dropping weight hit her belly. She smelled lemons and cotton and clean male sweat. "To New York? Your job? Any of it?"

He regarded her thoughtfully. She liked the way he answered questions. She was used to the regular *How are you?* questions and *Fine* responses, giving away nothing beneath the surface. In a way, she had the same issues Hawke had admitted to. Her relationships weren't as deep as she wanted, but she'd never given thought to it before. Hearing his story put some things in perspective, but it was scary to dig any deeper.

She didn't know what things she might find that needed to change.

"Maybe. When the time is right and I want to," he said.

She couldn't help the laugh that escaped her lips. "You're a strange man, Hawke. What's your last name?"

"Rinaldi."

She squinted at him through her sunglasses. "You don't look Italian."

"My uncle. My parents were both dark-haired and dark-eyed, so they didn't know what to make of me. But my uncle had the German genes even though he spoke Italian. Probably where I got my German name."

"Hawke is German?"

He wrinkled his nose. "No, my real name is Hackett, but I always hated it. So I use a nickname."

"Hackett." The name rolled off her tongue and she grinned. "I like it."

"I don't. Neither did my uncle—he begged my parents not to saddle me with that one."

"Were you close to your uncle?"

"Definitely. Sometimes I felt as if we practically lived together." He shook his head. "Heard he was a real Casanova back in the day too. Dad said he had quite a love affair here."

Her skin prickled with awareness. "Wait—did your uncle live here too?"

"Kind of. He stayed here with us in the summer, and Dad gave him free rein when we weren't vacationing. Eventually, he moved to Sicily."

Suddenly, her ears roared and her heart paused and her breath stuck in her lungs. She could barely choke out her next words. "What was your uncle's name?"

"Raymond. Why?"

No. Was it possible? "Was your uncle around your dad's age?"

"Yeah, they were only two years apart."

"He didn't own a boat, did he?"

Surprise flickered in his gaze. "Yeah, he did. Would sometimes bring small tours out with people he liked."

She couldn't stop the questions, which shot like bullets from her mouth. "And was your uncle married?"

He shook his head. "No, he never settled down. I remember asking him about it once. He got this strange look in his eyes and told me it wasn't in the cards for him, but he was happy. I always got the impression there was someone but it didn't work out."

Everything faded away. Of course. It was like fate had stepped in and led her here, to this bench, at this moment, with Hawke. This was too big to tackle alone. She needed her sisters with her.

"Hawke, will you come to dinner with us? I'd like to talk

more about your uncle. My sisters and I have a mystery to solve, and I think you just gave us the missing piece."

His brow lifted but he nodded. "Is this the same reason you all reacted when I told you my father's name?"

"Yeah."

"Sure. I actually have plans tonight with a friend. Will tomorrow work?"

She wondered briefly if his plans included a girlfriend, then pushed the thought away. Hawke was attractive and interesting, but not for her. Bailey had already made her intentions known, if he was free, and she wasn't about to get entangled with that mess.

Not ever again.

"Of course. I appreciate it." She stood. "We better get back."

They picked up the pace, but their conversation unfurled at leisure, focusing on Dev's work. When he got to her door, he smiled. "Thanks for the company on the walk."

"Welcome. I'll let you know what time for dinner."

He nodded and left. Dev tore inside the house, shutting the door loudly behind her. "Guys!" she called out. "Get your butts in here now!"

It didn't take long for her sisters to emerge. Bailey looked grumpy and Pris yawned, her blond hair all in disarray. "What? I still had half an hour on my alarm clock," Bailey groaned.

"I have to tell you something big."

They stared at her, waiting, and she gave an excited laugh. "I found R."

Bailey dropped into the chair and Pris gasped.

"Tell us everything," Bailey demanded.

She did.

CHAPTER TWENTY

Olivia

When I arrived in Positano for my fourth summer, I felt like a tight wad of emotion was fisted in my stomach, lodged there by a nonstop chain of events that challenged my ideas of the world.

I'd decided to tell Mom about Rafe. I knew traipsing off for the summer with Aunt Silvia was a long shot—both my parents had declared no more disappearing overseas for summer break. I was going into my senior college year and ready to make a stand. I figured I'd have a heart-to-heart about my feelings for Rafe and my plans going forward.

But when I sat down to talk, my mother had a different conversation in mind.

She informed me that she was in love with her new boyfriend and getting remarried.

She said the house—the family home I'd grown up in—would be sold and she'd be moving to Boston to be with her new husband.

How had I not noticed how much my mother had changed? Her hair was dyed. She tinkered with makeup and had lost weight. She laughed louder and seemed to always be hurrying off somewhere. I'd just been so engrossed in my own life, I never put the pieces together.

But as I stared, stunned, and my mom went on about an upcoming wedding and how she hoped I'd be happy for her, dread shuddered through me.

She was leaving me behind. The divorce had been brutal, but I'd managed to make some sense of it these past few years. Now she had no problem dumping my ass for a new life she wanted to lead in a new city. When I asked about Dad, she chirped out happily that he knew all about it and was completely supportive. And then she dropped the words that should have made me ecstatically happy.

"I know you love to go to Positano with your aunt, Livia, so we both decided you can go! Things will be crazy here with me reorganizing and getting prepped for a wedding. And even though I'd love your help, I don't want to be selfish. Go and have a wonderful time, and when you get back, you'll be able to see our new place in Boston. Honey, you've grown up so much. I'm proud of you. Proud you've become an independent woman on her own path. I didn't have the opportunities that you did. Never waste them."

Speechless, I stared at my mother as my safe world broke apart for the second time. I should have been relieved, but instead I felt as if I was being abandoned.

I was almost twenty-two. Yes, I'd been ready to declare my independence with my vow of moving overseas, but suddenly I felt like a scared little kid. It was as if all my pumped-up confidence about my future melted away, and all I was left with was doubt.

So when I saw Rafe for the first time, and he took me into his arms, I broke. Tears ran down my face as I stared into his beloved face, so safe and comforting, and I swore I'd never screw it up. We were meant to be each other's haven and soul mate. We'd been tested with our long-distance relationship and had managed to make it this far.

One more year and we'd begin to live our lives together. I'd follow the course.

I told Rafe all about my mom and her big plans. He held me tight as I rambled, the scent of citrus and bougainvillea blossoms heavy in the air as we sat in the garden. He'd taken the day off to spend with me, and I was looking forward to rebonding and enjoying quiet time together.

"But this could be a good thing, no?" Rafe asked, stroking my hair. "I know it's awful to feel your mother is beginning this new life, but you have always worried she'd never support your decision to move here. Now that she has someone of her own, maybe she'll be understanding?"

He was right. I just hadn't figured out why the idea of her accepting my decision suddenly felt so . . . flat. Shouldn't I be giddy with excitement? I still had my dad to deal with, but he'd be more apt to support me if I secured a job after graduation. I wasn't a kid anymore and he only wanted me to be successful.

Why was I suddenly confused?

I kept my face buried in the soft cotton of his shirt and nodded. "You're right. It was just a shock."

"Of course. I understand. I've had my own changes here to deal with."

I lifted my head and stared at him worriedly. "What happened?"

His smile belied the seriousness in his dark eyes. "My father isn't well. It was a hard winter for him and he was sick. He never seemed to recover and is having trouble."

"Oh, Rafe, I'm so sorry. I thought he just had a virus or something."

"The doctors thought so, but he is still weak. He refuses to get an operation for his knee. It's been hard."

I squeezed his hand. "What are you going to do?"

"I'm going to take over the business for now completely. Let him rest, maybe get stronger and come back later. For now, it means I won't have much time off." His jaw clenched and frustration radiated from him. "I'm sorry, *dolcezza*, but I must step in now."

"Can you hire someone to help? I'm disappointed, of course, but more worried about you taking on too much."

"If it continues and my father can't go back, I will hire someone. But for now, I can do it on my own. We need the money."

I fell silent, my thoughts churning. I hated that Rafe had to worry and had so much responsibility on him. I knew he was four years older and used to taking care of his dad, but it also didn't seem fair. He'd never gotten the opportunity to travel, go to college, or decide if he wanted a different career path. I realized then how lucky I was. "Are you angry about being trapped?" I knew I'd be. I swore to support him completely as I braced myself for a torrent of Italian cursing and Rafe's admission that he hated feeling his life wasn't under his control. Instead, he cocked his head and looked surprised.

"No. I hate my father is ill. But I always knew this would be my future, and I never questioned it." His face gentled as he stroked my cheek. "It will be better when you're at my side. It gets lonely knowing you're so far away."

"Not much longer," I promised, hugging him tight. "One more year. But for now, we'll enjoy the summer and the time you do have."

He hugged me back and I tried desperately to focus on his muscled warmth and comfort rather than the alarm slowly growing inside me. Before, I'd never thought past being together. But now? Where would I work? If I was in Rome, was it feasible to go back and forth to Positano? Did he want to keep the fishing and touring business only for his father and his legacy? If not, would Rafe be open to moving elsewhere so I could follow my own path?

I'd seen Adam a few times for coffee or lunch. He believed by combining sharp business skills, I could secure a great job in a private gallery. There'd be a bit of sales—which I'd previously shied away from—but Adam convinced me it was different if I worked on something I was passionate about. He had a friend in Manhattan who owned a thriving gallery and was interested in meeting me, but I hadn't been able to confess I'd be moving to Italy after graduation. Instead, I'd nodded and agreed, figuring when I returned after the summer maybe he would have forgotten.

Adam. Things had gotten . . . complicated. Nothing had happened—I'd never allow it—but each time we got together, I noticed the way he looked at me. A spark simmered between us, ready to flame at the slightest touch, but neither of us ever crossed the line. When he'd asked about my summer, I'd simply told him I was traveling with my aunt and would be out of touch. He'd looked disappointed but encouraged me to use the time to visit art galleries abroad and gain some experience.

He never mentioned my boyfriend.

I was glad I'd insisted we never talk about my relationship, wanting to keep Rafe completely separate from my friendship with Adam. Maybe it was a dangerous game, but my gut said it was important that neither of them know about the other. I swore I'd tell Adam the whole truth when I got back to school.

The lies I'd told and endless questions swarmed like bees and gave me a headache. I desperately wanted to talk it out with

Rafe and be reassured it would all be fine. But he was upset and now wasn't the time.

Later. We'd figure it out later.

For now, I'd enjoy my time here with him and the beauty of summer.

CHAPTER TWENTY-ONE

Pris

She looked at her sisters and nibbled her lip. Somehow, she didn't have a good feeling about this.

"Um, guys? Anyone want to cancel? We can go to the beach instead and get one of those fancy chairs and umbrellas. Cool off in the water. Doesn't that sound like a better idea?"

They'd just gotten to Nocelle, a tiny town approximately fifteen hundred steps above Positano, and were staring at the crooked sign that led to the famous hike Sentiero degli Dei—the Path of the Gods. The walk was known for its stunning views and difficulty, mostly endurance-wise, as it was a three-hour journey. The path was 2,156 feet up, carved out of the steep cliffs and mountains twisting around the sea. Dev had been pumped last night after her walk with Hawke, focused on accomplishing one mandatory sightseeing experience.

Bailey shot her a puppy-dog look. "Come on, Pris, it'll be fun. We need an adventure—getting to the top will be epic! Imagine your pics."

"We can always go to a beach—this is unique to the Amalfi

Coast. We'd be crazy not to experience it. Plus, I heard you were running miles every day, so you better not be complaining," Dev said.

"You hate hiking," Pris reminded her. "You complain about the steps all the time. What if you get halfway there and collapse?"

Bailey giggled. "Then she'd be the biggest loser ever. She's not overweight, she doesn't have any health issues, and she's not even forty. If Dev can't do this, I'll never let her live it down."

Pris tamped down a sigh. And . . . there they went again. Dev jumped at the bait. "Oh, right, like you're some kind of gym rat? You eat junk all day—for breakfast you ate a bunch of pastries."

"Because they're the standard Italian fare for the morning! And how would you know if I eat junk? You don't track my diet."

Dev gave a sniff. "Are you kidding me? You'd beg Mom to make brownies or cakes or cookies every single night. No matter what type of candy I had lying around, you'd steal it. I had to rotate my stash every week to keep you on your toes."

"You're exaggerating."

"Remember when we'd go trick-or-treating and you ate all my Hershey bars? I think there were like a dozen you gulped down, got sick, and still lied about it. And the lame Starburst you left behind didn't make me feel better."

"You cried to Mom. The world doesn't like snitches, Dev."

"The world doesn't like thieves, Bae."

Pris put up her hands. "Stop. If I'm stuck with you for the whole morning, we're going to practice the game of silence. Let's allow nature to work its healing magic, shall we?"

"Fine," Dev muttered.

"Don't even pretend you didn't take my Kit Kats. I used to count them and there was always one less every night," Bailey said.

"Enough!"

They shut up. Pris tamped down a groan. "Fine, we'll do the hike. But we're rotating the backpack. I'll start."

"It's only some water and snacks," Bailey reminded her. "We're not hitting the Appalachian Trail. Why are you nervous?"

"I'm not. Let's go." She took the lead and set a steady pace. It was late morning, and the sun was beginning to rise higher and shine stronger. A slight wind soothed the sweat from her brow. For now, they were alone on the trail, but she'd read it was extremely crowded in summer, so she expected to meet groups of people as they moved forward.

She wondered why she didn't want to do this hike. It wasn't like her. Dev was right—she was in shape, so it wasn't a physical block. Normally she was easy to please and always went along with things. No conflict seemed worth fighting over, so she got used to swallowing her opinion because it was easier.

It was probably the phone call with Garrett last night. The memory stirred like the leaves on the thick trees lining the woodsy-type path. He'd been so distant. Asking the same polite questions, which she politely answered. How was the house? How was Italy? Were they going to sell? Was she having a good time? Was she getting along with her sisters?

He'd gotten livelier after she told him they were keeping the house. He'd initiated an argument warning against the idea, and taking Dev's side. She listened, then told him they'd already made up their minds, and the discussion was closed.

But why hadn't she told him the reasons behind the decision? How she believed it had been Mom's sacred place and they wanted something to honor her by? What was holding her back from talking truthfully with her husband—a man she still loved? It was as if their relationship had somehow become a cocktail party—it looked elegant, well-mannered, and physically beautiful. But underneath? There was nothing of value left.

Maybe there was nothing left to save. Maybe that was the true reason she was so damn sad and lost. She didn't want to accept this final loss—the failure of the one relationship she'd put a hundred and ten percent into.

Was that how Mom had felt when she got divorced? Did she wonder if it was her fault—and if she had worked harder, Dad wouldn't have cheated? Was that why she might have refocused on her college lover, because it brought her back to simpler days?

Maybe all women felt like this inside. Always on alert, waiting for someone to judge and point out faults. It was exhausting having so many thoughts and questions and judgments constantly spinning in her mind, taking up all the space.

She almost tripped on a rock and cursed.

"Watch it, sis. Hey, how's Garrett doing? What's he up to lately?" Dev asked.

Great. It was like her sister picked up on her mood and asked the one thing she didn't want to think about today. "He's good. Busy at work. Made partner, so that's his priority."

"You like that word. Good."

She glanced at Bailey. "It's a good word. Covers everything."

Her sister trudged beside her, matching her pace. She smelled of mosquito repellent and coconut lotion. Her hair was clipped up in a bouncy ponytail. As usual, her face reflected a genuine openness Pris had always been jealous of. It was easy for Bailey to share. She wondered how she'd scored that gene. "Why don't you dig a little deeper?" Bailey suggested. "How's your marriage?"

This time, she did trip, flailing her arms like a Muppet until she caught her balance. Bailey steadied her, and she refocused on the trail with a new vigor. Exercise was supposed to be good at flushing out the demons, right? She quickened her steps and felt her muscles strain to accommodate the incline. "It's good."

Dev snorted. "Don't be lame, Pris. You can't take the high ground that we never ask you crap if you never give us anything. We've been more open with you, and I frickin' hate getting touchy-feely."

"It's a long story."

"Good, we have three hours with nothing to do. Are you having problems with Garrett?" Dev asked.

Pandora's box shuddered. "We've been married almost twenty years. I'm not surprised there's a bump in the road."

"What kind of bump?" Bailey asked. "Sexual? Communication? Is he leaving his dirty clothes all over the house and pissing you off? Or is it bigger?"

A group of hikers passed them. The path was narrow, twisting up the mountain, so they all shuffled around to fall into single file. Bailey picked the questioning right up after they settled.

"Is he cheating? Are you cheating? Has he done something specific?"

She blew out an annoyed breath. "It's nothing specific, okay? He's working too much, but he's always done that. I think with Thomas being away at school, I'm more aware of his absences. As for sex, I don't know—I'm going through a thing. Probably early menopause."

"Sexual desire begins in the mind," Dev recited. "If you don't feel emotionally connected to your partner, it becomes harder to be physical."

"Have you told him he needs to work less? Focus on your relationship a bit more?" Bailey asked.

"Of course. I've told him several times, but he explains being partner gave him a lot more responsibility and I need to support him. Be understanding."

She felt rather than saw her sisters exchange looks. "What do you do when he's working, Pris?" Dev asked.

Her back stiffened. Here it came. The normal snide tone where they judged her for having too much money and too much time. "I do a lot of work with charities. It keeps me busy. I run the household, do the bills, shopping, et cetera. It adds up."

"No, I get that. But what do you do for yourself? What's your guilty pleasure? What makes you happy?" Bailey asked.

The tightness in her chest strangled her breath. She ground her sneakers into the dirt with more force and walked harder. Instead of telling her to slow down, she heard them trot behind her, trying to keep up. Sweat gathered under her armpits and her calves twinged, but she kept her gaze focused ahead—on the one thing she could get done and behind her. Finish this damn hike.

"I like to read. I run. I watch Netflix. I take a class at the gym. I lunch with my friends. Tons of stuff."

"It sounds like busy stuff," Dev said. "Busy stuff can leave us really drained. Don't you miss dancing?"

She gritted her teeth to keep from snapping. "That's a part of my past."

"But a part of who you are. You weren't just enjoying some classes, Pris. You were a damn prima ballerina with the New York City Ballet. You danced in *The Nutcracker*. You were going to tour the world and you said no to get married and raise a family. That had to affect you in some way, especially since you tried to just remove that part of yourself like it never existed."

The roaring grew in her ears. She clenched her sweaty fists and fought for control. Dev was pushing hard for a reaction and Pris refused to give it to her. She would not lose her temper over a choice she made willingly. How dare her sisters question her life?

"Exactly. I wasn't about to go teaching little kids to do a holiday dance every year and pretend that meant something. I walked away and never looked back so I could focus on a new life. A very satisfying life."

A short silence fell. Her tension began to dissipate as it lengthened. They were backing off. They understood now there was nothing wrong except her strained marriage.

"I don't think you're satisfied at all," Dev finally said. She huffed and puffed between words. "I think you're the unhappiest of all of us."

Okay, she was done.

Pris stopped, rearing up like a stallion ready to kick some ass. "Excuse me? How dare you judge my happiness? You—who have no personal relationships to juggle so your life can be clean and bland like one of your balance sheets?" She jabbed a finger at Bailey, who watched her with wide, surprised eyes. "And you? Who floats around like commitments are beneath her, and attachments mean nothing, when inside you're just afraid to love anything in case it's taken away! So, please don't pretend you both have it together. You know nothing about me or my marriage or my happiness!"

She panted, yet felt a strange release from saying it all out loud. Pris waited for the explosion, the threats and accusations back, but they both shared a satisfied glance and Dev grinned. "There we go. Finally, a real response, and none of that *good* crap."

Her jaw dropped. "What?"

Bailey laughed. "I like this Pris so much better. It's real. Come on, babe, keep walking, or marching, or running, whatever the hell you're doing. It's good to get that energy out. And it's time you tell us the truth. Aren't you tired of trying to live in a bubble? 'Cause we think you deserve more. A lot more."

She stared at her sisters in shock. They really did understand. Or they wanted to, and she felt seen for the very first time—as if all those awful, strange emotions finally had a place to go. A strange prickling sensation strained her eyes and she was suddenly fighting back the need to weep. Instead, she spun on her heel and kept her gaze on the ground ahead.

"I don't know if my marriage is going to make it. Every day, it's getting harder to be in my own skin. I think I hate my life."

Relief weakened her knees, but she straightened them back in order to keep climbing uphill.

"Now you can begin to fix it, Pris. Or blow it up. Both are good," Dev said.

"And we're going to help you," Bailey said. "Now, tell us everything."

She did. She spilled every last horrible secret on the rock climb that had her on hands and knees, and confessed she was lost as she walked on the side of a steep, sharp cliff where one false move would have her tumbling. There was no judgment from her sisters—no effort to try to give her a list of steps to accomplish in order to turn her life around. They listened, asked more questions, and gave support.

And they hiked. Dev and Bailey made no complaints as the sun burned and the sweat poured and their legs trembled with strain.

Finally, Pris realized what she'd been needing. Her family. The people who loved and knew her best—all faults included. The years and distance in the past all faded away and pinpointed to this moment.

And then they reached the top.

Pris looked out at the magnificent view and her insides began to shift. It was almost too much to take in—the sweep of cliffs and sea and sky blending together and dazzling her vision. The reverent silence even amid the crowds, who kept filtering in but spoke in hushed voices, as if they were in the Sistine Chapel. It was nature at its raw, naked self, sprawled like a queen displaying its treasure and reminding humankind they were helpless before such power.

Her throat tightened and her eyes stung. It was a holy moment for Pris, and the final realization she couldn't do this anymore; couldn't live a life of quiet, desperate silence. It was her fault for not asking for help.

It was her responsibility to finally fix it.

Bailey spoke first. "You have to talk to him, Pris. It's the only way. I know it's hard, and you're scared to say the words, but just tell the truth. Exactly how you did with us."

"Agreed," Dev said. "It's not that you owe it to him, even though you do. You owe it to yourself."

Pris nodded. "Yeah. I think you're right."

She breathed in the fresh, clean air. Stared at the rocks and azure sea; the boats bobbing gently along the shore; the sway of the mighty trees weaving a carpet of thick green leaves beneath her. Pondered her sisters' words and the way she felt now that she'd unburdened herself.

It was all going to be okay.

Her sisters flanked her, their shoulders bumping gently. Bailey lifted her phone. "Let me grab a few pics."

A woman's voice echoed behind them. "Would you like me to take a picture of the three of you?"

"That'd be great, thanks," Bailey said, handing her the phone.

They posed tight together, smiling at the camera, the great beauty of Positano unveiled beneath them.

And Pris knew this moment had changed her forever.

They thanked the woman and wandered about a bit. Took

more pictures. Took a break and ate their granola bars. Guzzled water.

Dev gave a long sigh. "Well, shit. Now we have to get back."

They all looked at one another and began to laugh. They took the return route at a slower pace. Pris no longer felt there was a race against herself, or that she was trying to outrun her demons.

"Our reward will be the lemon slushies," Bailey panted out as they reached the midpoint. "There's a place called Lemon Point and it's famous. It may be the only reason my legs are still working."

"I'm buying a treadmill when I get home," Dev declared. "I'm tired of sucking at fitness."

"A treadmill can't give you this type of workout," Pris said. "Remember *Rocky IV* when Rocky trained in Russia using nature as his gym? Meanwhile, the other guy used this top training gym with all these fancy machines. Who won, huh?"

"Rocky?" Dev asked.

Pris shot her a look. "Funny. I like how some of the movie classics remain timeless. Thomas loved *Rocky*. I used to repeat the mantra 'No pain' when I danced."

Bailey shot her a curious look. "You always looked dreamy to me when I watched you dance. Like you were in another world of rainbows and unicorns. I guess I never thought of you in pain."

That made her laugh. "Are you kidding? Sure, when I was involved in the actual dancing I was transported, but most of the time I remember my aching body, my bloody feet, and daily ice baths. It's a brutal world. Honestly, I think the only reason I didn't get an eating disorder or need therapy was Mom. She was constantly checking in and telling me my body wasn't a vehicle to sell tickets, but something I needed to treat like a holy temple." She wrinkled her nose. "Crazy, right? But it got to me. When my teachers would yell and correct and pick apart everything I did, I remembered Mom's words and how she believed I was more than a class. It worked."

Dev let out a breath. "Okay, that's so cool, you never told us that."

"Why didn't you want to talk about your dancing, Pris?" Bailey asked.

She thought about the question, her insides no longer raw and tender. Funny, just sharing all that junk had allowed her to poke at the wound, and it didn't hurt as much. It was like a scab forming over a cut that could finally heal. "Because it was all mine," she said simply. "A world I was a bit selfish about—something that belonged only to me and I didn't have to share. Dancing gave me purpose, and God, I loved it. I loved it so much."

"Makes sense you lost your way," Dev said. "You tried to replace it with other people, but I don't think that ever works."

Bailey shot her sister a look. "That's deep, Dev. I'm impressed."

Dev stuck out her tongue and ruined the moment.

They passed another large group, moving to the side of the steep cliff, then reshuffled. Bailey began to shift back and forth on her feet, doing a strange little dance.

"What's the matter with you?" Pris asked.

"I have to pee. Bad."

Dev lifted her brow. "Dude, they have no porta potties out here. You have to hold it."

Bailey bit her lower lip. "Can't. Gonna pee my pants soon. I have to go."

Pris widened her eyes. "You can't! There's nowhere to go out here! We're in the rocky section. Why couldn't you have gone when there were plenty of trees to cover you?"

"I didn't have to go then! I'll climb up that hill there and you can block me."

"You can't pee on the Path of the Gods!" Pris squeaked out. "That's illegal."

Bailey began to jump a bit more. "Doubt it. I gotta do a natural thing and it might as well be on a natural path."

"Oh my God," Dev groaned. "This is not happening. There are tons of people around; someone's going to come!"

"Then they'll get a surprise. Keep a lookout."

Pris watched in horror as her sister darted a glance back and forth on the temporarily empty path, then began to climb the rocky hill. There was no real covering, no thick shady trees, just a few small bush-like shrubs that were mostly sticks. Bailey squatted and began to work down her shorts.

"I can see your ass," Dev hissed.

"Nothing you haven't seen before."

Bailey's relieved groan cut through the air. Pris averted her gaze, sweeping the path for anyone, then stiffened. "People coming! Hurry up!"

A couple appeared in her vision, laughing together, carrying backpacks and wearing baseball caps. Urging her sister on, she watched as Bae finished up and stood, tugging her shorts up.

And then it happened.

Her foot must've gotten caught on a stone, because she suddenly went down. Dev shrieked and Pris watched in shock as her sister tumbled down the slight hill toward them, legs flailing as her shorts tangled up around her ankles.

Pris jumped toward her, breaking the last of her fall with her body and landing them both on the ground from the force of the hit.

The couple ahead let out a yell and raced toward them.

Oh no.

"Bae, are you okay? Are you hurt?" Pris asked frantically, trying to right herself and check for blood or broken bones.

Bailey groaned, her hand rubbing her head. "No, I'm okay, but that hurt."

The couple skidded to a stop in front while Dev tried to block them. "Is everyone all right? Should I call someone? We saw her fall from the hill," the girl gasped out.

"I'm fine. So sorry to scare you. I was just looking at . . . something . . . and must've tripped."

"Good, that could've been bad," the guy said, his voice deep with a southern accent. "Here, let me help you . . ." He trailed off, and that's when it hit Pris full force.

Her sister's shorts were at her feet, along with her tiny pink underwear.

And she was mooning the couple.

From the front.

The guy's eyes bulged out and he took a step back, hand flailing in the air. The girl realized it at the same exact time because she muttered something and grabbed her boyfriend's hand, leading him away. "Um, as long as you're good! See ya!"

Pris watched the couple practically run ahead, obviously desperate to put as much distance between them as they could. Dev helped yank Bailey's clothes up and Bailey finally refastened her shorts. She brushed off the dirt and remnants of her fall, then tossed her head with a snort.

"I bet if they were Italians they wouldn't have even blinked. Americans are so damn prudish. Like they never peed on a hike before."

Pris and Dev shared a look.

Bailey marched ahead with a new vigor. "Come on. I want my lemon slushie."

CHAPTER TWENTY-TWO

Olivia

I waited for Rafe by the boats and knew it was time we had a talk.

My stomach squeezed with nerves. Things were beginning to change, and the questions that had bothered me a month ago had now grown to epic, monstrous proportions. I just didn't know how I'd bring them up.

The moment I saw his beloved face, my heart jumped as if recognizing its other half. Features carved with weariness, his white teeth flashed in the darkness as he came to greet me. We folded into each other, and his muscled heat felt like coming home. "You look so tired," I whispered, pressing a kiss to his rough cheek. The scents of sun, sand, and salt drifted to my nostrils. I pushed his hair back, which immediately sprang back forward. "We can skip going out and go back to the cottage. Aunt Silvia is in Sorrento tonight with friends, so we have the place to ourselves."

"Do you mind?" He pressed his forehead to mine and took

in a breath. "It was a long day and I've been looking forward to being alone with you."

"No, Julia and Ava will understand. Let's go."

We held hands and climbed the steps leisurely as he told me about his day. "Dad was scheduling the appointments and double-booked me. I ended up with a very angry family who insisted I take them on a private trip rather than refund their money. It was easier to agree."

"God, Rafe, you've been going nonstop since six a.m. You can't keep doing this. I thought Italy was the laid-back and take-a-riposte country."

He laughed. "*Sì*, but my business caters to tourists, and they do not like the ripostes."

"Do you know what Americans say to that?"

"What?"

"Screw them."

He laughed again and his demeanor lightened. We settled back at the house and cracked open the refrigerator, putting together an assortment of snacks to eat. We picked on salty olives, chunks of cheese, and crusty bread drizzled with olive oil and balsamic vinegar, talking quietly and soaking up each other's presence. There was a peacefulness I always experienced around Rafe, as if I could truly take a breath and just be. At the same time, the physical connection always buzzed beneath the surface. Everything would have been perfect if not for this restlessness still nipping at my nerves; the doubts that kept poking through my happiness and reminding me our lives together wouldn't be like our summers. I remembered my mom used to warn me when I'd beg to live where we vacationed that it would never be the same. "You still have to go to school in Disney World," she'd tease. "We'd need to work, clean the house, and have the same responsibilities we do back home. It's not as fun as you imagine."

I used to wave off her remarks, refusing to believe living in Disney wouldn't be the best. But lately, I kept wondering what our lives would truly be like day after day when we were finally together.

When our bellies were full, we took a blanket outside and lay on the grass in the garden. The moon was high and bright, and there was only a scattering of stars tonight. We snuggled together, my head on his chest, and soaked up the deep night silence.

"Rafe? Can I ask you a question?"

"Of course. What is it *dolcezza*?"

"I've been thinking more about our plans when I graduate. We haven't really discussed what would happen. Like, where I'd live or work. That kind of stuff."

"I know. I figured you'd want to decide what type of job you'd look for first. I know you mentioned museums or galleries, but you didn't seem sure. What do you want to do?"

"I always thought it would be more art history, but lately I've been interested in trying out a gallery. Selling paintings, working with local artists, that sort of thing."

He arched a brow. "Really? You always said you hated talking to strangers."

I laughed nervously. "I know. But I changed my mind. I may be good at it."

"You'd be good at anything, Livia." His husky voice washed over me with warmth. "There are many galleries around. We can begin making contacts. Maybe your aunt can help. After graduation, you can move in with Dad and me and we will find you a place to work."

I sifted through his response, wondering why his words didn't make me feel calmer. "Is there enough room for all of us? I'd hate to be an inconvenience to your dad. And will you still be working alone on this crazy schedule? I don't know; I was thinking of asking Aunt Silvia if I can stay here."

He nodded, but a tiny frown furrowed his brow. "Yes, if you're more comfortable. But when we get married, we'll be together in my house. I need to take care of my father—he can't live alone."

"Of course! Um, married? Oh, I thought we'd be living together or just, I don't know, trying things out."

He propped himself up on his elbow and stared at me. "Livia, I love you. I don't want you living with me unless we're married. I want a commitment. Don't you?"

"Yes! Yes, I guess. I'm sorry, I wasn't really thinking." But hadn't I thought of this beforehand? Hadn't I fantasized about being married and working together? When had the image changed? I only knew one thing for a fact, so I said it. "I love you too."

He relaxed. "I feel like I've been waiting forever and it's finally here. With your mom moving to Boston, and your graduation, everything is coming together."

"Rafe, what if I can't find a job close by? What if it's in Rome or Florence or Milan? What would we do?"

"I don't know," he said slowly. "I'm hoping that doesn't happen, because then we'd never see each other and we'd be back where we started. I'm sure you can find a job here—there are a few art places you'd love. If you work in the bigger cities, we'd have to rent a second place there, which would be expensive. But maybe part-time? And the other days you can help me with the business? Maybe take over the administrative stuff from Dad?"

My heart thudded madly in my chest. I sat up, my palms

suddenly sweaty. Why did it feel like I was about to have an anxiety attack? All these things I wanted suddenly seemed to sweep up and choke me. The big, free, romantic life I imagined wasn't reality.

"Livia? Tell me what's wrong? You don't look happy."

I bit my lip. "I'm just confused. Maybe because we've been planning this for so long I didn't think of all the specifics involved. It's just that I respect your business, but I want my own career. And in my head, I was thinking maybe you'd want to move to the city and start a new life there? Maybe hire out to keep the business and do half and half? We have options, don't we?"

Had I always known the answer, or did I really think I could change his mind? His face closed up, and those dark eyes filled with pain. I remembered what he'd been through with his previous relationship, and guilt flooded me. She'd left him for bigger things because she was selfish. Was I just as bad as her? Thinking of myself instead of the bigger picture? I'd once sworn I'd never hurt Rafe like she had, yet I was telling him I wanted more than he could give. The thought sickened me.

"Livia, I thought you knew. I can never leave my father's business. We've had it in the family since my great-great-grandparents. It's a part of who I am—my identity. I—I thought you said you'd be happy here in Positano."

Suddenly terrified, I reached out to touch him. His muscles stiffened under my touch. "I did! But I also thought you could maybe move the business somewhere else. A place where I can work too, and we can build a new life together. That's a possibility, right?"

"I could move, yes, but I've built a reputation here. I'd need to find another high tourist spot, a place for my boat, and a new home. I have to think of my father and how he'd react to leave everything behind. Do you understand?"

I did. That was the worst part. I'd lived in a fantasy world, caught up in an image I'd spun since that first summer where young love trumped all. And I did love him, with my entire soul. But the idea of giving up my own dreams to settle here for the rest of my life? If I was brutally honest, I knew I wasn't ready.

College had changed me. I wanted different things than I had before, or at least the opportunity to see what else was out there before I fully committed.

My helpless silence spoke for itself.

Rafe pulled away and stood, as if needing the distance. Already, I ached at the space between us, the fissures from the past summer cracking and expanding until we were two different people staring back at each other, wondering how we'd gotten here.

Finally, he spoke. His voice came out flat. "I was afraid this would happen. I was stupid to think you'd want this once you began to open up to the world. What was once exciting to you—this place and me—has become a trap. And you are right. You are right to think this way, yet I kept lying to myself it would be okay because I was selfish."

"No." I jumped to my feet, desperate to touch him, to explain, but the space between us had become a big, cold void I was unable to cross.

"Yes, Livia! Look at me. I have none of your ambitions. I am happy here, in this place, working a simple job. But you are so different—with your education and need to see and explore the world. This is what you should be doing. I've kept you tied to me with my own silly dreams because I love you, but love isn't supposed to be a cage. You need time for yourself. Time to see what you really want."

"I want you," I said brokenly, stumbling forward, reaching out to him. Suddenly, my fears about our future didn't seem as important as losing him. I'd sacrifice all of it as long as we could stay together. I couldn't be the one to cause him such pain, or bear it myself. "I changed my mind, Rafe. We'll work it out. I'll find a job here in Positano, or close by, and we'll have Aunt Silvia's house and yours. We can do this, just like we planned."

He shook his head. Pure resolution shimmered in his gaze. "No, *dolcezza*. I've done this before and the fallout was terrible. I can't do it again."

"Please, Rafe, I can make this work."

Oh, the bittersweet regret in his eyes made my knees buckle. "This hasn't been fair to either of us, and it's my fault. We have the next two weeks together, and then you go back to school. I think we need to take a break from each other in your senior year. You need to stop pausing your life until summer and really figure out what will make you happy."

"You make me happy," I whispered.

"You make me happy too," he said roughly. "But maybe something can make you happier and you never gave it a chance. It's not fair to me either. If I know you never had a chance to choose, I will always have regrets. I will always wonder if I took advantage or you stayed because of guilt, or fear. Do you understand?"

I did, but at the moment, all I knew was Rafe was breaking up with me. The pain of knowing he wasn't mine splintered my body apart. Yet, my mind grabbed onto the opportunity, sensing it was the only way to finally lay my doubts to rest.

"Yes, but there's no one else, Rafe. Do I need to prove that to you? Should we be punished for questioning how we'll live our future? That I want bigger things?"

He launched into a litany of Italian, so fast I couldn't understand. "This isn't a punishment, Livia. And it's not your fault for wanting a career for yourself. We should have given ourselves more space last year, when I realized things were beginning to change. For real love to work, it needs honesty, and space. We've given neither because we're afraid to lose each other. If we continue, we'll blow this up all on our own, and I'm not willing to do it. Are you?"

His words touched a deep place inside me, and I found myself nodding. As much as I wanted to fight the decision, I knew he was right. I hugged myself tight for comfort. "What are the new rules? Can we still write?"

His jaw locked. "It's better if we don't. Let's allow some space and see where we are at the end of your senior year. If we still feel the same, we can begin to plan our lives together."

"And if not?" A touch of bitterness leaked into my voice. "If you're the one who finds a woman who's better suited to you? If you fall in love with someone else and forget about me?"

His eyes softened. "We vow honesty to each other either way. No matter how difficult."

Frustration welled up. "I hate it."

He stepped forward to take me into his arms. I folded myself into his embrace and clung tight. "Me too. But we need this, Livia."

"What if something happens and I need to speak with you?"

He pressed his lips to my ear and caused a shiver. "I will be here for you. Forever. No matter what happens, even if we break up, even if you love another. My heart will never close off to you. Will you remember that?"

A sob caught in the back of my throat. "Yes. But I'm not going anywhere."

And I reached for him, tired of trying to prove my feelings, refusing to say goodbye like two star-crossed lovers in a movie. I kissed him with everything I had, and he kissed me back. We sank to the blanket and I pushed every doubt from my mind as I let my body show him where words failed.

Two weeks later, I said goodbye for the final time to embark on my senior year. My plan was simple: return to Rafe and prove we were meant to be together. I needed to believe that we'd work things out and compromise so we both got what we needed. I was determined to show the world that love could conquer anything, including age, time, and distance. I would stay true. I wouldn't make any mistakes or missteps.

Looking back, I realized it had always been more complicated than a simple decision or holding tight to an image that was more dream than reality.

Looking back, I realized how very wrong I was.

CHAPTER TWENTY-THREE

Bailey

When they sat down and got settled at Adamo ed Eva—a glorious restaurant set above the cliffs—Bailey realized she might never be able to go back to Taco Bell again.

Like . . . ever.

The clean white square tables, colorful flowers, and stunning sunset view seemed to bring her to a whole new level of sensory awareness. They sat on a panoramic terrace where the buildings embedded in the cliffs felt close enough to touch. She was always conscious of her body and sexuality—it was a part of who she was and used well in her acting and creative pursuits. But the pure sensuousness of Italy, the stripping down of everything but simple pleasures in sight, taste, sound, and texture—forced her to surrender to a strange mix of emotions she'd never truly recognized.

Perhaps it was being here with her sisters. The hike this morning had been transformational, not only for Pris but for her. She'd finally felt bonded again with her sister. It was a heady feeling. Sure, the tumble down the hill had been disastrous, but she hadn't been hurt anywhere but her pride.

If only Dev still didn't smirk at her each time their gazes met. Unfortunately, her sister had a long memory.

Hawke announced he was buying dinner and would have no protests. "I get to dine with three beautiful women, so I'm the winner here," he said. His tone held no cheesiness or false element, so she valued the compliment. Dressed in a beautiful white linen suit, he struck her as a native, with the brimmed hat tilted low on his head, giving him a sexy vibe.

She wondered if she'd start an affair with him. Of course, they only had two days left, so it would be more of a two-night stand.

Bailey wasn't sure. There was a good energy between them, but something bothered her. Until she figured out what it was, she wouldn't make a move.

They ordered a bottle of white wine and an assortment of fish and started off with tagliarini pasta. The delicate noodles and light sauce made the fruity wine sing. Bailey fell into foodie heaven while they chatted and caught him up on the details of the hike. Thank God, Dev left out the embarrassing part, but of course she couldn't help the gleam of glee flashing in her eyes.

"What's left on your agenda?" he asked, expertly twirling his noodles and spearing them into his mouth neatly. "Any last-moment requests I can help with?"

"We haven't gotten to the beach yet," Pris said. "I'd like to do that tomorrow."

"I have that scheduled for Friday so we can spend our last full day in complete relaxation," Dev said. "We still have the boat ride to the Blue Grotto and tour of Capri."

"Spiaggia Grande is the main beach here, of course. But I'd

recommend seeing something a bit less crowded. Fornillo is a great beach and not jammed with every other tourist."

"Oh, I love that idea," Bailey said. "We're doing the necessary sights, but I always prefer getting an inside look at an area."

"We don't have much time," Dev pointed out. "Or I would have added that to our schedule."

Hawke grinned, his eyes sparkling with humor. "You should extend your stay," he said.

"We have our return tickets already," Dev said. Bailey almost groaned at the prim tone of her sister's voice. She was the absolute worst at doing anything that was even slightly impulsive. It was exhausting. She didn't want Dev to miss out on amazing opportunities because of the stick up her butt.

"We could always change them to a later date," Pris said, blotting her mouth with a napkin. "If we wanted to."

Dev looked up in surprise, but her response was cut off by the arrival of their food. Grilled octopus resting in a tangy olive sauce, topped with fresh greens. Sea bass on a bed of mashed spinach, drizzled with fragrant oils, sun-dried tomatoes, and fingerling potatoes. Giant prawns overflowing the plate, their shells still steaming, the scents of lemon and butter drifting to her nostrils.

They looked at the food with pure reverence.

Then feasted.

"Dev mentioned you wanted to talk more in detail about my uncle," Hawke said.

Bailey glanced at the tote bag slung over the arm of Pris's chair. All Mom's love letters were ready to be revealed as proof. They were all hoping that with more details, they'd be able to confirm Raymond was the guy. It seemed like everything pointed in that direction, but still her heart beat frantically at the idea of finally getting close to solving the mystery.

Pris took the lead. "Yes. Dev explained you were speaking about your uncle, who lived next door with your dad. I know we've been kind of mysterious, but we actually came here to track down someone our mom was close with. His name began with *R*."

"Ah, and that's why you looked disappointed when I told you my father's name was Gio."

"Exactly. It's kind of personal, so we didn't want to say anything then. But it sounds like your uncle may be the man we're looking for."

He nodded, chewing his food thoughtfully. "Understood. Why do you think my uncle is a match?"

"We have a bunch of clues," Dev said. "We know he lived in Positano, his name began with *R*, and he had a boat here. He'd give tours and do some fishing. He seemed to be crazy in love with our mother and they had a passionate affair. She came every summer to see him for a good four years. Then they seemed to break up, but we think she returned to see him again about thirty-five years ago."

"Could be Uncle Ray. What else?"

They all shared a look. "That's it," Bailey said. "We don't have that many details."

Hawke cocked his head. "Do you have specific dates they met? That might help."

Bailey sighed. "Nope. The letters are full of emotion but little detail. At least, no detail as to where he lived, who his family was, or his permanent job. But if we met him, we'd know his heart and soul."

Hawke smiled and his voice was gentle. "I bet you would. Letters can get extremely personal. Much deeper than an email or text." He took another sip of wine. "Let me tell you what I can about Uncle Ray. Like I told Dev, I always suspected he had a great love affair and something happened because he never got married. He spent every summer here with my dad in Positano and used the house in the off-season. He had a boat here, but touring wasn't his full-time job. He just loved sailing and being on the water, so he'd take people he knew or tourists who he felt a connection to. Then, for some reason, he decided to leave. He gave up his share of the cottage to me, so I now own it in full. He moved to Sicily a while ago." His eyes darkened. "Hmm, interesting. I always wondered why he suddenly left."

Bailey dragged in a breath. Excitement prickled her nerve endings. It just *felt* right. "Mom wrote him a letter where he responded he'd meet her here on her sixty-fifth birthday. That was May fifteenth. Do you have any idea if he visited Positano then?"

"I don't. I try to speak with him regularly, but it's hard. Many times he doesn't respond—he was always fiercely independent." His gaze grew thoughtful. "I'm assuming your mom never got to meet him for her birthday?"

Dev shook her head. "She died a few months beforehand." Her hand shook a bit as she raised her glass. Bailey had the same reaction as she thought of the heartfelt possibilities that had never occurred. "I wonder how that was for her. Did she worry that he'd never know she got sick? Or did it all happen so fast, she had no time to think about anything? She died of pneumonia. Unexpected. A cold turned serious and sent her to the hospital, and she was just . . . gone. We're all assuming this man, maybe your uncle, never found out what happened to Mom."

The dinner plates were cleared, and Sacher torte was served—a deep, rich chocolate torte with hazelnuts and strawberries. Vanilla bean gelato paired with the dense cake perfectly. Hawke switched to espresso, his fingers cradling the tiny cup with a simple sort of elegance.

"I think there's only one thing left to do," he said slowly.

"What?" Pris asked.

"I'll call my uncle and ask him."

Dev groaned and rolled her eyes. "I can't believe I didn't even think about that. We are the worst detectives ever."

He laughed. "Easy to get swept up in the glamour of a mystery."

"We even brought the love letters in case you needed clues," Pris added.

"I'm sure those letters are precious to all of you. Rarely does a child get to know a parent on such an intimate level. We're too involved with the roles—we distance them from us." His gaze warmed, maybe with his own memories. "Meanwhile, they're only human."

Pris sucked in a breath. The words hit her full force, stirring up the messy emotions in her gut. Hawke was right about the role she'd assigned to Mom. Bailey felt as if her relationship with Mom was so different from the others'. She didn't have the trouble of seeing her through a lens. She'd spotted the sadness when Mom thought no one was looking. The letters only helped her make sense of it all. To Dev and Pris, the letters complicated things because then they wouldn't be able to put her up on the high pedestal they loved so much.

Love was messy.

Hawke paid the bill and they all walked home happily. The orange half-moon glowed as if it were full of secrets and magic. Bailey fell into step next to Hawke, enjoying his masculine presence. She liked men: liked their smell and deep voices, muscled bodies and simplistic way they looked at the world. It was women who were the complicated ones, full of thorns and contradictions amid the pure passion toward the ones they loved.

Bailey was glad she'd never succumbed to the temptation of committed love. Her life was so much easier and happier than others'.

"I'll call my uncle when we get home," he said.

"Sounds good. I'm exhausted," Pris announced.

"That was a long hike," Hawke said. "You should sleep well tonight."

Dev sighed. "I hope I do. Sometimes I get awful insomnia. I stare at the ceiling for hours and go over mathematical equations."

Hawke laughed. "Better than sheep. I have bouts of that too."

"Dev, you need to focus on your breath. Let your thoughts flicker across the movie screen in your mind without getting attached. Meditation and yoga will help you so much," Bailey said.

"No, thanks. One sleepless night I came close to a breakthrough with the bell curve and the current securities issues."

Hawke cocked his head. "Yeah? Now, that would be worth insomnia."

"You two are hopeless," Bailey said with a shake of her head. "I thought you said Positano changed you, Hawke. To become less attached to the trappings of the world."

His lip twitched. "Oh, it did. But the bell curve is sacred."

They laughed. The warm air caressed her skin, and the stars shone from the sky like diamonds. She felt drunk on being part of this place and knew it had little to do with the wine. Her nerves rippled with awareness. Her heart sighed. She craved to grab a bit of such vibrant energy and ingest it whole.

They arrived at the cottage and Hawke plucked his phone from his pocket. "Ready to give him a call?" he asked.

Bailey nodded, breathless with excitement.

Hawke dialed and, after a long pause, spoke in rapid Italian. Bailey loved the musical quality to the language and made a vow to learn it. His thumb slid over the button and he lowered the phone. "Sorry, but he's not answering. I left him a voice mail it's urgent. As soon as he calls, I'll contact you."

"Feel free to knock on our door anytime," Pris said. "We really appreciate it."

"Do you have our cell phone number?" Dev asked.

"Let me take yours—"

"Oh, you can have mine," Bailey jumped in with a smile. "In fact, if you're up for one more cocktail, we can hang out a little longer. For some reason, I'm not as tired."

He hesitated, but the charming smile appeared fast enough that she didn't worry. "Of course. I need to check on Lucifer, so you can come to my place."

"Great." She sent a wave to her sisters. "See you guys in the morning. Hope you sleep well."

"Yep, have fun," Pris said.

When she glanced at Dev, she stiffened. Her sister shot her a disgusted look that made Bailey's cheeks heat with shame. As she flicked her judging gaze back and forth between Hawke and Bailey, Dev's words held a dripping venom she recognized well. "Yes, Bailey. After all, you deserve to have some fun, don't you?"

It was the same tone Dev had used in the past few years. A tone that had been lacking over the past two days as they grew closer.

Guess she blew that.

Temper warred with the need to smooth things over in front of Hawke. She tossed her hair, spun on her heel, and grabbed his arm. "Thanks, see ya!"

He didn't say anything as they walked next door. He opened the door and motioned her inside. Lucifer was meowing in welcome or annoyance—she wasn't sure which—his tail twitching as he examined his new guest.

Hawke stroked his back and the cat seemed immediately calmer. "See, I told you I wouldn't be gone long. You better not have marked any territory in here just because you're pissed I actually had a social event."

She reached out to pet the cat, but Lucifer jerked back and shot her a disgusted look—as if she was beneath him. Hawke sighed. "Sorry, he does that with everyone. Don't take it personally."

Bailey laughed. "I have thick skin. You need it if you're going to perform." Her gaze took in the sleek, simple design of his home. Like their cottage, it was an open concept, but his décor matched the outside. Navy blue and white accents livened up dark wood furniture. A few of the pieces seemed hand carved in a variety of mahogany, birchwood, and cedar. The kitchen boasted modern appliances, a giant farmhouse sink, and comfortable seating around a high countertop, painted in gorgeous Italian tile of a Tuscan landscape. A flight of stairs led to the second floor. She wondered how many bedrooms were tucked up there—this house was definitely bigger than theirs. "Your home is beautiful. It suits you."

"Thank you. I've tried to make it comfortable and did some renovations. There are two bedrooms and my office upstairs."

She tilted her head. "Thought you were in semiretirement, taking a break from the world?"

"I was. Am. Let's just say, I've been toying with the idea of returning."

"Why give this up?" she asked curiously. "You're living the dream. Not caught in the awful rat race or social networks. The world's not telling you who you are and who you should be."

"Do you feel like that, Bailey? Trapped in the constraints of the world?"

Startled at the direct question, she hesitated. "Not really. I mean, I like to challenge assumptions of myself, but I feel the world has more good to give than bad. I wish there wasn't so much pressure, though. To succeed. To get married. Have kids. Be someone."

He walked into the kitchen. "I like your attitude, and I agree with you. It's even harder when you're young. Something about age makes things seem clearer. Wine? Espresso martini?"

"Wine, please. Red if you have it." His comment burrowed under her skin. "You speak like you're an old man. And I'm already thirty-two. Some people think I look like I'm twelve."

He grinned, expertly uncorking a bottle and pouring a glass of ruby-red liquid. "I'm forty-two. A decade is sometimes a century. Want to sit in here or outside?"

Usually, she loved being outdoors, but something about the sleek couch looked inviting. "Here's fine. Sometimes the bugs get at me."

With an easy grace, he picked up both glasses and settled in the corner of the couch. He handed her the wine the same moment Lucifer jumped up on his lap. The cat dug in with his paws to make himself comfortable, then settled in. "Spoiled devil," he muttered, but she noticed he petted the animal. He was a bit like Dev—direct without mincing words—but it was obvious he had a big heart.

He began to appeal to her even more, so she began testing boundaries between them to gauge his interest. Tucking her legs underneath her, she leaned forward to take her wine, allowing her neckline to gap open. She catalogued his odd reaction and surprise shot through her. His gaze glanced over her, taking note but revealing no reaction. He didn't look embarrassed, but the distance remained firmly between them.

Interesting.

"I think age really isn't a good indication of maturity," she said, falling back into their conversation. "Experience and travel are more important factors. For instance, I've been in the creative arts since I was a teenager. I've met a number of dynamic people. Moved around a lot. Done theater. Even charity work." Not wanting him to think she was bragging, she gave a self-conscious laugh. "My point is just to challenge your perception. Is a thirty-two-year-old who's worked one job and never been in love more mature than me?"

She got caught up in the power of his deep gray eyes, but it wasn't in a romantic or passionate sense. No, this was his genuine interest to get past any barriers and see who she was. Not so much a woman as a person.

At least, that's how it felt. She was so used to experiencing it with physical attraction or a shared experience like working on the same play. Hawke was different.

"You're so smart," he murmured, his smile heartbreakingly gentle. "Have you been in love before, Bailey?"

Snapping back into herself, she recognized the statement as her opening. He needed her to make the first move; that was obvious. "I thought so, but now I realize I wasn't. I think I'm more in love with the world than a person. With life experience. It's like this rush comes over me and I want to steep myself in it, whether it's Italy or a play, or a simple dinner with friends." Her voice trembled slightly as she opened up to him. "Sometimes, I wonder if I feel things completely differently from everyone else. Does that make sense?"

"Yeah, I think we all wonder that at some time. The fact that you even question it shows you're self-aware."

"Have you been in love?"

Shadows leapt in his eyes. "Yes. Once before, but I had my priorities mixed up."

"Is that the reason you moved to Positano?"

"One of them." He took a sip of wine, his fingers still stroking Lucifer. "Do you ever *want* to be in love?"

A barrier shot up at the direct question. Inside, it was as if a line got crossed, and her wires imploded.

No, she didn't.

But she refused to tackle the undercurrents of her answer, so she slid a few inches over on the couch, so they were close enough to touch if either of them reached out. "I think there are so many things better than love." Her gaze caught his. Her head bent forward, and she felt her hair sliding lushly over her shoulder. The air grew heavy and hot. "Like passion. Grabbing a moment. Not expecting a future is a powerful thing, Hawke. A type of freedom I like to embrace. I wonder if you agree."

Her tongue touched her lower lip. Once again, his gaze caught the gesture, but there was no pupil dilation, no intake of breath. She waited, wondering why her heart wasn't pounding in excitement, or why there was a lack of tension coiled in her belly. No, it was as if she was more curious about his reaction than her own, and that was the most puzzling thing of all.

He looked at her directly when he spoke. "I bet there are a thousand men out there who fell in love with you, Bailey. And I think you're an exciting woman. But it's not what I'm looking for right now."

His rejection didn't even sting. The truth in his words and warmth in his eyes immediately soothed any sense of discomfort. And she realized at that moment, she hadn't really wanted to sleep with him. It was just the way she pursued a deep connection with the male sex, the only way that she knew how to express it.

She'd never questioned her response before. It'd been easier to just go with it because it felt right. But maybe it was time to dig deeper.

"Okay."

He laughed then, and she laughed too. "But I still want you to stay and finish your drink with me. I like talking with you."

An actual blush heated her cheeks. "Thanks, same here. As long as it's not the bell curve."

"I'm sure I can come up with other topics. Now, tell me about your theater work."

She continued their conversation with ease. He listened well, which allowed her to open up because there was no judgment—just curiosity. He asked about her sisters, and Bailey ended up telling him personal things. Pris's current marriage struggles. The strained relationship between her and Dev she hoped to heal. The way they'd been so close and drifted so far over the past five years. It was very freeing being able to tell a relative stranger all about her family dynamics, yet feel safe doing so.

They sat and drank their wine and talked for a long time, until Lucifer began to gently snore, and sleep finally beckoned. "I better go; it's late."

He walked her to the door and she turned. "Thanks, Hawke. For everything."

He leaned down and pressed a kiss to her forehead. "I'll call or come by as soon as my uncle calls."

She returned to the cottage, sneaking in quietly, and settled on the couch. A door shut from the hallway, and she held her breath, hoping Dev or Pris didn't come to check on her. But the house fell into silence and she relaxed.

Bailey fell asleep feeling completely at peace, excited for the morning and what it held in store with her sisters.

CHAPTER TWENTY-FOUR

Olivia

My life soon became consumed by school, art, work, and Adam.

I returned home and told Adam simply that my boyfriend and I were taking a break. At his interested look, I quickly let him know I was hopeful to get back together after graduation and that I still wanted to be just friends. He backed off and agreed, and we continued hanging out.

Adam got me a job at an art gallery in Chelsea, and I fell in love with the unpredictability of Manhattan and the sophistication of the art world. My job became as important as my studies, and I burned the candle at both ends. The little time left I gave to Adam, for long phone conversations and dinners in Manhattan every Saturday night.

As Adam and I grew closer, the life I envisioned with Rafe began to slowly fade. I still missed him. At night, I'd imagine his dark-eyed gaze and beloved face; the way he spoke in a lilting voice; the sweet comfort offered as he wrapped me in his arms until I felt as if nothing could hurt me. I dreamed of Positano and the colored houses sprinkled over the hilltop; of hot sun and rocky beaches and the musical play of Italian drifting in the air.

But Adam was different. He pushed me toward things that scared me, believing I could do them. With each obstacle I conquered, more of my fears melted away. And though I was sometimes haunted by the thought of not seeing Rafe again, another part wondered if it was truly the type of life I was meant for long-term.

For the first time, I began to wonder if being in love was really enough.

One night, I'd finished up at the gallery and met Adam for a late-night meal. We'd taken the train in that day, so before heading to Grand Central Terminal we walked past Bryant Park. Springtime teased pedestrians with a mild early March day, so the assortment of colorful vendor booths was mobbed. Adam got us two frozen hot chocolates, and we meandered through the brightly lit space, browsing through books and candles, handmade jewelry and an assortment of crafts.

We stopped at the ice rink. Skaters crisscrossed over the smooth surface while soft music filled the air. "Let's skate," Adam suddenly said.

I blinked. "I don't know how."

"Who cares? It's the last weekend before the rink closes. Live a little, Liv."

It was his regular teasing remark when he dared me to do something I'd normally shy away from. Briefly, I remembered that night I skinny-dipped with Rafe, and how surprised he'd been. Rafe had never thought to change me; he accepted me exactly the way I was. But Adam created an urge to do more, be bold, grasp at the brass ring with both hands instead of comforting me when I wanted to stay home.

How could two men be completely different yet touch me so deeply?

The bolt of pain hit sharply, stealing my breath. I closed my eyes halfway and tried to deal with the sudden swirl of guilt and regret. Tears suddenly stung.

"Liv?" A warm palm cupped my cheek, tilting my head up. I looked into his golden gaze, filled with concern and something more, something that lit up my insides and replaced the fading sting of pain. "I'm sorry, I was just teasing you. We don't have to skate."

"That's not it. I was thinking of someone."

"Your ex-boyfriend?"

I shuddered at his soft question. "Yes."

He hesitated. Unconsciously, I leaned into him. He smelled like spice and sandalwood, exotic and masculine. He lowered his head, his gaze still gripping mine. "I don't want you to think of him anymore." I waited, transfixed, as his lips stopped inches from mine. "I'm crazy about you, Liv. And I just want you to think about me."

He kissed me. Soft, warm lips savored mine. I melted into him while the crowds rushed around us and the lights twinkled and the scream of a police siren blasted through the air. None of it mattered. We kept kissing, and when he finally pulled away, it was decided.

We were together.

• • • •

Dear Livia, amore mio,

My hands are shaking as I write this. I have waited so long and practiced this letter in my head for several days and sleepless nights. Since we said goodbye, I've held tight to the bond we formed that first summer afternoon, when I saw you standing by the water, blinking in the sun, a shy smile on your lips. My heart leapt in my chest and instantly became yours. It always will be.

I think of you and wonder how you spent this last year. I picked up the phone a thousand times. I wrote you letters I ended up tossing away, knowing I needed to keep my promise of no contact. It was the only way to truly know our hearts. For me, nothing has changed.

I still love you, dolcezza. I want to spend the rest of my days with you. My father has retired and now I must take care of him. During this time apart, I realized we can solve any of our problems as long as we are together. The real question is, do you still want to be with me? To move here and start a life together?

Does your heart still belong to me?

I know it is possible you have changed and grown in a new direction. I know it was a risk when I told you to be free and find what you truly want. For me, it has always been you. But I would rather lose you completely than take parts of you because you are doubtful. We have always been truthful with each other, dolcezza. And though it will hurt deeply, I still only want your happiness. I can take anything as long as I know you are living the life that satisfies your soul. No matter what, I will be here for you. Always.

Forever yours,

R

Dear R,

When I received your letter, I carried it with me for two full days, afraid to read your words. I still dream about Positano, and you. I still think about the time we spent together, the way you seemed to hold my very heart in your hands, and the way you helped me grow into a woman I always hoped I'd be.

When I finally read your words, a piece of my heart crumbled and became forever yours. Because as much as I wanted to return to you, fate put me on a different path and I am torn apart but must tell you the truth.

I've gotten a job in an art gallery in Manhattan. I love my work and feel more fulfilled than I ever have. Besides being surrounded by new and emerging artists, I find I'm good at talking with people and making sales. I will be graduating with a 3.9 GPA. My mom is now settled in Boston, but we've grown much closer. It's as if now she's fully happy, she's able to support me in ways I've never known before. We talk all the time, and I've come to care about my new stepdad. My own father is also doing well, and dating again. It's as if all those years of unrest had to happen to come to this point. I've been thinking about that a lot. How people come into our life and change it in so many ways. That is who you will always be to me. My first love and my best friend. The man who loved me as I was; who gave me the strength and support I needed to grow into the woman I am right now.

But you asked for the truth and I must give it to you. I have met someone. A man who had been a casual friend and slowly became more. I never meant to betray or hurt you, Rafe. I struggled and fought my feelings for a long time, but I knew in order to be fully yours, I had to explore this path with him so I can eventually return to you with a whole heart.

My choice backfired. I fell in love with him. I fell in love with New York City, and being part of the art culture I've spent so many years studying from afar. And as much as I'll always wonder if one day I'll regret my decision, I must stay here and follow this new path.

Oh, Rafe, can you find a way to understand and, perhaps, forgive me? I feel sometimes as if my body has been wrenched in half, the agonizing sorrow for betraying you, and our vow. But even worse would be for me to return and then rip us apart by my doubts and regrets! I cannot lie to you and say there is no one else. I can't say any longer that Italy is the place I see myself for the rest of my life.

How do I express my grief and pain in hurting you? My shame at doing the same exact thing I accused your ex of doing? Perhaps you'll never be able to forgive me, and that will be my punishment. And I don't blame you. I'm the one who failed us. I can only ask that maybe one day, you can find a way to accept my limitations and go on to have the life and love you deserve. Even if it's not with me. I will never forget you.

Livia

Dear Livia,

You are forgiven. Yes, my heart is broken, but to hear of your happiness, to know you are pursuing your passion and have healed the rift with your mother, is worth everything. You have been a gift in my life who will never be forgotten. My bright spot, my joy, and now a dream I will carry with me forever. I will always be here for you if you need me. And I will always love you.

R

CHAPTER TWENTY-FIVE

Pris

Pris stood alone, staring out her open balcony door. Dev had gone to bed. Bailey was at Hawke's. The night sky was dark, and a deep hush of silence blanketed the world. Her mind caught and seized on various memories, as if spurred from the first honest conversation she'd had with her sisters earlier today. It had jarred something loose within her, and now the demons were free.

About time.

She'd studied for years at the School of American Ballet, ever since she was eight years old, gaining her spot when she begged her mother to go to an open audition. She'd danced in the iconic *Nutcracker* ballet at nine, thankfully small enough to score a coveted part. She was one of the lucky ones—invited to be a part of the New York City Ballet—and slipped eventually into a primary ballerina role.

The years dedicated to dance fulfilled her, yet kept her from all the other experiences that marked a normal teenager. There were no late nights at clubs, dating boys, or sneaking alcohol at school parties. Her world narrowed to the people she interacted with at ballet—the instructors and fellow dancers and investors. When Garrett saw her dance one evening and asked to meet her, she felt as if her world had been cracked open—as if she'd been an oyster kept tight in her shell and Garrett forced her to change into a pearl. She'd never been in love before and it had consumed her, even more than dancing.

Pris hadn't believed it was possible.

The year they spent together was both beautiful and maddening. Her performance and rehearsal schedule was brutal. He'd just passed the bar and been offered a position at a prestigious Boston firm. On paper, it didn't seem to work—they were in two different worlds and had opposing responsibilities. But he'd fallen just as hard—and they realized someone would have to give in, in order for it to work.

Pris remembered sitting across from her mother at the kitchen table, spilling out her heart, desperate for advice.

"Mom, I don't know what to do. If I stay, I'll be traveling all over the country for Swan Lake. *It's my dream, but I didn't realize I could love someone this much."*

Her mother gazed at her with such raw regret and pain, Pris froze with dread. It was as if her mother knew the outcome of her dilemma, and there wasn't a happy ending.

"I know about that type of love," her mother said slowly. Her usually bright blue eyes were shadowed, and her fingers shook as she reached across to grasp hers. "Is there a way Garrett can be with you? Do a long-distance relationship for a while? At least, until Swan Lake *closes?"*

"He just passed the bar and got a job at Fitzgerald & Watkins. He'll be working nonstop hours and not be able to travel." Pris shut her eyes with despair. "I don't think we can

survive that type of stress. And I know ballet has been my everything, but the idea of losing him? I'd die, Mom. I never knew I could love someone like this."

Garrett had swept in like a hurricane, tossing her neat life into chaos. But it was a chaos that filled her soul in a new way—a way dancing never could. Suddenly, her priorities shifted. She'd been yelled at by her instructor for losing concentration. Pris knew she couldn't afford to make any mistakes, or the chance to be cast in the next performance would be minimal.

The real problem was her sudden disinterest. All she wanted was to be with Garrett.

She needed her mother's sane advice. Craved to be told what was the right thing for her future. The decision that would not keep her up night after night with regret.

"Pris, sometimes opportunities come into our lives we're not prepared for. The heart and head can be on separate pages, and there's really not one that's right and one that's wrong. It just . . . is." A sad smile touched her lips. "If you love Garrett and believe you'll lose a bigger piece of yourself by walking away, you need to follow that instinct. You can never regret love. It's the other things that will always make you wonder."

Relief rushed through her. Finally, she was being told what to do. Which choice made the most sense. "You're saying to choose Garrett."

"I'm saying you need to do what's right for you," Mom corrected. "But a lifelong soul mate is rare to find. Easy to lose. Maybe there will be other opportunities for ballet down the road."

She sifted through the words, even though her gut told her once she left the ballet world, there would be no more chances. It was a competitive, cutthroat environment built on the youngest, the best, and who worked the hardest. Sacrifice was consistently required. A full-force love affair took too much of the space that dance demanded for excellence.

Pris ignored the sliver of uncertainty at the idea of leaving years of ambition and passion behind. But her mother was right. To lose Garrett at this point would be too much. This was a sacrifice for love.

"I know what I need to do, Mom. Thanks."

Her mother hesitated, searching her gaze with a bit of desperation. "Be sure, Pris. And once you decide, commit to your choice fully—no holding back. If it's Garrett, give him everything you are."

The memory faded. Mom's words still rang in her ears, like she was right beside her. Funny, Pris had always viewed the encounter differently. Believed Mom was urging her to choose love over a career because she had no regrets loving her father. But what if she was thinking of someone else? A man she'd given up but never forgotten? A man who made her doubt and, perhaps, regret her choices?

Viewing things through the new lens offered her a deeper understanding of the impassioned way her mother gave advice. Commit one hundred percent. Don't look back. All the things she'd believed she'd done but had only buried them deep underneath the surface, waiting for the what-ifs to rise and explode and cause chaos.

Which they had done. If only she could have allowed herself to grieve her career, to be intentional and kind about her sacrifice, maybe she wouldn't have had this pent-up resentment toward Garrett.

But she was tired of living this way. Tired of steeping herself in the frustrated rage that did nothing but erode her marriage day by day.

It was time to get real with herself and make some changes. To make some choices. Her sisters were right. She'd been a passive participant in her life for too long, refusing to be real with herself, and her husband.

Not anymore.

She looked down at her phone and realized it was time. She only hoped he picked up.

Pris took a deep breath, relishing the fresh air, then rang his number.

His familiar voice saying her name flooded all the aching, empty places inside her. She realized how strong the connection with her husband still was. Even with their difficulties. Pris just didn't know what she was going to do about it.

"Hey. How are you?" she asked.

"Fine. Worked late again. Closed the case, though, with a big settlement. Finally, I feel like there's been justice done."

Happiness washed through her. His liability case had taken up both his time and his passion—a faulty electronic had caused his client brain damage, which also caused the loss of his family. Garrett had been the only one at the firm wanting to take the case because of the challenge. "That's wonderful news. You've worked so hard, Garrett. I'm proud of you."

"Thanks. Did you have a nice day?"

"Actually, it was full of surprises. I had a long talk with my sisters, and some hard truths came to the surface."

"Ah, well, that's good. I was hoping they'd decided to sell the place instead. Dev really is being the most rational one here. I'm glad you and Bailey finally got on board."

Irritation ruffled. Why should she be surprised? They talked nothing of emotions to each other—only banal items of everyday life. Of course he'd expect her big truth would have to do with selling the house. God, she was so tired of it all. "No, we're keeping the house. It's part of Mom's legacy and I feel at home here."

"Even though it's not practical?"

Sadness leaked into her voice. "The best things in life rarely are."

A pause hummed over the line. "Are you okay, Pris? Are you at least having a good time?"

She opened her mouth to utter her usual. *Yes, of course. Italy was beautiful. She was good. She was fine. She was both.*

Instead, she told the truth. "I don't think I've been okay for a long time, Garrett. But you know that."

His sigh spilled into her ear. "Yes, we both said as much at dinner that night. I thought you were going to Italy to figure things out."

The words escaped her mouth without thought, the safety of the dark and the distance allowing her to be raw. "That's the plan, but I don't know how it's going to work out. I have to tell you something."

"You can tell me anything."

Silly tears stung her eyes. "There's something inside me that's not right. Like a missing piece in a puzzle that I can't seem to find."

"Do you know what that piece could be?" he asked slowly.

"No. It used to be you. The way I used to love you filled up all the spaces until there was no room for anything else, not even ballet. And when Thomas was born, the same thing happened. It was like this powerful burst of love and need so strong it almost crippled me. There was nothing I wanted more than to love you both. Does that sound pathetic? That I could be so needy?"

She heard the harshness of a gasp. "God no! Not needy, just the opposite. Generous. Giving. You gave so damn much there was nothing left. Is that how you feel?"

She closed her eyes, and for the first time, the heaviness in her chest lightened. Just a touch. "Yes, yes, I think so."

"Why didn't you ever tell me this before?"

"Because I didn't want to know. I did what all the magazines and TV and female leaders warn against. I gave up all I had for love and didn't leave myself enough. Thomas doesn't need me like he used to. Neither do you. So I filled my days with busy-work and became a ghost."

It was horrible, the things coming out of her mouth—the burst of writhing snakes at the pit of her core she was finally spilling to this man she still loved. But she also felt free, and powerful, saying her truth, and she didn't want to stop. "I became a ghost because it was easier not to fight for anything else. I gave up, but now, I don't like myself very much. And I don't know if you can help me anymore. I don't know how you can love a woman who's not really here."

She rested in the silence, waiting for his answer. "Do you blame me?" he finally asked. "I pushed you to give up ballet. I'm the one who never looked up from my own goals to even ask how you were doing, assuming we'd be enough despite your sacrifices."

"You were. For a while."

"Yeah, for a while."

"See, when I chose you, I think I expected the same in return. And I think watching you grow and succeed and be fulfilled by your career—as much as I was happy for you—I became jealous. Resentful. Because I wanted that for myself, but I'd given it up."

"Makes sense. But that leaves me pretty helpless. How can I turn that resentment you have for me back to love?"

Her heart shattered at the broken notes in his voice. Yes, he still loved her. On some level, they both wanted to find their way back to each other, which gave her hope. "I love you, Garrett. The resentment is really toward myself—I just didn't understand that before. But having this time in Italy, being able to slow down and be honest with myself, things are beginning to change."

His voice was grit and gravel and full of emotion. "Pris, I still love you. I know you suspect there's someone else, and I'm not going to lie and say I wasn't tempted. Because I've been so damn lonely."

She held her breath, knowing it was time they both leveled with each other. "Did you? I need to know."

"I've never slept with another woman. There's never been anyone else I loved other than you. I don't want to lose you, but we've drifted so far apart. I'm also afraid if I try to tell you how to make yourself happy, I'll fail again. Do you understand what I'm saying?"

She did. For the first time, Garrett wasn't trying to fix the problem with answers or advice or concrete analysis. He wasn't trying to win an argument or win her back. A sense of peace washed over her, the knowledge that she was responsible for herself first, then her relationship.

She imagined him rubbing his head, thick hair mussed over his brow. Imagined his blue eyes that rivaled the stunning sea, and that feeling of home she used to get when their gazes locked and he claimed her. "Yeah, I understand."

"Good. There's something else, Pris. Something I want you to remember. I don't think it's about fixing anything. I think it's about finding your own happiness. I'm hoping that leads back to me, but that's a decision you have to make. Because we can't do this to each other anymore."

"I know."

They sat on the phone together in silence. The sounds of their breathing mingled and fell into a steady rhythm. There was no pressure to say anything, and a closeness vibrated between them that had been missing for a long time.

"I think I want to stay here longer."

"Okay. Do you think you'll find your answers there?"

A whisper of a smile touched her lips. "I don't know. But I feel Mom's presence, and my sisters and I are really talking for the first time. I did the most amazing climb, and at the top, I felt like I'd accomplished something."

"Tell me about it. About the climb."

She did. She told him about her dialogue with her sisters, and the time with Hawke, and how they were still trying to track down R. Garrett listened, and his presence filled her with a contentment that soothed her soul.

"I can't promise anything, though," she finally said. "I don't want to pretend I can fix myself in a week or two."

"Neither of us expect it. But we need to build a new foundation here if this is going to work, and it starts with you, Pris."

She said her goodbye and he whispered her name again. "What?"

"Will you call me tomorrow?"

Pris smiled. "Yes."

She hung up, her mind whirling with a cyclone of thoughts that kept her up for a long, long time. But inside, there was a beginning of calm seeping through her veins, reminding her that she might not be at the end of a journey, but just starting a brand-new one.

Finally, she slept.

CHAPTER TWENTY-SIX

Olivia

I married Adam when I turned twenty-five and got pregnant on our honeymoon.

Life became a whirlwind of work at the gallery, late-night dinner parties with a mix of interesting, eclectic people culled from both the business and art worlds, and settling into the role of wife and prospective mother. Since graduation, I felt as if I kept being pushed forward with a momentum that held no pause for reflection. I'd given up a quieter life of contemplation, thought, and figuring out who I wanted to be for a dynamic lifestyle with my husband in the center of it all. He quickly climbed the ranks to work as a top-level manager with a team beneath him. He went on multiple business trips, recruited sharp new minds for the company, and created a reputable name for himself in many circles.

Being in his presence brought a vibrant excitement of possibilities—the primary traits that had made me fall in love with him. He was the opposite of Rafe—a man of the world and its trappings, with an enthusiasm for a diverse crowd of people, opportunities, and adventure. I felt lucky to be his partner and swept up in a world I used to feel so uncomfortable in. Now I was the queen to his king, being invited to art exhibits and cocktail parties and mingling with important people in all industries. When I looked at Adam from across the room, usually surrounded by a fascinated crowd of people—including gorgeous women—he'd meet my gaze and smile intimately, reminding me I was the one he loved and wanted. We'd become a power couple, and I was a bit giddy from the ride. It was as if I was living my own chapter of Camelot.

We moved out of our apartment and bought a big house in Westchester, right on the seams of the city. It was a short commute to New York City but gave us a real lawn and backyard to raise our son or daughter. I made arrangements to take a short leave of absence from my job, planning to go back part-time until I found my footing. I'd never thought of settling down so early—I felt as if my career was just beginning to take off—but Adam was completely supportive of my choice to work and raise the baby.

Priscilla Avery Clayton was born on a cold winter's night on February 13. When I first held her and looked into her wide, confused blue eyes I knew my life would forever change. I studied her flushed pink, wrinkled skin, her tiny rosebud mouth that emitted the shrillest of screams, the frustrated fly of her fists when she wanted to feed, and tumbled into a passionate, raw, emotional love I'd never experienced.

I was a mother. A new part of me emerged—one full of protectiveness, fear, and a desperate need to make sure she had everything she ever wanted. It went beyond physical; I became obsessed with checking on her constantly at night to make sure she was breathing. Adam wanted to begin getting back to our normal social life and kept pushing me to find a sitter, but I had no interest in squeezing back into fashionable clothes and chattering about things that made no sense to me in my new world. I would rather read baby books, take Pris for walks in the stroller, and prepare organic baby food so she got all her nutrients.

I put off returning to work, and time began to blur—the days and nights filled with caring for Pris. Adam began to blame me for how I changed. He wanted the woman I was before, the adventurer who adored travel and dinner parties and interesting, academic conversations. But I blamed him for becoming a father and not even recognizing how this tiny human had changed everything. How could he sleep the same and focus completely on his job? How could he not feel like his purpose and reality had blown up to new proportions but, somehow, become better?

We began to fight. He spoke about the economy and questioned the burgeoning graffiti artists suddenly becoming so popular. I talked about Pris's new word she uttered or the expression on her face when she saw the next-door neighbor's new puppy. He wanted more sex, but the exhaustion of my routine, and the changes in my body, made me dread his increasing demands and pouty rants. I finally convinced Adam I needed to quit my job and be a full-time mother.

As time passed, I enrolled Pris in Mommy and Me groups and then ballet classes, and fell into a new world. Adam seemed to move further away. It was as if we began circling each other instead of connecting, except when he wanted sex. And even then, I felt as if something was missing between us, making me pull back from him even more. I tried to talk to him, but he only accused me of becoming one of those obsessed moms who'd become boring and one-dimensional.

It hurt. I tried to get him more involved with his daughter. I knew he loved her—I clearly watched his expressions and laughter when he held or played with her, or actually came home to sit with us at dinner. But then he was off again, his attention fading away, and he'd hand her over and leave the room, both of us forgotten.

I began to think about Rafe more often. His face would float in my mind, and I wondered what he'd think of Pris. Was he married now with his own children? Was he happy? Did he ever think of me? I toyed with writing to him again, just to see how he was. His memory kept me company late at night, while my husband snored beside me, the physical space between us so much more than in bed. I'd tucked Rafe's letters away in an old antique trunk I kept hidden at the back of my closet under some bedding. Sometimes, I'd take them out, smooth the crinkled paper, and reread them. I'd remember that young girl who loved so passionately and fully. I'd savor the innocence and purity of what we had throughout those summers, and how he'd changed me into a better person.

But there could be no regrets, because Pris was the greatest gift I'd ever been given.

Still, guilt pricked when his memory took the place of Adam. I wanted another baby, but Adam remained resistant, afraid I'd fall even further away from him and too deep into Mommyland. I made a decision to try to repair the breaks within my marriage. Slowly, I began to meet him halfway, agreeing to a regular babysitter so we could go out on Friday nights. I exercised and lost some weight so I could get back into my old clothes. I flipped through glossy art magazines and began sketching again. I stopped reading Rafe's letters and made a conscious effort to push his memory out of my brain. And by the time Pris turned four years old, I felt as if our marriage was beginning to heal. We grew closer day by day and I had hope we were stitching back the loose threads to make us whole again. Even our lovemaking held the depth it had when we first fell in love. I was finally beginning to be truly happy again.

Until the day I found out Adam was having an affair.

CHAPTER TWENTY-SEVEN

Dev

Bailey had slept with Hawke last night.

And Dev was about to lose it.

The frustration and anger whipped up inside her, ready to explode, like she'd just swallowed a Mentos and washed it down with Coke. She'd heard her sister sneak in way past midnight, just like she had when she was young. Bailey couldn't be quiet if she tried. The rest of the night Dev spent tossing and turning and stewing.

Why was she so pissed about it?

They were both single. Both available. Both attractive. It would be weirder if they *didn't* have an attraction to someone on this vacation. Maybe she was a bit jealous because Hawke intrigued her, and it was yet another conquest her sister would never appreciate. But as the darkness ticked toward dawn, Dev realized it was much bigger than that.

She had issues with the entire way Bailey lived her life. And those choices all circled back to that one horrible act she'd done when they were teenagers. The one Dev still couldn't seem to get over.

But it was also about Hawke. Bailey was constantly leaving a trail of broken hearts behind. Dev liked Hawke, liked his directness, and she was afraid her sister would enchant him for the next two days, keep him on the hook long-distance, and then eventually dump him. Hell, what if she used Hawke as a way to amuse herself when she came here to visit? Didn't he deserve to know the full story of what was involved if he began an affair?

Normally, she'd explode before she had her coffee and call Bailey out, but this time, she tamped down her irritation and raw emotions, feeling the need to process what she was thinking. They ate breakfast together and Dev made a list of things they'd need to go to the beach. She even ignored Bailey's snark when she teased her about adding relaxation to her itinerary.

When there was a knock at the door, Bailey rushed to answer it. "Hawke, good morning."

"Morning." He looked alert and freshly showered in his floral shorts and white T-shirt, but she caught his solemn expression even from a distance. "Wanted to let you all know I spoke with my uncle."

Dev slid off the chair and walked over. "What did he say?"

"I'm sorry, but it wasn't him. We had a long talk, and he finally told me who the woman was he never got over. Her name was Marjorie. She wasn't American—she lived in Rome and they had an affair, but she married someone else. He didn't know your mother."

She shared a disappointed glance with her sisters. "Well, at least we narrowed the field down by two," Pris joked. "Only thousands more men to check out."

Hawke gave a sympathetic smile. "I promise to keep asking any of my friends if they heard anything. You may want to check the boat-tour companies. Didn't you say he ran a business?"

"It sounded like he did boat tours with his father, but we

didn't get a name, or even know if it was a business or temporary job," Dev said.

"Can't hurt to call some places and ask if there's anyone there whose name starts with R."

Dev studied him to see if he was mocking, but his face was serious. Her blood warmed at this relative stranger who'd begun to care about them enough to want to help. She glanced back and forth at him and Bailey, trying to catch that morning-after giddy vibe her sister usually exuded, but Hawke only radiated the same casual confidence he usually did. He didn't seem to need to touch Bailey or make googly eyes. Interesting.

"Well, I won't keep you from your beach day. You know how to get there?"

They all reassured him that they did. Bailey smiled but turned back toward the kitchen, going to refill her coffee, so Hawke left.

"Be right back," Dev said. "Save me the last cup."

On impulse, she ran after him. "Hawke?"

He stopped, staring down at her. "Dev?"

She couldn't help the tiny smile that curved her lips at his teasing tone. "Can I talk to you for a minute? I'll make it quick."

"No need to hurry. Come on in, I need another cup of coffee."

She followed him inside his house. Her gaze swept over the interior. She noted the colors were clean, he was organized—his kitchen had many interesting objects to stave off clutter—and the room smelled like him. Lucifer prowled over, rubbing against her leg and mewing. Hawke retrieved a full mug, then cocked a hip and looked down with surprise. "Huh. He usually doesn't do that. You two must've bonded over the rooftop incident."

She grinned and knelt down, giving him a stroke. "I seem to

understand cats. I like their directness and attitude. More interesting than dogs."

"Yes, they are," he murmured. When she raised her chin, she found him staring at her with that piercing gaze that made her a little wriggly, like she was getting a heat rash. Lord, she had to get herself back together. This was embarrassing—she'd come over to focus on Bailey. "Let's go outside. It's a beautiful morning."

Lucifer ran ahead and jumped on the chair cushion, settling into his space in the sun. Hawke placed his coffee on the porch railing, bracketing both palms on the thick beam. His muscled body looked as lean and graceful as the cat's. "What'd you want to talk about?"

Dev began to pace. "I wanted to warn you about something. Actually someone."

"Bailey?"

She jerked back at his calm answer. "Yes. You shouldn't get too attached. Bailey might not be who you think she is."

She fought back the prick of guilt and told herself she was just telling the truth. After all, Hawke deserved to know before he fell under her sister's spell and got hurt like all the other men she'd seen her sister leave in her wake. Dev waited for him to turn around, but he kept staring out toward the horizon. "Hmm. Who do you think she is?"

She hesitated at the odd question. Settling herself beside him, she surveyed the sprawl of colorful houses on the sloping hill; the slash of sun over the water, setting the glossy surface to a million sparkling blinks of light. She drew a deep breath of air into her lungs, enjoying the sharp scent of lemon and floral in the air. "I think she likes to play games with men. I also don't think she does it to hurt them on purpose. It's how she always was—men were just there, always attracted to her. Always falling over themselves to please her. She dislikes getting involved for too long, so be warned if you're looking for something deeper from her. Bailey doesn't do relationships."

Hawke didn't turn, challenge her statement, or act surprised. His quiet presence unsettled her. He seemed so unlike the type of man Bailey would fall for. Then again, they were in Italy, and it was just like her sister to engage in an affair with their next-door neighbor. The bitterness lingered, which only pissed her off more, because, God, when would she be done with it? How had Bailey managed to hurt her so deeply over a silly decision she said she regretted? Was Dev so damaged she couldn't recover from this one rejection?

Maybe she needed some damn therapy.

"It's an interesting theory," Hawke finally said, as if they were engaging in a philosophical discussion rather than a warning about how Bailey was apt to hurt him. "Thing is, I disagree. I think that's exactly what your sister wants you and everyone else to think."

Dev blinked. "Trust me, you just met her. I've known her for years. I'm not trying to be a bitch, I just want you to know what you're getting into. Honestly."

His mouth softened into a smile. "I know you're not a bitch, Dev. Actually, Bailey admires you the most."

A snort escaped. "Riiiight. Sorry to bust your bubble about sisterly love, but we're complete opposites. If it wasn't for blood, we'd probably never speak. She thinks I'm a stuck-up, anal-retentive control freak who sucks all the fun out of a room."

His brow arched. "Ouch. She used different words."

"I can't wait to hear."

"Said you were fiercely loyal, extremely intelligent, and braver than her or Pris. Explained how you go straight at an issue whenever problems come up. Also, that you underrate yourself."

It took a while to process his words. Dev shook her head,

stunned by her sister's description. "Okay, were you high when this was said, or was Bailey?"

Hawke didn't laugh. "Neither. I'm sorry, I just see the light in her eyes when she speaks your name. There's a regret there, and shame. I have no idea what happened with you two, but Bailey hasn't forgotten."

Her insides tightened. "How do you know all this? From spending the night with her?"

"By listening. We stayed up late and talked. Just talked. She opened up about your relationship. I hope you don't feel your privacy was invaded—it wasn't gossip. I think she needed to share."

All the breath left her lungs. "Did she tell you what happened between us?"

"No. Just that she made a decision that affected both of you. One she regrets every day."

Hearing those words from him shook her to the core. She wrapped her arms around her body to hug herself. All these years and it took a stranger to allow her to lift the barrier. To find out Bailey didn't just brush it off as Dev being overdramatic.

She leapt over that brick wall built inside herself and spoke her truth. "She betrayed me. I haven't been able to get over it. The thing is, to her it wasn't wrong. I believe she didn't think long enough about what she was doing to regret it."

He nodded. "Sounds fair. Hard to get over something so personal, especially with family we trust. I only sense Bailey doesn't avoid relationships or responsibility because she doesn't care. She cares too much. It screws her up inside and she hasn't found a way to process that yet."

Dev bit her lip. Considered. Sifted through his words. "Are you a shrink besides a financial mogul?"

His lower lip quirked. "Not even close. But I pay attention. I put myself into deep self-analysis after I left my job. I learned going into the abyss, even though it's uncomfortable, gives me something extremely valuable. The good stuff is the monsters in the closet."

She snorted. "I'll keep mine locked up, thank you very much."

He laughed then, and she smiled back. "Don't blame you. Took a while to get past my blocks, and I still have too many to count."

"Bad ones?"

She was teasing, but not completely. He interested her beyond his attractiveness and confidence. She liked how he seemed at peace with himself, but not in an annoying guru-type way.

"That's the thing about blocks. You tame them, and new ones crop up. Keeps life interesting."

She shook her head and the words popped out before she could stop them. "I just can't picture you with Bailey."

Oh shit.

Dev clapped her hand over her mouth and smothered a groan. Crazily enough, he began laughing again. "I'm so sorry, it's none of my business. I came with my warning, you gave me something to think about, and I'm going to shut up now."

"Don't want you to shut up." He treated her to a full, direct stare, and heat crawled under her skin, into her cheeks, throwing her off balance. "And I told you, Bailey and I aren't sleeping together. We're not the right fit. She knows it too. Just ask her."

"Oh, okay. I will. I mean, if she wants to talk about it." Lord help her, she was actually babbling. She had to get out of here. "Thanks for hearing me out. I better go."

"I'm interested in you, Dev."

She blinked. "Huh?"

The crooked grin charmed her. "I'm a bit fascinated with

you. I know you're here with your sisters, though, so I don't know how you feel about me taking you out. If you'd even be interested."

"Wait—you want to take me out?"

He frowned. "Why? Does that seem surprising? Do you have someone back in New York?"

"No! I mean, no, it's not that." She bit her lip and tried to act like she got asked out all the time by handsome, successful Italian men. Well, maybe she never got asked because she never noticed? She had a terrible way of focusing only on the path ahead of her, which was always work. Her voice sounded mournful, but she didn't try to deny it. "I'm leaving soon."

"I guess there's no way to extend your trip?"

Excitement rippled through her. What would it be like to blow up her schedule and date Hawke? Just cancel her ticket and forget about all the tasks she'd planned to accomplish this summer before her August class?

Was she crazy? She couldn't do that. It didn't make sense.

"I don't know if I could."

He nodded. "Understood. You have an important career—I respect the hell out of that. If you have time for dinner, lunch, a walk—anything—let me know?"

"Sure, thanks. I'd—I'd like that." They smiled at each other and the corniness struck her. What was happening? She began to walk backward, her legs a bit wobbly. "Gonna get back. Talk later?"

"Yes."

She returned to her house, mind spinning. Hawke liked her. Wanted to date her. And he hadn't slept with Bailey.

Why did it feel so . . . right? Like the moment she met him, they'd clicked in a certain way. He seemed to get her. She was brisk and too direct and not too flexible. She wasn't gorgeous like Pris or charming and captivating like Bailey. But he liked her. And it made her giddy.

Her head spun from his revelations. Not only about Bailey.

But herself.

Why would Bailey say that stuff about her? Did she mean it? Was it possible her sister truly did regret her actions because of the way it affected their relationship? She'd always waved it off and acted as if Dev was sensitive and overreacting, refusing to see her point of view. After a while, Dev had stopped listening and numbed out every aspect of her sister so she wouldn't get hurt again. Was it too late to try to heal them?

Because it would take an actual calm conversation. It would mean digging into the skeletons, and neither of them had ever been good at resurfacing the past.

And maybe it was time right now.

Her heart pounded, but she set her shoulders back, flung the door open, and threw the next words out like a general calling for battle. "Bailey!"

Her sister jumped and whirled around. The dish towel dropped from her fingers. "You scared me! What?"

"Why'd you sleep with the guy I loved?"

She analyzed the sheer shock in her sister's wide eyes. The way her mouth fell open like a guppy and she stared back, unable to talk—a pretty rare feat. Pris had a similar expression, her hands clenched together as if she was about to prep for war.

"Wh-what are you doing, Dev? You want to talk about this now?"

Dev nodded. "Yeah, I do. Right now."

Bailey pulled out a chair. The sound of wood dragging against tile was a loud squeak. She dropped into it, a bit unsteady, and finally met her gaze. Then nodded. "Okay, let's do this. I've said this a million times before, but it never seemed to make a difference. I didn't know you loved him. I didn't know he mattered so much to you or I never would've done it. I never meant to hurt you."

Dev had heard the words a million times before, but this time she was able to spot a bigger picture. "When did you ever hear me say I didn't love him?"

"After you broke up! We were in our room and you confessed you'd both decided to go your separate ways, and I asked if you were okay and you said you were fine because you had never loved him anyway! You said you were grateful it happened sooner rather than later. I can't believe you don't remember this!"

The images dragged her back, through the mud and slog of time, without the blurred edges of selective memory to cushion her fall. The lacy quilt. The purple pillows. The posters and candles and assorted trinkets crowding every white surface of her furniture. Sitting on the bed and telling Bailey about what happened. Acting brave and disdainful of her feelings while her insides shriveled in pain and the fear that she was unlovable—would always be less than her sisters. Her sister's passionate anger toward Liam, which Dev bravely waved off as if he was beneath her and meant nothing.

Lies. All lies to hide her true heart from her sister. Had she really not seen the truth?

"I did, but I didn't mean any of it. I was hurting, Bae. Dying inside of humiliation because he was the first guy I truly loved. Was I supposed to sob on your shoulder and rage against the unfairness? Was I supposed to fall apart and be weak, showing how he'd hurt me?"

Bailey gasped, a combination of incredulous confusion and fury. "Yes! Damn you, yes, I'm your sister and you were supposed to tell me the truth so I could comfort you!"

Pris stepped forward. "Guys, why don't we take a break for a bit and—"

"No, Pris." Dev's voice was completely calm as she faced her oldest sister. "This is between Bailey and me and long overdue. You can listen, but you can't play mediator."

She waited to see if Pris would argue, but her sister nodded and retreated, her back touching the wall.

"That's not me. It never was me. And I figured you knew I was putting on a brave face because I hated to cry and fall apart. That was your role, Bae."

The realization hit slowly. Bailey pressed her palm to her mouth, stifling a tiny cry. Her blue eyes filled with anguish. "Oh my God. I didn't think about it like that. I assumed you'd come to one of your rational conclusions that he was nothing special and moved on."

Yes, it made sense now. The fogginess cleared and what was left was not the absolute truth like she'd always believed. It was more neutral—a truth seen by both Bailey and herself from two different worlds. "Can you tell me again how it happened?"

Her sister's shoulders slumped. "I ran into him after a party. I ribbed him about you a bit, and he laughed it off, which, to me, only confirmed your story—that it wasn't a big deal. I'd been drinking, and he came on to me, and before I knew it, we were having sex." Misery etched her delicate features. "That's all it was—a one-night stand. I left and figured we'd never see each other again. I knew it was stupid and I was never going to tell you. But then he showed up at our house, and you walked in and everything blew up."

Her words died out into a pulsing silence. They'd never gotten this far before. Each time Bailey began to tell the story, the rage and pain twisted inside Dev so brutally, she lashed out, unable to hear once again how she was unworthy. So ridiculous how a man could hold such power over her thoughts, or seep into her most intimate relationships and change them.

"Did you want to sleep with him?"

Bailey jerked her head up and stared at her in confusion. "I guess so. I wouldn't have if I hadn't wanted to—it's not like he forced me, Dev. I won't lie to you."

"No, I know, I just wondered if it didn't mean anything, why do it in the first place? Because on some level, if you didn't tell me, you felt guilty about it."

She watched her sister's face with curiosity rather than the normal vicious blame. It was so much clearer to her now. How funny she could have such a revelation about her own way of looking at things along with her sister. Dev knew they'd always been different. What if they'd been able to truly talk about it? If Dev had been able to be honest about her emotions and take that risk to let her sister in? If Bailey had just stopped to really think about why she was doing it?

Different. Things would have been so different, but as with anything in life, could they have ever truly avoided the trajectory they were on? Would something else have thrown them a curveball, forcing them on a different path, leading to this exact moment when they might be finally able to forgive each other?

"I don't know," Bailey whispered.

"I didn't think so." She said the words gently, without any sting. "I should have told you how I loved him. How he made me feel worthless when we broke up. How I was always comparing myself to you and Pris and found myself lacking." She dragged in a breath. "Finding out you slept with Liam was the final straw. It was proof I was nothing next to you. Even worse, I believed you didn't care about me at all. You acted like I was overreacting."

Oh, it shamed her to admit that pain, but like a wound cleaned with alcohol, it burned fast, then bled clean.

"You can't be serious," Bailey said. "I was a mess. You were the one who had everything together. Mom was always telling me to be more like you or Pris. And the reason I became so bitchy toward you even though I should've begged for your forgiveness? It's what you said."

"What'd I say?"

"That I wasn't your sister anymore."

Her voice was tinged with raw pain. The truth hit her full force, causing her to step back as if slapped. Yes, she'd said it. Meant it at the time, thinking Bailey would laugh it off like she did everything else. But there in her sister's eyes, she saw the fear, the rejection, and the anguish.

"I didn't mean it, Bae. I swear, I didn't."

Bailey swept at her leaky eyes, sniffing. "My head knows it. But the way you looked at me with such hatred? I thought maybe you were telling the truth. And after that, everything changed. You never really spoke to me again—not in the way you used to."

"You're my sister," she said fiercely. "Always." Bailey nodded. "I'm so glad we're finally talking about this, but it leads to something else. I want to talk about Hawke."

"What does Hawke have to do with anything?" A bit of heat crept back into her gaze. "Are you going to ask if we slept together? Are you still judging me on this stuff?"

"I went to speak with Hawke just now. He told me you didn't sleep together, but I want to know why. Because you made a proactive decision not to? Because it wasn't the right time? Or because he rejected you? It's important I know why, Bae."

Pris looked confused as she glanced back and forth. "What does it matter if Bailey sleeps with Hawke? They're both single. Am I missing something?"

"Exactly," Bailey said fiercely. "I hate the way you try to

make me feel ashamed over my choices. It's messed up. I'd never butt into your love life or judge your decision to sleep with a guy or not! I cannot believe you went to speak with him about me—that is so . . . uncool!"

Frustration coiled inside Dev, squeezed with a slow-building tension that suddenly erupted in a desperation to get her sister to finally see what she was doing. "Oh my God, it's not about sex or your female prerogative to have it! It's not even about Hawke. This is how you solve every problem, Bae—with men. Can't you see it? Aren't you exhausted from hopping in and out of encounters and pretending none of them touched you? Don't you know why it's always your go-to?"

It was the first time Dev spotted real uncertainty in her sister's clear blue eyes. She jumped up from the chair and stepped back as if fearful of being attacked, but Dev stood rooted to the spot, the lash of her tongue reaching beyond her sister's retreat. "I'll tell you. You think you're this seeker, and open to the world in any form, but you're more scared of love and attachments then me and Pris together. You have this habit of moving to a new place, getting a job, and immediately focusing on some guy, all the while telling yourself it means nothing. But you're lying."

"You have no idea what you're talking about." Bailey began to pant, shaking her head wildly. "I give my full self to whoever I'm with at the time, but I never feel the need to stay. I'm happier moving forward, seeking a new experience, a new relationship. Why is that wrong?"

The white-hot anger began to dull as she stared at her younger sister. God, she really believed it—believed she had this wandering spirit that was above them all. Above her own heart. "It's not that it's wrong; it's just not true," she finally said. "Why did you really sleep with my boyfriend, Bae? You said it meant nothing, right? It was just sex, and you didn't realize it would affect me."

Her face paled. "I thought we just talked about that and we were good. I thought—"

"No, we are good. I know you believed that, and it made all the difference. I swear, I've forgiven you, and hope you forgive me for cutting you out of my life. But did you ever really think about why it was so easy? You didn't even really want him. I've watched you. You sail into a room, and within the space of one conversation, you decide if you want to have an affair. You set up the terms before they even know what's going on in your head. And you set up the goodbyes, usually by moving to another job, another place, with another excuse."

Pris stayed silent, but it wasn't with horror. She seemed to grow more thoughtful as she stared at Bailey, and pieces seemed to slide together to make a full picture.

"No," Bailey said. But her voice had weakened. Doubt flared in her eyes.

Dev stepped toward her, but it wasn't in warning. It was in support. "We've started to dig deeper—all of us. Stuff is coming up and it's been uncomfortable. Is Hawke a distraction for you? Are you really attracted to him? Do you have any feelings for him? Or is he just convenient to keep avoiding your shit?"

Pris rubbed her head. "We need wine. I'm getting wine." Her footsteps clattered over the tile floor as she yanked open the refrigerator and poured three glasses of white, not seeming to care that it wasn't even noon.

Dev prepared for her sister's hot objections, or defense. She didn't blame her either. There were so many patterns of behavior from all of them that couldn't be solved within one conversation or one week in Italy.

Pris handed Bailey a glass and she sipped, fingers shaking around the stem. Then she met Dev's gaze dead on. "I was completely neutral on sleeping with him. Hawke rejected me, and we ended up talking all night. Later on, I was so relieved, because I realized I'd never wanted to have sex with him in the first place. I wanted . . . connection. I just didn't understand how to get it."

Pris dropped in the chair next to her, squeezed her hand, and took a gulp of her own wine. "I get it. Physical stuff is so much easier in some ways. It's like going halfway, but keeping the most important parts locked up and safe. I spoke with Garrett last night. Told him the truth. I don't know how to fix it, but for the first time, I feel like I'm really here and not just a ghost of myself. I like it."

Dev took the third chair, drank her wine, and glanced at her sisters. "Hawke wants to take me on a date."

Bailey and Pris gasped. "Oh my God," Bailey shrieked. "That's so romantic! I swear, I kept thinking about how similar you two were."

"Even as you planned to sleep with him?" Dev asked with a teasing grin.

Bailey punched her arm. "Stop, I told you I didn't really want to. Thank God he had the hots for you instead. What are you going to do? We're leaving in two days."

"I want to stay," Pris announced.

Dev stared at Pris in astonishment. "You what?"

"I want to stay." Stubbornness carved out the lines of her face. Her eyes snapped with a fire Dev rarely caught. "I need more time to figure things out. Think. Walk. Sit in the sun or sail on a boat and be close to Mom. And I want you both to stay with me, because I think we need the time too, more than anything."

Dev gave a half laugh. "That's crazy. We have stuff to go back to. I'm teaching this huge course in August and have all this prep to do. We already have tickets."

"We change them," Pris said. "We choose us for once and know it will all be waiting for us when we get back. I don't know what happened here with Mom and this man she loved, but I'm starting to believe it was more than just a physical affair. It went deeper. And I still don't think she cheated on Dad, but there's something about being in this house together. It makes me feel . . . stronger. More me. I just know I like who I am when I'm here, and I need a little more time."

Bailey shook her head and finished her wine. "This is crazy," she muttered. "But yeah, I'm in. God knows, after this morning I feel like I need a week just to recover."

Pris laughed and turned to her. "Please, Dev," she pleaded, tightening her grip. "I know this is hardest on you. But you can do some work here, and see Hawke, and we can build on what we've done with each other. I love you. I hate the way it's been between us, and I hate that I didn't fight to mend things. I just pushed our problems aside and pretended there was nothing to do, but I was wrong. Let's fix this now. I want my sisters back."

Dev groaned and rubbed her temples. Bailey and Pris stared at her like matching puppy dogs. Already on overload from the emotional upheavals, her heart was achy and tender, and her brain was shutting down from too much sensory overload.

So she looked into her gut.

And found the answer.

"I'll stay," she said. "But I'm not promising you any more of these touchy-feely sessions. And I get to plan the agenda for the rest of the trip without any bitching."

Her sisters shrieked and laughed and hugged her, promising her they would do as she said.

As soon as they settled, Dev got on the phone with the airlines to get the best price change possible.

CHAPTER TWENTY-EIGHT

Olivia

Looking back, I kept wondering how different things would have been if I hadn't surprised my husband for lunch that day.

It's funny how one decision sets off a firestorm of effects that can change a course forever. If we hadn't taken that shortcut. If we hadn't picked up that phone call. If we hadn't gone to that party. I realized I could spend all my time analyzing how it would have all worked out differently if I hadn't hidden in his office to surprise him with a picnic lunch while Pris was in pre-K. If his secretary hadn't been away from her desk and unable to warn him.

If Adam hadn't come into his office with that woman, shut the door, and kissed her while I stupidly watched from his desk chair.

The fallout was movie-worthy. The shocked wife. The beautiful mistress. The begging, apologetic husband.

The rest of the day followed the script. Adam swore he didn't love her, that when we were having problems he'd been weak and fell into the affair. He'd been trying to break it off, but she kept pursuing, hinting that she'd tell me if he didn't continue. I listened, numb to his excuses, only thinking about how if he'd lied so easily to me once, how many times had he done it before. Wondering what I was going to do about Pris.

I threw him out of the house and spent the next few days crying and mourning the loss of trust in my marriage. The bigger obstacle was what came next. Could I forgive? Did I want to try to save what we had? I'd believed things were better between us, but now I questioned every one of Adam's actions.

The world I'd built had been ripped apart, and suddenly I wondered who I was anymore. The quiet, reflective girl of my youth? The dynamic, thriving career woman caught in the excitement of change? The doting mother whose love for her child was her only focus?

Or someone new? Someone not yet formed from the ashes of grief and my husband's decision to cheat?

Maybe my next action was wrong, but I did it anyway. I called my aunt Silvia and asked if I could stay in her home for a little while. When she agreed, I made arrangements to bring Pris to my mom's. Then I told my husband I needed some time alone to figure out what I wanted and that I was going to Italy.

I ignored his pleas for forgiveness and vows he'd broken up with her. At this point, I realized saving our marriage was bigger than his cheating and had nothing to do with him.

It had to do with me and my decision to move forward. Or not.

Two days later, I arrived in Positano, on a rainy May afternoon. I dragged my lone suitcase up the familiar stairs, my gaze hungrily roving over the spill of colored homes, the sloping hillside, the sparkle of the sea as it grew smaller with every step ascended.

The cottage welcomed me with a rush of happy memories. I

imagined Aunt Silvia flitting around as she got dressed for the evening, the blinding sunset sweater wrapped over her shoulders, a cloud of rich perfume floating in the air, and her throaty laughter echoing through the rooms. I walked into the garden, the rain misty on my face, and breathed in the scent of earth and lemons and sweet bougainvillea. The colored petals were blooming in a tangle of lushness. The quiet dimness of the day settled around me, a touch of melancholy making me sigh.

This was the place where it began. And yet, it was all still wrapped up in Rafe. I hadn't written to him about my plans to come to Italy. Half of me was hoping to be strong enough not to contact him and to allow him his own life and privacy. I didn't even know if he'd want to see me after the way I broke it off, and I didn't blame him. For now, I'd be here in Positano alone. I'd figure out if my marriage was worth fighting for. I'd decide who I wanted to be in this next phase of my life on my own terms.

I walked back into the house and softly closed the door behind me.

CHAPTER TWENTY-NINE

Bailey

They walked past the beach and toward the small hut-like buildings that housed the ferry office and various boat companies offering tours. After calling every company listed that employed anyone of a certain age who had a name beginning with *R*, they found two possibilities. Arranging to meet both prospective candidates, she and her sisters were disappointed again. One man was decades too young, and the other was a cranky old man who believed Americans ruined his homeland and shooed them out with a litany of creative curse words.

If he *had* been Mom's mysterious lover, they agreed it was better to never know. No way Mom could fall for such a bitter grump. Plus, she was American.

Research complete, they settled on a group outing to the Grotte di Suppraiano in Praiano. Pris had been stuck on the Blue Grotto in Capri, but Hawke had mentioned the Grotte di Suppraiano would be less crowded and was just as beautiful. They also had the opportunity to swim in if they chose. Bailey loved the idea of having such total freedom in a mystical place but decided to stick with the boat. Her sisters agreed.

After the drama of the previous morning, Dev's planned trip to Fornillo beach was exactly what they needed. They'd lounged under red-and-green-striped umbrellas, sipping icy lemon cocktails as they overlooked the rippling blue water. The small pebbled beach was half as crowded as the main one, perched at the bottom of a plunging cliff—the reward for the long snaking hike downward. The water was cool and salty. They'd waded in to their ankles, discovering the steep decline of the sea floor as they were suddenly plunged in past the shoulders. Bailey and her sisters spent the afternoon lazing in the sun, people watching, and eating delicious salads and sparkling wine from the Hotel Pupetto.

Today, they were back to Dev's sightseeing agenda.

A young man named Paolo greeted them at the shore. He had deep olive skin, a mop of chocolate-brown curls, and dark eyes filled with a zest Bailey immediately appreciated. He flirted respectfully, lavishing them with compliments Bailey soaked up as her due, being in Italy, and got them settled in. There were only two other groups with them—a family with two kids, and an older husband and wife with lovely British accents.

Bailey got comfortable in her seat and dragged in a deep breath of sea air. So much had happened within the past twenty-four hours. She still felt unbalanced since the confrontation with Dev. After all these years, she had her sisters back. For real, this time.

But it had come at a cost.

The truth Dev had hit her with took its toll. Learning she might have been slipping in and out of affairs without true intent bothered her. Her foundation had shifted, and she was beginning to question all those previous decisions she'd once been so sure of. At first, she'd waved off the accusations even as she intended to own them in front of Dev. Hearing she was loved, and forgiven, was huge, and she had no intention of screwing it up by protesting Dev's opinion.

Until she went over the evening with Hawke.

And realized Dev might have been right.

Why had she so distantly analyzed engaging in an affair with him? Yes, she'd catalogued his attractiveness and the fun factor of an overseas affair. Hell, most women didn't pull apart every intention when passion was involved.

But it wasn't passion that had led her forward. It was more of a habit—a routine she engaged in when a man seemed interested. When was the last time she truly felt as if she could fall in love? Was she lying to herself by pretending to let life flow without controlling it, when all the while she was keeping herself in a tightly locked box?

She watched as the boat pulled away and cut through the azure-blue water. Paolo spoke over a microphone, but she allowed her mind to keep drifting, caught up in the beauty of the rocky cliffs and colorful houses. Bailey had always believed she'd discovered the true secret to life—unattachment. It never bothered her. She never felt lonely or like something was missing. Drifting from job to job, place to place, man to man, all seemed like part of her adventure. She never questioned it.

Until now.

Underneath the perfect glossy surface of her life lay some serious scratches and nicks. Some from her childhood. Some from the divorce. Others from her sisters—those ones were starting to heal.

But Bailey hated fear, so she'd begun to dig a bit deeper, and she realized the last time she'd truly felt closest to happy in a relationship was with Will. She kept going back to that night when they made love and he asked her to come back soon. Her heart wanted to say yes, but she believed her freedom was more important than any relationship. She'd convinced herself it was her duty to walk. To flee now and pull the Band-Aid off quickly. To limit the pain she'd give to him when she did leave him. One day.

Will was still texting her. She figured he'd get tired of being dissed and move on to another actress to do her play. Instead, he sent her silly little memes about Italy, random quotes of Shakespearean poetry, and musings about his day in the classroom. He'd taken a part-time gig at SUNY New Paltz teaching intro to theater. She enjoyed the way he saw the kids who were passionate about their art and wanted to dive deep. Will had more layers than she'd imagined. Or maybe, more specifically, than she'd wanted to explore.

But now she was questioning herself. Had she really wanted to break up with him? Besides a physical attraction, they'd formed a deep bond, through both their similar lifestyles and their passion for creative pursuits. His conversation kept her engaged. He embraced who she was and didn't try to change her.

So, why had she left?

Bailey didn't have an answer. But it spoke of the larger question Dev had posed. And maybe it was time to figure out what she really wanted.

"You okay?" Dev asked, bumping her shoulder lightly.

She turned and smiled. "Yeah, just daydreaming. The sun and the water are relaxing."

"I know. The last time I reached this type of relaxation was color-coding the cans in my pantry. Extremely satisfying."

Bailey laughed. "Well, this may not beat it, but I'm sure it's a close second."

"Are you mad at me? For what I said yesterday?"

Startled, she swiveled her head to meet her sister's light brown gaze. Dev would have never asked such a question before. The fact she even thought to check brought a strange sting to Bailey's eyes. "No. It gave me a lot to think about. I just don't want to fight with you anymore."

"Me either. How about when we feel the habitual urge to tear each other apart, we go for Pris instead?"

"Deal."

Twin smacks on the backs of their hands hit at the same time. "I don't need either of your shit," Pris muttered.

"Damn ballerina strength," Bailey said, rubbing the sore spot. But they were all giggling by the time Paolo announced their arrival at the caves.

"There is a short lineup today," Paolo said, his deep lilting voice pouring into the mic. "We picked the perfect time to visit, as the sunlight will be hitting full force. This allows us the opportunity to see the unique emerald green of the water. We will stop for photo opportunities for everyone."

"Oh, look at the kayaks," Pris said, pointing to the group entering the cave and disappearing through the large mouth. "Paolo, do you need to be a strong swimmer to do this?" she asked.

"*Sì, signorina*," he said. "There can be strong tides, so I always recommend taking a boat unless you have had good swimming experience. There are two natural caves accessible from Marina di Praia—a village beach surrounded by rock walls. The other one is Africana Grotto, also quite beautiful. Many tourists stay at the Maria Pia and can walk down straight from their rooms. Amazing, *sì*?"

Paolo continued sharing a variety of interesting information, and then it was their turn. The small boat glided into the opening, and they were swallowed into a surrounding rocky wall. A strange energy seemed to shimmer in the air, and even the kids remained quiet, as if to decipher what was happening. The water glowed in a myriad of colors, exploding her vision with rich emeralds and turquoise in tiny bursts of color. A distant hum, maybe the wind, vibrated through the space.

Bailey reached over the side of the boat and dipped her hand in the water. It closed around her skin in silky smoothness, and she thought of her mother, picturing her face. Had she experienced this same moment so many years ago? Had she tried to swim in, her lover by her side? Had she felt the same way Bailey did, surrendering to the power and beauty of nature, yet overwhelmed by an unknown future that yielded no promises?

A tingle ran down her spine. The air seemed to sigh with her mother's voice, and Bailey smiled, reminding herself it didn't matter. Her mother had had her own experience, one Bailey would never share. But right now, she felt closest to Mom, as if her hand was holding Bailey's as sweetly as the water.

Paolo spoke in low tones, filling in some historical details, then paused the boat by the opening so everyone could take their pictures. "Would you take one for us?" Pris asked, handing him the camera.

He smiled, flashing white teeth, and Pris put her head in between Bailey's and Dev's shoulders. He snapped the picture. "*Perfetto.*"

When they exited, the kids began to chatter excitedly. Dev shook her head. "That was all sorts of amazing. Isn't it odd how a simple cave can suddenly affect your outlook on life?"

Bailey blinked. "I was thinking the same kind of stuff. And about Mom."

"I was thinking about Mom too," Dev said.

Pris thrust the camera between them. Her hands shook a bit. "Um, guys? Look at this."

"Oh, our picture came out great," Bailey said. The three of them were smiling happily, the sun catching the gleam of colors on the water.

"I felt like Mom was there with us," Pris said slowly. "Which is cool, since that's what we were all thinking. But do you see it?"

Bailey squinted at the photo. "See what?"

Pris traced her finger along an outline. "This shadow? Right behind us?"

It took a few seconds, but then Bailey gasped. Goose bumps broke out over her skin and she stared in both shock and fascination as the shadow suddenly seemed to have the shape of a person—clearly a head hovering right above them.

Dev's jaw dropped. "It's Mom."

"Is that crazy?" Pris whispered, hand still twitching. "I mean, that's crazy, right?"

"No," Bailey said. The acceptance washed over her and a smile tipped her lips. "It's not crazy. Mom was there with us. I felt her."

"So did I," Pris said. "But you know I'm not into that stuff."

"Neither am I," Dev said. "But this time, I'm agreeing. And I don't want to ruin it by overthinking either."

"Neither do I," Bailey said softly. She reached out and put a hand over her sisters'. A surge of happiness caught her full force, and she swore right then and there, she'd never take their relationship for granted again. Her sisters might be pains in the ass but they were hers. And somehow, Mom thought it was time they all knew she was looking over them.

They spent the next hour exploring various sites along the sea. Paolo kept them entertained with facts and fun stories, and they took a ton of pictures, each one more stunning than the last. When they finally pulled back into Spiaggia Grande, Bailey was ready for a big lunch and some serious wine. They tipped Paolo generously and chatted a bit.

"It was a pleasure having you ladies today," he said, dark eyes gleaming with appreciation. "What hotel are you staying at?"

"We actually have a place here. Our mom passed it down to us," Pris said.

"Many of our homes here have been from many generations," Paolo said with a smile. "It is nice to keep a part of our families with us, *sì*?"

Bailey nodded. "It is. You did a wonderful job. Have you been working with tour groups a long time?"

"*Sì*, my *papà* and his *papà* always had worked on boats, and now I run it with my brothers. I'm off to the university in the fall, though. I wanted to stay, but Papà insists I get a degree first before I decide. I'm studying business."

Bailey liked his energy and openness. He seemed so young for the way he looked at things, though, unless it was the culture. Americans just didn't speak about respecting family in the same way.

"How old are you?" Dev asked.

Bailey wanted to roll her eyes at Dev's direct questioning, but she was curious, too.

"Twenty-two." His gaze locked on Bailey. "And you?"

She laughed. "Thirty-two."

"A perfect age gap. How long are you staying, Bailey?" His rich voice hinted at obvious interest.

She ignored her sisters, who practically tittered over the attention. "Another week."

"I'd be happy to take you out on another boat ride. On the

house." He slid his card into her palm with a smoothness that she appreciated. "Or take you to dinner on land."

Oh, he was deliciously handsome, charming, and . . . young. A bit too young. "*Grazie.*"

"*Prego.* Call anytime, *signorina bella. Ciao*, Priscilla. Devon."

He shot them all another dazzling smile, then retreated to his boat. Bailey walked away, her mind already calculating the possibility of going out with him just for his company. A date was nothing. And though he might be young, she was only here for a week more. One night of passion in Italy wasn't a crime, and . . .

What was she doing?

She stopped walking. A strange despair shot through her, mixed with confusion.

"What's the matter?" Pris asked.

Dev was still walking, her tone teasing. "*Dayum*, if he looks like that, what about his brothers? Well, there goes another hot man falling at your feet, Bae. Must get so exhausting collecting phone numbers and deciding who's worthy and—" She stopped, cocking her head with worry. "Hey, what's up? Why do you look like that?"

Bailey swayed on her feet. "Because for the first time, I realize I'm doing the exact thing you accused me of. Rationally reviewing the benefits and drawbacks of sleeping with him. Or dating him. It's like there's this host voice in my head from one of those game shows, droning on about all the possibilities, but I feel . . ."

"How do you feel?" Dev prodded.

"I feel detached. Oh my God, I think something's seriously wrong with me."

Her sisters walked over and flanked her. "Do you always feel like that with every man you meet?" Pris asked. "Or are you just starting to notice when you're *not* connected?"

Bailey sifted through the past, thinking over the various men she'd dated and gotten involved with. "I didn't feel that way with Will," she finally said. "There was this spark right away, and it only got stronger when we had a conversation."

Dev nodded. "Okay, so it's not all the time. That means you're able to discern if there's truly interest or you're just switched off but going on autopilot."

Her sister's logic made her snort. "Did you see Paolo, guys? I'd be dead not to be attracted."

"Bae, you can be attracted to someone or appreciate them without wanting to jump into a date. Don't you know that?" Pris asked.

"Not really. I guess I feel I need to give every guy a chance if he asks."

Dev blinked. "Um, yeah, that's exhausting, dude. No wonder you're all mixed up. Being free with the universe and opportunities is one thing. Dating every guy who shows an interest is another level. *Jumanji* level."

Pris giggled. "Paolo hit all my buttons, but I don't feel the need to explore it."

"You're married!" Bailey said. "I'm single."

"So what? You know what you need? An intervention," Dev said briskly. "From now on, the next four men who hit on you or ask you out, you say this word: *NO.*"

"Just *no*? What if there may be a potential for something great?"

"Then he'll keep asking and you can say yes on the fifth time," Dev said.

Pris sighed. "Dev's right. Just say no. You need to give yourself permission to be okay with yourself for not jumping at every opportunity. I don't think I realized you put such pressure on yourself, Bae."

"Which is another reason you get involved with men who are easy to leave," Dev added.

"Is Will that theater guy?" Pris asked. "You mentioned him once or twice. When did you break up?"

Bailey nibbled at her lip and began walking again. "Right before I came here."

"Why?" Dev asked.

"I thought it was time. I was afraid he was getting too attached."

Dev made a noise under her breath. "Him? Or you? Man, Dad did a number on you too, huh?"

"I have no issues with Dad," Bailey said in surprise. "I'm not like you guys. I forgave him."

"Forgive, sure. But his actions got into your psyche and may have made you question what's real and what's not. You were little during the divorce, Bae, but it still affected you."

She stared at Dev. The words were brisk and honest, delivered in her usual no-nonsense tone. But the easy acceptance of them gave her the permission to ponder the idea. She hated tossing any blame around to Mom or Dad. Bailey believed each individual has her own choice on how to live. But maybe ignoring it and forging forward left some remnants behind that she hadn't dealt with.

"I never really thought about it," she said faintly. "I hate people who think everyone else is the problem."

"That will never be you," Pris said. "But it's time you gave yourself a break." She dragged in a breath. "Maybe it's time we all do."

They walked in silence, letting the gorgeous scenery soothe

them. Mega-yachts perched behind them and littered the shoreline. They began the steep incline of steps, and suddenly Pris turned, her face filled with excitement.

"Let's go out tonight."

Bailey raised a brow. "We go out every night."

"No, I mean, let's go party! Let's go dancing! They have this fabulous club called Music on the Rocks—it sounds really cool, and things have been so intense lately. I think we all need a break to have some fun."

"I had fun on this tour," Dev said with a bit of defensiveness.

Bailey smiled. Pris got so excited when she was amped up to do something she believed was a bit naughty. "I'm in. I agree, let's get our groove on."

Dev sighed. "Fine, I'll go. But I didn't bring anything sexy or clubby with me."

"We have time to shop right after lunch," Pris said firmly, more bounce in her step as they climbed. "Why don't you invite Hawke?"

"Huh? You think he'd want to come to a club?" she asked doubtfully.

"Duh, yes, he'd probably love to go dancing with you, idiot," Bailey said fondly. "Ask him."

"I don't want him to intrude on our time," she said slowly. "I told him I'd be careful about that."

Affection surged through her at Dev's uncomfortable expression. This was new to them all, trying to honor one another without walking on eggshells. She figured it'd get easier with time and more natural. For now, she was grateful Dev cared enough. "Let's do dinner together and Hawke can meet us at the club," Bailey offered. "A perfect compromise."

"Agreed," Pris chimed in.

Dev nodded. "Okay, I'll ask him."

Bailey enjoyed the look on her sister's face. She'd rarely seen Dev interested in a man—her sister preferred to hide behind a stoic facade—but right now, it was obvious she was both nervous and excited.

They were all stretching themselves in different directions.

Bailey hoped they'd all end up in a better place when they finally left, but the trip wasn't over, and she knew fate had a wicked sense of humor.

For now, she'd wait. Think a bit. And dance.

CHAPTER THIRTY

Olivia

I was in Positano for two whole days before I went to see Rafe.

I'd tried. But being here, so close to him and the memories of us, was too much to overcome. I'd avoided the main beach and boats in favor of long walks, quiet moments in the cafés, and browsing through the shops. I sat in the garden and sketched. I thought.

Yet, every hour spent here only led to my feet walking the path to his front door. Hands trembling, heart beating wildly in my chest, I knocked early that evening and waited. Prepared to greet his wife and children. His dad. A close friend or a woman he was dating. Anyone but the man who answered the door.

"Livia?"

His voice held the familiar lilt as he said my name. Shock reflected from his face, and I took the moment to greedily devour his presence. God, he hadn't changed. Yes, he was older, but age only added to the full power of his presence. His muscles seemed leaner, the creases around his eyes and mouth more pronounced. Chocolate-brown curls still flopped over his brow in an unkempt mess that made my fingers tingle; I ached to run them through the strands. But it was his eyes that drew me in, captivated, and held me prisoner.

Dark, and deep, with a sooty blackness that both welcomed and blamed me. I held my breath as we stared at each other, caught up in another time and place, and my throat tightened with emotion.

"Rafe. I'm . . . sorry. Sorry I didn't write and tell you I was coming. And I wasn't going to. I knew I shouldn't. I'm only here for a week, and I was going to leave you alone, but I just . . . couldn't." My words were mangled, and suddenly it was too much. What was I doing? Torturing us both with what-ifs and rubbing salt in a wound? I had to get out of here.

A half sob tore from my lips as I turned. "I'm sorry. I shouldn't be here. I have to go—"

"Livia. Wait." His hand shot out and grasped my wrist. The immediate contact sent chills and burns up my arm, and I knew then it hadn't been a lovely fantasy or a dream from a young girl. The connection was there between us, flaring bright and wild, dragging me back.

Slowly, I turned.

A warm smile curved his full lips, and joy gleamed in his eyes as he looked at me. "Stay."

I'm not sure who moved first. I ended up wrapped in his embrace, those strong arms around me, my cheek against the soft cotton of his shirt.

And I felt like I had come home.

CHAPTER THIRTY-ONE

Dev

When they walked into the club, Dev tried to ignore the flutters in her belly when she caught sight of Hawke.

She'd been ridiculously happy when he quickly accepted her invite. Now her gaze ate up the sheer yumminess of his quiet masculinity, even surrounded by flashing lights, gyrating bodies, and the edgy vibe of the crowd. The simple jeans, snug black button-down, and shiny leather shoes only added to his persona of a man who knew who he was. She found herself drawn like a lightning bolt to a socket, gliding across the floor to stand in front of him.

"Hi."

His lower lip tugged. He shifted his weight as he gazed down at her with piercing gray eyes. "Hi. How was dinner?"

"Amazing. We went to Zass. There was an opera singer who sang like she was from the Met and I had stuff I couldn't pronounce but it ended up being amazing pasta with squid. The view was spectacular."

"Sounds perfect. I can't wait to hear about your day and the boat tour."

"I can't wait to tell you." She laughed a bit self-consciously. "I need to dance off some calories. I think Pris is tipsy already." She jerked her head toward her giggling sister, who was pointing at them in true juvenile manner.

Hawke grinned. "Zass also has a great wine list. Can't blame her. I'll keep looking for an open seat, but for now, can I grab you a cocktail?"

"A round of water for all of us, please. I think we all need some hydration."

"Got it. Be right back."

He cut easily through the crowd and to the bar and seemed to get the bartender's attention quickly. She shook her head as Pris and Bailey came over. "Hawke's getting us some water. We don't want to get sick."

Pris was already swaying back and forth to the pumping beat. "I want a piña colada!"

Bailey pressed her lips together. Pris turned into party-girl central when she drank, which was usually a crack-up, but Dev had to make sure she was safe. "After you drink your water, we'll get you one. With a paper umbrella and everything."

"Oh, good. A pink one! Bae, let's dance."

"But I— Oops, here we go." Bailey hurried after Pris, who'd already pressed herself into the cluster of dancers and immediately picked up the rhythm. Ballet had made her a fantastic dancer. She was able to hear the beat and coordinate every step into this fluid movement of body and sound. Dev watched them with a touch of envy. She was a terrible dancer—way too in her head.

Hawke appeared by her side carrying the waters. "Follow me. Saw a guy at the bar who's leaving and we can grab his table."

They scored two deep blue cushioned chairs outside. Dev

studied the amazing club, which was set in an actual cave and boasted an open air structure—no windows separated the inside from the outside. Poised on the edge of the cliffs, the spread of rocks, sea, and sky unveiled before her in spectacular glory. She should've known even a club would be different here—more of an experience than a simple evening out.

She caught sight of Pris and Bailey wriggling their hips to the beat. The music mixed with the distant roar of the waves. "Do you want to join them? I'll man the chairs."

"A little later. I just want to settle in for now."

"You look great."

His compliment was uttered with a sincerity that made her heart squeeze. It had been so long since a man had looked at her like that. Pris had discovered the short black dress in one of the shops and immediately shoved it at Dev. The slinky fabric skimmed over her body like a hug; a touch of shimmer shot through the threads. "Thanks. What'd you do today?"

He took a sip of his own water and pondered. "Work. I had a client who needed babysitting. Afterward, I took a walk, then a nap with Lucifer."

She studied the lines of his face, the thrust of his jaw, the shadow of stubble. "Do you nap often?"

"Only on weekdays," he said seriously.

"Did you make your client happy?"

His brow creased. "For today. He'll be unhappy tomorrow."

"Does that bother you?"

"It used to. Not anymore. I've found ways to remind myself it's not about me personally. It's about the profit, but as much as I want to trick myself into believing I can magically guarantee a perfect retirement, I can't. I can only go with my gut, my instincts, and my experience. For some it's enough. For the others, we're not meant to work together."

She blew out a huff of air. "How do you manage, though? Does your company just allow you to have this casual attitude? It's another reason I'm concerned about leaving academia. I don't want to jump from a limited career into a world that values stress as a badge. I feel like I'm always teetering on the line of workaholic to begin with."

"I was on that path for a long time. But I don't regret it—I needed to experience that type of world in order to know I didn't want it. I think you're damn smart, Dev, and you know what you want when you see it."

"And if I make a huge mistake? Mess everything up?"

He leaned forward and caressed her cheek. His touch was warm and gave her tingles. "You try something else. Fix the mess. But you have to love the work. You'd hate that corner office with a cushy title if you weren't in the trenches."

"How do you know so much about me?"

Her heart beat so hard she wondered if he heard. "It's weird, but I feel like we've known each other before. We seem to . . . fit somehow." He dropped his finger and gave a half laugh. "Wow, I'm not going to be surprised if you make a quick exit. I sound like a nutcase."

"No, you don't. You just said the truth. That'll never scare me away."

He leaned forward as if he were about to kiss her.

Pris screeched her name and dropped into the space between them. "Do you have my piña colada?"

Dev laughed and handed her the glass. "Drink this first. Isn't this place incredible?"

"I'm obsessed," Bailey said, draining her own cup. "Hey, why don't you guys go dance while we hold down the fort?"

"Oh, I think we're good."

Hawke stood up and held out his hand. "I think we both need to lose some excess energy. What do you think, Dev?"

All her shyness about being a bad dancer faded away. After all, did she really care? She was with an interesting, gorgeous man at a club in Italy. So, she sucked. Dev doubted he—or anyone else on the floor—would notice. She reached out, and his grip was warm and strong around her fingers. "Let's do it."

They danced. They lost their seats, but it didn't matter, because the music kept luring them back, along with the energy of the crowd, the gorgeous view, the echo of waves hitting rocks, the sultry night air beckoning them to lose control just this once.

Dev did.

They made their way back hours later. Hawke led them home, and even though her ears had a slight ring in them, she felt light and airy inside, like there were all these lovely spaces where before it had been cramped and tight. They broke into a rendition of "That's Amore," singing at the top of their lungs, collapsing into giggles when Pris's voice cracked on the high notes and Dev repeated the same line twice.

When they reached the cottage, Bailey and Pris went inside and left Dev and Hawke outside alone.

"Thank you for inviting me with you tonight," he said.

"Thanks for coming." Dev was tipsy but not drunk. She knew she wanted things, but she was the careful sort. But tonight, with a sky full of stars, daring buzzed in her blood. "Hawke?"

"Yes?"

"I really like you."

He didn't laugh. Just leaned forward, his breath a sweet rush over her lips. "I really like you."

"And I'm thinking I'd really, really like to kiss you."

"Dev?"

"Yeah?"

"That's the exact same thing I was thinking."

And then he kissed her. She looped her arms around his neck, and pressed her body against his, and fell into kissing him. Slow and sweet, lazy and thorough; there was no rush and no sense of time. No ending or beginning. Just her and Hawke wrapped up in each other and a moment in time she sensed she'd never forget.

Drunk on him, on Italy, on her newfound feelings, she was swept up until the moment when they finally broke apart.

His breath came heavy. His voice was gravelly and sexy. "Get some sleep. Can I see you tomorrow?"

"We're heading to Capri tomorrow for most of the day."

"Tomorrow night? After your day with your sisters, will you have coffee with me?"

She smiled. "Yes."

"*Buona sera.*"

A sigh spilled from her soul. "*Buona sera,*" she whispered.

Dev floated back inside, where her sisters were waiting on the couch for her. Pris was flat on her back, legs up in the air, stretching her bare toes back and forth, with a silly grin on her face. "You were kissing!" she announced. "I just know it!"

Dev broke into laughter and squeezed in next to Bailey, who laid her head on her shoulder. "I agree with Pris. I think there was kissing tonight."

"We did."

"Was it good?" Pris asked seriously. "'Cause I remember my first kiss with Garrett. It was different from anyone else I'd ever kissed and I knew in that moment I was going to marry him."

Dev wrinkled her nose. "I'm not there yet, but it was good. Very, very good. He's special."

Bailey hummed under her breath. "Romance is so magical,

isn't it? Do you think Mom felt like this? When she fell in love with R?"

"I think so," Pris said. "It showed in that letter we found."

"Do you still love Garrett like that?" Bailey asked.

Pris scissored her legs and frowned. "Yes. It just got lost in responsibility and marriage stuff. Maybe we're crazy to believe things can remain the same, but the core is still there for us. Isn't that enough?"

"I hope so," Bailey mused. "What do you think, Dev?"

She tugged at Pris's long blond hair, beginning to braid it. "I've never really been in love before," she admitted. "Not grown-up love. I mean, I thought I loved Liam, but now I know it wasn't the real thing."

"How come? Were you afraid?" Pris asked.

"Nope. I just wasn't interested. I liked work better. Relationships feel awkward. I hate first dates and the getting-to-know you phase."

"But you did so well with Hawke. He jumped right over Bailey straight to you!"

They laughed at Pris. "True, I finally won a hot-man competition," Dev teased. "But it was different with Hawke. It was natural."

"That's how you know it's right," Pris said. "You deserve this, Dev. Try not to overthink it. Just enjoy him and how he makes you feel."

Before this week, those words would have sent Dev into a flurry of panic, or off on a major defensive mission. She didn't do flow, or romantic interludes that made no sense. It wasn't who she was. But lately, Dev wondered if it was time to take a chance on something bigger. Riskier. But with bigger rewards.

Hawke's face drifted past her vision, and she gave a girly sigh. "Yeah. Okay."

"Oh, she's a goner," Bailey said. "Did he ask you out again?"

"Tomorrow night. For coffee."

"Perfect. We get your days, and he gets your nights! Don't you love when everything falls together?" Pris said.

Dev finished the sloppy braid and tied it into a half knot. "Perfect."

"Perfect," Bailey recited, yawning. "How about we get up early to see the sunrise? Won't that be exciting?"

"Oh yes, let's do it!" Pris said. "I'm not sleepy at all."

"Neither am I," Dev murmured, the solid warmth of her sisters pressed against her a bit like being in a pack. The memory stirred, bringing her back to when they were young and would play hard, then collapse into a pile together, out of breath and energy and ideas for the moment. "Sunrise it is."

They slept.

CHAPTER THIRTY-TWO

Olivia

After our first meeting, I spent every day with Rafe.

He took me out on the boat and I helped with the tours, assisting him while I happily digested his spiels on the caves, the history of Positano, and funny stories I'd heard before about him growing up here. The full season hadn't swung in yet, so he had extra downtime. We went to Praiano and lay out on the beach, greedily soaking up the sun while enjoying the space and quiet of minimum tourists. We ate dinner with his dad, and I saw how good Rafe was with him and his failing memory. His dad now needed a cane to get around. But he remembered my aunt, and I'd laugh at some of his stories of the carefree days of partying and dating Aunt Silvia.

Mostly, though, we soaked up each other's presence, greedy for the time. Content to be together again.

Today, we sat in the garden. I'd found my old sketchbook in the closet and showed him the one I had done of him that day, years ago. He challenged me to do another one, but I'd refused, claiming I was way too rusty. He asked to keep the sketch, his eyes glinting with melancholy, and I agreed. I liked the idea of him having something I made for him.

We relaxed on a giant blanket, watching the clouds, our hands brushing together now and then. Nothing physical had happened between us. Rafe knew I was married, and we both respected the line, even though I'd told him the reason I was here.

"I imagined you'd be married with a child already," I said. "I was always so jealous of all the women that buzzed around you."

He laughed. "When you were around me, I didn't even recognize other women. After you left, I wasn't interested in dating for a long time. Eventually, I tried to put myself out there, but my father required much of my time, and I hadn't found the connection I was looking for."

"Do you want kids?" I asked softly. "One day?"

"*Sì*. Very much so. I always saw us—me—with three."

I ignored the way he stumbled over the word, but my palms began to sweat. The idea of having a baby with Rafe made my insides light up.

"Do you have a picture of your daughter?" he suddenly asked. "I'd like to see."

"Yes." I fished out the wallet from my purse and handed it over.

"I can't believe how much she looks like you," Rafe said as he stared at the picture. "Is she creative? Does she like art?"

"She loves to dance, especially ballet. To be honest, she's a bit obsessed." I wrinkled my nose. "Priscilla watched *The Nutcracker* a million times, and she's always practicing, almost as if she's listening to some teacher in her head. I set up a little dance studio for her and got a wall mirror and a barre. I'm sure it's just a phase, but who cares if it makes her happy? I'm happy I can afford the lessons."

He tilted his head, his lips quirking in a smile. "That's beautiful. Imagine finding something you love so much at a young age. The creative blood must run in your genes."

"It better because Adam doesn't have a drop. He relates to computer code and spreadsheets."

I stopped, horrified I'd said his name. I'd confessed the truth to Rafe the first night we were together, and he'd listened without judgment, not saying one bad word about Adam. I think he knew I was only here temporarily, but we couldn't seem to stay away from each other. It was as if I breathed wholly when I was with him.

"I'm sorry, Rafe. I didn't mean to say that."

"What, the name of your husband? He's a part of your life. The father of Priscilla. We can't pretend he doesn't exist—that's not fair to any of us."

"You're right. I don't want to make things worse between us. Not when I just found you again."

He reached out and touched my cheek. I almost reached for him to hold his hand to me, desperate for contact, but he let it drop and the moment disappeared. "I told you I'd always be here and I meant it. You're important to me." A sigh spilled from his lips. "But I also can't pretend I don't have feelings for you. I'm not a saint. Nothing has changed for me."

I cursed the leap of joy that rushed through me at his words. The feeling of rightness again, as if my journey away from him had been necessary for me in order to end up back here. Where I truly belonged. "I can't pretend either that I'm feeling just friendship. I know I hurt you, though, and I can't do that again. I'll never forgive myself."

"It is not for you to decide, *dolcezza*, is it?" he murmured.

The familiar endearment speared me in half with pure longing. We stared at each other for a long time, savoring the intimate moment, the pulse between heartbeats and the possibilities that lay stretched ahead of us.

"Will you go back to him?"

The question stole my breath, because he'd razored straight to the heart of the matter. Was I willing to go back to Adam and work it out? Or was there something else for me, another life I was meant to live? A life with Rafe I'd rejected, but perhaps, had always been meant to be?

Maybe now it was.

"I haven't decided," I said truthfully. "We have a child together. I made a commitment to him. It's bigger than what I want. I'm trying to do the right thing."

He seemed to ponder my words, his features closed up in deep thought. "But isn't following what you truly want the right thing?"

"I used to think so, before I had a child. Now everything is about her."

He glanced one last time at Pris's photo and handed it slowly back to me. "I always knew you'd be a great mother."

The tinge of pain in his voice pummeled my chest like fists. "It was never about not loving you enough," I finally said. "Or choosing Adam over you. I only knew I felt on the verge of something big—a discovery of who I was and how I wanted to be in the world. I got caught up with it. I understand now why you pushed me so hard to be free my senior year. Because if you hadn't, I may have come back to you, but it wouldn't have been real. I would have resented what I left behind."

"I know. You were too young. I knew from the beginning, but I fought it." A wry smile twisted his lips. "We didn't do anything wrong, *dolcezza*. Some things just . . . are. I'm glad you're with me now. And eventually, you will make the decision that is right for you. No one else. *Va bene?*"

The crippling tension and constant questioning drifted away and left my insides light. "*Va bene.*"

Rafe reached out and took my hand. I didn't pull away, and everything seemed perfectly back in sync, as if I'd never left.

Maybe, in my heart, I never had.

CHAPTER THIRTY-THREE

Pris

She breathed in the heated quiet of late afternoon and closed her eyes, tipping her head back. The scent of lemon mixed with floral blooms. The lazy buzz of a bee whispered in her ear. Her feet were bare and warm from sunshine. Her belly was pleasantly full from the plate of spaghetti vongole she'd indulged in. Not usually one of her go-to meals at restaurants, but the memory of her mother made her order it. Mom had always adored the simple dish, and whenever they went out for Italian she'd order it amid everyone groaning and teasing her about her unadventurous foodie spirit.

But even that dish had been leveled up, and Pris finished every bite.

Bailey was taking a siesta. Dev was out for a walk with Hawke. And it was time for her to do some work.

With a sigh, she opened her eyes and pressed the point of her pen to her paper. What else did she like to do? The list was supposed to contain all the things that made her happy so she could begin to pinpoint what direction she wanted her life to take. It sounded like an easy enough exercise, and she'd eagerly begun, but after half an hour, her list still included a few sparse items.

Dancing
Yoga
Helping others
Fashion and styling
Running

That was it.

She sucked.

Pris groaned and looked at the other column of jobs she'd done over the years. Besides ballerina, she'd worked and headed multiple charity boards, tried her hand at a fashion blog that fell flat because she wasn't engaging enough (and hated posting pics of herself), and ran various large functions for the charities she headed. Pris knew they were important. Those events were planned out a year in advance and were the primary fundraisers everyone counted on. But when she looked deeper, she still couldn't figure out what brought her joy.

It always came back to dancing. But she'd turned her back on it long ago, afraid to open the door and cause more heartbreak. Had she been wrong? She'd dismissed teaching as a cop-out, but now she wondered if it'd been an excuse. Watching others follow and fulfill their dreams made her feel like a quitter.

Which was ridiculous, because she'd made a proactive choice. Wasn't it time she accepted the past and tried to build a better now for herself?

Maybe she could teach yoga?

Her phone buzzed and she threw the notebook down and picked up. "Garrett? Everything okay?"

"Yep. Wanted to check in now since I'll be in court late, then headed to Gus's Tavern for dinner with Roy. Didn't want to miss your call."

Warmth flushed through her. They'd spoken every night, and the vibe felt different. They discussed things beyond the activities of the day, even though he loved hearing about their daily adventures, and spoke about things they hadn't touched on in years. How Garrett sometimes felt trapped by his own success and responsibilities. The way she felt less than whole after Thomas left, because he'd taken a piece of her with him. They laughed over better memories from when they were young. It felt in a strange way as if they were dating again, but it was only their voices connecting over thousands of miles.

To Pris, it was romantic. Like getting to know her husband all over again.

"What are Frick and Frack up to?" he asked.

She laughed. "Bae is napping and Dev went for a walk with Hawke. I think she's really crazy about him."

"Is that good or bad? Having an affair in another country can cause some issues if they want to pursue it."

"I don't know, but it's nice to see Dev happy. Maybe she's just living in the moment."

"Dev? Are you kidding? Isn't she the ultimate planner?"

"Yeah, but things are different here." Pris tried to explain the way being in Positano, where her mother had once lived, had given all of them a new perspective. "I know it sounds crazy, but all of us finally admitted things to one another. Personal stuff. Stuff I don't think we even realized ourselves."

"Like us?"

His low voice reached out to her and lingered. "Yes. I told them about us. "

"Did they give you any advice?"

"No. It was nice. They just . . . listened."

He let out a breath. "Yeah. We've forgotten how to do that with each other. This house is empty without you, Pris. But I feel like you've been gone a long time even when you were here."

"I feel the same about you. I don't want to do that anymore. I want us to both start to choose each other. Is that something you can do? Even if your job comes second?"

"I'm going to damn well try."

"Me too. I'm sitting here in the garden and making lists of things I love. Trying to figure out what direction I need to take. I thought about taking art classes, becoming a yoga teacher, or starting my own not-for-profit."

"You can do anything you set your mind to. But aren't you missing the thing that you love the most? Ballet?"

The memory of her worn pointe shoes floated in her vision. Sewing them so carefully along the seams to extend their wear. The feel of her toes as they slid home. The freedom of giving in to her body by using movement and music rather than her head. Longing cut deep and raw, but this time, Pris let herself feel it. "I do miss it. But I'm forty years old, Garrett. An old lady in the dance world. My time is over."

"I'm not talking about performing. What about signing up for ballet classes again? Getting back in shape for you—not anyone else? Or teaching? God, Pris, you're so damn good with kids. It doesn't have to be elementary. You can teach middle school or high school. You have contacts."

"Who'd want a ballerina out of her prime who's been out of that world?"

"You danced with the New York City Ballet! You took my and everyone else's breath away. Do you think that's normal, Pris? That's a piece of immortality, but you've let it define you. It will never be the same, but you can have ballet in your life in a new way. Don't you want to try?"

She looked at her notebook. She thought about the work she did to fill the time and the feeling of purpose she constantly craved—the same purpose that had slowly wrung her out day by day, until there was nothing left for her to give. Either to herself or to Garrett.

He was right. She was limited only by the story she spun for herself and her past. As for pride? Why did she care? She did nothing wrong by walking away and choosing a life with her husband. Her mistake had come from pretending it was all or nothing, by identifying herself so closely to her past career that she'd left no room to find other parts of herself.

"I'll think about it," she said.

"Good. Did Thomas send you that picture at the Tower of London? He's such a joker."

She laughed, picturing her son pretending to scream from the top of the tower with his buddies. "Yeah, he seems to have some good friends. The last time we talked he actually said they were going to get a pint."

Garrett laughed, and they spent the next few minutes talking about their son. When he was ready to hang up, she was surprised to realize there was a flare of longing burning in her chest. A need to look into her husband's bright blue eyes; touch his face; be held by him.

"I miss you," she said.

His voice was a low rumble of sound. "Miss you too, sweetheart."

She clicked off and smiled. Sat for a long time in the garden, pondering her choices. Looking at her list. Thinking of Mom and her own path. Realizing just because she'd embraced motherhood, it didn't mean she had no regrets. All this time, Bailey had been right. Pris looked at her mom as a mother, a parent, a person with no right to live in the gray zone, because that's where she'd placed her father, and there was room there for only one parent to screw up.

"I understand, Mom," she whispered.

The birds twittered and the bees buzzed and the sun shone.

Pris made her decision, opened her email, and began to write.

CHAPTER THIRTY-FOUR

Olivia

I spoke with Adam and told him I needed a few more days. My mom had already checked in with me and said it was no problem to keep Pris a little longer. She was having a wonderful time keeping her entertained in Boston and spending some quality time with her. I talked with Pris on the phone, her precious voice rushed and excited as she told me all the things Grammy had shown her, and when we hung up, I sank to my knees and cried for a long time.

I knew I'd been tired and more emotional than usual, dealing with on-and-off nausea, but I had a big decision to make. Or not. I also realized I could go back home and try a temporary separation with Adam. If we both wanted it to work between us badly enough, we might be able to repair the broken pieces.

But the more time I spent with Rafe, the more I knew I was lying to myself.

I'd never fallen out of love with him. I'd veered off course because I'd been too young and couldn't make the final commitment. But now I knew this relationship had been so much more than a summer affair or a bittersweet first crush.

This was a forever love.

Yet, I faced the same obstacles. Adam and I had a child together, and I couldn't just move to Italy to be with Rafe. I needed to think about the fallout if I suddenly declared to my husband that I was in love with another man and headed to Positano with Pris. Then again, Adam had made his choice to take another woman to bed during the most difficult time of our marriage. Wasn't that when true character and loyalty were tested? Could he ever love me the way I needed him to if it was so easy to be intimate with another woman while lying to my face?

My mind became a jumbled mess, but beneath it, I knew there was an answer. I needed to be brave enough to really admit what I wanted and to accept that it would be hard either way. Piecing together my broken marriage would be the hardest thing I took on. And if Rafe was truly my soul mate, I'd need to find a compromise with Adam—maybe dual custody with half the year in Italy? Yes, it would be messy, but the thought of Pris growing up here, speaking Italian, living a simple life beyond all the trappings back in New York, called to me. It felt . . . right.

I spent the day on my own. I sketched, journaled, and sat with myself to ask the hard questions I rarely faced. I alone owned the capacity to create a life I loved and needed. And yes, Pris was everything, but I also knew she needed me fully committed to whatever future I chose. That way, I could be the best mother.

I saw Rafe that night. We dined at a quiet café overlooking the rocky coastline. The air held a deep-seated longing neither of us could hide. I reached for the bread and he gently clasped my wrist, his thumb pressing into my palm. The touch seared through me and I gasped at the familiar heat between us. His dark eyes glittered with emotion, and within them, I saw his unanswered question.

He released his grip and shuddered, as if trying to gain back control. "You leave on Saturday," he said quietly. "Are you going back to him?"

The tangle of doubt and grief and guilt suddenly loosened. I looked into his eyes and felt the truth bubble up from within to spill over my tongue. "No. I'm not going back."

A sharp breath expelled from his lips. "What are you going to do?"

I squeezed my eyes half shut, terrified but knowing now what I needed to do. "I'm going to tell Adam the truth about us. My feelings for you. And I'm going to bring Priscilla here for the summer. I want her to experience Italy and I want to see if this is something we can make work even if it's complicated." A sob caught in my throat. "I know it's crazy, Rafe. I know it may blow up all over again and we won't be able to patch together a life, but I want to try. I owe it to myself, to you, to us. I want to . . . try. If you want it too."

The fierce joy carved out on his face told me his own truth. "Livia, it's always been you. I will take anything you have to give me, don't you realize this? Yes, I want you and Priscilla and to see however we can be together."

My heart leapt, and we stared at each other over the flickering candlelight, poised for a whole new chance. This time, everything felt different. It was still hard, there were still obstacles and a difficult road ahead, but there was also less doubt. Yes, I still loved Adam, and he was Pris's father, but Rafe completed me in some way that was a gift.

I couldn't walk away from it again. This time, I knew exactly what I wanted.

We left the restaurant and went back to the cottage. As we had years ago, we made love, rediscovering each other, falling back together with whispers and soft caresses. My body welcomed him as fiercely as my soul, and I wept with completion as we came together. Later, we lay together in a tangle of naked limbs, talking late into the night, afraid to break apart for fear it was all a dream and we'd wake up alone again.

"I love you, Livia."

I held him tight. "I love you too."

His voice broke. "You will come back? I won't lose you again?"

I kissed him softly on the lips. "I will come back."

He nodded, his body relaxing against mine.

Finally, we slept.

CHAPTER THIRTY-FIVE

Dev

The scream stopped her cold.

Heart racing, she flew down the hall and flung open the door to Pris's room. "Oh my God, are you hurt? Do you need medical attention? Did you see a spider?"

Bailey bumped into her back, pushing her farther into the room. "What's the matter?"

Pris was lying on the bed, jeans open over her hips. "I can't get into my jeans," she whispered in horror. Her long blond hair was spread out on the quilt, giving her an angelic look. Slender feet wriggled back and forth as she began twisting with obvious effort. "They don't button!"

Bailey muffled a laugh, but Dev glared. "You scared me, idiot! So, buy a bigger pair."

Pris squealed, staring at her like Dev had suggested she marry an alien and have three-headed babies. "What's wrong with you? These are my favorite jeans, already worn in—I can't buy a bigger size! Oh my God, this is awful. What will I do?"

Bailey looked a bit evil. "About time you have the same issues as the rest of the female population. Dev and I deal with our curves every day, so it's time you slip on your *big*-girl panties. No pun intended."

Dev burst out laughing. It was satisfying to see her gorgeous older sister finally wrestle with her pants not fitting.

"You both suck! What am I supposed to wear on the scooter?"

"Got any yoga pants?" Bailey asked innocently.

Pris threw a pillow at her. Bailey grabbed it, climbed on the bed, and began using it to smash Pris, who shrieked like a toddler and tried to cover her face.

Yeah, Pris would be the first one to be killed in a horror movie. It was a wonder how she'd thrived in the competitive ballet world, but maybe her ruthlessness was only confined to dance.

Dev broke up the fight after getting in a few good slugs, and gave Pris a pair of her stretchy pants.

Of course, Pris looked like a model in them, whereas Dev sometimes felt a tad dumpy in the same pair. The thought caught but didn't hold this time—just floated off into outer space. She realized the past few days she wasn't as harsh on herself, and the usual self-flagellations didn't hold any sting. She held herself to a high standard that had always seemed to work, especially with her career. But maybe she could give herself a break now and then regarding the things she couldn't control. Was this what falling hard for a guy did? Made sharp edges all gilded and rosy?

She actually liked it.

Hawke seemed pretty satisfied with who she was—inside and out. Not that they'd slept together or even really fooled around. Their relationship consisted of kisses, deep conversations, and late evenings together with Lucifer. Sometimes they took an afternoon walk, and Hawke began introducing her to a variety of neighbors he was friends with. She loved the easy warmth with everyone she met and began to settle into herself. For the first time, Dev wasn't identifying herself only through her work. It was a huge part of her life, and she loved dissecting interesting elements of the financial and teaching world with Hawke, who never got bored. But it was the other subjects he teased out that surprised her.

Her sharp wit didn't piss him off but made him laugh. Her usual defenses were met with quiet patience. When they were together, the hours stretched long and languid but also held a sharp urgency, tempting her to reach deeper to keep building the connection. Time was both their enemy and their friend. She had never felt so off her game and plugged in at the same time.

Bottom line?

She was a mess and she didn't care.

Three days left. This time, the ticket would need to be used. The three of them had met with the real estate agent and everyone decided to have the paperwork ready to go, but to hold back until they wanted to rent the house. Pris might want to bring Garrett. Bailey might decide to come back in between jobs. The money that had once been so critical to Dev didn't seem as urgent. Now it was personal. She wanted the house to be used in the right way, like Mom would have wanted.

Plus, it was near Hawke.

They headed out to the scooter place, where Pepe greeted them and got their Vespas ready. They found helmets and did a brief tutorial, and everything went smoothly except for the argument between her and Bailey regarding who got the orange Vespa and who got black.

Orange was too flashy anyway. If Bailey wanted to act like a toddler, let her. Dev was the grown-up.

More confident after spending a week getting used to the roads, they zoomed out to the famous Amalfi Coast. Pris was way too slow, so Bailey took the lead and Dev kept a steady pace in the middle. The scooters hugged the twisty cliffs and the sea spilled underneath them in a blinding Listerine blue. The colors hit her vision all at once: burnt sienna, clean white, turquoise, deep burgundy, and bright, sunny yellows. Earthy rock blended with lush green trees. The streets once packed with touring crowds in Positano now opened up to vast, open space. Italy was a sensual, delicious contradiction for the senses, and Dev realized she'd fallen in love here, just like her mother. She was vibrantly alive and happy. She never wanted it to end.

The wind tugged at loose strands of her hair and caressed the bare skin of her limbs as they rode, refusing to stop until her butt was screaming and she was desperate for a drink. They pulled over to take pictures at popular spots and stopped for a brief lunch. Pris insisted no carbs for at least twenty-four hours, so they ordered salads, gulped Pellegrino, then took off again.

The trip reminded her a bit of the walk on the Path of the Gods. The longer they rode, the faster they left the past behind them and built something brand-new. Bailey's laughter carried on the wind, and Pris's shrieks now held bubbles of excitement. The handlebars and the zigzagging road beneath the wheels were her only focus.

They finished their drive at the Hotel Prestige in Sorrento and ate dinner. Dev sipped wine and watched the sunset fall over the skyline, a slow creep of color bleeding into the horizon. The silence felt reverent; humble; a place to rest within the trip and herself. Bailey reached out for her hand and Dev squeezed it. The world seemed laid out before her, a gift she never wanted to forget.

She felt like she'd swallowed a taste of magic.

The trip home was long and more difficult in the dark. They went slower, bodies tired, returning home late in the night. Dev took a shower and changed into comfortable clothes.

"Are you heading to Hawke's?" Bailey asked, already lounging in sweats.

"Yeah, do you want to come? Hang a bit?"

Bailey smiled. "No, but thanks for the invite. I'm going to draw. I took a lot of pictures, but my head is full of images I want to get down on paper."

"Mom loved to draw." Dev sat down for a moment beside her. "I used to catch her sometimes sketching us, and then I'd yell at her to stop."

"I remember that! I always wondered if she missed working in the art world. Raising kids and leaving what you love behind must've been challenging."

"Like Pris?"

Bailey nodded. "But I'm hopeful for her. She's been talking to Garrett every day and she looks happier. Or at least, determined to change."

"I think we all are."

"Did you talk to Hawke about what happens when you leave?"

Dev shook her head. "Not yet. For the first time, it's like my head has nothing to do with my decisions, and it's so nice. Is this what it feels like to be you?"

Bailey laughed. "Probably. I think if I was a little bit more like you, and you were a little bit more like me, we'd rule the world."

"Damn straight."

"Get going and see that man of yours. Don't be afraid to have an honest conversation with him, Dev. It may be hard, but I'm beginning to wonder if hard is sometimes worth it."

She sighed. "Maybe."

As Dev headed to Hawke's, she thought about her sister's words.

And wondered what was going to happen next.

CHAPTER THIRTY-SIX

Olivia

After I said goodbye to Rafe, I put my plan into action.

First, I called Aunt Silvia and told her everything. I asked if I could use her home for the summer and bring Pris, and she was immediately supportive. "Darling, you are always welcome at the cottage! When I pass, it will belong to you. I'll be happy leaving it to someone who loves the place as much as I do."

"Thank you, Aunt Silvia, but I don't want to think of a world without you in it."

Her booming laughter made me smile. "Others might not have the same high opinion of me, darling. As for your marriage, I'm terribly sorry. But I find life is a long time, and bad things sometimes bring opportunities for second chances. You fell in love with Rafe at nineteen, and I think it was a lifelong connection. It doesn't happen often, but when we find our true mates, it's a gift. Be happy, my darling. Pris will thrive in Italy, and I'm sure you can work something out with Adam."

I prayed she was right, but I hung up feeling more confident.

Then I drove to my mother's to pick up Pris and finally tell Mom the entire truth. We sat in her kitchen over cups of tea while Pris played, and I began with that first fateful summer. I talked nonstop, and she listened, occasionally interrupting to ask me questions. When I finished, she stood up, went to the refrigerator, and grabbed a bottle of wine. "I think we both may need this right now," she said, taking out two glasses.

I laughed. Mom rarely drank but always had a bottle of Riesling ready for emergencies. "None for me. I've been throwing up on and off. All the emotional nerves, I guess."

"That's understandable." She gave a generous pour and sipped. "I'm trying to decide if I should call Silvia and bitch her out. I can't believe you both kept this from me, but suddenly it all makes sense. Your crazed need to go with her every summer. God, your father would have had a heart attack if he knew it was about a boy. He never liked Silvia much either."

I sighed. "I needed to keep it a secret. Especially since I'd planned to move there after graduation—you both would have freaked."

"I still can't believe Adam did this to you and the family. At least Pris is little. When your dad and I broke up, you were so lost. I regret I didn't help you more. I felt as if I was falling apart and all I could do was try and survive, but I left you alone too much. I'm sorry, Olivia."

Her apology touched me deeply. I reached out and squeezed her hand. "It's okay, Mom. I can understand things better now. You did the best you could, and it worked out. I love seeing you happy."

She smiled at me with gratitude. "Do you feel ready to make such a leap? Is this man worth giving up your life here? And what about Adam? He may not agree to this, Liv."

"I know. We're meeting for dinner this week to talk. I can't go back to this marriage and fight fairly when my heart is with Rafe. I have to believe that Pris will be okay."

"Then you'll do what needs to be done and Pris will be fine. She has two parents who love and support her. I'll help you any way I can."

"Thanks, Mom."

When I got back home, I had another bout of nausea and wondered if I should see a doctor. I was positive it was stress—and it wasn't like I had a virus where I was attached to the bathroom. I just felt completely off.

I flipped through my calendar to see when I could fit in a checkup, then paused.

I always wrote down when I got my period, but this month was blank. I mentally counted down, realizing I was more than two weeks late. I'd completely lost count with the Adam situation and going to Italy.

I was never late.

The knowledge rolled over me like a slow wave that turns into a tsunami. I sat staring at the dates on the calendar as my vision blurred.

No. God, please, no.

Trying not to panic, I grabbed Pris and put her in the car seat, then drove to the local pharmacy. I bought two pregnancy tests and a lollipop for Pris, then settled her in front of the television with her treat.

Skin cold and clammy, I ripped open the package with shaky fingers and peed on the stick. Then I closed my eyes, sank to the ground, and waited.

After I glanced at the results, I quickly opened up the second test and redid the entire thing.

The results were the same as the first.

I was pregnant.

CHAPTER THIRTY-SEVEN

Dev

He was waiting on the front porch.

Lucifer jumped off his perch to rub against her legs. Throaty purrs emitted from his mouth, making her feel special. She scratched his head and murmured back to him.

"He's gotten attached."

Dev straightened up and took the chair next to him. He handed her a glass of wine while Lucifer jumped in her lap to get comfortable. "Don't worry. He's too cool to show it."

Hawke laughed, sipping his own drink—a splash of bourbon on the rocks with two ice cubes. He was a wine connoisseur but preferred something richer in the late evenings. Dev liked gathering these tidbits of information to create a fuller picture of who he was. He wasn't a man to overly share, but he answered all her nosy questions with an easy directness that drew her closer. "You say that now. You won't be hearing the agonized howl of a cat's broken heart."

"I didn't think a ten-day affair could get so intense," she deliberately teased. "Maybe he'll replace me with a sweeter, more tamed companion."

"Nah, he'd get bored. His name isn't Lucifer for nothing."

Her nerves tingled as his gaze met and drilled into hers. "We're not talking about the cat anymore, are we?"

His lip quirked. He swirled the amber liquid. Ice cubes tinkled against the glass. "No, we're not." He took a sip and seemed to reset. "Tell me about your day."

She decided not to push. They had time. She relaxed into the chair, stroking the cat's fur. "Rode Vespas along the Amalfi Coast."

"Pepe take good care of you?"

"Of course. There may have been a small argument regarding scooter colors, but I was the bigger person."

"Bailey got the orange, huh?" She laughed. "I wish I could repeat certain experiences for the first time. Seeing Amalfi from the seat of a Vespa is one of them."

"It was amazing. We rode for hours. Then we stopped at the Hotel Prestige and watched the sunset. You were right. The spot was perfect—nothing blocked the view."

"Good. Next time, I'd take you to Termini. It's this beautiful small town on the Sorrento Peninsula like a hidden gem. The sunset views are killer."

"I'd like that."

He smiled and she smiled back. "I wanted to mention something. I had lunch with a friend of mine today. He's lived in Positano a long time and knows most people. I was telling him about your mom and he mentioned a guy who may fit the bill. It's his friend's dad. About your mom's age. Worked on boats here for years, then moved to Amalfi. Seems he got married later than most and now has two kids. His name is Rocco. Worth checking out?"

Her heart beat faster. Any type of lead was exciting, especially since they were running out of time. "Definitely. How can I contact him?"

"I have his number so you can call. He speaks English. If it seems like he's the one, you can always arrange to see him before you leave."

"Perfect. Thanks, Hawke, this is great."

He fished the note out of his pocket and handed it to her. "That's the number. Let me know if you need help. Mention David Veroni—that's my friend."

She gazed at the number on the paper, twisting it in her fingers. "Do you think it could be him?"

"Don't know. But I've always believed in the long shot."

His hand touched her hair. A sigh slipped past her and the air warmed. She addressed the unasked question between them. "Are we a long shot?"

"I don't think so."

She shook herself out of her trance. Time to get real. Shifting her weight, she narrowed her gaze on him and swore to focus. "Let's go over the pros and cons of pursuing this relationship. Unless you want to end things right here? I get on the plane, we chalk up our time to a lovely gift, and we move on with our lives."

"I veto that option." A smile curved his lips as he continued to stroke her hair, his fingers so very gentle. "I happen to feel like Lucifer. You're irreplaceable."

Her tummy tumbled. Damn his quiet charm. Dev cleared her throat. "Oh, you're good."

He chuckled. "Give me the other options, please."

"Fine. We continue with a long-distance relationship and put no restrictions on the other."

"You're saying we can date and be with other people, yet still see each other when it works out?"

"Correct."

"I veto that too."

Happiness bubbled up within her. She tried to tamp it down, reminding herself there were still many alternatives to consider. "Moving on. We do a long-distance relationship but agree to be monogamous and see if we can bring this connection with us into our real lives."

His gravelly voice was all business, but his hands were personal. "Clauses? Stipulations?"

"We create a schedule on when we talk, including Zoom, email, text, or phone. We agree to a certain number of meet-ups that's fair to both of us. We give ourselves a timeline to renegotiate or see where we are. I'm thinking we begin with six months, and if we're agreeable, we move to a year."

"You are the sexiest woman alive."

Her cheeks flushed. "Thoughts?"

"I like that option."

"So do I."

"But I'd like to tweak the timetable. Let's say three months virtual long-distance with all the inclusions you mentioned. The last three months, we become more personal. We have one date per week minimum."

She tilted her head, confused. "A Zoom date?"

"No, I'm planning to move back to the city, Dev. I'll be working at the firm again."

Her jaw dropped. Suddenly, the possibilities this could turn real between them overwhelmed her. "I—I can't believe it. But I thought you were set on staying here. Aren't you afraid to go back to it again after what happened?"

His carved features reflected a serious intensity as he stared into her eyes. "I've been ready for a while now but wanted to move at a slower pace. I miss my job, but I've learned how to create a better balance in my life. Figured out my priorities and what I want. This time, I won't let my job own my soul. And I'll always have this place to fall back on when I need a break." Hawke leaned in. "But I don't want to scare the crap out of you. I can do slow. You don't need to promise me anything or feel pressured. This is the right move for me, either way."

She waited for the panic to hit. The pressure of having her tidy schedules threatened. Her career suddenly vulnerable to a more demanding personal life. The idea he could want more from her than she was ready to give.

Instead, there was nothing but a simple joy that flowed through her veins, quiet and clean and full of hope. "I think we may have reached an agreement for both parties."

A grin overtook his face, and he pressed his forehead to hers, his hands cupping her cheeks. "You wanna sign?"

"Yeah."

His lips pressed gently to hers. "You wanna stay?"

She sighed and leaned into his muscled strength. "Yeah."

Hawke reached out and gently removed Lucifer from her lap. "Sorry, buddy, you've been trumped."

Then he did something she'd once believed would only happen to Bailey.

He picked her up and walked upstairs to the bedroom, where he shut the door behind them.

CHAPTER THIRTY-EIGHT

Olivia

There are moments in life that are turning points. Some are brought by external factors and can be transformed by sheer grit, bravery, and a hunger for something more.

Other times God seems to be laughing above like we are a sitcom for his amusement, because there are no choices left—just a road before you that must be walked because it is the only route available. A road of acceptance.

It took me a while for the shock to wear off enough for me to think. I was pregnant with Adam's child. A baby I'd ached for when I imagined our marriage was strong. Now this baby was the ultimate sacrifice. I saw my future so clearly now, where before there was an exciting purpose to explore a love of a lifetime—a life with Rafe.

But this was another type of love. Already, I felt the connection between us, my hand resting on my flat belly. A brother or sister for Pris. The gift of a life given to me to care for. It was all mine if I did one simple thing.

Walk away from Rafe a second time.

I went to the gynecologist the next day, who confirmed the news and sent me happily off with some prenatal vitamins. I was seeing Adam for dinner, and I had no idea what I'd do. Did he even want another baby? Maybe he'd used the time apart to realize he didn't want to be married any longer. We could raise both children together but separate. I could still go to Italy for the summer with Pris, then return home to have the baby. There must be options I wasn't thinking of because my brain was foggy.

But first, I needed to talk to Adam.

We went to our favorite restaurant, a tiny Italian place with good food, dim lighting, and privacy. Seeing him after the time apart was strange. My gaze took in his slightly rumpled clothes and tired eyes. He looked different, almost as if he'd aged these past three weeks. A certain arrogance that had always been part of who he was had been ripped from his demeanor. "You look wonderful," he murmured, mouth curved in a soft smile. "I missed you, Liv. How was Italy?"

I fiddled with my napkin, overwhelmed by emotion. A part of me still loved him. There was a familiar solidness to us as a couple, even with everything that had happened. Rafe brought out a different type of love, one coaxed from my very soul, as if I'd found my other half. With Adam, it was more of building a life together that fit. There was a connection from the familiar, and from loving and raising Pris.

I hesitated. "It was good. I took the time to think about some things. How are you? How's work?"

He gave a half shrug. "Busy, as usual. Pete offered me the senior-level promotion I've been looking for."

"Congratulations."

"But I'm not taking it."

I blinked. "Why? That's what you've been working so hard for, isn't it?"

"It used to be. Not anymore." Silence fell. He took a sip of his bourbon and cleared his throat. "I have some things I need to say, Liv. I'm ashamed of the man I've become. Of what I've done to you. To us."

My eyes widened. Adam wasn't the emotional type. He shied away from tears, professions of everlasting love, and deep inner sharing. He always said showing up and keeping your word was a better proof of love than flowery sentiments. But the man before me seemed softer, more vulnerable.

I swallowed, my hand rubbing my belly in circles under the tablecloth. "You broke us, Adam. I don't know what we could ever get back. What made you do it? Was it the woman you fell for? Did you just want more sex? Was I not enough for you?"

He rubbed his head. "You've always been enough for me. I began losing myself, Liv. I wish I could explain. It was like work was consuming me, and then I felt there were these leftover pieces to give to you and Pris, and nothing for myself. I was a selfish prick. I had to work with this woman on a deadline, and one thing led to another. And even though I felt guilty and sick about losing you, I still did it. I swear to God, she meant nothing to me. I kept thinking it would blast me out of my cage and I could get back to you." Misery etched his face. "Stupid. I ended up ruining the only things I treasure. You and Pris."

I thought of Rafe and how I'd never told my husband about Aunt Silvia's house in Italy. How I'd kept a piece of my life a secret, because it was all for me. And I had now officially cheated on my husband. It didn't matter that he'd done it first. Perhaps I was just as guilty as Adam.

"Maybe it was a sign," I murmured. "Maybe you were looking for a way out instead. We had a hard time, Adam. I don't think you liked the person I became after Pris was born. And I don't know who I'd be if we did decide to get back together. It's time to be honest with each other. Is this something we want anymore?"

His blue eyes lit with a fierce determination, and he leaned forward, his voice raw. "Yes. Yes, you and Pris are what I want. Please listen to me, Liv. I know it's only been a few weeks, but I've changed. I started seeing a therapist to figure things out. I finally realized nothing matters more to me than my family, and I spoke with Pete this week. I not only turned down the promotion, but I told him I wanted to pull back on a few projects so I have more time at home. I used work as an excuse to shut myself away. I realize if we have any chance to make this work, I can't be that man anymore. I want more for all of us."

A strange grief washed over me. My husband was finally opening up and sharing some honest truths. But a part of me only wanted to keep him vilified, an easier way for me to justify leaving him to be with Rafe. I wanted black-and-white decisions, but like the baby I now carried in my belly, things were so much more complicated.

"I know you needed time away to process things. Is there still a chance we can work our way back to each other? I'll fight for us, and for Pris. I know it will take time and there's no quick fix. But I'll show up, every day, and regain your trust. If you let me."

A sob choked my throat. Dear God, what was I going to do? I'd never imagined Adam like this—open and real, willing to fight for me. He'd turned down a promotion. Yes, he'd been unfaithful, but if there was a chance I could keep our family together, didn't I owe it to my children to try? Remnants of emotion between us still burned. Could they be reignited?

There was one more thing he had to know.

"Adam, I found out yesterday I'm pregnant."

Shock flickered over his face and was replaced by pure joy. He sprang from his chair and came over to me, dropping to his knees. "Liv, are you sure? My God, are you feeling okay? What did the doctor say?"

His hand rested on my thigh. I gazed down, studying the cowlick at the top of his head, the tears in his amber eyes, and the face of a man who seemed honestly moved by the news of the baby.

And in that moment, his reaction changed everything.

I was pregnant. I had a responsibility to see if I could make this work. How could I go back to Rafe with a newborn in tow and try to make a life there for us? How could I turn my back on Adam, who wanted a chance to make it right for all of us?

"We're both fine. I'm only six weeks, still early."

He lowered his head and kissed my fingers. "Baby, please give me a chance to make this right. This time, I won't screw up. I'll be a good father. I know my priorities now and I love you and this baby you're carrying. Don't do this alone."

I closed my eyes and saw an image of Rafe. I watched myself run toward him as he caught me in his arms. Saw us walking the hillside paths of Positano as my children skipped at our side. Envisioned slow, sleepy nights watching the stars, and sailing on the boat, and creating a simple, beautiful life together. And I was happy.

Then I said the words aloud and the image shattered into tiny fragments around me.

"We can try."

....

Dear R,

My dearest love. How do I begin a letter like this? When I imagine your face as you read these words, I can't breathe, and I'm dragged back to that painful time so many years ago when I had to tell you I wasn't coming back to Italy.

I'd picked a different life and a different man. It led me away from you, but I'd already given a piece of my heart away—the piece that would always be yours. It seemed like fate had finally blessed us when I returned and found you still loved me.

Everything I told you was true.

I swear on all I hold dear that I was coming back to you, my love. Nothing would have stopped me, except the one thing I love more than you.

My child.

I'm pregnant, Rafe. I found out when I got back home and saw my doctor. I'm six weeks, and carrying Adam's baby. When we met so I could tell him about you, about my decision to leave, I realized he deserved a chance to be a father to this baby. My decision affects so much more than me.

We both broke our vows. Now it's time I try to forgive for the sake of our children.

Yet, here I am once again, walking away from a man who I believe is my soul mate. Were we never meant to be? Or am I living with you in another reality, an alternate world where we will always be together?

There are no words to explain, or ask forgiveness. There are only my choices and the pieces left from both of us.

Forgive me, my love. Forgive my weakness and my love for this child that encompasses my very being. Forgive my need to fight for my marriage. Most of all, forgive me for betraying the man I will always love.

Livia

I sent the letter and waited. My belly grew, Adam moved back in, and we began to patch together the broken fragments of our relationship, slowly, day by day.

Rafe never wrote back.

I tried calling him a few times, but he never answered. I wrote a few more letters as a tiny piece of me hoped we could salvage something—even a friendship. I knew it was over and he would never contact me again. I grieved his loss and mine silently, and the day Devon was born, I swore to give my all to Adam and my family, because this choice must be worth it. My marriage would succeed. My daughters would be happy. I would be complete.

So, I wrote my final letter, then began a new chapter and decided not to look back.

CHAPTER THIRTY-NINE

Bailey

"Are we ready to call?"

Bailey looked at her sisters and nodded. Dev held the phone in front of them, hit the speaker button, and dialed.

"*Pronto?*"

Dev's voice was calm and somewhat businesslike. "Hello, may I speak with Mr. Rocco Esposito?"

"*Sì*, this is him."

"Hi, my name is Devon and I'm calling because a friend referred me to you—David Veroni? My mother had a home here in Positano for years, and she recently passed away. My sisters and I are trying to track down some of her friends. I wondered if I gave you the name if you'd remember her?"

"*Mi dispiace.* It is hard to lose a mama, but how nice you want to know her better."

"Yes, David mentioned you ran a boat business? She spoke of a man who was a dear friend who did the same. I was wondering if that could be you."

"I ran a boat-tour operation for many years. Small. We take tourists to grottos and beaches. What is your mama's name?"

"Olivia Moretti. She came every summer in the mid-seventies with her aunt. Silvia Agosti."

His laugh was robust. "*Sì*, I remember Silvia. Everyone knew Silvia! Very beautiful. Long red hair, no? I met her a few times."

Bailey's breath caught in her lungs. She shared a glance with her sisters, who looked just as excited and nervous. "Yes! That's her! What about her niece—Olivia Moretti? She would've been in her early twenties then."

"Ah, let's see. It doesn't sound familiar. What did she look like?"

Pris gave a detailed description.

"Ah, *sì*! I met her. She came with Silvia to a party."

Bailey practically jumped up and down in anticipation. "Did you date her?" she burst out.

Another deep laugh. "No, no! I only see her once."

She ignored the flash of disappointment. He might not be the R they'd been searching for, but finally they were speaking with someone who'd seen Mom. "Can you tell us anything about her? Any detail is appreciated."

His sigh echoed over the line. "I will try to remember, but it was long ago. She was sweet. Quiet. She said she loved to sit in the garden and draw. Or write. Wanted to be an artist. Silvia said she was very talented and creative. Adored her. And I could see how much your mama loved it here—she said it was a magical place."

The sting of tears surprised Bailey when she imagined her mother sitting in the same garden, caught up in dreams of her own.

Pris spoke up. "*Signore*, would you happen to know if she

was dating anyone in Positano? Or brought him to the party? We think he worked at the harbor with you at another boat company. His name begins with an *R*."

A tense silence fell as they waited for his response. "No, she was alone that night. Mentioned no boy." His voice held sympathy. "*Mi dispiace*, I don't remember anyone I worked with named R, but I am an old man now. Seventy-five years young, they say. I say they lie."

Bailey's spirits plummeted. She'd felt so close. "We understand."

"I will keep thinking on this. If I remember, I will call you. You leave me your number and I will ask some people, *va bene*?"

"That's very kind of you. Thanks." Dev rattled off their number twice and finally hung up.

Bailey sighed. "Another strikeout. But at least he remembered Mom."

Pris smiled. "She sounds like you, Bailey. Now I have this image of her right outside, sketching in the garden."

Pleasure shot through her. "Me too. But I feel like I'm going to spend the rest of my life freaking out over *R* names, wondering if they connect back to Mom."

"We still have two days," Dev insisted. "Who knows what can happen?"

Bailey grinned. "Well, look at you. Believing in magic and all that good stuff. How's Hawke?"

"Fine."

"Did you finally do the walk of shame?" Bailey teased.

Dev stuck out her tongue. "Leave me alone."

Pris wagged her finger in the air. "I was up and I heard you creep in around six a.m. You did."

"Oh my God, I will not discuss this like a juvenile," Dev said. Her cheeks were hot, which made Bailey and Pris laugh.

"Damn, I always shared with you," Bailey said. "And I gave details!"

"And now we're grown-ups and should act like it. I will say we discussed our future and came to a mutual decision."

Bailey flopped on the couch and pulled her knees up. "Tell us."

Dev tried to keep a straight face, but Bailey caught the wild look of happiness glinting in her eyes. "Hawke is coming back to Manhattan to work in about three months. We'll do long-distance, and then get a trial run when he moves back to New York."

Pris clapped her hands. "That's the best news! Man, it was like fate or something. Who comes all the way to Positano and finds her soul mate, plus he lives in New York?"

"Pretty lucky," Bailey said.

Dev cocked her head. "What about you, Pris? Have you decided what you're doing about Garrett?"

Pris paced gracefully back and forth. "I don't want to say this trip magically made all of our problems go away. But something's changed between us. I think it was me." She peeked over as if waiting for them to interrupt, but they kept silent. She continued. "It was exactly what you guys said. I never shared my feelings with him—nothing beyond temporary things like irritation, or sadness, or stress. None of the deeper stuff. I think I didn't *want* to feel it? Being here is a reminder I get to choose what makes me happy and what I want from my life. I lost my power along the way. Garrett's not to blame for that, but he also has to be willing to deal with the changes."

"Does he seem up for meeting you halfway?" Bailey asked. "You complain that he's always at work. Do you think he can change too?"

"Yes, if we both want to. And he says he does. These past few nights I've felt closer to him. We talk about everything like we did when we first fell in love. It's like we're getting to know each other again."

"And you? You mentioned pursuing a new career. Any ideas?" Dev asked.

"Well, I actually made a list of stuff I loved, to try and figure things out." She rolled her eyes. "Unfortunately, there wasn't that much, but I decided to contact one of my old friends from the New York City Ballet. We were on the phone for a while, catching up, and she says she always has spots for guest teachers or lecturers. She opened up her own ballet school and invited me to come by."

"You're kidding! Pris, that's amazing," Bailey said. Seeing her sister even mention ballet was a huge deal, and just by the expression on her face, it seemed right.

"What was the stuff on your list?" Dev asked.

Pris recited them. "Not much to work with, huh?"

"Actually, you're missing a key thing that you've always thrived on. Competition."

Pris stared at Dev in confusion. "What do you mean?"

"Dude, you run endless miles every day for—how long?"

"A few years," Pris said.

"That's a big deal. Have you ever considered entering the NYC Marathon? Or training for one?"

Bailey gasped. "What an awesome idea! I agree with Dev; you need a challenge for yourself. Running would be perfect."

Pris opened her mouth, then shut it. Surprise flickered across her features, along with something else Bailey spotted.

Excitement.

"I never thought of that," Pris said slowly.

"Well, think about it," Dev said. "Competitive running is a

huge pastime. Combine that with teaching dance, and you may have found a new direction."

Pris nodded. "I'll think about it. I have no idea where it would lead, or if I even want to teach. But it's time I open myself up to more opportunities. I'm tired of believing my only role was as wife and mother. I'm so much more than that."

Bailey's chest tightened. She was so proud of her sisters. How had they made such leaps and bounds in only two weeks?

Because they'd finally been truthful with each other. And themselves. It was like Mom had been guiding them here all along.

Pris sat next to her and gave her an affectionate squeeze. "What about you, Bae? Will you be making any big changes?"

A touch of shame hit her. She wasn't leaving Italy with a new love or an old flame. She still had no real job prospects lined up, or even an idea of where she wanted to settle next. As usual, she was caught in between, but this time, it didn't fill her with a sense of passion and adventure. It felt a bit . . . empty. She forced out a laugh. "Guess I didn't get the memo we should've been working on transforming into butterflies. But I'm excited to get back. Find a new play. Maybe take a few art classes and work part-time at that café I love. I'm good."

Oh God, she sounded pathetic.

Dev leaned in, her gaze fastened on hers. "Bae, I'm sorry I was such a bitch."

She blinked. "You already apologized for that and we moved on."

"No, not for the asshole Liam incident. Or calling you out on your stuff. I'm not sorry at all for those—I meant every word. I'm sorry for making you feel less than just because you're not like me."

"What do you mean?"

Dev sighed. "You're comfortable seeing how things unfold, and there's nothing wrong with that. I'm someone who needs a secure nine-to-five job. I need to know where to go and what to do when I get up in the morning. But does that make me right? Or better? No. It just makes me judgmental and mean. You're different and it's time I supported you rather than trying to make you feel bad for it."

The apology healed the wounds that had been deeply slashed so many years ago. She respected Dev so much—the way she lived her life with high goals and no apologies. The way she allowed herself to fall for Hawke against all rationale. Knowing that Dev really did support her meant . . . everything. "Thanks," she said softly. "I really appreciate it."

"Is Will still texting?" Pris asked curiously.

She nodded. "Yeah. I may talk with him when I get back. He's insistent about this play he wrote for me to star in. I've been thinking about what you guys said, and I want to make sure I broke up with him for the right reasons."

Maybe that was her big change—allowing herself to be vulnerable. It wasn't about losing her free-spirited ways, or knowing she'd never be like Dev, happy in a job that constricted her independence. Or like Pris, pursuing marriage and a family. It was about accepting deeper parts of herself she was suddenly able to see. Maybe that was enough.

Her sisters had helped with that. Now it was time to do her own work.

She stood up. "Okay, enough analysis. Let's get on with the agenda. Dev?"

Dev grabbed her planner, opened up the page, and frowned. "Hmm, weird. I could have sworn I had the museum tours and cooking class but it just says *beach*."

Pris jumped up. "Getting changed now! Beach day!"

Bailey did a little dance, jiggling her hips. "You're a genius, Dev! How did you know we desperately needed another day to lounge around?"

Dev bit her lip. "I don't remember doing it." She scrunched up her face and studied her book. "Is that . . . Wite-Out? Did someone change my planner?"

But Dev was shouting to an empty room.

Bailey was already getting changed, trying not to giggle.

CHAPTER FORTY

Olivia

I got the news after my third daughter, Bailey, was born. Aunt Silvia had died.

There was no funeral. She'd requested to be cremated with no ceremony, intent on allowing her spirit to fly free with no mourning. She'd never wanted unhappy, crying faces to follow her into the afterworld.

I received the deed to the Positano cottage in the mail with a note from her lawyer. It had been closed up for a while and winterized. A local checked in regularly and was automatically paid from the estate. She also sent me the sweater I'd loved so much. I immediately pulled it around me, the threads soft from age, the blinding golden colors of sunset a reminder of her bright spirit. The scent of sandalwood and exotic spice drifted to my nostrils, bringing me back to that special night when we were both getting ready to meet the men we loved.

I grieved in private, tucking the deed away with Rafe's letters in my trunk. When my hand brushed the crinkled paper, the memories hit hard, making me double over with such a painful loss, I couldn't breathe. But I kept my promise. I didn't read the letters or think of Positano. I buried all of it under a hand-stitched quilt and hid it in the back of the dark closet.

I believe there are two paths in life, one playing out now, and the other in another timeline. Sometimes, the barriers blur and I can almost feel myself with Rafe, sailing on his boat, eating dinner as we watch the sun sink, raising tanned children who run free and speak English and Italian, uninhibited in ways my own children can never be. As I cart Pris to dance class and Dev to gymnastics and Bailey to preschool so they can learn how to socialize well with others, appreciate achievement, and be well-rounded, a slice of me wonders if it truly matters, if this is a matrix-like snow globe where we run as fast as we can but never get anyplace that will make us truly happy. I remember holding hands with Rafe while we lingered for endless hours waiting for a fish to bite. The slow crawl of time. The simplicity of our joy. The stripped-down version of myself and the life apart I chose with Adam. Eventually, the thoughts fade away and I snap out of it. I fall back into this current moment, go over all the things left to accomplish in my day, and push the image of the boy I loved away. Better to think of it as a misty girlish dream rather than a reality.

It was better that way.

Years passed, one after another. I lost my father first, and then my mother way too soon. I threw myself into raising my girls, and life was busy. Adam and I bloomed for many years, especially when Bailey was young—intent on both living up to our vows to rebuild a strong foundation. And we were happy for a long time, until time and neglect began to erode the good.

I found out he cheated on me when Bailey was thirteen years old and in her temperamental years. Somehow, he'd begun slipping back into allowing work to become his prime focus. Was it all his fault?

Taking another woman to bed? Yes.

Growing apart? No.

I found my own outlet—my daughters. I became embroiled in school activities, dating, shuffling car rides, and the other million tasks that ran a household. Pris was attending daily ballet classes and moving toward the goal of attending the NYC Ballet school, so my calendar was demanding. As Adam spent late nights at the office, I stopped nagging him to come home for dinner, finding it almost easier to do my own thing and be available for what the girls needed. I realized they adored their father as a distant figure who occasionally swept in with kisses, compliments, and the deep conversations that intrigued them. To them, he was a hero in the shadows, appearing when they needed him most.

Maybe there's no such thing as villains or victims in a relationship. Maybe it's just about two people doing their best, compromising, forgiving, until it becomes too much; until giving in to our own inner selfishness is easier. Do we ever make a conscious choice to hurt someone, or does it just happen in tiny increments—daily choices that erode a foundation until it becomes easy to fool ourselves, to believe this one tiny choice won't matter.

And then it's too late to fix.

This was my marriage. An intricate map of twists and turns, where I hurt him by shutting away the deepest part of myself and he tried to fill his own void, not knowing why he felt so empty. Husband and wife who sleep in the same bed, brush their teeth at the same sink, birth children, yet are strangers to each other.

I was the boring one, but I'd accepted my role without bitterness. Because as I watched my girls grow and bloom and come into themselves, I knew it was worth it. The sacrifice of

Rafe from my life had a purpose. And even with the affair, as much as it hurt, I was able to accept Adam's faults because he still gave the girls what they needed, even if it was on his terms and he got more kudos than he deserved.

Adam came back to me after I found out about the affair. He was apologetic and hoping to see if we could revitalize our marriage a second time.

So, we tried, but this time was different. Neither of us had the motivation or fierce focus we'd had the first round. Slowly, we began to let each other go, finding a balance within our relationship and being parents.

Sometimes, as I stared at the young women before me, whom I adored with a ferocity that could never be described, I wondered what their own choices would be one day. Pris was giving up everything for a life of dance, cutting away all the other parts to smooth the way to success. Dev used her logic to make all the hard decisions, preferring balance sheets rather than her heart. Bailey was my artist, a free-spirited adventurer who was in love with the idea of love but seemed unable to ever settle. I caught shades of myself in all my girls—in their passionate, mirrored gazes. The fierce focus and zeal for a satisfying career. The freedom of creative expression in quiet, solitary moments. The lure of passion and possibility around the next corner. They were taking the world by storm on their own terms, and nothing could stop them.

At least, that's what I believed.

Time gave me a very different perspective, but like everything else in my life, it was too late to fix.

CHAPTER FORTY-ONE

Pris

Pris sighed and looked around at the cottage. Half-packed bags lined up for tomorrow's early departure. A bittersweet sadness flowed through her at the idea of leaving. So much had happened here, and Mom had been a testament to all of it. These past two weeks had changed everything.

The thought of seeing Garrett again stirred hope. She hoped they could continue to grow together rather than apart, but knowing next week she'd be starting a new adventure for herself was key. She'd signed up to begin ballet classes again and get back in shape, and was meeting with a trainer to learn about the marathon. She was ready to embark on a new journey to find what fulfilled her. The past—or the years lost—no longer mattered so much.

Because they weren't lost. She had her precious Thomas. A marriage worth fighting for. A life that was still so good, it was time she woke up and began living it.

Dev groaned. "I'm not looking forward to those stairs."

Bailey laughed. "Oh, come on, your legs are like rocks now! Where'd you make reservations for our final dinner?"

"The Mirage. I got us a sea view and the menu looks sick," Dev said.

"You could have invited Hawke," Bailey mentioned. "We don't mind."

Dev smiled. "Thanks, but I wanted it to be just us tonight. Kind of our farewell. I'll see him tonight after dinner." Her gaze skirted over the cottage. "This turned out to be an amazing vacation, but I wish we'd been able to solve the mystery we came for. Do you think we'll ever figure out who R is?"

"We may never know the full truth about Mom and R, but maybe we weren't meant to." Pris spoke slowly, her brow furrowed in a frown. "I feel like we were meant to find her house. *Our* house. At first, I thought I needed to protect her legacy. I didn't like the idea of us thinking she was unfaithful, or not the perfect Mom I always saw. But now? I feel like this was always about us."

"Us?" Dev asked, tilting her head.

Pris smiled. "Yeah. Us. We were broken and no one knew how to fix it. We lost Mom but we gained one another. And I kind of feel like she's been here, guiding us back, and this house was part of it all. Is that weird?"

Bailey sighed. "Not at all. Sounds perfect to me. Why do we always try to make it about a guy anyway?"

Dev laughed. "Truth. Even though I found one when I wasn't looking. I guess I'm learning the best-laid plans don't always work out."

Bailey fell back in exaggeration. "What did you say? Plans may not work? I'm sorry—can you repeat?"

Dev punched her in the arm. "Cut it out! I'm taking a risk here, but I'm going to try."

Pris beamed. "That's all we want you to do. Hey, if you ever need a reminder, I can text you this picture I snapped on the beach." She scrolled quickly through and showed her the screen. The picture showed Dev with a straw hat perched low on her brow, sprawled out on a red-and-yellow-striped lounge chair, mouth hanging open in an obvious snore.

Bailey cracked up, which got her another punch. "I told you to delete that!" Dev yelled.

"Never. I'm printing it out for my Christmas cards this year."

"You both suck."

Bailey jumped to avoid another attack and floated toward her room. "Gonna sit in the garden before dinner and do some sketching."

"I'll join you," Pris said. "I want to soak up as much as possible before we leave. I feel closest to Mom in the garden."

"So do I," Bailey said.

Dev grabbed her phone. "I'm going for a short walk with Hawke. Just going to change real quick."

"Okay, meet you outside, Bae," Pris called. She grabbed a water bottle and headed toward the front door.

Then stopped short.

A man was standing outside, behind the screen door. His hand was raised to knock, but he lowered it when he caught sight of her. "Hello? Can I help you?" Pris asked, walking forward. In Boston, she'd never open the door to a stranger, but Positano was so friendly, strangers invited you to dinner daily.

She swung the door open and paused.

The man stared back at her and, immediately, goose bumps prickled her skin. His hair was a mop of salt-and-pepper curls. He was taller than average and seemed fit. His face held thick brows, a full mouth, and a broad, slightly crooked nose. But it was his eyes that mesmerized Pris. Deep and dark, like staring into a midnight abyss. Full of emotion. Sadness. Longing. Regret. It was all there contained in his gaze, and suddenly, Pris began to shake, sensing all the days before had led up to this one right here, in this moment.

"My name is Rafael Sartori. I was a friend of your mother's."

The water bottle slipped out of her hand and crashed to the floor. She tried to get her voice to work. Finally, it came out in a squeak. "Please come in. Let me get my sisters. We've been looking for you."

He bent and retrieved the bottle, pressing it back into her hand. Pris called out.

"I told you I'm coming I just—" Bailey trailed off, clutching her sketch pad to her chest.

Dev came around the corner and just stared.

"This is Rafael Sartori," Pris said, her voice a tiny bit stronger. "He knew Mom."

The silence in the room felt explosive.

Finally, he spoke. "I'm here to tell you about Olivia Moretti. About what happened." He paused. "About us."

CHAPTER FORTY-TWO

Olivia

It's the first day of summer.

I woke up thinking of him today, as I often do, but this time I dragged out the trunk from my closet and lifted the lid.

The house is quiet. Bailey still comes in and out depending on who she's dating or what job she picked up, but even then she has her own room and I rarely see her. Adam and I have been divorced for years now, finally agreeing the girls could handle the split.

I kept going back to the irony. Bailey was just a little younger than I was when my parents decided to divorce. I'd been set on giving them a different upbringing, sure Adam and I would make it, but we did our best. Mom was right. Sometimes, it's better to let go and focus on being happy as individuals. Mom definitely did better than Dad, though. Till the very end, I always believed he regretted the divorce and missed Mom.

I pulled out the quilt first, setting it aside, then lifted the pile of papers. My hands shook only a bit as I sat on my bed with the stack of letters. Slowly, as if unwrapping a precious gift, I began to read through them.

His lilting voice sang in my head with each word. The memory of his scent rose to my nostrils, as if imprinted on the crinkled paper. But it was always his eyes that haunted me—dark and sooty, full of warmth and a love that had always been fully for me.

I wondered if he was married with children. If he'd stayed in his father's house and took over the business. If he was well and happy.

I didn't plan to begin writing the letter. I reached for the familiar stationery that sat in my bedside drawer along with my favorite pen, and the words poured out of me, the scratch of the ink flowing over sheer crisp white.

I signed my name and paused, rereading the note.

Odd, if I had an actual cell phone number, I'd be able to text him. If I had an email, I could make sure it was delivered right to his inbox. Technology had changed everything. My girls laughed at me when I needed their help with remotes and phones and the damn computer that kept me a perpetual student. But we'd been right to stick to letters. It was more personal than a voice over the phone. It was an outpouring of the heart, unedited, raw, and unfiltered.

It was what Rafe deserved from me.

I sealed it up, wrote out the familiar address, and put it aside to bring to the post office later. I didn't expect him to write back, but I needed to put the connection out there. Just writing to him gave my insides space and light, and I got dressed with a smile on my face.

He was out there, hopefully happy, hopefully living a great big beautiful life. It felt right to reach out now, after all these years, to let him know I'd never stopped loving him. Age changed perspective. I saw things so clearly now, the good and bad, the wrong and right, and everything in between. It was too late for any regrets, and I refused to have them.

Now I could only sit back and watch my daughters choose their paths. If only I could help heal the breaks within their relationships. Dev had frozen Bailey out of her life because of a fight over a boy—but I knew it was bigger than that. A betrayal between sisters cut deep, and no matter how much I tried, they refused to mend the break. Pris had given up her career for love and given me my first grandchild, but something in her eyes haunted me, a regret that seemed so awfully familiar. When I tried to talk to her about it, she always waved it off with a laugh. But I still wondered.

Is this the fate of a mother? To worry and wonder about her children no matter the age? To beg and borrow and steal from God in order to give them everything? To help them make the right choices when I knew myself it would be impossible—because without pain there isn't real joy?

I sat with the questions while I got dressed, went to the post office, and mailed the letter.

I got no response to either my questions or my letter, until years later.

• • • •

When the letter arrived, I didn't open it for a long, long time.

I carried it with me in my pocket, occasionally running my fingers over the sharp edges to remind myself it was real. I had written to Rafe off and on for the past few years. The letters were never returned, so I had no idea if he was throwing them out unread or choosing not to respond.

It didn't matter. He'd become my confidant, a friend to reach out to in the middle of the night. I shared everything with him, holding nothing back, as I had those summers we spent together. Writing to him gave me hope and breath. I was happier than I'd been in a while, even if our connection was only imaginary.

Finally, I sat down that evening, poured myself some hot tea, and read the letter.

Dearest Livia,

For too long, I was unable to accept your letters. It was best for both of us—to finally let go of a past that was too beautiful, it may have ended up destroying us both. I had done my best to keep those summers locked away. Even that one precious week when I believed you'd come back to me is a memory best not to revisit. I convinced myself our time together was a dream, but when I saw my name on those envelopes, I realized I alone could ruin a life that I'd rebuilt after you left. I couldn't do that, dolcezza. Not even for you.

But now, I find myself at a crossroads. I still think about you. I still wonder what could have been. I still want to gaze upon your face one more time.

So, yes, I will meet you here for your 65th birthday.

R

A mix of emotions slammed through me, so tumultuous I could only hang on until my breathing steadied.

He was agreeing to see me.

Something about my sixty-fifth birthday called to me. I'd begun dreaming I'd spend it in Positano, at Aunt Silvia's house, close to the memory of Rafe's presence. I'd written to him and asked if he'd be willing to meet me, never expecting a response. But now it was going to happen.

I'd see Rafe on May 25. My birthday.

Tears sprang to my eyes, and I threw back my head and laughed. I wished I could call Aunt Silvia or my mother to share my secret. I wished I could gather my daughters and tell them about my past, and beg them for forgiveness if I wasn't enough because a piece of me had always belonged to him.

Instead, I cradled his letter to my heart. I had plans to make. Tickets. Arrangements to have the house ready when I arrived. And get better from this blasted cold that I couldn't seem to get rid of. I had to be healthy for the trip.

I was going to see Rafe.

CHAPTER FORTY-THREE

Dev

Rafael sat down on the couch. Pris was doing her elegant pacing again, and Bailey perched on the opposite side of him. Dev decided to stand, arms crossed in front of her chest. Her insides were jittery with nerves and excitement.

They'd found him.

Or, he'd found them. She couldn't stop her greedy gaze from cataloguing each one of his features. A canvas bag lay beside him he was holding tight, his fingers in a deathlike grip.

She wondered what was in there he cared about so fiercely.

Dev cleared her throat and took control. Pris and Bailey seemed a bit struck mute, so she did what she did best. Ask questions.

"We've been looking for you since we arrived," Dev began. "We never knew about this house, or Mom's relationship with you, until we found your letters. We wanted to come to experience the place where she spent her summers. A place she really loved."

"Ah, she kept my letters." He nodded. "I always wondered. Your mother loves this place very much."

"How did you find us?"

He blinked and Dev was struck by his beautiful dark eyes, framed by lush lashes. "You met my son, Paolo. He gave you a tour of the grotto."

Bailey gasped. "Oh my God, that was your son!"

"*Sì*. He now runs the business with my other son. I have been retired a while. We were talking and he mentioned he gave a tour to three beautiful girls who had a family house in Positano. A home inherited by their mother. I would have never thought anything about it, but when I asked my son the names, he mentioned Priscilla." A flicker of emotion crossed over his face. "It is a unique name, but I pushed it out of my mind. It is too much of a coincidence, no?"

"You knew my name," Pris breathed out.

Rafe nodded. "I saw your mother when you were about four years old. She showed me a picture. But I never intended to come here. It was only yesterday I met a friend who mentioned the same three girls looking for a man by the name of R who once ran a boat-tour business, living in their mama's house. I knew then. I decided to come."

"Thank you," Bailey whispered. "There's so much we are hoping to learn. Things only you'd be able to tell us."

"I don't understand why you are here." A frown creased his brow. "Your mother could answer all your questions. She made the decision not to meet with me months ago, and I respected it. So, why are you looking for me?"

A cold chill ran down Dev's spine.

He didn't know.

The knowledge hit her full force. Of course he didn't. Mom had died before she could meet him on her birthday, so Rafael assumed she'd changed her mind.

Oh God.

She shared a horrified glance with her sisters, then lowered her voice to a gentle tone. "Rafael, our mom died back in February. She got pneumonia and was gone before any of us could even talk to her." Tears stung her eyes like tiny bees. "She didn't meet you because she couldn't. Not because she didn't want to."

Dev would never forget the look on his face. Grief crumpled his features, and agony shone in those dark eyes. A painful sound emitted from his throat, and he covered his face with his hands, muttering a word over and over.

Dolcezza.

He'd loved her. The proof was evident in his reaction and his broken whisper. Whatever had happened, her mother had been deeply loved, and the knowledge soothed her soul rather than inciting betrayal. Bailey had been right. Life wasn't a map of strict boundaries of black and white. It was a mess of gray areas that mushed together in no evident pattern. All Dev knew in this moment was that their love had been real and had made Mom who she was.

Bailey was the first to reach out. She closed the distance and put her arm around him as he cried. Pris was next, her hand tentatively laid on his arm. Dev took the time to go into the dining room and fish out the letters from Pris's bag. She knelt in front of him and he lifted his head.

"These are your letters," she said softly. "She kept them in a trunk in her bedroom. We've been trying to piece together her past, but this is all we had to go on. All I can say is you were a huge part of her life. She never forgot. She always loved you."

He took the letters, smoothing out the pages, and dragged in a breath.

"I will tell you everything. But I think this will help."

He opened his bag and slipped out a pile of papers tied with a frayed green ribbon. "I kept her letters also. All of them. They will show who your mother was. How special she was to me."

Dev took them like the precious gift they were. Bailey was freely crying and the emotion in the air was electric.

Pris stood up slowly. "We need wine. Rafael, can I interest you in some wine?"

A smile touched his lips. "*Sì*. Lots of wine, *grazie*."

CHAPTER FORTY-FOUR

Olivia

Fate stepped in one final time.

I wasn't able to get to Positano for my birthday. The cold that had lingered turned to pneumonia and put me in the hospital. The illness sank so deep into my lungs, and exploited a weakness in my heart that couldn't hold up under the infection.

I died without seeing my girls. I couldn't tell them to be strong; to forgive one another; to follow their hearts without apology.

I couldn't tell them about Rafe. I couldn't get word to him about my illness and the real reason I'd never show up to meet him on May 25.

I never got to see his face one last time and let him know he'd always been the one.

Was this punishment for my mistakes? Proof we were never meant to be together in this lifetime? Or just the cruelty of life—random and sometimes unfair, ready to spring out and rip apart what you believed you controlled?

It didn't matter any longer.

I thought about my precious girls; those beautiful summers in Positano; the booming laugh of my aunt Silvia. I saw my mother beckoning me with love and the births of Pris, Dev, and Bailey with Adam at my side.

Rafe's face was the last image I saw before I closed my eyes.

And I smiled.

CHAPTER FORTY-FIVE

Bailey

The sun set and they missed their reservations.

The four of them sat together, sifting through letters their mother had written. Reading some aloud. Steeped in another time, when young love had changed her. Each letter Bailey read revealed another piece of her mother, until the entire puzzle finally clicked together.

Rafe shared the story of their first meeting, through the summers of college, and what happened afterward. Sometimes he'd pause, struggling to harness his emotions, and then slowly continue. He was generous with his stories, as if he realized they were greedy for everything.

It was the story from a romance saga.

Bailey thought about her father. Remarried with his own new life. Had he ever suspected Mom loved another? Or had he been so wrapped up in his own wants and needs, he hadn't taken the time to figure it out, or care?

Bailey would never know. She'd never tell Dad about Rafe. There was no need to hurt him at this point, or have him question his entire marriage. That would only bring unnecessary pain.

"Did you show up on her birthday?" Bailey asked.

"Yes. I came here to the house. Waited in the garden for hours, until dark. The place was still shut down, and I knew she wasn't coming."

"I'm so sorry," Pris said gently. "I can't imagine how Mom felt knowing she couldn't tell you why. It happened so fast. She complained of a cold, which went into her chest, and suddenly she was admitted with pneumonia. We had no chance to even get to the hospital to see her before she passed of complications."

"I am sorry for all of you. To lose her without a last conversation must have been hard. But you know now how much she loved you." He smiled. "You all look so much like her. Your mannerisms are similar."

Pleasure shot through Bailey. He motioned to the discarded sketchbook. "Do you draw too?"

Bailey nodded. "Yes. I heard Mom sketched a lot in the garden."

"It was her favorite place. I brought something else." He fished around in his bag and brought out a piece of sketch paper. On it, his image was captured beautifully. He lounged on the chair in the garden. Curls falling over his face. Laughing. Sunlight streaming faint shadows over him. Mom had captured his essence—the joy and love as he looked at her.

"It's so beautiful," she choked out, reaching out to touch the image. "When did she draw this?"

He wrinkled his nose. "Summer of 'seventy-eight? We'd spend a lot of time in the garden. She loved to sketch—I always believed she'd become a great artist herself."

"She loved her job at the gallery," Dev said. "But she never pursued her own craft."

"I think she was happy it was just for her," Bailey said. "I used to catch her sometimes. Sitting alone, sketch pad in her lap, looking off into space with a tiny smile. She looked happy."

"Yes. That was so like her."

"What about you, Rafe? Are you still married?"

"*Sì.* I have two sons, who run the boat business. I met my wife a decade after your mama left. For too long, my heart wasn't open to try again, but my wife broke me down. She is good. Kind. A wonderful mother." He smiled and Bailey was struck by his gentleness. "I love her."

"Mom loved our dad too," Pris finally said. "I think it's okay to love two people differently. One may not be better or worse."

"I can't help but feel guilty," Dev said. "I was the reason she didn't come back. Do you think every time Mom looked at me, she remembered what she gave up?"

Rafe shook his head, his mouth firm. "No. In fact, I think it was the opposite. I think every time she looked at you, she felt pride and a certain peace I couldn't give her. Your mother wasn't meant to live here with me. I believe we were sent to each other to learn lessons on how to love without expectations or barriers." His gaze probed, resting on each of their faces as if searching for their innermost thoughts. "Your mother was a big part of my life. If I hadn't met her, I wouldn't have the life I lead now, and it's one I love and treasure. And she wouldn't have the three of you. You see, it's not about regrets or what-ifs. It's about choosing what's best at the time, and we both did that. We made each other better. More whole, so we could go back into the world and carve our own path. Do you understand?"

And suddenly, looking into his gentle brown eyes, Bailey understood. Life was so much bigger than the tiny little worlds built around people's expectations and identities. It wasn't about taking the wrong road, after all, or being afraid to make mistakes or go after what you want. It was about daily choices to live your life to the fullest, even if they weren't easy.

Maybe Mom and Rafe were never supposed to be. Maybe they were meant to love each other for a specific time. Because it was the jagged edges and sharp corners that created character—the pain from love and loss—the pleasure from giving in to something you wanted more than anything.

Yes, she'd died before she could see Rafe again. But somehow, Bailey sensed it was meant to happen that way. Maybe the past had to remain there, frozen in time and memory like a perfect, bittersweet taste that lingered forever. Maybe a face-to-face meeting would have changed it all, forcing Rafe to make a decision that could have hurt his own family.

Mom and Rafe had made their own choices.

Now it was time to make hers.

A sense of peace washed over Bailey. She glanced over at her sisters, who looked like they'd reached the same type of conclusion. Pris nodded, and Dev looked as if she'd come to her own revelation. Bailey reached out and took their hands, needing the connection, and there was no hesitation between them.

They all squeezed back in a united front.

Evening had settled in when Rafe finally stood. "I must go. Do you leave tomorrow?"

Bailey nodded. "Would it be okay if we stayed in touch? Is that weird? If you don't want to—"

"I would like that very much." He smiled at each of them, raw emotion in his dark eyes. "I know your mama would be so happy right now. To know you are here, in one of her favorite places, together. Here is my cell phone number."

They exchanged theirs quickly and he walked to the door.

"Thank you for this. For letting me know and spending the time with me. I am here for all of you if you need anything."

They hugged one last time and then Rafe disappeared.

Bailey stared out into the night. She was full of a mix of pain, elation, sadness, but most of all—joy.

"Well, that was a hell of a finale," Dev said.

Pris and Bailey laughed. Pris wiped away a tear from her cheek and shook her head. "I'm a mess," she groaned. "I feel like I watched *The Notebook* five times in a row!"

Dev winced. "Ugh, I hate that movie."

Bailey rolled her eyes. "Are you even human? Then again, you never understood *The Way We Were*. Now I know why Mom sobbed uncontrollably. It had a bigger meaning."

Dev snorted. "I prefer *Silver Linings Playbook*. Now, that was a love story."

Bailey and Pris stared at her.

"What? It was direct and to the point."

"With a mental illness?" Bailey asked.

Dev shrugged. "Whatever. Should we go and get something to eat or are you guys too wiped out?"

"No, let's grab something at the café quick and finish packing," Bailey said. "You want to spend some time with Hawke and tell him what happened."

"Plus, we need some processing time. That was heavy," Pris said.

"We did it, guys," Bailey said. "We met R. We got the truth."

"Yeah," Pris said. "The outcome wasn't what I expected, but I'm okay. Actually, more than okay. God, did you see the way he looked? He really loved her."

They pondered in silence.

Bailey took a deep breath and told the truth. "I love you guys. Can we promise each other we won't go back to the way things were? I need you."

Pris put her hand in the circle like they'd do when they were little and had made one another a promise. "I need you too. We need one another. It's a pact."

Dev put hers in. "Pact."

Bailey made the circle complete. "Pact."

She'd gotten her family back.

EPILOGUE

Ten Months Later

Pris

She rushed through Times Square and to Forty-Fourth Street. Ignoring the massive crowds and lineups, she pushed into the throng in front of Carmine's and waved a hand. "Meeting someone!" she called out. The hostess nodded, and Pris spotted the table immediately toward the back.

Pris reached them, laughing as she dispersed hugs. "I'm so sorry I'm late! I couldn't get a cab anywhere," she said.

"Totally fine, we just ordered our wine," Bailey said. "You cut your hair! It looks so good!"

Pris touched the shorter bob and wrinkled her nose. "Thanks—it was time. I feel so much freer this way."

"Dude, you look gorgeous as usual," Dev said. "How did rehearsal go?"

"Really good. I think some of the girls will get in, but you never know. It's not as much about classical training as stage presence now."

"You're enjoying teaching, then?" Bailey asked.

"I am." The waitress came by for their order, then came back with a glass of Chianti for Pris. "It was definitely a learning curve, but it's been a few months and I'm getting into it. God knows, it took me three months of nonstop work just to feel like I can get myself into shape."

Dev laughed. "Especially after not being able to zip your jeans after our trip."

"Nightmare. But I feel fit now and better able to teach. And of course, my coach beats my ass regularly."

"Are you entering the half marathon?" Bailey asked.

She nodded. "I'm going for it." Besides training for her first official big race, Pris had scored a part-time job teaching ballet for a renowned studio. The kids were there for serious career pursuit, and she enjoyed helping them level up their skills. She'd gone in specifically to support some of her students who were rehearsing for a big production at a local theater. "I realized even though I enjoyed running fundraisers for charities, I do better on a more personal basis. It's like I go home now and feel accomplished."

"I get it." Dev slathered some bread with butter. "That's why I'm sticking with teaching for now. I turned down the last job offer at Schneider & Partners. Everything looked great on paper, but my gut warned me I wouldn't be happy. The interview board had already advised it's more than a full-time job, and I'd be working round the clock."

Bailey winced. "That sounds awful! Good for you, Dev. The students at NYU are lucky to have you."

"Thanks. Jordan is leaving next year, so I'll be up for chair. I have a good shot at it. Hawke was supportive either way, but I think he's secretly relieved I didn't take the job."

Pris looked at her sister, taking in the natural glow of her skin and light in her eye. "And how is Hawke doing?" she teased.

On cue, Dev blushed. "Fine. We're good."

Bailey laughed with delight. "Did you move in together yet?"

"Next month we're making it official."

Pris shrieked with glee and Dev turned redder. "Okay, guys, calm down. It's not like I just got a date for prom."

"This is even better! He's coming with us in July, right?"

Dev nodded. "Yes, we're both taking the time off. I can't wait—only two more months."

Pris couldn't wait either. Garrett was going to join them this time, and he was looking forward to seeing the cottage they'd all fallen in love with. With Dev's teaching schedule, July was the best month to take off for travel, and they'd all put in vacation requests months ahead, carving out two full weeks to spend together.

"I already spoke with Roberto, so the place will be all set," Dev said.

"Perfect. Bae, tell us everything about you. What's your next project?" Pris asked.

Her sister retained the same open enthusiasm, but there was a new quietness that radiated from her. As if she were more focused. "Well, *Bedding My Baby* was a huge success. Will couldn't believe how it blew up—something about a romantic comedy nowadays resonates. Suddenly, he's been in demand and so have I. I have an opportunity to do a play for this indie theater gaining popularity. I think I'm going to take it."

"That's great. You were amazing in *Bedding My Baby*. I swear, Bae, you were made for the stage," Pris said.

"Yeah, all that drama you court ended up being worthwhile," Dev teased.

"Rather flow with my emotions than check a flowchart for them," Bailey retorted.

Pris laughed. "You guys never stop. What's going on with you and Will?"

Bailey regarded them thoughtfully. "We're taking it slow. Will and I agreed to be monogamous with each other and be honest with our feelings and where we're at. I like going deeper into a relationship—I've never done that before. I'm not one to slap a label on what we are to each other—and I'm certainly not thinking marriage at this point but . . ." She trailed off.

"What?" Dev asked.

"He makes me happy. I think I'm just . . . happy."

Pris smiled. "It's nice, isn't it?"

"Yeah. It's also nice to know I'm in this. Usually, I have one foot out the door. I thought it was smart, but now I see it was cowardly."

"You've never been a coward, Bae," Dev said quietly. "You're a force to be reckoned with."

Bailey brightened and threw her shoulders back. "Yeah. I am!"

They laughed and the waiter came by to drop off their plates. The food was served family-style, so the platters held chicken parmigiana, escargot with garlic and oil, and spaghetti vongole. Pris stared at the magnificent food on the table, then at her sisters. A rush of emotion slammed through her—fierce and strong and beautiful. She raised her glass.

"A toast. To Mom, on her birthday. Happy birthday, Mom," Pris said.

Bailey and Dev clinked their glasses to hers.

And Pris smiled at them, grabbing onto the moment, silently thanking her mother for . . . everything.

Olivia

I understand everything now.

I realize we don't have to be one person or another. We are all of them, and supposed to change as we live—we pick the people we can love who will accept us, support the change, grow with us. And I believe there are certain people you are meant to love to get to the next phase—people who allow us to grow and become what we are meant to be—but they are never meant to be ours forever.

Yes, it's sad, but also . . . reassuring. It means there will always be someone just for us, at the time we need them the most. And isn't love forever? Isn't a memory everlasting, frozen in time, reminding us of all the beautiful things in life to be grateful for? That's how I like to look at it. But if you never open up your heart, afraid to take risks because of the possibility of blowing it up or making huge mistakes—you will live half a life. That is where regrets come from.

There are no more regrets for me. I have loved two men with my heart and my soul. I have raised my three girls with a passion and purpose that filled me. I have walked this earth and done my very best to make the most of every moment.

It is enough.

I watch my girls as they talk and laugh and toast me. They are happy. They have found one another again and are living their lives to the fullest, as I've always dreamed for them. Somehow, Positano has both healed and pushed them to be more. To be their authentic selves, messy and imperfect, yet so beautiful. There is so much beauty within the pain.

I hadn't seen that before, but now I do.

I smile and look into their beloved faces.

And know everything is exactly how it should be.

ACKNOWLEDGMENTS

I wrote this book during the pandemic. The story of three sisters who go on a search to discover their mother's hidden past was a light that helped me through some dark times. It was as if each morning, I was able to take a breath and escape into the beauty of Positano, the sweetness of first love, and the exquisite pain that comes from life itself when we open our hearts to others.

I believe in the power of stories and the ability to heal, even if it means a few hours of escape from harsh reality. I hope I did my job and was able to offer that for you within the pages of this book.

Though the story originated from my sometimes maddening, sometimes magnificent Muse, a team helps get a book to the next level. A big thanks to the team at Berkley for all of their hard work and talent—my editor, Kerry Donovan; the copyeditor; editorial assistant Mary Baker; my marketing and PR team, Jessica Mangicaro and Tara O'Connor. Gratitude to my agent extraordinaire, Kevan Lyon, and my first-round content editor, Kristi Yanta.

Special thanks to Mary Leo for helping me get the details of Positano correct and reading the first draft.

High five to my amazing assistant, Mandy Lawler. Thanks to Nina Grinstead and Mary Dube at Valentine PR for their talent at helping me think outside the box. A big hug to all of my supportive readers, bookstagrammers, bloggers, and book clubs—I am forever grateful for your help in loving and sharing my books.

The Secret Love Letters of Olivia Moretti

JENNIFER PROBST

DISCUSSION QUESTIONS

1. Priscilla, Devon, and Bailey are all very different women. Did you relate to one of the sisters more than the other characters? How did their different personalities and beliefs about their mother cause discord between them?
2. Do you agree with Olivia's decision to keep her romance and the Positano home a secret from her daughters? Why or why not?
3. Olivia makes some difficult decisions throughout her relationship with Rafael. What did you see as the turning point in their relationship? And how did each decision she made about their possible future affect her?
4. Positano becomes almost an additional character in the story. What were your favorite scenes? Have you ever visited Italy? To which region would you most like to travel?

5. When Priscilla takes a walk on the Path of the Gods, the physical hike becomes a personal journey for her. Did you have any strong feelings about the fate of her marriage and her choice to give up ballet?
6. When Devon meets Hawke, she believes he's interested in Bailey. Were you surprised he had a stronger connection with Devon rather than Bailey? Why? In what ways were Hawke and Devon well suited?
7. Devon and Bailey were estranged due to a decision Bailey made years ago. Can you relate to Dev's feeling of betrayal? Or did you think she should have forgiven her sister sooner? Did you see Hawke's arrival as a problem for the sisters?
8. Which of the sisters did you feel changed the most after their trip to Italy together?
9. Olivia's love story is interwoven throughout the sisters' story. Did you like having her point of view included in the story?
10. Did you agree with Olivia's decision to give her husband a second chance? Why or why not? If she had decided to stay with Rafe, how do you think the story would have changed? Would she have been any happier, in your opinion?
11. What were your feelings about Rafe? Do you agree with him responding to Olivia's letters? Do you think if he'd met her for her sixty-fifth birthday, they would have ended up together?
12. Life is a series of both choices and surprises that throw us off our path. Do you think Olivia and Rafe were soul mates? Or was it just the bond of first love? Discuss.

13. Each of the sisters faces a challenge in her life when she decides to go to Positano. Do their journeys resolve their conflicts? In what way?
14. *The Secret Love Letters of Olivia Moretti* has strong themes of love—how many distinct love relationships can you identify in the novel? Did you feel more strongly connected to one relationship than another?
15. Olivia and Rafe relied on their written correspondence to communicate with each other. Do you believe old-fashioned letters are more powerful than verbal or digital communication? Have you ever written a love letter? Had one written to you?

DON'T MISS
JENNIFER PROBST'S

OUR ITALIAN SUMMER

AVAILABLE NOW!

Francesca

"No, I said the deadline is Wednesday. That gives you two days to give me a decent hook or I'm pulling you off the account."

I ignored the glint of resentment in the young man's green eyes, wondering if he thought his charm and good looks trumped talent. In many places, they did. But not in my company.

I gave him credit for smothering the emotion immediately and forcing a smile. "Got it. I'll get it done."

I nodded. "I know you will."

He left my office with his shoulders squared, and I wondered what would eventually triumph—pride or the drive for success. He was young and had promise, so I hoped the latter for him. Pride was good in some cases, but working on a team to retain high-powered advertising accounts required the ability to do what it took, whether it was working with someone you didn't care for or swallowing the innate instinct to push back at the boss you hated.

Of course, he didn't hate me. At least not yet. It was hard to take orders from a woman who was blind to looks, charisma, or flattery. I'd learned that lesson early—and ran my F&F Advertising with a ruthless efficiency and cold-mannered sharpness that made me one of the best in the business. I'd even managed to snag a spot on the Top Ten Women to Watch in Business list from *Fortune* magazine.

Too bad I had no time to enjoy it.

I glanced at my watch, my mind furiously clicking over the day's crammed schedule. I'd have to work late again, but it'd be worth it once I nailed this new account. I headed to the conference room for a meeting with my team, my sensible low-heeled shoes clicking on the hardwood floor. Layla and Kate were already perched at the polished table, laptops fired up and endless papers strewn around.

"Morning, boss," Kate said, motioning toward the chair next to her. "Figured we'd be eating lunch in again, so I had Jessica get your usual."

"Thanks." I took a sip of my Voss water as I sat beside them. I lived on water and grilled chicken salads, which was the easiest fuel to shove into my body on limited time. "Where's Adam?"

"Running late," Layla said, shooting me a smile. "But I don't think we need him for the brainstorming session. Better to get his feedback on the social media after we have a few solid concepts."

"True. He didn't look too thrilled with our new product."

Kate quirked a brow. "He's been begging to sell something sexier than kids' lemonade."

Layla snorted. "I told him anyone can sell sex—it's not even a challenge. If he makes this work, he's a genius."

I laughed. "You always did know how to motivate him, Layla."

My valued art director preened. "Plenty of practice in the ranks of hell. At least it was good for something."

Layla had graduated at the top of her class and planned to

take Manhattan by storm. Unfortunately, like me, she ended up with a slew of crap jobs, and being a black woman in the industry meant encountering prejudices to overcome. We'd worked together for a few years before I ventured out to create my own company, and I knew she'd be the perfect art director for F&F Advertising.

I trusted her with both my business and my personal shit. It was the best decision I ever made.

Kate was my advertising manager and my other right hand. She wore tailored designer suits, and her blond hair was pulled back tight in a chignon, emphasizing her classic bone structure. I had to admit, when I first met Kate, I thought she was too beautiful and quiet to be successful in such a cutthroat business, but she soon proved me wrong, and now I never discriminate based on looks. I made sure I hired a diverse, multicultural team, treated them like royalty, and offered enough incentives for promotion. It proved a good move, since I had low turnover and a core of hard-won talent.

Lately, I'd been thinking of offering them both a full partnership. My little boutique company was finally on the verge of exploding, and I needed people I trusted by my side. I had been intent on not bringing in partners, but now I saw that if I wanted to really grow, it was time I took the leap. Plus, I considered these women friends. They'd proven their loyalty, and we worked well together.

But that tiny sliver of doubt still crept through me. I'd gotten here by relying on my own drive, talent, and gut instincts to give clients what they need, twenty-four seven. I was the final say on everything for my company. Giving up that type of control made my skin prickle, like I was about to break out into hives. I'd heard horror stories of being pushed out by once-trusted partners and overruled on important decisions by lack of majority. What if Kate and Layla decided to team up and I found myself the odd woman out? Power sometimes had a funny effect on relationships. Did I really want to take such a chance? Even with these women I trusted and called friends?

I needed more time to think it through. Until then, I'd just push forward.

I shook my head and refocused. "Let's get to work. We only have two weeks until the presentation. I've been looking over all the reports from the research department and there's a few things we need to zone in on."

Layla jumped in. "Lexi's Lemonade is organic. That's the main buzzword."

"Exactly. Statistics show kids drive popular drink sales by pushing their parents to buy. We need to find a way to bridge the gap and get the children to beg the moms to buy it."

"And the moms need to feel good about giving in," Kate added.

I brought up a picture of the label on my screen and tapped it with my fingernail. "Packaging is huge. The recycled box is earth-friendly and colorful. It needs to compete on the shelves with Capri Sun, Honest Kids, and the endless others. We need to find a unique inroad."

"At least it tastes good," Layla said. She pursed her red-painted lips. "Can you believe Kool-Aid still sells a shitload? Man, I loved that stuff growing up. And what a mascot. Genius."

"Hmm, but I don't think we want a mascot for this product," I said. "We need to gain children's attention with the ad, then slam it home that there's low sugar and no preservatives. The double hook."

"Shock value?" Layla threw out.

I nodded. "Possible, but not too much. I think funny."

Kate cocked her head. "Kids nowadays are immune to shock value with YouTube and video games. I agree, funny may be the way to go."

Layla groaned and opened up her email. "I'll get Sarah started on kids' comedy and what generates the most sales."

"Good, let's start throwing everything in the pot for possible scenarios," I said. The rush of adrenaline warmed my blood as the challenge of a new creative account settled in. This was what I lived for, the elusive hunt for the perfect hook to please a client and sell the product. It never got old.

We started brainstorming and my phone vibrated. Glancing quickly at the screen, I noticed my mother had called twice without leaving a voice mail. I held back a groan. Typical. If I didn't pick up, she just kept calling and refused to leave a message. Soon, a text came through.

Frannie, please call me. I have an important question.

Impatience flickered. She was always calling me with endless questions, from how to work the television remote to what movie to rent at Redbox to whether I'd read the latest article about coconut oil healing all ailments. Once, she'd called half a dozen times to tell me she had a thirty percent coupon at Kohl's and didn't want it to expire.

She'd never really respected my work or how far I'd come, still treating me like I had a disposable job that allowed me to leave when I wanted, relax on weekends, or delegate my work when I wished. Her constant refrains echoed through my mind.

I don't understand. Aren't you the boss? Why can't you take some time off?

I grabbed my phone and typed out a text. Busy now. Call you later.

I got back to work and shortly thereafter Adam came in. His

curly brown hair was a bit mussed, and sweat gleamed on his forehead. "We have a problem," he announced, crashing down into the chair.

"You decided you're too fancy to work on branding Lexi's Lemonade," Layla teased, used to Adam's dramatics. The man was a bit over-the-top but a genius when it came to creating click-worthy social media campaigns.

"No. The IG ad for Dallas Jeans is tanking." He slid his iPad down the table with it opened to the screen. "Consumers hate it. We need a rebrand."

My heart rate rammed into a full gallop. I had no time for any failures that weren't scheduled. "It's still brand-new," I said, glancing down at the ad. "Maybe we need some organic growth first."

Adam shook his head. "Not with this. It's only going to get worse. I have a few suggestions on what to tweak, Frannie. I know you're busy so I can work with Layla and get it handled."

"No problem," Layla said. "I can make the time."

I hesitated. I was already overworked and overscheduled. I should just let Adam and Layla take care of it, but the Dallas Jeans ad was something I'd helped create. If it bombed, I needed to be involved in fixing it. "No, I can work with you."

Kate blinked. "What about Lexi's Lemonade? We don't want to get behind. It may be better to let them handle it, Frannie."

I squared my shoulders. "I know the client best, including Perry's preferences. I'll stay late a few nights and knock it out."

Kate and Layla shared a glance but held their tongues. They'd been pushing for more control, advising me to hire more people and to work lead on fewer clients. I knew they were trying to help and that they craved more responsibility, but I still had an uneasy feeling that if I stepped back too much, they'd eventually decide they didn't need me.

I tamped down on the tiny flicker of fear coursing through

my bloodstream. That annoying, buzzing voice whispering the million ways I could fail. My entire reputation was based on running F&F Advertising and thriving at every level. I'd finally managed to secure some national-brand clients and needed to show they'd made the right decision in placing their dollars with a smaller firm.

Why did it feel like the entire world was waiting for me to fail? Successful women were still looked upon as dangerous, and one big mistake was gleefully gossiped about, with news of it spreading like wildfire.

I cleared my throat and took a deep breath. "Now, let's get to work," I said firmly.

They didn't protest.

• • • •

Hours later, I collapsed in my office and buzzed Jessica. "Any messages?" I asked.

She rattled off a few I could put off until tomorrow. "Your mother called twice. Said you'd promised to call her back."

I groaned, rubbing my temples. "I forgot, thanks. Go on home. Thanks for staying."

"No problem. Have a good night, Frannie."

My stomach growled. I reached inside my desk drawer and nibbled on a Kind bar. Better get it over with. I dialed my mom's number.

"Hi, Mom. Everything okay?"

"You never called me back." Her voice held a slight sting designed to instill guilt. It worked. "You weren't at Allegra's track meet."

Shit.

My daughter's schedule was as jam-packed as mine, with tennis matches and races across the county. I'd missed the last few and swore I'd be there for the invitational. Her time was stellar and she had a good chance at getting a scholarship for both her running and her grades. This meet had been key. "I'm sorry," I said with a sigh. "We had a crisis here at work, and I literally just got to my office. Why didn't she call or text me?"

"Because she wanted you to remember on your own."

The whiplash of guilt stung deeper. Another test I'd failed. How could I be a rock star at my job and such a loser at home? "What was her time?"

"I forgot but I wrote it down for you. She beat her record in the eight hundred and got a medal for first in the fifteen hundred."

Pride flashed through me. "That's amazing. Is she there with you?"

"No, she went home on her own. But I wanted to invite you both to dinner this week. Allegra wants to try out a new dish and we've had no family time together. How about Wednesday?"

I closed my eyes, resenting the requests she threw at me. She had nothing on her schedule and assumed I should jump at any invitation. "I can't, Mom. I've got a hell of a week coming up with this new campaign, and I need to work late."

An impatient sigh huffed over the line. My nerves prickled with annoyance. "Again? This is a difficult year for Allegra, and she needs you home, at least for dinner. Plus, I can't freeze the grass-fed beef since it's been in the refrigerator and I got it specifically for you. It's expensive."

"Then make it for yourself, Mom. It has less hormones so it's better for your health."

Mom snorted. "I'm too old to care what I eat anymore. Why can't you come home and eat like a normal person, then go back to the office? At least we'll have some time with you."

I ground my teeth, remembered my last dentist appointment, and tried to relax my jaw. My mother had spent her entire life catering to Dad and me, creating domestic chores like a lifeline. And though she always said aloud that she was proud of my success, deep down I wondered. Instead of trying to support me through my struggles as a single mother, she turned to her skills as a master guilt-trip artist and exposed all my own crippling doubts. Did she resent my choice to become a career woman? To raise Allegra without a father figure? Or did she wonder what type of life she would've had if she'd embraced more than the four walls of her home?

I'd never know. We rarely got into deep conversations. It was easier to stick to mundane topics and trick ourselves into believing we had a connection—the sacred mother-daughter bond that movies love to exploit in sickening, shallow sweetness. I preferred the truth, even though it sometimes tasted bitter.

"I just can't. I have endless things to do and little time."

"One day you may find there's no time left, Francesca. And that you gave work more power over you than it should have."

It always came back to this—I'd never win, no matter what I did or how hard I tried. We viewed the world differently, and she had no interest in trying to understand me. For too many years, I had longed for an acceptance that never came, until I swore I'd stop looking for her approval. The hurt that sprouted from my mother's words was more humiliating than anything.

And still I couldn't stop leaping to my own defense. "I'm sorry if I own and run a profitable, successful company and can't get home for dinner. I'm sorry I'm such a disappointment to your high standards."

"Stop using that tone and putting words in my mouth!"

Oh God, we were going to fight again. And it would take up too much energy and precious time. I drew in a deep breath and focused on keeping calm. "Do you want me to text Allegra and see if she can join you for dinner? I was going to tell her she can invite friends over and order pizza, but maybe she'd like to visit."

I tried to ignore the disappointment in her tone, reminding myself she didn't have a million balls in the air to juggle other than dinner. "I'll text her. You're busy."

I managed to hold my tongue. "Thanks."

"What about Sunday? Surely you have a few hours to be with us on the Lord's day. There's something I need to discuss with you and it's important."

I hadn't been to church since I was fourteen, when I finally declared my independence and refused to go anymore. "Fine, I'll come Sunday."

"Good. Make sure you congratulate Allegra when you see her. She worked hard for that trophy."

The direct hit caused me to wince. She acted like I didn't know how to treat my own daughter. "Of course."

We said goodbye and hung up.

I sagged over my desk. Tension knotted my stomach and squeezed my lungs, compressing my breath. No, I would not allow this to happen again. The last attack must have been a freak occurrence. Too much stress, too little sleep, too many cups of coffee. I had a thousand excuses for the crippling anxiety that had washed through my body last week and driven me to my knees, fighting for breath. Thank God it had happened when I was alone in my office, where it would remain a secret. But even now, just the thought of another breakdown clenched my muscles in fear.

I closed my eyes, fighting to slow my rapid heartbeat. For a few frantic moments I couldn't breathe, and I tried not to lose it, but then the air hit my lungs and I gulped it down gratefully.

What was happening to me lately? I'd always thrived in

stressful situations, but maybe the Lexi's Lemonade account was bothering me more than I thought. Maybe after I put in the necessary hours and secured the campaign, I'd stop having these ridiculous attacks.

Yes, I'd just control it for now. Lately my nights were spent staring up at the ceiling and worrying. My body had begun to rebel, and I had no time for it. Next month, I'd see a doctor and get fixed up. It would all be fine.

I grabbed a bottle of water and took a few sips while my mother's words still churned in my brain. She'd be the first one to crow *I told you so* if she knew about my anxiety attacks and would probably cite my refusal to spend time on my health and appearance as the cause instead of old-fashioned work.

Even at seventy-five, my mother was beautiful, with firm, smooth skin in a gorgeous olive color; thick hair that had once been coal black but had turned to gray; and a trim, lean build that never seemed to thicken, even with her advanced years. She took pride in her appearance and was always tugging at my hair or begging me to wear makeup.

I'd inherited none of my mother's fine traits. My hair was pin straight and limp, so I'd begun wearing it short, with a shaggy, fashionable cut. Even my attempts at highlighting failed at coaxing the dirty-blond strands to sparkle, but I invested in a top-notch stylist so at least the color had some range. My eyes were plain brown. Not brown with gold specks, or an inky depth to give them more mystery. Just mud brown.

Mostly, I didn't care. I realized early on that not having my mother's beauty was an advantage. I had good skin and bone structure, thank God, enough to achieve a passable pretty. Since I was average height and weight, not too curvy or too skinny, I was able to dress in a wide variety of ways depending on the person I chose to reflect. I wasn't beautiful enough to cause men concern or women jealousy, and not unattractive enough to feel awkward. I built on my advantages young, learning what to accent and what to tone down, from my wardrobe to my speech, until I'd perfected the look of a female executive going places. Marriage had never been on my radar, not when meaningful, exciting work, money, and travel were at stake.

Dad would have understood. Would have cheered from the sidelines to see his only daughter reach the pinnacle of success in this cutthroat business. He'd always been driven to succeed like me and spent most of his hours building his own business. Dad moved from general construction to building homes, until he'd created a small team and cultivated a stellar reputation. He used to tell me to stay on budget and stay on time and clients would pour in.

Mom consistently complained about Dad's absence and long work hours, but she was the only one who didn't understand. I knew he wanted to give me better opportunities. He introduced me to a glimpse of a world with no borders if I was smart enough and driven enough to leap for it. He used to tell me I was just like him—born with stars in my eyes and wandering feet, always looking for more. He never tried to curb my dreams or make me feel like I wanted too much. He understood.

God, I missed him. His death was a bitter loss I still lingered on, especially late at night when there was no one there to soothe the doubts. The heart attack had taken him hard and fast, but the worst of the grief was the knowledge that he'd never been able to hold his granddaughter. He would've doted on Allegra.

The thought made me reach for my phone to call my daughter.

When she didn't answer, I knew she was mad at me.

I'd broken another promise.

The familiar guilt slammed through me, but I took the punch like a seasoned boxer, already comfortable with the thousands of ways I'd failed at being a mother. It was so much easier when she was a baby. Sure, the lack of sleep and endless exhaustion sucked, but coming home to her precious giggles and obvious adoration made up for all of it. I was able to give her what she needed most of the time. A bottle. A blanket. Changing her diaper. Playing. Food. It was like a checklist to follow that guaranteed a high degree of success and boundless love.

Now?

I couldn't remember the last time she hadn't looked at me with utter naked resentment. As if I'd personally done everything I could to ruin her life. No matter what I tried—discipline, being her friend, ignoring her dark moods, offering advice—it was all wrong. And not just a little. Every day my failure was evident in her venom-dripping voice or the cold judgment in her big brown eyes, which had once offered reverence.

She'd always been extremely close with my mother and liked to visit or cook dinner over there. Maybe some extra time with my mother was good for Allegra, especially since I'd been working so much lately. Allegra wouldn't be pressured or pushed or grilled—my mother didn't believe in that. At least, not for her granddaughter. She loved to fuss and spoil and pamper, and Allegra adored every moment.

I had to stop worrying about everything so much. I was in a good place, and it had happened under my own drive, discipline, and hard work. Allegra would eventually see all my successes and be proud when she got older. Looking back, she'd finally realize she had more opportunities to make a difference in the world because I pushed both of us.

I refused to have regrets about my choices.

And I refused to fail.

Photo by Matt Simpkins Photography

Jennifer Probst is the *New York Times* bestselling author of the Billionaire Builders series, the Searching For . . . series, the Marriage to a Billionaire series, the Steele Brothers series, the Stay series, and the Sunshine Sisters series. Like some of her characters, Probst, along with her husband and two sons, calls New York's Hudson Valley home. When she isn't traveling to meet readers, she enjoys reading, watching "shameful reality television," and visiting a local Hudson Valley animal shelter.

CONNECT ONLINE

JenniferProbst.com
JenniferProbst
AuthorJenniferProbst
JenniferProbst.AuthorPage